J.H

A French Affair

Also by Katie Fforde

Living Dangerously
The Rose Revived
Wild Designs
Stately Pursuits
Life Skills
Thyme Out
Artistic Licence
Highland Fling
Paradise Fields
Restoring Grace
Flora's Lot
Practically Perfect
Going Dutch
Wedding Season
Love Letters
A Perfect Proposal
Summer of Love
Recipe for Love

Katie Fforde

A French Affair

arrow books

Published by Arrow Books 2014

4 6 8 10 9 7 5 3

First published in Great Britain in 2013 by Century

Arrow Books
Random House, 20 Vauxhall Bridge Road,
London SW1V 2SA

www.randomhouse.co.uk

Addresses for companies within The Random House Group Limited can be found at: www.randomhouse.co.uk/offices.htm

The Random House Group Limited Reg. No. 954009

A CIP catalogue record for this book
is available from the British Library

ISBN 9780099539193

The Random House Group Limited supports the Forest Stewardship Council® (FSC®), the leading international forest-certification organisation. Our books carrying the FSC label are printed on FSC®-certified paper. FSC is the only forest-certification scheme supported by the leading environmental organisations, including Greenpeace. Our paper procurement policy can be found at
www.randomhouse.co.uk/environment

MIX
Paper from responsible sources
FSC® C016897
FSC www.fsc.org

Typeset in Palatino by Palimpsest Book Production Limited,
Falkirk, Stirlingshire

Printed and bound by
CPI Group (UK) Ltd, Croydon, CR0 4YY

To everyone who loves antiques whether
they make a living at it or not.

Acknowledgements

This book needed a lot of people to make it happen and I'd like to thank them here. From the beginning, the lovely and very helpful Sheena Brand who gave me the original idea by telling me about her inspiring father Colin Brand, and how she and her sister Jill inherited his spot and took on the challenge of becoming antiques dealers when they knew very little about them. Then, by coincidence, my friend and neighbour Jonathan Earley took me to the antiques centre where Sheena and her sister Jill have their pieces. There I met the quietly spoken but utterly charming Peter Collingridge who was inspirational.

A chance meeting at a literary festival took me to the delightful and enthusiastic Natasha Roderick-Jones. She agreed to be my research assistant and took me to Newark Antiques Fair and introduced me to the very helpful Di and Ron Aldridge (where they argued about the language of antiques dealers and taught me how to bargain). I still don't know anything about antiques but I still yearn to learn more.

Later on, when I needed to visit France for research purposes, Jo Thomas told me about Chez Castillon, took me there, where I met Janie Millman and Mike Wilson. They have to be the most welcoming and nurturing and generous hosts ever. They helped with my research and gave me space to get a lot of writing done. The fact that I was there with Judy Astley, Kate Lace and Jane Wenham-Jones did not make it any less creative or indeed less fun. (Considering the wine, it's amazing we all got so much done.)

If you're thinking about a writing course, do check out the Chez Castillon website, www.chez-castillon.com.

Desmond Fforde, Briony Fforde and all my family do so much to make my life easier. I am truly grateful.

I also must thank my wonderful publishers for their continued support. In no particular order, Georgina Hawtrey-Woore, Selina Walker, Charlotte Bush, Amelia Harvell, Jen Doyle, Sarah Arratoon, and everyone else at Cornerstone who seem to devote their lives to looking after me. Also, Richenda Todd who picks up the dropped bricks with such tact – thank you.

Not forgetting endless support from Bill Hamilton and Sarah Molloy at A M Heath – I am so lucky to have you!

Writing a book is quite hard enough but without the love and support of everyone listed and a lot of people not listed, it would be quite impossible. Thank you.

A French Affair

Chapter One

'I'm saying this more in horror than in anger, sweets, but are you really going like that?'

Gina shot her sister a look that combined irritation, amusement and a touch of exasperation. They were in the car on the main road to Cranmore-on-the-Green and turning back to revamp her outfit was not an option. Sally's little girls were asleep in the back and Gina found it easier to drive if they were not singing and squabbling and spilling cartons of juice in her car. She wanted to get as far into the journey as possible before they woke up.

Now, she said, 'Seeing as we're actually on our way, I *am* going to go like this. What's wrong with what I'm wearing anyway? I've got a jacket in the boot.'

Sally, eighteen months younger and making the most of the Indian summer, was wearing a long skirt, drapey top, gladiator sandals and a great many beads. She brought off the hippy-chick look irritatingly well. Gina felt herself being judged.

'It's very corporate,' Sally pronounced. 'A black

trouser suit and a crisp white shirt might be fine for your business meetings but this—'

'It is a business meeting.' Gina glanced at the sat nav. 'Anyway, most of my clothes are still in those cardboard boxes the men give you when you move. At least the shirt is clean and ironed. Nothing else I currently own is.'

'It's not exactly a business meeting,' said Sally, having cast an eye over her children to make sure they were still asleep. 'It involves a significant letter. From our mad Aunt Rainey.'

Gina felt she should suppress Sally's excitement just a bit. 'It is business. Our dear departed aunt had a space in this guy's antiques centre. That's business, isn't it? The letter is just something about that. Probably.'

Sally tutted at Gina's down-to-earth attitude. 'Yes, but it's contact from beyond the grave.' She said this as if she was Yvette Fielding announcing an especially spooky edition of *Most Haunted*.

Gina giggled. 'Rubbish! We just got letters from her solicitor. It would only count as being beyond the grave if we had a séance.'

'Do you think that's a good idea?'

Gina was laughing properly now, even as she shook her head. 'Honestly, Sal, you're barking. I do not think a séance is a good idea. Besides, it's completely unnecessary because we have letters. Actual paper, here-in-the-real-world letters.' She sent Sally a loving if somewhat despairing look. 'I do wonder sometimes if being an artist and a stay-at-home mum has rotted your brain.' She paused for a second. 'Not that you don't do a brilliant job keeping it all together on no money. But some of your ideas are a bit out of left field.'

'Well, you have to keep yourself amused somehow when you're hunting for little garments under the bed and stopping the girls from killing each other.' Sally sighed.

Gina felt a pang of guilt for the brain-rot remark. 'You're such a brilliant mother, Sal, really you are. The girls are a real credit to you.'

'But? I feel a but coming on!'

'Nothing about you, but I do think this meeting will just be signing a document so the antique centre can get the space back or something. It won't be anything exciting.'

'So, you don't think there'll be actual money then?'

Gina shook her head. 'I don't see how there could be. You saw Aunt Rainey more often than I did but I think we'd have known if she was rich, surely? She didn't own a house and she never seemed to have much cash.'

Sally sighed again. 'I miss her, you know. Aunt Rainey was a real character, always talking about the Beatles and all those old bands as if they were her best friends, but she was a lot of fun. I wish I'd seen more of her really but having the twins so soon after we moved down here, it wasn't easy.' She smiled.

'She came to tea a couple of times, always dressed like an ex-rock chick, and I thought how much the girls would love her when they were a bit older but, well, she died.'

'She was a lot of fun and quite eccentric. And if you're not careful, you'll end up just like her,' Gina added.

'I wouldn't mind. She was great.'

'I know. It was a compliment. Sort of.'

Sally regarded her sister as if not knowing quite how to take this. Eventually she changed the subject. 'So, what was he like? This Matthew Ballinger?'

'I haven't met him, have I?'

Sally waved a hand, as if this was a minor detail. 'But you spoke to him. What was his voice like?'

'OK. Nice, even. Although he sounded a bit grumpy . . . You're doing it again, aren't you?'

'What?' Sally's outraged innocence reminded Gina of her nieces when confronted with some huge mess or other.

'Matchmaking,' said Gina, trying to sound firm. 'That's why you're fussed about what I'm wearing. You've got to stop this.'

Her sister looked out of the side window, possibly slightly embarrassed. 'Well, it's time you had a boyfriend again.'

'No it's not. I'm on a break from men. The last one was a real disaster, who actually took money from me as well as all the other crap you know by heart now.'

Gina paused. Being lighthearted about her failed relationship wasn't yet easy, even if she was well and truly over him. 'That was part of the reason why I moved down from London, in case you've forgotten. I'm not going there again, not for a long time.'

'Where? London?'

Her sister growled.

Sally allowed Gina a second to calm down. 'That wasn't the main reason though. After all, London is massive. You could have avoided Egan if you tried.'

'Oh, I tried! But when you know all the same people you're bound to run into the one man you really don't want to see.'

'That's just an excuse. You really moved because you wanted to see your nieces grow up,' said Sally comfortably.

Gina smiled in agreement. 'I do. And there's the fact that business is so dire and my only big client left has come down here too. Also the rent on my flat had shot up and with the recession I had to regroup. All of which you know.'

'You've missed out "and you pestered the life out of me",' said Sally.

'That too.' Gina laughed.

'You'll love it down here though. I know you will.'

Reluctantly, Gina agreed. 'I know I will too. I already love waking up in my cottage and seeing fields at the bottom of the garden instead of the back end of a dodgy fish and chip shop.'

'There will be things you'll miss though,' said Sally generously. 'You were in the seething metropolis and now you're—'

'In the sticks? Missing being able to get a good curry?' Sally had never before acknowledged a single downside. Was she now feeling responsible for her sister's happiness?

'We have a truly brilliant balti, but maybe you'll miss the buzz? I hope not. I'm so thrilled that you moved. We all are.'

'Not just so I can babysit?'

'Of course not! As if.'

Gina chuckled. She loved her nieces and although she found them fairly exhausting she always liked spending time with them. 'I think I am a country girl at heart and it is so much cheaper renting here than in London.' She paused. 'But no matchmaking, you hear? If ever there comes a time when I think I might be ready for another relationship – say in about ten years—'

'When you'll be forty, nearly past child-bearing.'

'—I'll either let you know or go on the internet.'

'That's so unromantic!'

'Good. I've had it with romance.'

'You haven't really. Everyone has a romantic side, they just don't want to acknowledge it.'

Gina raised her eyebrows and tried not to smile. It was her sister who was the romantic. She herself was a hard-bitten businesswoman who had a living to earn. She had absolutely no space for romance in her life, now or at any time in the future. Falling in love had been a disaster. From now on her head would rule her heart, and just to be sure, she'd avoid relationships altogether.

'Now I know that you are never going near another man, is it safe to wonder what this Matthew Ballinger might be like?' Sally continued. 'Is he young or old? Same age as Aunt Rainey, do you think?'

'He sounded middle-aged. And no, I couldn't tell from his voice if he was married or single.'

'I didn't ask!'

'Did Aunt Rainey ever talk about him? When she came to visit?'

Sally screwed up her face in thought. 'Not that I can remember, but I had the babies and they took up most of the conversation, one way or another.'

'I asked Dad on the phone if he knew anything about him. He didn't. He did say that Rainey was prone to having younger men hanging round after her though.'

'Perhaps he's one of her young lovers.' Sally sighed. 'Maybe when I'm sixty-odd I'll have young lovers.'

Gina laughed. 'Not if Alaric is still around you won't!'

Cranmore-on-the-Green was a Cotswold town known for its historic, picturesque buildings, antiques, tea shops and tourists. Now, on this bright, autumn day, it was bustling with people taking advantage of a few days of late sunshine.

Gina and Sally had found a huge car park seemingly miles from the town centre and, after a few minutes of struggle and 'want to walk', they managed to get both girls strapped into the double buggy. The little party then made its way through the crowds.

'You've never been to the French House, have you?' said Gina.

Sally shook her head. 'No. Cranmore-on-the-Green doesn't have a supermarket, so I don't need to come very often, and there are so many antiques shops and centres I wouldn't know it if I had seen it. I always send Alaric's parents there for a little trip out when they stay. They love it. But I've got a little map so we should be able to find it quite easily.

'It's a shame he couldn't have the girls,' she went on, steering the buggy into the road to make way for a group of elderly women who had obviously had lunch in the pub and were now trying to find the coach park.

'No, it's good that he couldn't,' Gina said firmly. 'He had to meet a client which might result in a good commission.' Gina felt her artistic, romantic sister and brother-in-law needed to be a bit more businesslike and sometimes became over-businesslike to compensate. She secretly thought of them as the Flopsy Bunnies, 'improvident and cheerful'.

'Yes, but not everyone likes children and we do

want this meeting to go well,' said Sally, hefting the buggy back on to the pavement.

'Oh come on. They're adorable. Anyway, we're only going to be five minutes, I expect. Here we are, the French House.'

'Goodness!' said Sally. They stared up at the building, which was old, stately and huge. It was different from the Georgian buildings on either side, the windows being closer together and taller. A curtain of Virginia creeper covered the walls with scarlet and a couple of slightly rusty brackets supported a sign proclaiming it was indeed 'THE FRENCH HOUSE'. A couple of bay trees in tubs stood on the front steps, which led to a pair of large double doors. The sign needed repainting and the bay trees had lost their original lollipop shape but to Gina the faint air of neglect made it look beautiful and romantic.

'It sort of looks French, doesn't it?' said Sally.

Gina nodded. 'I suppose it does.'

Sally sighed. 'We'd better see if we can get the push-chair up the steps and through the door.' The house didn't look as if children ever went into it.

A bell jangled as they arrived in the entrance. Gina noticed there was quite a large hole in the carpet but the brass on the door was brightly polished. A pleasant-looking middle-aged woman came up to them. 'Hello, I'm Jenny. Matthew is expecting you. Would you like me to mind the buggy? He's upstairs.'

'Thank you, that would be very kind,' said Sally, after more introductions.

After some discussion about which twin wanted to go with Gina, they each picked up a golden-haired moppet and followed Jenny up a grand-looking staircase. As Jenny knocked on one of the doors at the top of the stairs, Gina straightened her shoulders. She didn't know what lay ahead but it was all a bit daunting.

Chapter Two

Matthew Ballinger stood up from behind his enormous desk as the party entered, looking astonished and not at all happy as the tide of femininity swept into his office. He was very tall with dark eyes and hair to match. The hair needed cutting and the eyes seemed wary. For an instant he gave Gina the impression that he was an antique himself but then she realised this was crazy – he wasn't even that old. It must have been because the room, which was not large and was crammed with furniture, looked like the set for a Dickens novel and made her think Matthew Ballinger should be wearing a high collar and tail coat. He cleared his throat.

Gina, feeling sorry for him, held out her free hand. 'Hello! You must be wondering what on earth has happened. We're Gina and Sally Makepiece – you're expecting us. The girls – Persephone and Ariadne – are extras. They're twins,' she added, as if knowing this helped. And she'd stuck to their maiden name, Gina realised, wanting to keep things simple.

A look, which she interpreted as absolute horror

masked by good manners, crossed his face. 'Matthew Ballinger. How do you do? Do sit down. I'll find some more chairs.' He was obviously well out of his comfort zone.

In spite of his reticence, Sally gave Gina several knowing looks while he was finding another chair. Her facial expressions and mouthings indicated she felt he was 'gorgeous!'

Gina barely had time to roll her eyes and frown before the chair was produced. Her sister really was way out of order sometimes. Besides, a sort of saturnine cragginess didn't always translate to 'gorgeous'. Although, she had to admit – purely objectively – that he wasn't bad-looking.

When Gina and Sally were seated, with Persephone and Ariadne on their knees, Matthew Ballinger retreated behind his desk. 'Sorry, I wasn't expecting so many of you.'

'You don't need to worry about the smaller versions,' said Gina. 'They're only here for the outing.'

'Couldn't find anyone to look after them,' said Sally apologetically, giving Persephone a hug.

'Right, well,' said their host, producing a file. 'I've got a letter from your aunt's solicitor which presumably is the same as the ones you've got? And then there's the one we have to open together.'

'Yes,' said Gina, knowing if she'd been entrusted with a letter like that her curiosity would have got the better of her. She'd have at least put it up to the light. Sally would have had it over a steaming kettle in minutes. Perhaps Aunt Rainey had known that. How could he be so calm about it?

'So, shall we open the letter then?' said Sally after a few desperate seconds of waiting.

'We might as well,' Matthew said, producing the envelope. He picked up a letter opener, slit the envelope with agonising precision and cast his glance down the page.

'Oh dear,' he said eventually. 'It's . . . it's a bit complicated. Look, would you like a cup of tea or something?'

Gina and Sally looked at each other. Complicated? What did that mean?

'We don't need tea. We'd like to—' said Gina.

'I still think a drink would be best,' Matthew interrupted, getting up and heading for the door. 'I'll see if there's some squash for the children.'

'Juice!' said Sally. 'They can't drink squash. E numbers,' she explained. 'Makes them hyperactive.'

He shuddered visibly. 'Jenny?' he called down the stairs. 'We couldn't have some tea, could we? And some juice for the girls.'

'Juice,' said the twins, almost in unison. 'Want juice!'

Gina wanted to press Matthew but he was looking so forbidding that she didn't know where to start. Sally was distracted by the girls, who were getting visibly restless. Since her abilities as a mother included conjuring skills, she was able to produce a couple of rice cakes from her sleeve to placate them.

An old clock on the mantelpiece ticked loudly, slowing time with its measured pace. Something in the room seemed to sigh. Gina wondered if it had been her. It could have been the furniture.

At last the door opened and the Nice Lady they had met downstairs came in with a tray.

'This is Jenny Duncan,' said Matthew Ballinger. 'She's the backbone of the place.'

'Oh, we've met, Matthew,' said Jenny. 'I have a pushchair the size of a family car in my cubby hole.'

The moment she spoke there was an eruption. Following the tea tray was what looked like a rather thin donkey. The girls began to scream.

Sally's maternal instinct told her to lift Persephone up out of harm's way but because of the size of the harm, it wasn't possible. Gina, in charge of Ariadne, decided to carry her out of the room. She didn't think she was in danger but the screaming was deafening her.

'He won't hurt you!' said Matthew loudly but only just audibly. 'It's only Oscar.'

Then Oscar started to bark. The sound was so deep and terrible it seemed to come from the bowels of the earth. Gina hadn't thought the girls could scream any harder but somehow they managed it.

'Quiet!' said the Voice of God, which turned out to be Matthew.

For a second or two there was silence. Oscar looked away, embarrassed, as if the bark had nothing to do with him. The girls, unaccustomed to being told what to do, especially by strangers, stopped screaming more from shock than obedience.

'Jenny, if you wouldn't mind removing the dog?' said Matthew. 'And you two,' he said to Ariadne and Persephone, although Gina felt he was addressing her and Sally as much as he was the girls, 'if you stop making such a noise we can get our business done quickly and efficiently and then we can all get out of here.'

As one, the girls began to weep, silently but wetly. Big fat tears slid down their cheeks from wide-open eyes. Gina remembered that Sally had always been able to do this as a child and wondered if it was a gift they'd inherited.

'I'm sorry,' said Sally. 'I can't concentrate while the children are so upset. We'll have to do this another time.'

'It shouldn't take long,' said Gina, who wanted to get it over with.

'I think maybe Mrs – er – Sally is right,' said Matthew. 'Another time might be better. Maybe in the evening, when the children are asleep?'

'Brilliant idea!' said Sally. 'Let's meet at Gina's house. Then if the children aren't asleep, they won't be my responsibility. Their dad can sort them out. Card, Gina!'

Gina was used to being the sister who was in charge. She felt in her pocket for a business card, glad she'd been organised enough to get them done immediately she moved. She handed one to Matthew. 'It's not far at all – only about twenty minutes away. How about tomorrow night? Sally, would that be OK with you?'

Matthew took the card and looked down at it. Just for a moment Gina wished it wasn't quite so funky, but she was a PR person and she needed to present the right image. It just didn't seem right this time, in such a dignified and old-fashioned setting.

'Oh yes – but let's get the girls out of here!' Sally begged. The silent weeping was beginning to be audible. Gina knew from experience the screaming could start up again at any moment.

'About eight suit?' said Matthew.

Gina nodded. Ariadne had drawn breath for a shriek. As Oscar gave her a look of mild curiosity, Ariadne let rip. Gina ran out of the room with her charge. It was like being a moving car alarm, she thought.

A few minutes later, after a quick struggle with the pushchair, Gina, Sally and the twins were outside the French House.

'Quiet!' said Gina, who had been impressed by how well this had worked on them before. The noise subsided. 'I don't know about you,' she went on, 'but given we can't have a bottle of Pinot to help us recover, I'm going to need a bloody big pink cake!'

It took a little while, plus cake, ice creams and some sparkly hairgrips, before the party felt calm enough to discuss their recent experience.

'I know the girls are a bit hysterical about dogs,' said Sally, 'but you must admit it was a giant.'

Gina nodded. Even she had felt unnerved when that monster had trotted in behind the tea tray.

'And Matthew was hardly less terrifying,' said Sally, whose talent for exaggeration had been enhanced by chocolate gateau.

'I think he was just a bit overwhelmed by us all,' said Gina. 'He wasn't expecting four of us and we did rather take over the place.'

'Well, I think he's a Mr Rochester: all dark and brooding.'

'And sinister?'

'Oh, not sinister!' said Sally, affronted by the suggestion. 'Mr Rochester was gorgeous, wasn't he!'

'Sweetie,' Gina chuckled, 'I know you're really talking about Matthew here. But he's an antiques dealer, which means he's probably gay, or married. And even if he isn't either, I'm still not interested. How many times do I have to tell you I'm taking a break from men? You wouldn't push drinks on an alcoholic.'

Her sister regarded her through narrowed eyes. Sally, in spite of being short of both money and time, was both in love with her husband and happy, and she wanted everyone else to be happy too. She felt the only way was through the love of a good man, but before she could launch into her well-honed speech about success in business meaning nothing if you had no one to share it with, Gina said, 'So, Matthew's read the letter now and we haven't. I hope that doesn't put us at a disadvantage.'

'I don't suppose it will,' said Sally, retrieving yet another hair-slide, from the floor this time. 'After all, Aunt Rainey wouldn't leave something in her will to a stranger when she had us.'

'She was eccentric,' said Gina. 'Maybe she would.'

Sally shook her head. 'She did live in France a lot in the sixties and dye her hair well past the age when orange was a good colour for her, but she had all her marbles. That's why Dad got almost everything and we got mysterious letters.' She glanced at Gina. 'And an intro to Matthew at the same time.'

Gina didn't rise to the bait. She got up and retrieved her coat from the back of her chair. 'Well, we'd better get going. I want to get home before it's dark. Spooky country roads and all that. Besides, the parents will be dying to know what went on today. I'll ring them.'

'I'm not sure they'll be all that interested,' said Sally, who had never forgiven her parents for moving to Spain just when she became pregnant.

Gina, who had also felt a bit let down at the time, nodded. 'I'll tell them anyway.'

The little girls stared out of the window singing to themselves on the journey home. Gina and Sally didn't talk much. Gina was thinking about the chaos that was currently her home and wondering which bit she should tackle first. Sally had a vacant expression on her face. Gina knew from experience she was probably working away at something in her head and briefly envied her for being an artist. Gina loved her work as a freelance PR but public relations, although stimulating and creative in its way, lacked a decorative side. She felt this missing element far more than not having a boyfriend.

When they arrived at Sally's house, Alaric carried his daughters inside while Sally made the usual offers of supper and a bed for the night.

'Honestly, I must get back,' Gina had to say at least three times. 'I've just about got a path between my bed and the door but I should make a bit more space.'

'You're not going to do that this evening. Stay with us. Alaric can bath the girls and we'll open a bottle of wine.'

'Tempting though that sounds I must do something useful. That's the trouble with being freelance, you don't get time off in the same way. And I should do some unpacking. I'll see you very soon.' She started the car engine.

Her sister spoke through the open window. 'At least we know one thing . . .'

'What?'

'My gaydar, which you know is impeccable, tells

me he's not gay! And before you ask, you know perfectly well who I'm talking about.'

Gina laughed and drove off, leaving her sister waving madly in front of the little cottage she had made a home. Gina couldn't imagine why on earth her sister felt so sure Matthew Ballinger wasn't gay. Just because he wasn't camp didn't mean a thing. Nor did the fact that he had a dog the size and colour of a donkey. He did run an antiques centre, and even though she hadn't looked that closely, all the bits and pieces in his office had looked well kept and lovingly arranged. Although, thinking about it, she remembered a rather dodgy china dog, all Chinesey, with huge, rolling eyes. Would a gay man put up with something so ugly in his work space? Maybe Sally had a point, but it was nothing to her. Gina had forsworn men.

Chapter Three

Matthew rang the following morning to ask if he could bring Oscar with him that evening.

'Normally he'd be all right at home, or I'd leave him with Jenny, but she can't have him and there are so many firework parties at this time of year. He hates bangs.'

As Gina had been sure when she'd heard his voice that he was going to cancel, she found herself saying, 'Oh, that's fine. Bring him. The girls aren't going to be here after all. I'm not that keen on bangs either.'

'Good. I will. Thank you. I'll see you at eight then.'

Gina sat where she was for a few minutes after they had disconnected. What had Aunt Rainey been thinking of? What on earth had been going on in her mind when she wrote those letters and left the strange instructions with her solicitor? Was she, Gina, going to experience more life changes than she'd already taken on? And if so, was she up for it?

Gina went through to the sitting room which was also her office. The little cottage, though enchanting, didn't have room for a separate work space. Her friend Dan, a property search consultant who had found her new home for her, had been concerned about that, but she had reassured him that when the cupboard-cum-second bedroom was no longer full of stuff to unpack, she could move up there.

It was going to be tough setting up her business in an area where she only had one business contact. The first thing she'd done when she'd arrived the previous week was to get herself online and her post redirected.

Her client would pay the bills for a month or so but would not cover anything extra. She had to find some more work as soon as possible. At least as a public-relations person who specialised in marketing she had plenty of ideas as to how to do that, and she decided a leaflet was the answer. When times were hard it was more important than ever to make sure your name was out there, and she would do this by getting her leaflet to every business in the surrounding area. Later that day, when she was at last happy with her copy, she looked up a local printer and drove over to see him.

Sally arrived at quarter past seven that evening, laden with baskets and boxes.

'This is so you can do a makeover on my house?' asked Gina while she and Sally were still kissing each other hello.

'I know you've only just moved in and won't have had time to do a thing to make this place anything like a proper home. I'm just here to help.' She looked around critically.

'I've been frantic all day working!' said Gina, wishing she didn't sound as if she was apologising for attending to the practicalities of life and not the aesthetics.

People meeting the sisters for the first time often assumed that Gina was the stronger character, but now she surrendered to the soft and scented bulldozer that was her sister on a mission.

Gina moved boxes, found chairs and rugs and generally assisted as Sally performed the sort of miracle usually seen on television with a staff of thousands and a celebrity to help.

By ten to eight Gina slumped in the only armchair and looked about her. 'Wow!' she said.

'Hmm, not too bad, given I didn't have long,' said Sally, looking around her with a satisfied-bordering-on-smug expression.

Tea lights glowed on every surface. A rug lay in front of the fireplace and Gina's work area was covered with a deep red cloth studded with tiny mirrors which reflected the candlelight. What had been a desk looked like a cross between a dresser and a shrine. The papers were in a box Sally had converted into a filing tray; the computer had been relegated to the bedroom.

Gina's pillows had been wrapped in more red tablecloths – a student trip to India meant Sally had dozens of these – so the sofa and armchair looked deeply inviting. There was a bunch of Michaelmas daisies and Japanese anemones from Sally's garden on the windowsill as well as more tea lights.

Sally twitched a cushion. 'Looks OK, doesn't it?'

'Frankly I think it looks like a bordello, but a very cosy one,' said Gina.

'Now all you need is a fire. Does the fireplace work?' said Sally, ignoring Gina's comment.

'Yes, and the landlady had the chimney swept.' She paused. 'But it's not that cold and the heating works OK. Do we really need a fire?'

'It'll make the place look more welcoming,' said Sally, rummaging in the only basket not yet empty. 'Matches, matches, come to Mummy.' She looked at her sister impatiently. 'Now find some glasses, do. I've brought wine.' Sally was setting the scene and it had to be perfect.

Gina found the glasses and a cloth to polish them with in case they were dusty after the move. She didn't bother to protest that it was a business meeting and not a party because she knew Sally wouldn't listen. As far as Sally was concerned, where there was more than one person gathered together it was a celebration, the space had to look pretty and if it was after six o'clock there had to be wine. She had inherited their mother's gift for hospitality. Gina hadn't to the same extent; although she liked people to be comfortable and for the place to be tidy, she couldn't dress a room quite as well as Sally could.

Once Sally had the makings, including candle ends, newspaper and kindling, she looked up at her sister. 'OK, over to you. Light the fire.'

Gina smiled as she knelt on the hearthrug. Her sister could do the pretty bits but Gina could get a fire going quicker than anyone.

When the wood Sally had brought had caught and the fire was going nicely, Sally gave her sister a critical inspection. Gina was wearing jeans and jumper.

'This is fine,' said Gina, brushing bits of stick off herself. 'The jeans are clean, the jumper is newish and I've put mascara on. Look.' She batted her eyelashes to demonstrate. 'If I put any more on he'll think I'm weird. I wasn't wearing any make-up when we first met.'

'I know,' said Sally grimly. 'You never do. You are thirty, you know, maybe it's time to stop relying on your wonderful natural complexion.'

Suddenly worried, Gina peered into the mirror. 'Do I look old?'

'Of course not. Anyway, you look great in candle-light. Now let me just have a final check that everything is perfect . . .'

By the time there was a knock on the door, a little after eight, the cottage looked cosier than it had for years and certainly since the short time Gina had lived in it. Even by Sally's high standards it was extremely pretty and inviting.

In the flurry to create the perfect *Country Living*

effect Gina had forgotten to mention Oscar. She'd forgotten about him herself until she opened the door. Fortunately Sally managed to stop herself imitating her daughters as Oscar loped into the cottage; she kept her exclamation down to a small squeak.

'Matthew, welcome,' said Gina, to give her sister time to breathe deeply. 'Sally has insisted on making the cottage look dressed for a party, not a meeting, so I hope you're up for a glass of wine.'

Oscar, not waiting for an invitation, flung himself in front of the fire, thus taking up most of the floor space.

'Thank you, that would be nice,' Matthew said.

'Why is your dog so big?' Gina heard Sally ask as she went into the kitchen to fetch the drinks.

As she came back in again she heard Matthew reply, 'Because he's mostly Irish wolfhound and big is how they come. And although he's huge, he's terrified of bangs. It makes it difficult to leave him alone at this time of year, with firework parties going on at all times.'

'Oh I see!' said Sally, softening somewhat.

Gina handed him a glass of wine and then one to Sally, who was sitting in the armchair with her feet curled under her. Spiders made Gina do that, not dogs the size of hearthrugs.

'So what's the rest of him?' asked Gina, having seated herself on the kitchen chair. She didn't feel she knew Matthew well enough to sit next to him on the sofa.

'He's technically a lurcher,' said Matthew, 'but he's

mostly wolfhound, which makes him largely unsuitable for lurcher-like activities.'

'Largely is about right,' said Gina. 'And I'm not going to ask about lurcher-like activities because I'm sure I don't want to know – but he's lovely,' she added, suddenly realising she did like him. He was a gentle giant. Matthew was certainly a giant – he and Oscar took up most of the room – but was he gentle, like his dog? She dismissed the thought swiftly. He certainly seemed less imposing than he had in his office.

'Oscar dearly loves a good fire,' said Matthew. 'It was kind of you to light one.' He was perched on the edge of the sofa, as if he wanted to make a quick getaway.

'That was Sally's idea actually. She said it made the place cosier. I felt it might be a bit hot.'

'We can always open a window,' said Sally, who seemed to have summoned up enough courage to put her feet on the floor now.

'So what about Aunt Rainey's letter?' said Gina, who was feeling more and more anxious. She had forgotten her sister was afraid of dogs and felt guilty for inflicting such a big one on her. And Matthew seemed ill at ease too. In fact, only Oscar seemed remotely comfortable.

'I took the liberty of taking photocopies so we've all got one.' He handed the girls a piece of paper each.

They both studied them for a few seconds.

'Actually,' said Gina. 'I can't read in this light.' She looked at Sally, knowing she would hate it if Gina ruined the effect by turning on the overhead lamp.

'Nor can I,' said Sally, 'but Matthew, you're near the lamp. You read it aloud. It'll go in better that way anyway.'

'OK,' he said, and began. '"My dears . . ."' He looked up, making it clear he would never use an expression like that.

'You're probably wondering what this is all about. Let's just say I'm a meddling old woman but indulge me! I want my lovely nieces to discover the joy of the antiques business. Some people call it "the Disease" but it's such a delightful one, I have no qualms in infecting others with it. So, I'm giving the girls £500 to start off with and I'd like you, Matthew, to take them on, let them have my space and what's left of my stock, guide them through the first tricky months and if you make a profit within four months, you will all get a bit more money. Have fun!'

Matthew stopped reading and looked at them both.

'Go on,' said Sally.

'That's it. That's all it says,' said Matthew.

For a few moments, the only sound to be heard in the room was Oscar's gentle snores and the crackling of the fire.

'Aunt Rainey was a little bit crazy,' said Gina eventually. 'Wasn't she?'

'Well, she was pretty eccentric,' said Matthew. 'But she did very well and was a real asset to the centre. She was an erratic buyer but she always found interesting things. People came in regularly to see what she'd got her hands on.'

'But how exactly does an antiques centre work? There didn't seem to be many people around when we came the other day,' said Sally.

'It's not like a department store with every stall manned. Owners rent space and take it in turns to man the centre. We always have two people on duty, but sometimes people come in to check their stock. We have about ten traders in the French House in total.'

'So why aren't they there all the time?' asked Sally. 'You'd think it would be easier to sell your own things if you're actually there.'

'Dealers have to buy stock, restore it possibly, and most of them have stock in other centres too. It may seem odd if you're used to ordinary shops but it works perfectly well,' said Matthew. He was back to perching on the edge of the sofa, frowning at them both.

'I don't think we can do this,' said Sally, having thought about it for all of thirty seconds. 'We know nothing about antiques and I don't imagine it's something you can just pick up.'

Matthew made a noise which sounded as if he was about to agree but Gina interrupted.

'I disagree,' she said. 'I think we should give it a go. I certainly need the extra inheritance, and you do too, Sally.'

Sally looked at Gina in amazement. 'Sorry? Run that by me again?'

Gina felt herself flush slightly. Generally she was the sensible sister and for her to support this mad idea was very out of character. However, whilst Sally had been asking Matthew questions, she'd been thinking about Aunt Rainey's letter. She obviously wanted them to take over her stall – she wouldn't have written specifically to say so if she hadn't. She might have been eccentric but she wasn't an idiot. And for some reason she was determined that they work with this rather difficult man – who was obviously reluctant to have her and Sally inflicted on him. But she wouldn't be daunted. 'I just think we shouldn't dismiss it out of hand,' she said quietly but firmly.

Sally frowned. 'I'm sure we could get the will changed – convince the lawyers she wasn't of sound mind or something. And it can't be a lot of money, can it?'

'I wouldn't have thought it would be enough to be worth wasting it on trying to get the will changed,' said Matthew. He shrugged. 'I don't suppose anyone would know if I just sold her stock for you. No need for you two to get involved.'

There was another long silence before Gina said, 'That would be cheating.'

'Yes,' said Sally. 'I'm not as law-abiding as Gina, but if Rainey went to all this trouble to get us involved, then that's what she wanted. We can't just go against her wishes.'

Gina sensed her sister, in one of her characteristically lightning changes of mood, was coming round to the idea.

Matthew sighed. 'The antiques business is not exactly thriving at the moment. It will be very tough to make any money and there's a lot to learn.'

'I'm sure. But we're quite capable of learning new things,' said Gina, wondering why she was suddenly so determined to take on another challenge.

'I didn't mean to imply you weren't,' said Matthew. 'I'm just trying to think what's best.'

'Look,' said Gina, 'I do understand how daunting it must be for you. We're two strangers and our dead aunt wants you to teach us what you've probably spent your life learning. I do completely get that you don't want to take it on.' She paused. 'On the other hand, if you could find it in you to do that, we would try our very, very best to make a go of it.'

There was another agonisingly long silence. 'I don't want to seem obstructive,' Matthew said at last, 'I just don't want you going into this whole business thinking it's going to be like it is on *Bargain Hunt* or whatever, when it's a lot more mundane than that.'

'But?' prompted Sally, helping herself to crisps.

'Well,' said Matthew, almost as if the words were hurting as they came out, 'although I wasn't related to Rainey, she was very good to me. When my father died a couple of years ago, she was a rock. If this is what she wanted, and you really are up for a lot of hard work and disappointment, I will take you on.'

Gina let out a long breath. She could tell it had been a big effort for him – and why wouldn't it be? Why would Matthew want to take two sisters he knew very little about under his wing when he was obviously a serious type of person, who took his business very seriously too? But they could be serious as well, especially Gina. 'That's very, very kind.'

'We'll try really hard not to let you down,' said Sally.

Matthew looked down at Oscar and rubbed him at the base of his tail with his foot. Then he sighed. 'I miss Rainey. She wasn't like a mother to me or anything like that but she stopped me getting too gloomy. She encouraged me to get Oscar although everyone else said I'd be mad to get such a big dog. But it was the right decision. If she wants me to do this, then I owe it to her to carry out her wishes. She was very wise.'

It was a long speech for someone who didn't seem in the habit of making long speeches. The room was very still. A log shifted in the grate and Oscar groaned in his sleep.

'Then let's drink to our new partnership,' said Gina, raising her glass.

'Yes. Here's to us,' said Sally.

'To us,' said Matthew more quietly. He was obviously still getting used to the notion.

They all clinked and then Sally said, 'We're like the Three Musketeers!'

'Are we?' said Matthew, looking puzzled.

'Well, not really—' began Gina.

'Oh, OK, we're not going to have sword fights or anything but there are three of us,' said Sally. 'And Oscar can be D'Artagnan. He was a dog.'

Gina was used to her sister coming across as slightly dotty and stole a glance at Matthew. He might pull out of the arrangement or condemn Sally as a complete idiot.

'Oh, I remember. Dogtanian,' he said. 'On children's telly?'

'That's it,' said Sally. 'I knew dogs had something to do with it. *The Muskahounds.*'

'Right,' said Gina, getting up and adding another log to the fire, patting Oscar at the same time. 'Now, what's the first step in our new adventure?'

'You'll need to come over to the centre and we'll see what stock Rainey left. I'll find you some space and we'll see how you get on,' said Matthew. Whilst not sounding exactly enthusiastic he did seem serious about helping them. 'What usually happens is that the dealers rent space – an area or a cabinet, depending on what they deal in – and then serve in the centre to pay rent. If you're really good at selling' – he directed this at Sally – 'you could do more hours.'

'I am really good at selling,' she said bluntly, 'but I'm terribly short of time, what with the twins and all that. I'll do what I can though. I'd enjoy it,' she added a little wistfully.

Gina was aware that her sister, who loved being a mother, sometimes felt the lack of another life. 'I'll help out whenever I can,' she said, glancing at Sally and then Matthew. 'I'm used to doing pitches so I expect I can sell too. But what worries me is I'll have absolutely no idea what I'm selling.'

'I'll have to give you a crash course – both of you,' said Matthew.

'What's the best way to learn?' asked Gina, who liked to do things properly.

'By doing it,' said Matthew. 'There isn't a correspondence course – well, there probably is – but if you're going to deal and not just collect, you have to learn by doing.'

Sally got up. 'More wine? Or should I make some tea?'

'No thank you, nothing more for me,' said Matthew. 'I've got an antiques fair to go to very early tomorrow morning.' As he got to his feet, so did Oscar, causing Sally to step back a bit but not actually jump on to her chair.

'I should go too,' she said. 'My girls wake horribly early.'

Gina smiled. 'It seems I'm the only one not getting up at dawn.' She stretched a little. 'I'm going to feel very smug tomorrow.'

Matthew raised his eyebrows. 'I think you should come with me to the fair. I'll pick you up at six thirty. We need to be there by seven.'

This was like a verbal bucket of cold water. Gina opened her mouth to give him all the reasons why this was a totally unreasonable suggestion but there were so many, she didn't know where to start and so she shut it again.

'Absolutely,' said Sally excitedly. 'We should make a start on this straight away.'

'But we haven't seen what Rainey has already,' Gina pointed out, having at last thought of a sensible objection.

'She had very eclectic tastes,' said Matthew. 'I'll steer you away from anything too radical. And bring cash if you can, or we can stop at a cashpoint on the way. You don't have to buy anything; it would just help you get your eye in. But this is a good local market, not too big. The perfect place to start.'

Gina clung to her wineglass for support. 'I just think we should feel our way into this a little and not go on a buying trip before we've even seen the centre properly.'

'Oh, for goodness' sake, stop being so sensible,'

said Sally. 'Golly, if I could go off on a spending spree to a market I'd be ecstatic.'

'To an antiques market?' Gina demanded, not convinced.

'Well, I'd rather it was fabric or paint or stuff like that, but I'd go like a shot. Really, Gina, if we're doing this, we should get on and do it.'

Gina reached out for Oscar's head, which was level with her chin, and rubbed it thoughtfully.

'I'll pick you up at six thirty tomorrow morning,' Matthew repeated as he nudged Oscar towards the front door. There was a firmness about him that made Gina feel that arguing would be pointless.

Gina closed the door behind him and then confronted her sister.

'I never guessed that was going to happen,' said Sally.

Gina bit her lip. 'It is a bit of a shock. But a good shock, I think. I feel weirdly positive about it, as if it's the right thing to do.' She looked at Sally, suddenly guilty. 'Is it all right with you?'

Sally shrugged. 'Well, my gut reaction wasn't positive, but I'm up for anything that gets me away from my lovely girls, just for a little bit. And you never know, we might make that profit and get that little bit of extra money Aunt Rainey promised us.'

And with that she flung her scarf round her neck, grabbed her bag, blew a kiss at her sister and was gone.

Chapter Four

Pride meant that Gina was up, washed and dressed when Matthew knocked on her cottage door the next morning, but with her toast and marmalade clasped uneaten in her hand and her coffee cooling on the side she could barely bring herself to smile. Only her professional PR-girl grit made it possible.

'Hi. Time for a cup of coffee before we go?' she said, trying not to sound desperate.

Matthew shook his head. 'No. Come on.'

Figuring he wasn't a morning person either, she slung her bag over her shoulder, picked up the coffee and followed him to his beaten-up old Volvo. The seats were all down at the back, presumably to leave room for a substantial chest of drawers or small dresser should he need it. No large furry face looked out at her.

'No Oscar?'

'Jenny's minding him. I need the space.'

They got in and buckled up. He gave her an inscrutable look.

'Do you always take your coffee with you when you travel?' he asked.

'Only if I'm not driving. I never drink and drive.'

He didn't respond to her joke and she decided it wasn't really all that funny. But she felt there was absolutely nothing wrong in taking one's coffee with one, if one hadn't been given time to drink it.

'How far are we going?' she asked a bit later. She'd finished her breakfast and, having buried her dirty mug in her handbag, was now trying to get marmalade off her fingers by wiping them on her scarf.

'Not far. And there's a public loo near so you can wash your hands.'

She chuckled. 'I hate having sticky fingers. I would have put something else on my toast only I couldn't find anything.'

'Are you settled in properly now?'

'No. It'll take me ages but I've got my work stuff sorted.'

'What is it you do again?'

Gina paused for a second before replying. People – people like Matthew Ballinger, who even on very brief acquaintance she knew to be old-fashioned and a bit stuck in the past – were often very sniffy about public relations.

'I'm in PR,' she said brightly.

'Which is?'

His comment was non-committal but Gina knew she had been right. She took a breath and gave him the answer she always gave people who thought PR was a waste of time and money. 'I help people promote their businesses so they do better, employ more people and thus keep the economy going.'

There was a moment's silence before he said, 'I see.'

Gina sighed. He obviously didn't. He clearly disapproved of PR. He probably disapproved of a lot of recent inventions like social networking, the internet, Google, which was probably why he dealt in things that were at least a hundred years old. Then some imp made her decide to enlighten him. 'I expect the antiques centre could do with some PR.'

He gave her a horrified glance. 'We do not. We manage perfectly well without it.'

'Really? You said business wasn't very good at the moment. Maybe you need a bit of help?'

'Not that kind of help, thank you.'

'Well, if you change your mind, you know where I live.'

'Indeed.'

They drove the rest of the way without speaking. It wasn't exactly a companionable silence but it suited Gina. She watched the countryside flow past as they sped along.

After about forty minutes, they entered a large market town and Matthew parked the Volvo in the municipal car park and pointed the way to the Ladies. 'I'll wait for you,' he said.

The Ladies was surprisingly clean and Gina was glad of a moment to freshen up before facing the unknown.

'Just follow my lead,' Matthew said as she rejoined him. He guided her through a passage where a bakery and a pub kept their dustbins.

'Obviously you'll only take me to the very nicest places,' she said, picking her way past empty barrels, plastic bread crates and less savoury debris.

He stopped, turned back and smiled.

He did have rather a charming smile, she thought as they emerged into the back entrance of a large hall. She hoped Sally never saw him smile or she'd never leave off her matchmaking.

The hall he led her to was full of people setting up trestle tables and arranging their stock. They all seemed to know each other, exchanging banter and insults with the same ease as they asked after each other's families and how business was going.

'It's open to the public from about ten till four but the trade all come early,' he explained.

Everyone seemed to know Matthew but while they were all friendly, Gina couldn't help noticing that he didn't seem one of the gang. They treated him more with respect than friendliness, and eyed her with what she felt was deep suspicion as if she had a label saying 'I'm not really one of you' round her neck. She tried to overcome it but found herself trotting behind Matthew like an anxious child.

Then, attracted by some scent bottles, she stopped at a stall and let Matthew stride on to where a man had some pieces of furniture. Gina picked up a bottle engraved with deer and with an embossed lid. 'This is pretty.'

'It is,' agreed the seller, a woman wrapped in layers of cashmere. 'It's Bohemian.'

'Lovely. Probably beyond my price range though.'

'I'm looking for about four hundred,' said the woman.

Gina put it down again. 'These are delightful though, aren't they?'

'Very sellable but pricey.' The woman paused. 'You came in with Matthew Ballinger?'

'That's right,' Gina agreed.

'He'll never fill his father's shoes,' the woman went on. 'That's the trouble with Matthew.'

Gina suddenly felt defensive. 'What do you mean?'

'His father had a special gift. He could pick up a piece and tell instantly if it was a fake or not. It made things easy for him.'

'What, in a sort of psychic way?'

The woman shrugged. 'More likely years of experience. Anyway, things are harder for Matthew.' She narrowed her eyes. 'Dealer, are you?'

Gina was about to say no, of course not, when she realised she *was* a dealer – albeit a very new one. That was why she was here. 'I'm a learner, and it's very early days. I'd better find Matthew.'

In the time it took to find him and wait for him to shake hands on a deal, she realised what a very terrifying thing she and Sally had taken on. She wished her sister was there for moral support. It would have been fun with her. As the morning progressed she became more and more anxious. Matthew always seemed to be talking business with people and she didn't want to be hanging on his sleeve all the time, but if she didn't watch him in action, she'd never learn. And it was so hard. Too hard.

It was still quite early when they left the hall. As she and Matthew drove back, the Volvo (which she discovered was almost obligatory if you dealt in antiques) full of small but beautiful bits of furniture, she decided she should tell him she didn't want to go ahead.

'Matthew?'

'There's no one else in the car.'

'I don't want to do it.'

'Do what?'

'Become an antiques dealer. It's too difficult.' Gina felt herself becoming rather desperate. 'How can I sell things I know nothing about when the person buying them probably knows far more than me? How can I buy them in the first place? I was at a total loss this morning.'

'I did tell you it wouldn't be easy.'

'I know,' she said meekly.

'But you wanted to give it a go for Rainey's sake.'

'That's how we all felt last night: you, me and Sally. But I didn't really appreciate how hard it would be.'

Matthew didn't speak for a while. Then he sighed. 'Give yourself a chance. It was the first fair you'd been to. And nobody knows everything.' He was being generous, Gina knew, but he had had years to learn his trade – and if what that dealer had said was true it hadn't been easy for him.

'But I didn't know *anything* – except I couldn't afford to buy a scent bottle for four hundred quid and sell it at a profit.'

'Well, that's a very good thing to know. You could have got a bit off that price but scent bottles are specialist items. You need to know where your buyers are.' He smiled. 'You're being too hard on yourself.' It was the nicest thing he'd said to her and Gina felt some of her determination beginning to return.

'I'm not bad at selling, actually. But selling things to experts, when I know nothing, and expect to make money – well, I just can't.'

To her surprise she spotted a glint of amusement in the corner of his eye. 'You won't be selling to other dealers, not at first. You'll be selling to ordinary punters, collectors, people looking for a present for their cousin's ruby wedding – cranberry glass probably. Very popular for ruby weddings.'

'Oh,' said Gina. 'You know, I hadn't thought of that.'

'It's my fault. I introduced you to the professionals before you'd seen the casual buyers. Have you got time to come to the centre now? After I've bought you breakfast, of course. Second breakfast,' he amended. 'Then we'll go to the centre.'

He parked the car at the back of the French House, took her down a side street and then opened the door to a shop, the window of which was full of tins of tea, coffee and cocoa, Continental delicacies, grinders and teapots. The bell jangled as they went in.

It was the aroma of coffee that hit Gina first and she stayed in the shop part for a few seconds to enjoy it before following Matthew to the café in the back.

'What would you like? A cup of coffee? I recommend the cheese scones too.'

Gina sat on one of the high stools at the bar while Matthew placed the order and chatted with the girl serving. He was obviously a regular customer. He came back with a loaded tray.

'Coffee's never quite as delicious as it smells but this is pretty near it,' she said when she'd taken a couple of sips of her cappuccino.

'It's the thought of this afterwards that gets me out of bed before dawn.'

'Did you have a successful trip? You seem to have bought a few things.' She spread butter on to her scone and took a bite.

'Yes, I got a couple of nice pieces at reasonable prices. The trick is to buy stock that will sell quickly. If there's always something different to see, buyers keep coming back. But if they know they're going to see the same massive wardrobe and dressing table they don't bother.' He frowned. 'We have a bit too much of that in the centre at present.'

'So small is beautiful?'

'A lot of the time. People don't have room in their houses these days for big pieces.'

'There's no room for anything huge in my cottage although I would rather like a dresser. There's space along the wall in the kitchen.'

'We'll have to look out for one.'

Gina shook her head. 'I don't suppose it would be sensible to buy something I might not have room for in another house.' She was surprised to find herself sounding wistful. She'd never minded living in rented housing before and yet now she suddenly realised she wanted a home that was hers, that she could buy furniture for. She thought of Sally's tiny cottage that she'd made such a pretty, cosy home. She wanted to do that too: paint walls, upholster old sofas and strip floors. She shook herself back to reality.

'Some dealers furnish their houses with their stock. Everything in it is for sale,' Matthew said. 'They keep things for a while and then move them on.'

'Do you do that?'

'No. My father did but I rather resented favourite chairs and sideboards disappearing. I once had my desk snatched away before I'd finished my homework. I haven't done it in my own home.'

'People I met today spoke very well of your father,' Gina said cautiously.

'Yes. He was a wonderful character. Friendly, outgoing – hugely knowledgeable.' He shot her a glance. 'I know a fair bit about antiques but otherwise I take after my mother.'

Gina smiled. 'Is your mother still alive?'

'No. She died when I was in my early teens and I'm an only child, which threw me and my father together rather.'

'How sad. Not about you and your father but about your mother dying so young.'

'Yes, it was sad, but we got over it.' He flashed a smile. 'You can see why we were so fond of Rainey. She and my dad were a right pair. She'd come to dinner, dripping in scarves, making cocktails, putting on music she'd brought with her, talking, laughing, trying to find me girlfriends . . .'

'And did she succeed ever?'

'Not really. I'd rather find my own on the whole.'

Gina chuckled. She was enjoying herself, she decided. Matthew seemed in a good mood this morning; nothing like the grumpy, reticent man they'd first met. 'So where do you live? Near the centre?'

'Very. In a flat on the top floor. Very handy for

work.' He smiled that charming smile again. It made him seem so much less intimidating.

'And does Oscar manage in a flat?'

'He doesn't know it's a flat. He thinks the whole house is his personal space. Now, do you want more coffee? Another scone?'

'No, thank you. That was delicious but very filling.'

'Right, I'll show you my empire.'

Something in the way he said that made Gina wonder if in fact what he described as an empire was really a burden. He was an odd character. Reading people was part of her job but she realised she couldn't fathom him. He'd gone back into his shell.

'Jenny will have opened up and taken Oscar for a stroll,' Matthew said as they approached the French House. Looking up at it, Gina thought it must have been a magnificent family home at one time.

'Jenny is a godsend,' Matthew continued. 'She's always willing to open up, close up, do whatever's needed. She did it for my father and now she's doing it for me.'

'Has the French House always been an antiques centre?'

'Yes, for as long as I've known it. It was thriving in Dad's day – well, we still do OK now but times have changed . . .' He sounded wistful and Gina thought again about what the dealer had said. Had his father expected him to follow in his footsteps?

she wondered. There was nothing worse than always feeling second-best, not that she or Sally had ever felt this in their family.

'Did you want to be an antiques dealer?' she asked as they approached the door.

'No. I wanted to be a linguist. But I used to work for my dad in the holidays and so I sort of fell into antiques.'

'That seems a shame. I mean, to have to follow your father into the business when you wanted to do something quite else.'

'You can't really *be* a linguist,' he said. 'I did languages at university but I didn't know if I wanted to be a translator or an interpreter or what. I used to go with my dad to France and help him haggle. It seemed as good a thing as any to do with my French. Dad didn't force me into it, if that's what you're thinking. Now, let's go upstairs so you can leave your bag, then we'll unload.'

As they moved up through the centre to the top of the building Gina couldn't help feeling the place had a rather neglected air, as if everyone had gone away to do something more interesting. She and Sally had noticed it wasn't the most vibrant of places when they'd come here the other day and looking at it again Gina felt quite sorry for it – and Matthew. The atmosphere might have been because trade was bad but it couldn't help that there were so many other antiques businesses in Cranmore-on-the-Green. She wondered what it would take to make the French House a bit more profitable?

Oscar was in the office waiting. The moment he saw Matthew he reared up on his hind legs and put his paws on his master's shoulders.

'Golly, he's so big!' Gina laughed. 'He's the same size as you, very nearly.'

Hearing her, Oscar got down again, gave Gina an unenthusiastic sniff and flung himself to the floor.

'I'm sorry, he's not very forthcoming with people he doesn't know.'

'I wonder where he picked that up from?' asked Gina.

'Sorry?'

'Oh, you know, that thing about dogs being like their owners . . .'

Matthew scowled. 'Are you saying that Oscar and I look alike? Because my hair is not entirely grey and my eyebrows do not beetle, and I don't have a beard either.'

'I didn't say he was like you in looks.' Gina bit her lip. She didn't really know Matthew well enough to tease him but if she didn't, they might never get to that point. They needed to be able to work together, after all, and that would be harder if they had to be serious all the time.

He frowned at her in a way that told her he knew he was being teased and didn't mind. For a moment she caught a glimpse of the more relaxed Matthew she'd witnessed in the café. She hadn't imagined this side to him, then. She felt unexpected relief.

Gina helped Matthew shift the contents of the Volvo into a storeroom at the back. It was already quite full with an assortment of lamps and furniture arranged into sections, each with a sign by them indicating the different dealers in the centre, Gina presumed.

'I never saw any of these things,' she said, feeling foolish. She didn't feel bad about not trying to buy any of them but she should have at least spotted them.

'You develop an eye for anything you haven't seen before and what interests you. You will have been confronted with a whole hall full of new things. Also, Bert kept these things on one side for me. He knows I like French furniture and bought these with me in mind.'

'This is a nice little chest of drawers,' said Gina, taking one end of it as they lifted it out of the car.

'That's a commode. Nineteenth century. It's got some later paint and fittings, but it's in good condition.'

'This little bed is sweet,' said Gina, managing this on her own.

'It is. It's hand-painted, about nineteen hundred, in very nice condition.'

'And how much would you expect to get for that?'

'Somewhere around the five-hundred mark, I hope. Possibly more.'

Gina nodded sagely and picked up a large stone bowl. 'I'd imagine this was used for cream.'

'Yes, you're probably right. Be careful! It's heavy.'

'I must say, the Volvo is quite Tardis-like, isn't it? I would never have guessed all that would go in the back of an ordinary estate car.'

'That's why we antiques dealers love them.'

As they walked into the building together, both with their hands full, he went on, 'I'll give it all the once-over and price it before I put it out.'

Once everything was safely stored away Matthew said, 'Now, would you like a grand tour of the place?'

Gina looked at her watch and gave a small scream. 'Is that the time? I've got an appointment with the *Advertiser* in fifteen minutes. I want them to put my PR leaflets in their paper. I thought I had loads of time.'

'Well, don't panic. I'll take you home. Where is the appointment?'

'In Summerwick!'

'No problem. Jenny?' he called out into the depths. 'Can you mind the shop for a bit? I need to take Gina back.'

Minutes later they were speeding through the roads and lanes, Gina half terrified at how Matthew threw his old Volvo around and half pleased to think she wouldn't be late.

'Sorry, did I frighten you?' he said as they drew up outside her cottage.

'It was fine. You got me here. I've just about got time to change my top and then run into town. Thank you so much.'

He tipped his hand to her and drove off as she let herself in.

'That was really quite dashing,' she said to her reflection as she pulled a clean shirt down over the jeans. 'Matthew Ballinger is rather a surprising man.'

Sally had invited Gina for supper that evening to hear all about how she'd got on at the fair, and, as hoped, Gina arrived in time to help the girls with their bath and read to them. Alaric was cooking and Sally was finding homes for a large population of Sylvanian Families. As Gina read stories, cuddled up with the girls in their parents' bed, she knew her sister was finding the right home for each fuzzy animal. No throwing it all in a box for her. Would her attention to detail make her a good antiques dealer? Sorting fuzzy toys didn't seem like a transferable skill in this particular case, but you could never tell.

'The trouble is,' said Gina later, a glass of wine in her hand, her elbows on the kitchen table, having eaten a wonderful lentil curry, 'antiques are so diverse. I don't think we can possibly learn enough about them – even one tiny aspect of them – to make a profit in the time Aunt Rainey intended us to.'

'And you didn't have a chance to look at the stock she left us?'

Gina shook her head. 'No, I had to dash off. But the point is we wouldn't know if things were worth a pound or a thousand pounds.'

'Well, Matthew will know,' said Sally. 'We'll get him to price everything up and we'll sell it. It can't be that hard, can it?'

Gina sighed. 'I think it can. On those TV programmes the experts offer tiny amounts for things. Are they ripping the dealers off or do the dealers overcharge hugely? You see? We have no idea.' And whilst Matthew had seemed quite encouraging today, how long would it be before his patience wore out? He had his own part of the business to run, and the centre to look after.

'Are you staying over?' asked Alaric, a bottle poised over her glass.

'Yes please. I've got rather fond of your sofabed over the years,' she said. In fact she was fonder of her own bed but she needed to really put it across to Sally how difficult things would be and more wine would help. She was the one who had wanted to make a go of it but once Sally agreed to something she would often ignore the 'little things' like practicalities. If they were going to succeed in this venture it was important they both knew what was involved. 'This is going to be tough, Sally.'

'It'll be fine,' said Sally, true to form. 'Anyway, I plan to sell my own stuff and not just antiques.'

'You've really got good at them recently and they

are gorgeous, but I don't think Matthew will let you put things that aren't antiques in the French House. I think you need a specialist shop.'

Sally overlooked the compliments and cut to the chase. 'You mean everything there is over a hundred years old?' She sounded sceptical.

'That is the definition of an antique,' said Gina. 'Look, I don't know if Matthew stocks newer stuff, Sal, but I'm pretty sure he wouldn't allow cushions and lampshades.' She was annoyed to hear herself sound apologetic.

'He certainly seems very set in his ways,' Sally observed.

Gina wasn't as certain about this as Sally was but she kept her thoughts to herself. 'When do you think we could go over and see what's there?' she said after a tiny pause.

'When my darling husband can look after his beautiful girls,' said Sally, rubbing her husband's arm affectionately. 'When can you make it?'

'Almost any time. I haven't got a lot of work on at the moment.' Gina sighed.

'You sound worried, hon,' said Sally.

'I am a bit. We need to make this antiques thing happen. People are just not spending money on PR at the moment.'

'You can always move in with us. The girls would love it.'

'That's very sweet of you but it would drive you

mad after a couple of days.' Gina didn't add that it would drive her mad far quicker. But she was very touched by the offer.

'Well, you need never be homeless.'

Just for a second Gina remembered her life a couple of years ago. Business was booming, she had a boyfriend, she went on mini-breaks and stayed in lovely hotels. Then the boyfriend had decided that one girlfriend wasn't enough and somehow she had missed the signs. Apart from everything else, it made her feel so desperately stupid. And he still owed her money – quite a considerable sum actually.

'I could do tomorrow, couldn't I, my darling?' Sally held her husband's hand and toyed with his fingers. She liked to wrap her entreaties in little gestures of affection. 'The girls will be at nursery in the morning, so you could get some work done?'

Alaric raised an eyebrow. 'So I have to pick them up?'

Sally nodded. 'We can't leave them there all day, we can't afford it. But if Gina and I could have a day to sort out this business, it would be just fabby.'

Alaric agreed and Gina called Matthew. Tomorrow would be fine, he said with a lack of enthusiasm Gina felt was characteristic.

She went back to the table to find Alaric had cleared it of supper and retreated to his studio and Sally was making tea.

They sipped in silence for a few moments before

Sally said, 'You know, I find it quite hard to see Matthew and Aunt Rainey working together. She was so eccentric and off the wall and he's so – stuffy!'

Gina thought for a few seconds, trying to work out how Matthew and Rainey did get along so well. 'I don't think he's stuffy exactly. Just a bit of a young fogey.'

'Not that young. Forty if he's a day!'

Gina chuckled. 'Forty is still too young to be a fogey.'

'Whatever. What did our batty and unstuffy aunt see in him?'

Gina shook her head. 'We may never know. But she must have found something in him that was loveable. Maybe she needed someone to mother and he needed some mothering.'

Later, as Gina settled her hip bone so it missed the hard bit of the sofabed that night, she thought about how much she valued her sister. Sally was fun and positive and didn't see problems everywhere like she did. Tomorrow Sally and she would discover their Aunt Rainey had left them treasure and they would make their fortunes. Perhaps things would work out for them after all? It might even be fun!

Chapter Five

'I'd forgotten how full of old things these places are,' said Sally as Gina led the way up the stairs of the French House the following morning. 'When we came before I was too taken up with the girls to look around much.'

'Antiques tend to be old,' said Gina. 'It's kind of part of their job description.'

'I know,' said Sally, 'but I'm not sure I like them. I like things that are newish. It's all a bit old and moth-eaten here.'

Gina had to admit that the place did seem as if no one had been near it for years, but she suddenly felt territorial on its behalf. 'These things are clean,' she said. 'Look at the shine on that table.'

'Hmm. I didn't mean things were dirty. I don't know . . . it's just a bit – dead.'

Gina knew exactly what her sister meant. Once again, there didn't seem to be anybody around, neither stallholders nor buyers. She knew that the stallholders took it in turns and they wouldn't all be there at one time, but there was a distinct lack of bustle.

To Gina's relief, Sally managed to be calm in the face of Oscar, who to his credit didn't actually move when they went into Matthew's office: the door was open and as they were now part of things they felt they didn't need to knock. Oscar stayed in role as a large furry rug, which today was placed just to the left of the door.

'Actually,' Sally whispered to Gina as they tiptoed past him, 'he's so big he's not like a dog at all really. More a sort of cut-down horse.'

Matthew appeared not to have heard this remark and when he did look up from the books on his desk he seemed not to register they were there either. Even when he did, he failed to look delighted to see them, although he managed a polite smile and said hello.

'Hello!' said Gina. 'Did we disturb you? I thought you were expecting us.' This wasn't a good start.

'Sorry. Yes, I was. I got caught up with the accounts. Not exactly edifying reading.' He looked down at the page in front of him for a moment, then closed the book and got up. 'Let's go and find Rainey's stuff and see if it's enough for a cabinet.'

'Isn't Rainey's stuff still on display somewhere?' asked Sally.

Matthew shook his head. 'No. As I said before, dealers rent space, they put out what they want and they take turns to mind the shop and take money for all the stalls. When Rainey died, we had to pack up her things and add it to the case where she kept her stock.' He paused. 'Jenny did it. Maybe there's something in there that will make our fortune. Although to be honest, I think Jenny would have told me if she'd found anything valuable.'

'Maybe we should have a proper tour,' suggested Gina.

He stopped and shrugged, obviously not keen. 'OK.' He led the way into the middle of the house. Cabinets and larger items filled the wide passages and every odd corner between the doors of the rooms, which were all open.

Matthew went into one room. 'This is Harold's section – he's not in today. He's the expert in antique brass, which is quite a skill as it's not hallmarked.' He walked into another room full of furniture. 'There are some lovely English pieces here but the stallholder, Margaret, has a case in another centre and she's there more often than she is here.'

In room after room they were shown beautiful objects, and yet the lack of energy both women had recognised the moment they'd entered the French House was evident everywhere. It was more like a museum than a shop.

Eventually, they reached a storeroom at the back. It was smaller than the one Matthew had shown her yesterday and smelt faintly of turpentine.

'Here we are.'

Aunt Rainey's legacy was stored in an old suitcase, which, as Matthew lifted it off a shelf, appeared to be quite heavy. He put it on a table covered with a chenille cloth and pressed the catches. 'Now, what have we got?'

There was a silence as they all looked inside the lid. Gina felt a pang of disappointment. There was nothing that looked remotely valuable. Lots of it seemed to be old bottles. She exchanged a grimace with Sally.

'Now I know why she didn't put this stuff out before,' Matthew said after a couple of seconds. 'She's gone in for collectables.'

It didn't take an expert in body language to gauge how Matthew felt about this.

'And that's bad,' said Sally as if in confirmation.

He nodded. 'We like things to be genuine antiques here although we're not draconian about it. Rainey probably planned to put these with another centre.'

'Do people bring in a whole lot of new stock on the first of January, when it's reached its hundredth birthday?' Gina was trying to lighten the atmosphere but Matthew didn't smile. He sighed and took out the first item.

'Well,' said Sally with confidence. 'Even I know that's not valuable. It's a revolting model of a cottage that I wouldn't give house room. Next!' She was voicing her sister's feelings, only Gina felt her pronouncement wasn't exactly tactful.

Matthew gave Sally a look which made it clear she knew nothing. 'It's probably made by Goss and is worth over a hundred pounds,' he said before handing it to Gina. 'Look at it carefully, it's charming.'

As Gina inspected the model she did begin to see it had something about it. 'I sort of understand what you mean about it being charming but how can it be worth a hundred pounds?'

'Because people like them – collect them. Some of them are worth up to a thousand, or more if you're lucky. Now, what about this?'

'It's a corkscrew,' said Sally delightedly. 'I'm an expert already.'

Matthew handed it to her. 'OK, tell me something about it.'

Sally took it tentatively. 'It's the kind that hurts your hand if you try and open a bottle with it,' she said eventually.

Gina took it, for some reason eager to be able to say a bit more if she could. 'Well, it's old. I'd guess Victorian?'

Matthew nodded. 'What makes you say that?'

'I don't know. It just seems that way.'

'And what do you think it's worth?'

'I have absolutely no idea. About fifty quid? Or is that ridiculous?' It was like a quiz on a subject you had no idea about.

Matthew nodded and Gina felt ridiculously pleased. 'You might get that. You'd need to price it up a bit so you have room to come down. What can you tell me about this?' He handed Sally an item.

'It's a pig,' said Sally, 'but obviously there's more to it than that.'

'It's a jug,' said Matthew, removing a bit from behind the pig's neck. 'Quite modern but fun, I suppose.'

'Quite modern? What exactly are you talking, date-wise?' asked Gina, who found she wanted to learn about this quirky creature.

'About nineteen fifty I would guess, I'm not an expert. Too modern for me.' He did manage a rueful smile.

'Nineteen fifty is halfway through the last century,' said Sally firmly. 'That's not modern in the real world.'

'Probably not,' Matthew agreed. 'People have accused me of having an antique mind as well as an antiques centre.'

Gina sighed. 'I know I said this before, but you really do need a good PR person who'd put you on the map a bit.'

'We are on the map to people who know about us. We have a good reputation in the trade.'

'Yes, but what about new customers?'

'We manage,' he said firmly.

Gina wanted to shake him. No wonder his accounts were making him depressed if he was depending on dealers who already knew about the centre and a few odd people wandering in off the street to earn him a living. They'd never get themselves up the steps!

Sally, who'd been sorting through the contents of the suitcase with a slight frown, said, 'There seem to be a lot of old scent bottles here.'

'I think that was a new interest of Rainey's.' Matthew reached into the case. He picked up what looked to be a china cat. Then he took off its head. 'Quite sweet. You might get a hundred for this.'

'Rainey seems to have gone in for animals posing as something useful,' said Sally. 'But who'd have thought they would be so valuable?' She extracted what looked to Gina to be an empty bottle of Chanel No. 5. 'I think my girls have got something very like this in their toy box. I would never have let them have it to make potions with if I knew it was valuable.'

'It would need to be an early example to be worth much,' said Matthew.

'I'm still getting it back,' said Sally. 'They won't miss it.' She put both hands in the case, turning over bits and pieces, much more enthusiastic about old things now.

'Maybe we should get all this priced up,' said Matthew. He was clearly either bored or busy. 'There are some price tags over there.'

'But are you willing to let them go on display here?' asked Gina. 'If they're not old enough?'

He regarded her in a way that revealed nothing of his feelings. She was familiar with his ability to disguise his thoughts by now but it still maddened her.

'Yes,' he said eventually. 'It was what Rainey wanted, obviously. We should respect that.'

Gina didn't comment but she'd always felt it odd that people respected the wishes of the dead when they were quite likely to have ignored their feelings when they were alive. Still, Matthew might always have respected Aunt Rainey. 'That's very kind of you,' she said.

'It's OK,' he said brusquely.

Sally, who had the best handwriting, wrote the prices and Gina attached them to the pieces Matthew selected. She looked up enquiringly at a tiny blue bottle Gina had found hiding inside something else.

'Victorian again,' said Matthew, taking it gently. 'Somewhere between thirty and fifty. Put forty-eight on it and see how we do.'

'A lot of this pricing lark seems to be guesswork,' said Gina.

'More often than I'd like to admit,' said Matthew.

They took their items down to Rainey's section. She had a showcase in one of the smaller rooms.

'I'm surprised you kept it empty,' said Gina.

'To be honest it wasn't from choice,' said Matthew. 'We have a lot of very loyal customers and dealers, but we're not attracting new ones.'

'When we know each other better,' said Gina, 'I'm going to sort that all out for you.'

Matthew unlocked the case with an air of tired resignation. 'I doubt it,' he said.

While Gina was looking at Matthew, wondering why he was so downbeat when she felt sure that with a little energy and enthusiasm his antiques centre could thrive at least as well as any other centre, Sally was arranging the items in the case.

She seemed to have a knack for it. Instantly Gina felt she wanted to own the bits and pieces she'd faintly despised when they were in the suitcase.

'That looks nice,' said Matthew with masterly understatement.

'But the cabinet looks rather empty,' said Sally. 'Shall we get some more things out?'

'No,' said Matthew. 'Too many scent bottles wouldn't look right. We need a good mixture, or only scent bottles.' He paused. 'You need more stock.'

'Will you buy it for us?' said Sally instantly. 'We've got the five hundred pounds. You could make sure we had things we could make money on.'

'I could,' Matthew agreed, 'but what would you both learn from that? No, what you need to do is go to a proper antiques fair. Where Gina and I went the other day was tiny – it was a good place to start and local – you really need to go to Newark.'

'What's at Newark?' asked Gina.

'The biggest antiques fair in Europe. I owe it to Rainey's memory to train you properly and you'll really get a crash course there.'

'Oh my God! That sounds like so much fun,' said Sally.

'Don't forget it will all be old things,' said Gina.

'You know what?' said Sally, aware she was being teased. 'I've kind of come round to old things.'

'So when is this fair? I might have to rearrange work things if I'm going.'

'Next week, as it happens,' said Matthew. 'You've come into the business at just about the right time – from a buying point of view anyway,' he added.

'That's terribly short notice,' said Gina. 'We're not ready.'

An unexpected spark flared in Matthew's eyes. 'Rainey would say you're being a coward,' he said. 'And I don't think you are. I think you're up for a challenge.'

'I am – we both are,' said Gina. 'It's just so soon—'

'Newark is on when it's on. The next one isn't until after Christmas.'

'OK then,' said Gina before she could change her mind or question Matthew's reasons for helping them. Was it just in Rainey's memory or was he throwing them in at the deep end to prove a point – that they weren't cut out for this? 'We'll do it.'

Chapter Six

Matthew picked Gina up from her cottage in the early afternoon. They had agreed he would drive them up and they would spend the night at the B. and B. Rainey and he used to stay at. Sally had, at the last moment, been unable to leave the twins so was going to join them at the fair the following morning. Matthew seemed more relaxed than usual, even a little excited.

'We'll take as much as possible away with us but we can get anything big sent home. It'll be good to have Sally's car too.'

Having locked her front door, Gina followed him down the path. She was wearing trainers and, following instructions, had brought a huge bag with her, filled with plastic carriers. She was also carrying an overnight bag. 'No Oscar again, I see,' she said. She could feel herself picking up on his excitement, and realised that in spite of her anxiety about being able to make a go of the whole business, she was raring to go.

'We're not joined at the hip, you know. Although

he'd quite enjoy it. He's very sociable when he wants to be. I should have a smaller dog really, that I could take about more easily. Or a van,' he added, putting her bag in the boot and getting in beside her.

Gina chuckled, and then asked, 'Aren't you taking any pieces to sell?'

'No, this is a buying trip. I rarely take a stall at these things.'

He switched on the radio. 'You can choose the channel. Anything except Radio One. I'm too old-fashioned for that.'

'Don't you like to chat while you're driving?'

'Gina, the journey will take roughly three hours. If we try to make polite conversation for that long we'll both be exhausted long before we get there. And Newark is quite exhausting enough.'

Gina nodded. 'Fair enough.'

Matthew put the car into gear and they set off.

Three hours later, they drew up in front of an enchanting old farmhouse. Gina stretched her legs while Matthew retrieved their bags from the boot.

'The owner, Clare, is a lovely woman,' he said. 'She's been hosting antiques dealers for the big fairs for years.'

'Oh?' Gina took her bag out of Matthew's hand. 'Isn't it just Newark that's near here?'

'No, there are a few and they tend to be close together so people can go to all of them over a few days.'

'That sounds hard work.'

'It makes sense. If you come from London or the South and you've hired a van you want to fill it.'

As she followed Matthew through to the back door Gina thought being an antiques dealer was a tough way to earn a living. You had to travel miles to find your stock with no guarantee of making a profit on any of the pieces. And you still had to pay all your overheads. You'd have to be lucky and get some bargains if you were going to survive at all.

'Hello, we're here,' Matthew called out as they entered the house. The door wasn't locked and he obviously felt comfortable just walking straight in. A woman who could have been any age from fifty to sixty-five, with laughing eyes and a lot of necklaces, beamed at them from the centre of the large farm-house kitchen. A delicious smell of cooking pervaded the air. It was all very homely and welcoming.

'Clare, this is Gina Makepiece. She's Rainey's niece – one of two who are taking over her space in the centre. Gina, this is Professor Clare Elwell, who's been landlady to antiques dealers for ages in her spare time.'

Clare Elwell gave Matthew a hug and then took Gina's hand briefly and smiled. 'Welcome, welcome. You must be exhausted. You will both eat with me, won't you? I've got a lovely stew if you don't want to eat out?'

Gina glanced at Matthew. She hadn't thought about eating.

Matthew, who was making himself at home, putting his bag on a chair and stroking the cat, nodded in the direction of the Aga and raised an eyebrow.

Gina took it as her cue. 'If we wouldn't be imposing on you, I think it would be lovely to eat here,' she said.

'Rainey and I always ate with Clare,' Matthew said. He smiled a little shyly. 'It's nice to have you instead, Gina, it will stop Clare and me getting drunk and sentimental reminiscing about Rainey.'

'She and I shared a flat in London in the late sixties,' explained Clare. 'She was trying to be a rock journalist and I was studying. Now, Matthew, you open the wine for us like a darling, you know where it is, and I'll show Gina her room.

'Just come down when you're ready,' said Clare as they climbed a staircase lined with photographs and paintings. 'And let me know if there's anything else you need.' She opened the door to a very pretty double bedroom.

Gina glanced round the room, noting a radio by the head of the bed, bottles of water, biscuits, magazines and a selection of books as well as the usual tea- and coffee-making facilities. 'It's perfect. Everything I could possibly want.'

'We'll see you downstairs. No rush, Matthew and I will be very happy catching up and supper won't be for a while yet.'

After Clare had gone Gina couldn't help remembering the last time she'd stayed somewhere like this. It had been with Egan, before she had discovered that he had been taking money out of her account with her cash card and using it to woo other women. She forced the memory out of her head. He had admitted the theft when she challenged him and promised to pay her back. He'd even convinced her not to prosecute. For some reason she found herself wondering what it would be like to come here with Matthew as a boyfriend and banished that thought even more quickly. She needed a man like she needed a hole in the head.

It wasn't like a bed and breakfast, Gina thought, as she investigated the toiletries in the bathroom, it was more like staying with friends who had really comfortable guest accommodation.

She took Clare's advice and made herself a cup of tea while she washed and gave her hair a quick brush and then went back to the kitchen.

She looked around it happily. It was large, warm and just messy enough to be comfortable but not so messy you worried about hygiene. There was an open bottle of red wine on the table. Matthew was nursing a glass while Clare was stirring a large Le Creuset pot.

'Here.' He got up. 'Have a drink.' He was obviously very at home in Clare's house.

Gina sat down at the table and accepted the glass of wine.

'So you're new to this antiques lark?' asked Clare, peering into the Aga and then removing some baked potatoes.

'Yes. And I wouldn't be involved at all if it wasn't for Aunt Rainey.'

Clare laughed. 'So you called her that? Not Auntie Doris?'

Gina shook her head. 'Only if we wanted to annoy her. It's funny, Doris is coming back as a name but she obviously didn't like it much.'

'Well, when we lived together we spent a lot of time trying to give her a more hip name. I used to call her Rainey Rainbow anyway so we went with that eventually.'

'You don't happen to know why she never married, do you? Dad never knew but you probably knew her far better than her family.'

'She had loads of boyfriends, but they never led to anything until she went to France.'

'We knew she lived in France for quite a long time.' Gina leaned forward. 'Do tell.'

'I don't know much except that she had a wonderful lover,' said Clare. 'She used to come back and sleep on my sofa when she had work on. She'd never talk about him. Said it had to be a secret.' Clare smiled, full of reminiscence. 'She did say it was the best thing in her life, though.'

'Was she a rock journalist or antiques dealer then?' asked Gina.

'Rock journo.' Clare sat down at the table and Matthew filled her glass.

'She was quite successful for a while, wasn't she?' said Gina. 'I remember Dad saying.'

'She was for a bit but the work sort of fell away. As it does,' said Clare ruefully.

'Which was how she found herself doing what a lot of unemployable people do, dealing in antiques.' Matthew laughed. 'That's what she always told me.'

Gina couldn't help noticing how much more relaxed Matthew seemed. She had to admit he really was quite attractive, especially when he stopped being so taciturn – not to say grumpy. 'Was she successful?'

'She was. She didn't make a fortune but she earned a living,' said Matthew.

'I'd love to hear more about her,' said Gina, taking a crisp from the offered bowl. 'I have a feeling there was more to her than her family really knew.'

'That's probably true,' said Clare. 'She and I used to get up to all sorts in London. She used to invite me to gigs and we'd go round to the stars' dressing rooms afterwards.'

'You weren't groupies, were you?' Gina was rather shocked.

'We didn't sleep with all and sundry if that's what you mean, darling,' said Clare, a little amused. 'But we had a lot of fun.'

As Gina tottered up to bed, far later than was

sensible for someone with a very early start and a long day ahead, she realised she'd had a lot of fun too. She couldn't wait to tell Sally that their Aunt Rainey really had been a personal friend of the Beatles!

Chapter Seven

'I can see why you were worried about it being hard for Sally to find us,' said Gina at eight o'clock the following morning as Matthew drove into a car park the size of an airfield. 'It seems to cover to infinity and beyond, to quote Buzz Lightyear. Where is the building?'

Matthew appeared not to have heard of Buzz Lightyear. 'It's the site of the Newark showground and absolutely huge, but don't worry. We'll work out some way of meeting up with her.'

Knowing that Newark was the biggest antiques fair in Europe was one thing, actually seeing it in real life was different altogether. As Matthew slid his Volvo in between two others Gina said, 'Will you be able to find the car again?'

'People do lose their cars, but so far I've always managed to find mine.'

Despite the hour there was already quite a long queue waiting to buy their entrance tickets. There was a huge selection of people: men in tweed and corduroy; women dressed in woolly hats and shawls over their fleeces; young girls in tight jeans with leg warmers, already giggling; and every other sort of person in between.

Many had small carts, or trolleys, or home-made versions of the same. One woman had a tower of crates as high as she was, lashed together with rope. Others, and she was one of these, had large light bags slung over their shoulders. There were a few dogs too. Gina was disappointed not to see one set up with panniers – it wouldn't have looked at all out of place.

'Is this really the sort of place you'd come to if you couldn't walk?' murmured Gina to Matthew as, getting nearer the mobile ticket office, she spotted a raft of what looked like mobility scooters.

He chuckled. 'I promise you, people who can walk perfectly well hire those. The distance you have to cover makes it sensible. Others have bikes to speed up and down between the stalls. It does make it quicker.'

'Would you have brought a bike if I hadn't been with you?' Gina demanded, feeling instantly guilty.

'It's all right, I have a couple of friends who will lend me theirs if I feel the need. Here's one of them now.'

A tall man with curly hair, a beret and a pushbike came to say hello before joining the back of the queue. 'Mornin', Matt,' he said, revealing a cockney accent and a wicked smile.

'Jake.' Matthew nodded. 'This is Gina. She's taking over Rainey's spot in the centre.'

'Oh yeah, I heard that Rainey had died. Sad. She was a great woman. A real eccentric.'

Gina – in jeans, fleece and comfy trainers – sensed disappointment. 'My sister Sally, who's also taking over the spot, is much more like her.'

Jake laughed. 'Nah, you're all right.' He turned his attention to Matthew. 'Looking for anything special?'

'Just some good saleable pieces.'

Gina couldn't tell if Matthew was holding his cards close to his chest – she never wanted to play poker with him – or was simply telling the truth.

Jake pushed his arm playfully. 'Don't we all, mate. Let me know if you want to borrow the Dick Van Dyke.' He winked at Gina. 'That's the bike to you.' He moved off to join the line of people.

'He seemed nice,' said Gina.

'Yes, really nice and straight as a die. He's based over in Sussex so we don't do business that often but I've had some nice pieces from him and him from me.'

While Matthew was paying for their tickets, which were in the form of a label like those at race meetings, Gina heard her phone bleep. It was a text from Sally. 'Should be with you at about ten.'

As Gina tied her label on to the zip of her bag she told Matthew. 'She must have left the house at about five this morning,' she said in amazement. 'She's really keen.'

'Well, let's see if we can get you some nice pieces before she gets here, to start you off. Then I'll leave you girls alone for a bit.'

Gina contemplated objecting to being referred to as a girl but decided it was a waste of energy. 'Will we be able to get much with five hundred pounds?'

'I should hope so. That's quite a lot of money if you're going for small stuff.'

'What sort of things do you think we should go for?' She gazed around. There were row upon row of stalls and she could barely see to the end of them. She felt it would be very easy to get lost. 'There's so much here. I don't know where to start.'

'Here's as good as anywhere,' said Matthew, setting off down one of the avenues.

Gina followed, feeling completely out of her depth. As they walked, she looked left and right, trying to take in as much as she could.

'I think some art deco pieces would look nice with the scent bottles,' said Matthew. 'Rainey loved art deco.'

'I don't know the difference between deco and nouveau,' confessed Gina. 'In fact the amount I know about antiques could be written on the back of quite a small postage stamp.'

'Nouveau is more plants and natural things and deco is more geometric and was a bit later. But don't worry about not knowing anything. You'll learn.'

'Oh look,' said Gina, unreasonably offended by him saying she knew nothing, 'there are some lovely pieces on that stall.'

'Yes,' said Matthew. He stopped. 'Would you mind if I did the business for you? No offence, but you haven't got enough money to be able to waste it and any dealer worth his salt will be able to tell you're a novice and will get every penny out of you he can. He won't try that on me.'

'But how will I learn if I don't do it?' Gina did want his assistance but felt she had to take the plunge sometime.

'As I said, when Sally gets here I'll leave you to your own devices but it would be good to get some nice bits before then.'

Gina sighed. 'How are we going to work it, then?'

'I'll get you some choice pieces at rock-bottom prices.'

He made it sound so simple but Gina wasn't happy. 'But if you buy things we don't like – or I don't like – we won't be able to sell them. I have to choose the pieces,' she said firmly.

'But if the dealer knows I'm buying them for you he'll still charge more.'

Gina had to agree this was true. 'OK, we'll amble past, deep in conversation, and I'll tell you what I've liked when we're out of earshot.'

Matthew looked down at her. 'You are completely mad, you know that? Are you sure you wouldn't like me to just get some things I know you can make a profit on?'

Gina's business brain said yes, this was the sensible solution, but she felt if she started her career as an antiques dealer depending on others completely, she might never have the courage to break free. 'I'm sure. Let's do this.'

She took hold of his arm, leaning into it so she could look absorbed in him while really having a good look at the stall. 'Walk really slowly and pretend we're deep in conversation,' she said.

'What are we talking about?' said Matthew.

'It doesn't matter.'

'Yes it does. I can't be deep and meaningful if I don't know what I'm supposed to be feeling.'

Gina was surprised. 'You're not making a joke, are you?'

'Good God no! As if. I just need to get into my part.'

Pushing aside the thought that he might have a sense of humour, Gina applied herself to a subject that could be engrossing them. 'Could we be discussing where we're going on holiday?' It was the only thing she could come up with that felt safe.

'Not at Newark. No, we'll discuss whether or not to buy the huge armoire we saw earlier. Will it fit in the dining room or not.'

They hadn't seen an armoire but she got the point. 'Oh, OK. Let's do it then.'

Matthew threw himself into the part. He gripped her arm. 'Darling, I think if we threw out every other bit of furniture that armoire could look really quite important . . .'

She was momentarily thrown by his use of 'darling', then she reminded herself he was only playing a part. And if they weren't a couple, they'd have to be colleagues which could reveal her complete lack of knowledge. She picked up the line and ran with it. 'But what would we eat off if we threw out the table and chairs? We'd have an armoire we could almost move into and have to eat Christmas dinner off our knees!' Gina's often buried sense of the ridiculous burst forth.

'Don't forget to look at the stall,' prompted Matthew as they became level with it.

Gina did her best to peruse the stall while walking along. She spotted an interestingly shaped vase and what seemed to be an oddly sized tile.

'OK, can we go back the other way so I can have another look?' she said.

'Do you want to change arms? That would look odd.'

'No, I can look across.' Gina rather liked holding Matthew's arm. He felt strong and his overcoat, although old enough to have been his father's, was cashmere.

They turned and then set off again a few yards up the alley between two rows of stalls and then back again.

'Seen anything else?' said Matthew.

Gina had been wondering why she found it so nice hanging on to Matthew's arm as she walked. She put it down to her latish night and early start. 'Sorry,' she said, 'I was distracted by the thought of being with a man who'd throw out all the dining-room furniture for what is really just a posh wardrobe.'

'We'll make another pass then.'

Gina giggled at his fencing terminology but did remember to have a good look.

'OK, I saw some really nice coffee cups—'

'Cans.'

He was such a stickler. 'Cans then, and another vase, but really I think I need a closer look. Then you can get an idea of what I like and I might not mind you doing the buying.'

To his credit, he didn't sigh. 'Fair enough.'

As a couple, they wheeled into the stall. 'Oh *darling*,' said Gina, now well into her role. 'I really like those coffee cu— cans. They're so contemporary!'

The dealer raised his eyes and smiled. 'Late-eighteenth/early-nineteeth-century Wedgwood.'

'That old?' Gina's amazement was genuine. The cups had a blue and white chequered pattern with little emblems on the white squares. 'Really, you wouldn't be surprised to see these in Harrods as part of some new collection.'

'Indeed. But I think you'd probably want to give a whole set as a wedding present – darling – and this pair are probably beyond our price range.'

'Oh,' said Gina, who'd had a good scan of the stall, 'you'd have thought second-hand things would be cheaper.'

Her reward was a pinch on her arm. 'Anything else you like, my love?' said Matthew.

'I quite like that vase.' She indicated a rather odd-shaped article which, from a distance, could have been the outline of a woman with nothing above the shoulders. Closer to one could see a painting of a woman with butterflies for hair and a spider at the centre of her torso.

'I don't think Evangeline would though,' said Matthew.

'Evangeline?' Where on earth did he get a name like that for their fictional bride? she wondered. 'Oh, I always call her Angie. I forgot she had that weird name.' She pinched Matthew this time. Being clamped together had some advantages.

She was seeing a whole new side to Matthew and she rather liked it. Deciding it was time she spoke for herself, she unclamped herself and asked the stall-holder, who seemed good-natured and friendly, 'What about that tile thing? Is that expensive?'

'This is a Compton Pottery plaque, made about nineteen hundred,' he said.

'And how much is it?' said Gina, worried that Matthew would expose himself as a dealer by saying 'What's your best on that?'

'Two hundred pounds to you, love,' said the dealer.

'And a lot less to anyone else probably,' Gina replied. 'Come on, darling, let's find a nice chandelier.'

She was aware of Matthew shaking as they walked along, again clamped in a newly-weds' clasp. 'Are you laughing?' she demanded. 'That was my very best acting. I should get an Oscar.'

'You do have a certain comic talent and you mustn't mind if I laugh.'

Gina found she didn't mind at all. 'I'll forgive you.'

'But we're no nearer getting you anything for your stall,' he said, steering her to a relatively quiet spot whilst they took stock. 'Here's another plan. You go to a stall, on your own, and ask the price of anything you like. Choose a few things. Then back away as if it's all way too much. I'll spy on you from a distance and see how many of the things I can get at a reasonable price.'

'It sounds brilliant but how good were you at Kim's game as a child?'

'Sorry?'

'You know, there are a number of objects placed on a tray and you have to remember as many as possible after the tray is taken away. Children's parties? Didn't you play that?'

'I think that was probably more a game for girls,' he said disparagingly. 'But I do have a good memory for objects. It goes with the territory. Off you go. There's a likely stall over there.' He pointed to one full of little bits and pieces – much like the stuff Rainey had in her suitcase. Gina's eyes lit up. This was more like it, surely she could find something here to buy and at a good price.

She enjoyed looking at the objects and hoped Matthew was able to see which ones she was asking about. She found a small vase even she recognised as Moorcroft, which she hoped wouldn't be beyond the budget; she held it up, hoping she wasn't being too obvious, but wanting to make sure Matthew saw it in between the other people milling round the stall. Next she spotted a pair of candlesticks she just thought were pretty but turned out to be worth over a thousand pounds. She shook her head and a charming nightlight in the shape of a lighthouse caught her eye. It seemed a snip at fifty. She fell in love with a bowl decorated with fish but when she heard that was five hundred pounds she realised most of the stall was beyond her. She moved away to let Matthew work his magic but she doubted if he'd be able to negotiate enough to make them affordable. She glanced at her watch. It was nine thirty already. She spotted a coffee stall and decided that was as good a place to meet Sally as any.

She was looking longingly at some little carved birds when Matthew caught her up. 'I got you the nightlight and the Moorcroft. You owe me a hundred.'

'No!' she gasped. 'I can't believe you managed that. You're a genius!'

Matthew looked a little abashed. 'Just doing my job. Now, are you all right to have them in your bag?'

Gina put the parcels away safely. 'I'm meeting Sally at ten. I thought here was a good place. Can I buy you a cup of coffee? As a thank you?'

'If you buy me a cup of coffee every time I get something a bit cheaper for you I'll be awash. But one cup would be nice. We're in this together, remember, Gina. We're both under instruction from Rainey.'

Gina disconnected her phone. 'I've done my best to tell Sally where the coffee stall is but she said she couldn't relate to what I was saying.'

'Ring her back and tell her to wait by the entrance. I'll go and meet her there,' said Matthew, getting up. 'I'll borrow Jake's Dick Van Dyke. I've just spotted him round the corner.'

While she sipped her cooling coffee and ate the rest of the bun she hadn't been going to have, Gina realised she liked Matthew. She could see what Aunt Rainey had seen in him. He was mostly reserved and serious but had a kind heart and a sense of humour. She'd have to be careful how she conveyed this to her sister or she'd have them up the aisle in seconds, but she did feel they were part of a team now.

Sally arrived ten minutes later, breathless and laughing. 'He gave me a backie. Really, it was the last thing I expected from Matthew.'

An emotion she didn't recognise stabbed Gina for a moment. When she realised it was jealousy she leapt up and hugged her sister, determined never to feel like that again. 'He put you on the back of the bike?'

'I sat on the saddle and he pedalled. I haven't laughed so much for years. He's surprisingly good fun, isn't he?'

Gina chuckled. 'He is. But as he isn't with you, I presume he's biked off somewhere else.'

Sally nodded. 'Yes. We're on our own for a bit, he said. Isn't this place *huge*!'

'You must have set off at the crack of this morning.'

'A bit before, actually. You know how it is, when you know you've got to get up early you don't really sleep. Still, the girls will be as good as gold, I know. I promised them presents. I saw some amazing crystal decorations as we whizzed past,' said Sally. 'They're for Christmas really, but the girls will love them.' She paused. 'Hey! Why don't we buy some? If they're here, they must be acceptable at the centre, don't you think?'

The sisters set forth, clutching on to each other. 'I've got a couple of things already,' said Gina. 'They're all wrapped up; I'll show them to you later. We've got about four hundred pounds left to spend. Let's have a look at this stall.' She drew her sister towards a table full of what Matthew would probably call knick-knacks. 'And do let's try not to tell the world we know nothing about antiques.'

'I won't have a problem with that,' said Sally. 'I was good at drama at school.'

'I'll have you know I've displayed some pretty good acting skills myself this morning. Matthew and I played a married couple with complete conviction.'

Even before she'd finished speaking she realised she shouldn't have said that. Sally stopped and turned to her, an expression of glee on her face. 'Really?'

'It was only pretend. If we were at a stall together and weren't a couple, we'd look like colleagues and then I'd look a complete fool when I didn't know what I was talking about.'

'Oh, OK,' said Sally, reluctantly suppressing her excitement as she picked up a rather pretty cup and saucer before quickly putting it back down again when she saw the price. A glance at a couple of other items soon told them both that everything on this stall was beyond even a bargaining price. Not knick-knacks then.

'Why don't you take me to the decorations stall?' said Gina. 'If we get the girls' presents out of the way we can focus better on getting stock.'

'Good idea. It's outside. Not far . . .'

The stall took a bit more finding than Sally had thought but they had a good look round while they found it. 'I think we should definitely stick with small decorative items, like Rainey already had,' said Gina.

'I'm cool with that but really, I think we should

get some of these decorations too. I mean, they're small and decorative and Christmas is coming up.'

'But they're not antiques.'

'I think we should buy them anyway,' said Sally. 'Even if we don't sell them at the centre we could take a stall somewhere else.'

Gina shrugged. 'I suppose. After all, we have to make a profit, but no one ever said we had to sell through the French House.' Although she already felt a certain loyalty to it.

The stall was truly impressive. It didn't only have decorations but anything that could be made with crystals and a clever welding tool.

'These hair-slides are to die for,' said Sally, putting her purchase in her handbag. 'What else shall we buy? Those dress rings are terribly on trend.'

'We must keep some money for antiques . . .' Gina protested as Sally seemed to be getting carried away.

'They are sort of old,' her sister said. 'I had quite a chat with the woman who makes them. The bits of crystal are recycled. I think they're amazing.' Sally's eyes lit up in a way they hadn't been when they'd been looking at true antiques. These were much more her thing.

'Well, at least we can afford them and they are extremely pretty,' Gina conceded.

'Yes,' said Sally, 'and it's our stall. We should be able to sell what we like at it. If not, we'll work out some other way to sell them.'

Fifteen minutes later they had an awful lot of decorations.

Sally had got an amazing deal, Gina had to admit. She'd got about three hundred pounds' worth of decorations for a hundred.

'You have done brilliantly, but can we please buy some antiques. Now.' Gina felt they were somehow cheating Matthew with the decorations and she didn't want to quarrel with him – or put him out.

She led Sally to a stall that had plenty of the small, sellable items they were looking for. Sally immediately spotted a tea set, quirky and attractive.

'How much is this?' she asked the stallholder.

'How old is it first, though,' whispered Gina.

'Fifties, classic, very popular period now,' said the man. He was dressed mainly in denim and seemed quick to spot them as people ready to spend money and not just browse.

'Thanks, but not that old then,' said Gina firmly. Matthew had made it plain the 1950s were practically contemporary. 'Sally, we're supposed to be buying antiques only from now on.'

'Well, there's plenty here that's antique,' he said. 'What do you fancy?'

He did seem a bit more like a market trader than an antiques dealer but Gina had quickly discovered there was no type when it came to dealers; anyone or everyone could be one. It was a very egalitarian business.

'What about these, set of fish knives and forks, in their case, make a lovely present.'

'I don't think so, thank you,' said Gina. She hadn't been in the business more than five minutes but she had spotted there were sets of fish knives and forks everywhere and no one seemed to want them.

'Well now, girls.' The dealer leant in. 'If you want something really special, I've got something behind here I don't want everyone to see. Something that needs a really good home.'

Gina was instantly suspicious. 'Sorry, but why wouldn't you want your stock on display?'

The dealer became even more confiding. 'As you probably know, the antiques business is very competitive.' Gina had already picked this up, so it went a little way to reassure her. 'I don't want to give my local dealers the advantage. But you girls, I know you're not local to me, so I'd like you to have these pieces.'

Gina wasn't entirely convinced but was curious. So was Sally, it seemed.

'What is it? she asked.

'Come round the back and I'll show you.'

As 'round the back' was still very public the man did a lot of checking to see no one was listening, which Gina was sure was just showmanship. 'Tea caddies.'

Sally stifled a giggle and Gina bit her lip. All this cloak-and-dagger stuff for tea caddies – they should have been opium pipes at the very least or some sinister paraphernalia used in witchcraft.

'Well, they look nice,' said Gina. Maybe they would be the sort of good saleable items they were looking for. 'Do people collect them?'

'Oh yes. Tea caddies are very popular, but you don't often get this quality, not for the price.'

'Why not?' asked Sally.

The man looked offended. 'I thought I told you. If my neighbouring dealers had these for sale, people would go to them in future, not me. That's why I don't want them sold locally.'

Gina was still trying to work out if this made sense when Sally cut to the chase. 'How much?'

'Five hundred,' came the reply, without the usual hesitating and sucking of teeth they'd come to expect.

'Far too much,' Sally came back, just as quickly. 'Two hundred!'

'Are you trying to take the food from the mouths of my wife and children? Four hundred.'

'You must be joking,' said Sally, obviously well in the spirit of hard bargaining. 'Two hundred and fifty!'

'Come on, girl! Be fair. I can't sell you this very pretty pair of tea caddies at less than I paid for them. Three hundred and fifty.'

Gina wished she had the opportunity to do a crash course in tea caddies. It was just this sort of occasion that made their total ignorance such a handicap.

'We've only got two hundred,' said Sally. 'Take it or leave it.' She was amazingly tough.

The dealer's hand had gone out and Sally's had nearly met it, when the curtain was pulled back and they heard, 'Don't, under any circumstances, buy those caddies!'

Chapter Eight

It was Matthew.

'Hey, butt out, mate,' said the dealer. 'We're doing private business here.'

'These women are my colleagues,' said Matthew.

'What?' The man looked horrified, making Gina realise that it had been obvious that they were novices.

'So they won't be buying the caddies,' said Matthew firmly. Then he put a hand on a shoulder of both women and guided them away.

'I can't decide if that was incredibly overbearing or rather sexy,' whispered Sally, probably loud enough for Matthew to hear.

'I'm sorry if that seemed overdramatic but that man would have fleeced you,' Matthew said.

'So they were fakes? How did you know from a distance?' said Sally.

'Firstly, there are a lot of fake tea caddies about. And these were far too cheap.'

'But how did you know how much he was selling them for?' demanded Sally. Gina wondered if she was bearing a grudge for being cheated of her bargain.

'I'd spotted them earlier. When I saw you being taken behind the stall I knew he was up to something. The minute I set eyes on them I saw the hinges were wrong.'

Gina sighed. 'This is so difficult. I don't see how we can ever make money at it.'

'It's not a quick road to riches unless you're very lucky,' said Matthew, 'but some of us have been making a living from it for years.'

'But how long did it take you?' asked Gina, now thoroughly despondent. She'd been enjoying herself, but the immensity of the task they'd taken on overwhelmed her once again. They were going to be robbed at every turn.

'I did have the advantage of a father in the business,' said Matthew more kindly, 'but I didn't make money on my first deal. As an old hand at this antiques fair game, I say we need tea and somewhere to sit down. Then you can show me what else you've bought.'

He guided them to the café. When they all had tea and doughnuts he looked at them in a schoolmasterish way and said, 'So, show me what you've bought.'

Gina felt told off even before Sally produced the bags of Christmas decorations. Had there been a moment she'd have told Sally to keep quiet about these.

'Aren't they beautiful?' said Sally delightedly.

'They're OK, I suppose, but they're not antiques,' he said dismissively.

Gina felt the need to stick up for her sister. 'They're made out of antique materials,' she said.

'Even so, we couldn't sell them at the centre.' He was adamant.

Gina was about to tell him about their fall-back position of taking a stall elsewhere when she had another thought. 'What is the centre like at Christmas?' she asked brightly, trying to give the impression she'd moved on from the decorations.

'Well, Christmas isn't a good time for antiques dealers. It never has been. No one's thinking about buying furniture then, unless it's a new sofa to watch the Christmas specials on television from.'

Gina felt watching a Christmas special was the last thing he would ever do. 'But people do buy presents and not all antiques are furniture, after all.'

Matthew nodded in agreement.

'What's your point, Gina?' asked Sally defiantly, tucking the decorations back into their bag.

'I was just thinking – from a PR point of view – Christmas could be a very good opportunity for the centre.'

'How?' queried Matthew, a puzzled frown on his face.

Gina's respect for Matthew had been growing but just now she wanted to shake him. She'd countered her own negative feelings with creativity, and she wanted his mood to change too. Just because Christmas had never been a good time for antiques before, it didn't mean it couldn't ever be. 'We could do an event. Advertise it well, of course, and get everyone to put their small, gifty items on sale. We'd do mince pies, mulled wine, get people into the centre who've never been into an antiques shop in their lives.'

'Oh yes,' said Sally, practically knocking her tea over in her excitement. 'I think that's a brilliant idea, Gines. After all, antiques are so romantic and men never know what to get for their women. There are some darling things most women would love.' She paused. 'And we could sell our decorations,' she finished, deliberately not looking at Matthew as she said this.

He scowled. There was no other way of describing it, Gina felt. 'I'm really not sure—'

'It must be better than not doing it,' said Gina. 'If Christmas is usually a slack time, it can't do any harm. We'll have a theme – get the stallholders to dress up – drag the town into the French House, lured by music, the smell of spices and everything priced to sell.'

'I can't see how it would work,' said Matthew, which made Gina want to slap him.

Heroically restraining herself from violence, Gina pressed on. 'That's because you have no vision. Really, Matthew, give me a free hand and I could set up something brilliant that would really give the business a boost.'

'It is what she does, Matthew,' said Sally. 'And although I hate to say it, seeing as she's my older sister and all, she's very good at it.'

Mathew chewed the last of his doughnut and drained his cup before he replied. 'I'm not saying I agree but if the stallholders are happy then I might – and I mean might –' he looked sternly at Gina, who was trying hard to conceal her triumph – 'let you go ahead. You do know though, don't you, that we only have about two of us there selling on any particular day?'

'Yes, of course we do,' said Sally impatiently.

Gina thought for a moment. 'Well, then,' said Gina decisively. 'On this open day everyone would *have* to come in.' She smiled. 'Don't worry – I'll persuade them.'

It was mid-afternoon and, with a long journey ahead of them, Sally and Gina said goodbye to Matthew, who was staying on another night. He retrieved Gina's overnight bag for her and the sisters set off for the exit. They were both exhausted.

'It's like snow-blindness, isn't it?' said Sally. 'You just can't focus any more.'

'No. It all just merges into one object and you couldn't tell rubbish from pure gold – even if you did know anything about it.' She stopped to readjust her bag on her shoulder. It was feeling quite heavy now. As she gave it a hike her eye was caught by a cardboard box in front of a stall. It was almost a reflex now. She put out her hand to stop Sally. 'Would you mind if we just had a look at that box?'

It was a stall selling chandeliers and the box was full of pieces: a mass of cut-glass drops, pendants, pieces of crystal like giant diamonds in all sorts of shapes and some spikes, like crystal icicles. 'These are amazing!' said Gina. She was getting as bad as Sally but Matthew wasn't with them and they were so pretty.

Sally crouched down beside her. 'Think of what you could make with these.'

'Apart from chandeliers, you mean?' Gina recognised the light of creation in her sister's eye.

'Christmas decs – but not only for Christmas. Oh, do let's buy them. How much are they?' She smiled up at the dealer winningly.

'A hundred,' he said.

Sally stood up. 'What a shame. If you'd said twenty, we'd have taken them off your hands. But we haven't got a hundred.' She sounded worryingly professional, Gina thought.

The dealer sighed. 'I can't take twenty but if you make me a sensible offer—'

'Thirty,' said Sally immediately.

'Ninety,' said the dealer.

'That's hardly better than a hundred! Thirty-five.'

Gina looked into the box again. There were a lot of bits and pieces in it, although now she looked more closely some of it appeared to be random bits of plastic. She got up and joined her sister. It was time they were off. 'Come on, Sal, we haven't got all day.' Pulling her coat across she felt in the travel wallet she had tucked down her front with her emergency money in it. She pulled it out. 'What have I got here? Forty-five pounds. And that's all we have.' She gave him the money with one hand and shook his free one with the other. 'Deal?'

The man shook his head sadly. 'Deal!'

The girls picked up the box between them and staggered off.

'I can't believe we got all this for forty-five pounds!' said Gina.

'I might have got him down a bit further,' said Sally. 'I was doing well.'

'But as you didn't actually have any money . . .'

'I was sure you had some in your secret stash,' she said with sisterly insight. 'I can't believe you're still doing that hiding-some-money thing. It's so neurotic. Has anyone ever stolen your bag?'

'I left my handbag in a taxi once, if you remember,' said Gina. 'I've always put a couple of notes somewhere about my person ever since. Sometimes I put a credit card in there too.'

Sally shook her head at her sister's funny little ways. 'Come on, let's get these jewels home.'

After a bit of searching, and several goes at 'I think it's along here somewhere' from Sally, they eventually found her car and set off for home. Sally had given in to Gina's insistence that she drive, finally admitting she was tired after the long drive up.

'You seem to have come round to old things,' said Gina a bit later.

'I like them better if I can make something new out of them,' said Sally. 'I can make some sensational things with those bits and charge what we paid for the whole lot per item!'

'We could try to sell them at the centre if Matthew agrees,' said Gina. 'He might soften up about it if we have this Christmas market.'

'You think? He's very uptight and purist, Gina.'

Gina found herself feeling offended although she did realise her sister was right. 'Do you think this special Christmas market is mad?'

'Certainly not! Lots of people feel shy about going into shops if they know they're not going to buy anything. But if they could just buy something little – like a candy cane – they'll take the chance.'

'Victorian sweet stall, excellent idea,' said Gina. 'Hot chestnuts, mulled wine – or maybe cider? A bit more traditional English?'

Sally laughed. 'I love it when you get going on an idea. One minute you're all cautious and sensible, keeping money in your special travel wallet in case you get your handbag nicked – but when you are really into an idea you'll do anything!'

Gina glanced at her sister fondly. 'You have to think big, but I've already rejected the idea of having a living nativity . . .'

Chapter Nine

Gina's efforts to promote herself as a freelance PR hadn't had huge results, and her client had nothing for her at the moment. He was bringing a new product out which would mean a lot of work, but not until the summer. Therefore she decided to focus on the French House. She planned to go there the Saturday after the trip to Newark to arrange their couple of cases and to get to know some of the other dealers. There'd be three of them on a Saturday. It would give her a chance to get them on side about the Christmas event.

She couldn't decide if she was relieved or disappointed not to see Matthew's Volvo parked in one of the centre's few spaces.

She opened the door awkwardly, setting the bell jangling, and went in.

Jenny was there and took the box Gina was carrying. 'Morning! Are you here to work, or are you just delivering your stock?'

'I'm here to work, I hope. I want to sort out our stuff and put anything that's priced into the cabinet, but I'd love to do anything else useful.' Gina liked Jenny and knew how important it was to get her on side. 'If there's nothing else, I'm very happy to hoover, or make coffee for the others.'

'That's kind. I have had a quick run round with the vac but if you came in early one day, it would be lovely if you did it. Oscar produces rather a lot of hair but as he's not here today we won't have to keep doing it. Shall I show you where the coffee things are?'

As Jenny led her to a little kitchen at the back of the building Gina glanced around. Although she was more used to it now, it still made her feel a little depressed. She was even more determined to have the Christmas event, however hard it might be to persuade people. The French House so needed an injection of energy. After a brief glance at the kitchen, Gina rearranged the stock on what she now thought of as her and Sally's stall until she was sure she had the perfect look. She then went to introduce herself to the dealers who happened to be in. The first thing she would ask would be if they wanted a hot drink and how they liked it.

Her first target was Tiggy, an attractive woman in late middle age who'd been an actress. 'Still do it if they want me to,' she said, having accepted the mug of green tea gratefully. 'But this is my life now, really.' She had a husky, sexy voice and exuded warmth. 'So tell me all about yourself.'

'Well,' said Gina, 'I'm one of Rainey's nieces.'

'Oh darling, how we all loved Rainey. Such a loss to the world, but how marvellous you're taking on her pitch.'

'With my sister. It's probably a terrible idea really as we neither of us know a thing about antiques but it was a challenge, you know.' Gina felt it was right to be completely frank with Tiggy. She'd have been found out pretty quickly if Gina had pretended to know anything anyway.

'We've all got to start somewhere and if you've got Rainey's stock to kick you off . . .' said Tiggy, who'd confided she'd been christened Antigone.

'And Matthew took me and Sally – that's my sister – to Newark and we got some more things.'

'Splendid. I haven't been to Newark for a while now but the last time I did, someone came and bought all my stock. I was devastated.'

Gina frowned. 'But surely that's a good thing, isn't it?'

'In some ways, of course it's good. We're here to sell the stuff, after all, but it meant I had nothing else to sell and had to buy like mad to build up my stock again.'

'I see,' Gina said. Then: 'Tiggy, can I ask you something?'

'Anything except my age or my weight.'

Gina chuckled. 'It's nothing personal, but I was thinking it would be good if we had a Christmas event. Matthew told me Christmas wasn't a good time for antiques dealers on the whole, and as I'm a PR consultant in my day job, I thought: Here's an opportunity to *make* it a good time.'

'Hm, well, anything that would help to earn a crust,' said Tiggy. 'What sort of thing did you have in mind?'

'Well, I'd want people to sell small items, which could be presents, and we'd have mulled wine – or cider – and ideally I'd get people to dress up in Victorian costumes.' Tiggy was an actress – would she be open to this idea? 'My plan is to offer entertainment, to get people into the centre who wouldn't normally go into an antiques shop. I want them to see antiques as potential gifts, not just something you look at on telly.'

'I see where you're coming from and it sounds fun, but I'm not sure you'll convince everyone. Did you say Matthew had agreed to it?' said Tiggy as she rearranged a collection of very pretty blue and white cups and saucers.

'Reluctantly, but if we all made money, it would be worth it and he'd see that. After all, we haven't much to lose!'

'You have, actually,' said Tiggy. 'Mulled wine or whatever doesn't come free. But I'd be happy to make nibbles and things and I think some of the others probably would too.'

Gina felt cheered that she'd managed to get at least

one person – two if you counted Matthew – on side and moved on to her next prey, who dealt only in furniture. He, unfortunately, wasn't at all keen on the idea, even after Gina had offered Hobnobs with his coffee, but he did concede he didn't expect to do much business at Christmas so was willing to move his stock into storage, which was almost as helpful.

The other dealer in that day – a youngish man who told her he shared his stall with his teacher-wife and sold a mixture of small items: vases, decorative jugs, some jewellery – was keen. 'I think it's a good idea. It's a real shame we can't take advantage of people's panic buying.' He hesitated. 'Mind you, the wife and I are quite tied up round Christmas. We're part of a Gilbert and Sullivan group and we're doing *The Pirates of Penzance* early in January.' Gina could tell by his smile that this was a passion he was proud of.

'Oh, what fun,' said Gina. 'I don't suppose that means you'd dress up for our event? To add atmosphere?'

'Sure. And we'll have a few spare costumes too, which we could lend to other dealers, to make it a bit easier for them.'

Gina could have hugged him. 'That would be brilliant. And, I'm sorry, what was your name?'

'Andrew, and my wife is Sophie. She's here more in the school holidays.'

'Would you both be here if we did an event?'

He nodded. 'I should think so.'

'Excellent. You sell exactly the sort of things people would want to buy as presents. And I feel if people came in here once and saw how lovely some of the things are, they might get into the habit of it.' She smiled brightly. Her argument sounded so convincing, but was she just making up a scenario because she wanted it to be true? There was no way of telling. Still, three down, seven to go.

When she went back to her cabinet she was pleased to see a woman staring into it. From behind she looked pleasingly affluent. Gina was determined to sell her something.

'Can I help you?' she said in a friendly voice.

The woman turned and smiled. She was in her early thirties, well dressed and groomed. As Gina took in more of her appearance, she realised just how glamorous she was.

She was wearing a suede coat that went down to her ankles and looked as if hundreds of rare chamois had died to produce it. Gina wasn't an expert but she recognised the boots that graced those ankles were very, very expensive. Her jewellery was gold and chunky; her scarf was silk. It was all classic stuff that would look just as fabulous in twenty years' time. She'd have looked at home on the front row of a catwalk show.

She was also very good-looking, but now Gina looked at her more closely, she felt she was too perfectly made-up. It made her look older than she probably was.

'Is there anything you'd like to look at? You were showing interest in my cabinet before I appeared?'

'Oh yes,' said the woman. 'The scent bottles. Can I see them?' She had the barest trace of a foreign accent.

'Which one in particular?'

'All of them.'

Gina found the key and unlocked the cabinet, her fingers fumbling with the unfamiliar lock. She brought out all of Aunt Rainey's scent bottles and laid them on a nearby table. She wished she'd had a bit of velvet to display them on and made a note to get one.

As she watched the woman pick over the bottles in a way that made Gina feel they were very inferior, she remembered how off-putting it was to be watched by a salesperson too eagerly. She kept herself busy with a duster she found tucked in a corner and wiped the front of someone else's cabinet. She'd have to find out what other people did to avoid hanging over prospective customers with their tongue hanging out.

'I'll have them all,' said the woman.

Gina felt herself go hot and then cold. She could have managed to sell one bottle – they were all priced up – but what on earth should she sell the whole lot for? She rearranged them on the table. 'You'll have to give me a moment to work out a price—'

'I'll give you a hundred pounds for the lot.'

The woman obviously had no qualms about making a cheeky offer. Gina laughed.

'I'm sure you don't expect me to take that offer seriously!' She was doing frantic sums in her head. Was this person offering half what she expected to end up paying? In which case, should she ask four hundred, so two hundred would meet in the middle? Two hundred wasn't enough.

'I think it's a fair price.' The woman was obviously a seasoned haggler. Her calm assumption that she was in the right made that clear.

Oddly, Gina drew confidence from her as if it were catching. 'It's really not. Just let me tot up the individual bottles and I'll have a better idea.'

'Oh, don't be silly. You must give me a deal,' said the woman quickly as if trying to avoid giving Gina time to work out what was reasonable.

'Just to give me an idea,' said Gina, knowing she mustn't let herself be rushed into anything. It had just dawned on her that if she made a profit it would release the rest of their inheritance.

It seemed to take her far too long to add up the price tags but she found that if she sold the scent bottles separately, it would come to at least seven hundred pounds. She gave her customer a broad, confident smile. 'Sorry to keep you waiting but my absolute best on that would be six hundred.'

The woman raised a perfect eyebrow. 'Really? Well, I couldn't possibly pay all that.'

Gina knew it was a buyer's market but she was not going to lose out. She needed every penny and she would fight for it. 'I'm sure I can do something on it but not too much. I'm not a charity, after all.' Her smile came out again. This time it was just a tiny bit patronising. She hadn't only borrowed confidence from this formidable woman.

'I know that but I would be buying all the bottles. There should be a discount for quantity.' The woman obviously wanted the bottles very much or she would have walked away.

'Ten per cent is fairly usual.' Remembering Tiggy, earlier, she added, 'And taking all my stock isn't necessarily good for me. I'd get far more from the bottles if I sold them separately.'

'But how long would that take you? Cash in your hand is what you want if you're in business.'

Had Gina really heard a tiny emphasis on the word 'if'? Was the woman casting doubt on her business acumen? Something jogged Gina's arm. She looked down to see Oscar's head appear over the table, as if he were checking out the perfume bottles too.

'I hope you're not selling all those bottles too cheaply, Gina,' said Matthew from behind her.

'I said six hundred.'

She heard him sniff disdainfully. 'Well, if you don't mind giving the stuff away. Come on, Oscar.'

Gina was disappointed. She thought she'd come

up with the right figure. Obviously she hadn't. 'Well, I obviously can't improve on that. I'm afraid it's a case of take it or leave it.'

'I'd better take it then,' said her buyer. 'Can you wrap them for me?'

'Of course. Why don't you take a look round while I do it? I'll find you when I've done them.'

A little while later, Gina went to find Matthew, her hand full of used notes, her heart full of a sense of failure. 'So how much should I have got for those bottles?' she demanded when Matthew looked up from his accounts.

'Rainey would have been delighted if you got a couple of hundred.'

'What? But you said—'

He was smiling. 'I thought I ought to give you a helping hand.'

'So six hundred is good?'

'Bloody fantastic. You're a natural at this. Congratulations! Ring Sally, tell her the good news.'

Gina sat down on a handy chair. 'But adding them up separately, I'd have got more for them . . .'

'You had to do a deal. She was keen and obviously had money. You got some of it from her. Rainey would have been so proud.'

The good news began to sink in. Her first deal and she'd made a profit! 'Shall we go for a drink after we close up? I feel the need to celebrate.'

Chapter Ten

After he'd locked up, Matthew guided them through streets lined with ancient and historic buildings that mostly housed antiques shops, Oscar trotting obediently beside him. Gina had known that the town considered itself to be the antiques capital of the Cotswolds, but seeing just how many shops they passed on this short journey was a bit worrying. She made a note to suss out the competition soon. A quick glance told her that tidying up the frontage of the French House would be a good start.

Matthew seemed not to notice his competition as he led them to an old coaching inn. 'They know us here and are happy to let Oscar take up the entire hearthrug. They say he adds character.'

Gina laughed. 'Like animated horse brasses or a yard of ale?'

Matthew nodded. 'A touch of the medieval never goes amiss. I quite often grab a bite here if I'm too lazy to cook.'

Gina regarded him. Nothing she'd seen about him up to now indicated anything but a hard worker. He seemed to lead quite a lonely life. He obviously wasn't married, and there had been no hint in any of their conversations that he had a partner. She knew he was an only child and with his parents both dead he didn't seem to have any other existing family. She wasn't aware of any friends either, but then he was a very private man – why would he tell her about his social life?

Matthew opened the door and Oscar trotted straight in. He took up his favourite place in front of the fire, even though it wasn't lit, whilst Matthew found them a table and Gina went to the bar.

'So, here's to your first major sale and whacking great profit,' Matthew said, raising his glass.

'Thank you.' Gina smiled, proud of herself. 'And thank you for giving me that nudge at the right time, even if I did think you were telling me off.'

His gaze narrowed a fraction and he hesitated. 'I promise you, Gina, that if ever I do tell you off, you'll be in no doubt about it.'

There was something in his expression – a challenge? a warning? – that made Gina wonder what it would be like to be told off by Matthew. And this glimmer of something made Gina fleetingly see him as more than just an attractive but staid antiques dealer. She suppressed the feeling as soon as she realised she'd had it and sipped her drink.

'Well, I hope you don't ever feel the need to tell

me off,' she said. After a slight pause, she went on, 'I spoke to all the dealers who were there today—'

'There were only three.'

'Four. One came in to deliver something. And the man who only sells antique desks and tables—?'

'Alfred.'

'Well, he was the only one who wasn't keen on the Christmas event idea. But he said he was perfectly willing to move all his stock out of the way. The others were enthusiastic.' This was only a slight exaggeration. Tiggy had been enthusiastic but she suspected Tiggy would be enthusiastic about anything. 'The young man with the Gilbert and Sullivan fixation was definitely keen.'

'Andrew.'

'That's right. He said he and his wife Sophie would both be able to be there for the event.'

'Right. And did you tell them about having to dress up?' Matthew's handling of his glass indicated his own scepticism.

Gina nodded. 'I did and they're fine with it. I expect you know they're G and S fans and not only did they say they'd dress up, they'd even lend bits and pieces for the others.'

Matthew's look made her feel she was a child putting on a little show for the grown-ups but she decided not to take offence. She was getting used to his disapproving looks. They didn't always mean he was totally against an idea; it was his default mode, he just needed cajoling out of it. She pressed on. 'I need to locate a costume-hire firm although some people may have stuff. We don't want a corporate look, after all.' She paused. 'Do you think we should make sure everyone is dressed in the same period? Or is that all going a bit far?'

Matthew choked slightly before saying, 'Going a bit far.'

Gina had no difficulty interpreting this; he was laughing. 'I know you think I'm mad with my PR ideas, but it is something everyone has to think about. And I also think you should open on Sundays.'

Any amusement Matthew may have been feeling vanished. 'My father never opened on Sundays. He said Sundays were for families.'

He was exasperating. Surely he could see from the other dealers in the town that it was a missed opportunity. 'In the olden days, yes, they were. But nowadays a family is just as likely to go shopping as sit round the table doing jigsaw puzzles. In fact a hell of a lot more likely.'

'I don't think our dealers would – or should, even – give up their precious Sundays to sit in the centre waiting for someone to come in.'

Gina almost found herself asking Matthew what he did with his Sundays but managed to stop herself. She didn't want to look as if she were prying and nor did she want to confess that Sundays were pretty flat for her sometimes.

They were momentarily distracted by a blast of air, laughter and stamping of cold feet. A large group of men and women of assorted ages entered, half of them peeling off to the bar, the rest clustering around a large table towards the rear of the pub. They were clutching bags with various logos, including one Gina recognised as coming from one of the antiques shops they'd passed on the way to the pub. Another thing the French House was lacking: instant publicity. She sighed. Hell would freeze over before she could persuade Matthew to go down that route! She would, however, press her point on Sunday trading, even if it took her all evening.

'They won't come in if it's not open,' she said.

'I live in the centre and I have never been aware of anyone desperate to buy a sofa table on a Sunday,' Matthew countered firmly.

'No, but neither are you aware of the people who come up to the door, see the "Closed" sign and go away to a shop that *is* open. And what about all the tourists who come to Cranmore-on-the-Green for the weekend? They want to wander round the shops before they go back to London. Why not make it possible for them to wander into ours?'

'You're sounding personal about the centre now,' said Matthew. 'And today was only your first day.'

'I can see the potential, that's why. I'm not sure

why that woman who bought my scent bottles was here but she didn't look local. Her card didn't say. I expect she was here for the weekend. When people are on holiday they're in the mood to spend. They don't have time to browse in their busy working lives. If they need a table they'll just go to Ikea. But give them the opportunity, in their down time, to see how much more beautiful and stylish an antique table would be – they'll take it.'

'Forgive me, but you're very, very new to the business. I don't think you're really in a position to make these sweeping statements.'

Had Matthew's drink not been too far away for her to reach she might very easily have tipped it over his head. Instead she scowled at him. He might know 100 per cent more than she did about antiques but she knew about people and their spending habits.

'I may be a complete novice regarding the antiques business but I know people. Selling is what I do, or rather encouraging others to sell. People like shopping on Sundays.'

'I don't think—'

'You not thinking is what has put the centre on its downward curve. And don't tell me there isn't one – it's obvious.'

A few heads turned towards them. She realised she was talking rather loudly. Still, he just wasn't making the most of the centre and as a PR it was her duty to make him see that. She was sure Aunt Rainey would have done the same if she were still alive.

Matthew seemed unaffected by her vehemence. 'No one wants to work on Sunday. If you could guarantee there was going to be good business that would be different. But I think hardly anyone would come in.'

He sounded so dismissive, so unwilling even to give Sunday opening a try, she knew she had to take drastic action to get him to listen. She gripped his wrist and glared into his eyes. 'I will undertake to do all the Sundays between now and the New Year just to show you I'm right!'

'Really? You're very persistent.' He regarded her intently, making her feel like an antique that might well be a fake. She really hoped she wasn't one. Then his expression softened and she felt as if she'd won a battle. 'There won't be anything in it for you. The centre won't be able to credit you for your extra time, particularly when we haven't had a meeting about it, which is how things are usually done.'

'I don't care, I'll do it for nothing!' Gina's passion caused her to knock her glass with her hands and she only just caught it before it fell over. Chastened by this she took a breath. 'But I may need someone with me,' she added quietly. If she was right and Sunday was a good selling day she could get into a terrible muddle if she was there on her own. 'And stop laughing at me.'

Matthew was the picture of surprise. 'Did you hear me laugh?'

'No, but I know you well enough by now to be able to tell when you're cracking up inside. And I am right about this Sunday thing, you know.' She gulped her drink, wishing it was alcohol. She needed some confidence, even artificially induced confidence. Would every idea to help the French House be such an uphill struggle? Now he was laughing at her and it made her feel patronised and ready to kill him. She took some deep breaths to help herself calm down.

Matthew finished his drink. 'OK, we'll give it a whirl until Christmas. Things slacken off a bit afterwards anyway. If it turns out to be a good idea' – he obviously seriously doubted this – 'we can drop it again in January.'

Gina sighed with relief. She knew in every bone it was a good idea. She might not have won the war but she'd won her second battle – first getting Matthew to approve the Christmas event, now Sunday opening. She felt strangely exhilarated. 'Fine. I'd ask Sally to do Sundays with me but Sundays would be hard for her, with the girls.'

'My point exactly,' said Matthew. 'Would you like another drink?'

Gina shook her head. 'No, thank you. I expect I should be going really.' In spite of knowing this was not a date and not fancying Matthew or anything remotely like that, she somehow didn't want to leave his company. She found her bag and got to her feet.

Matthew rose too. 'Can I suggest you stay and eat with me? I want to talk about the woman who bought your bottles. I think I've worked out who she is.'

Gina became enthusiastic. 'If you're offering me gossip: definitely! But we'll pay for ourselves, yes?'

'If you prefer.'

When they both had plates of steak and ale pie in front of them, Gina said, 'So who is the mystery scent-bottle buyer?'

Matthew chuckled. 'I'm fairly sure she's planning to set up a shop in town.'

Gina's happiness diminished a little. 'Not an antiques shop?'

He shook his head. 'No. The sort of shop that sells vastly expensive bits and pieces for "the home". You know the sort of thing: scented candles costing over fifty quid, vile fake zebra-skin lampshades and faux-fur throws, whatever a throw is.'

'It's a blanket.'

'So why not call it a blanket?' he demanded.

'You sound as if you'd rather she was opening a sex shop. Why are you so indignant?' She was just relieved it wasn't more competition for the centre.

'The premises she's got her hands on used to be rented by a lovely old antiques guy. She offered more rent so he was out on his ear.'

Gina bit her lip, aware that instead of thinking, 'one

less dealer to take our business', he just thought about the person. In spite of her own concerns about there being far too much competition in the town, she had to admit it was rather lovely of him, even if it did mean his business wasn't doing as well as it could.

'It's sad about your friend. Why don't you offer him space in the centre?'

As usual his expression was unreadable but Gina though she detected ruefulness. 'I would have done but we don't currently have space.'

Gina felt stabbed with guilt. 'If you didn't have to give Rainey's spot to us you'd have had space.'

'But I did have to. And my first loyalty is to Rainey – or her descendants.'

Gina put her hand in her lap so she couldn't put it on his, which was lying on the table. 'I'm touched. It must have been, well, a bit of a shock, when Sally and I turned up with the girls that day.'

The corner of his mouth moved. He seemed much more relaxed now, like a man loosening his tie after a particularly difficult meeting. He didn't have that guarded look about him.

'It was a bit of a facer, I must admit. But then Rainey liked shocking people so I shouldn't be surprised really.'

'I wish I'd known her better. She was obviously much loved.'

'She was a wonderful person and I expect she wished you two madwomen on to me for the good of my soul.' There was a smile at the back of his eyes as he looked down into hers.

Gina couldn't help smiling back. 'We owe it to her to make a success of it then.'

'We do. And you've made an excellent start.'

'Thank you. Which was partly down to you.' She paused. 'I know you said you can only learn this business by doing it but are there any books I could read? I'd quite like to hurry the process up!'

He chuckled. 'If you're interested, I've certainly got some books I could lend you. I'll get them for you later when you go back for your car.'

'I'd really appreciate that.'

As they continued to eat, Gina realised she was enjoying his company. He didn't feel obliged to be charming and entertaining all the time, which was very restful. And now she acknowledged to herself he was attractive, it was easier somehow.

Oscar was still inert by the fireplace. The large party had now left and the pub was quiet. Gina suddenly yawned. 'Sorry! I don't know why that happened.'

He smiled. 'I'll get the bill.'

'No, we'll pay for ourselves. We're colleagues – remember?'

'I asked you. It was my invitation. Therefore you must let me pay.'

'Matthew . . .' She spoke gently. 'I really hate to be the one to break it to you but things have changed a bit since Queen Victoria died. Women are treated more or less equally these days. They have the vote and everything.'

'Really? When did that happen?'

Gina smiled. 'Tell me, if I'd been one of the male dealers you were having a meal at a pub with, would you have had a problem with him paying for himself?'

'Of course not, but you're a woman.'

'Thank you for noticing, but we're colleagues. It's fine for us to pay for ourselves.'

He raised an eyebrow but just then Oscar got up and stood in front of Matthew.

'Oscar thinks it's time we stopped arguing and went home,' she said. She handed Matthew a note which would cover her share.

Frowning slightly, he picked it up and walked over to the bar.

After a 'Bye then, Matthew, see you again soon' from the barman, they walked back to the centre in companionable silence. 'Will you be all right here while I fetch the books?' he asked, when they reached her car. 'Oh yes, of course you will. You've got the vote!'

Gina laughed as she watched him disappear into the house, Oscar following far more slowly.

Chapter Eleven

Gina spent most of Sunday sorting out her papers and concentrating on how to entice more clients. As the working week began, although the antiques books Matthew had lent her drew Gina with a siren call she managed to resist and focus – for most of the morning at least – on getting herself some paying clients. Doing free PR for the centre was all very well but it wouldn't pay her bills.

She switched on her laptop while she was still eating breakfast and to her surprise and delight there was an email from a charity courtesy of her one paying client and she instantly emailed back suggesting a meeting.

Then she allowed herself a look at perfume bottles on eBay before setting off to see her sister. Sally had rung after Gina got home from the pub on Saturday night and had had to be convinced that the celebratory drink and meal with Matthew didn't mean she should be choosing a wedding outfit.

'Oh. So nothing happened between you?' Sally had said after Gina had explained about her brilliant sale, and told her that the buyer of the scent bottles might be opening a shop. 'Well, Matthew might be being sniffy about that shop but I think it sounds as if it could be useful. I've made a really cool lamp using some of those bits of chandelier we got at Newark and her shop might be just the place to sell it.'

'I thought you were going to make Christmas decorations for our event.' Gina had been indignant. Had Sally's dislike of old things taken hold again?

'I am and I have, but some of those bits are quite chunky. I couldn't use them all for decs, but nor could I waste them. I've been experimenting a bit with my soldering iron – not easy in a house our size that contains small children – but among other things I've made some really fabulous lamps. They send rainbows all over the room.'

'Gosh, those are *beautiful*!' said Gina now. 'You are clever. They're not exactly antique-looking though, are they?'

Sally regarded her creations. She'd made three lamps, each very different from the other. 'To be honest, I'm not sure what to do with them now I've made them. I mean, supposing that shop doesn't open?'

Gina, perched on the edge of the kitchen table, studied the lamps, which took up the entire worktop. 'We'll find somewhere. They really are lovely, Sal.'

'So how much should I charge for them?'

Gina chewed her lip. 'Well, any shop would put a

big mark-up on them – possibly fifty per cent – so think what they might sell for, and make it top whack, then work backwards. Or take them to Liberty's and see if they'd like them.'

'The trouble is they might want to go on having them. I've only got enough chandelier pieces left for a couple of small lamps.' Sally tweaked one of her creations. 'Who'd have thought I'd turn out to be so good at soldering?'

'Who indeed? But would you like to spend all your time making lamps? If you would, I'm sure you could get more parts. You could buy them new after all.'

'To be honest it's creating something out of what's there that's the fun. I'm not sure I want to be a production line.' She hesitated. 'Although if it was earning good money I couldn't really say no.'

'The woman who bought the bottles left her card. Shall we get in touch and see if she wants them?'

'Maybe we should wait until we know more. We need to be sure she is opening a shop. Ah, here are Alaric and the girls. Peacetime is officially over.'

The next day, after a very satisfactory meeting with the charity, Gina took the very long route home via Cranmore-on-the-Green. Quite why she was so drawn to the French House she wasn't sure – perhaps because the antiques business was seeping into her blood? She had been poring over *Miller's Antiques Handbook*, the book Matthew said would give her most information fastest, trying to learn as much as she could. Now, she wanted to see if any of the dealers had new stock, who was on duty, what had sold and how people were feeling. It was the community of the centre that attracted her, she told herself, and nothing to do with its owner.

She parked the car in the public car park, aware the dealers' spaces would probably all be taken, and set off to the French House. On her way she saw a new shop being done out. This must be the one Matthew had talked about – rented by her scent-bottle buyer, Carmella Romera. Curiosity and a gap in the sheets of paper covering the windows led her straight to it. She couldn't resist a snoop and it would be good to see what sort of stock Carmella was planning on carrying.

She was just peering sideways to see if she could get a better view when someone moved into her line of vision. It looked incredibly like Egan, her devious, cheating, embezzling ex-boyfriend. No – it couldn't be! Her heart sinking, she looked more intently, hoping a shift of angle would reveal the man to be someone quite different. But no. It was definitely him. And just at the moment she took this in, he looked up and spotted her.

Instinct made her run. As fast as she could she crossed the road and dashed up towards the French House, trusting he'd lose her among the people bustling along. She flew up the steps to the entrance and burst through the front door before realising Egan wasn't following her and had probably never intended to. It still took her a few seconds to stop panicking.

'Hello! You're in rather a hurry, aren't you?'

It was a late-middle-aged man Gina hadn't met before. He had greying hair and was wearing a suit that was old but fitted perfectly. His accent proclaimed he was from the upper classes but his smile was friendly.

'Hello!' she replied, panting slightly, wondering how she could explain her explosive entry.

'You must be Gina, I think,' he went on. 'I've heard a lot about you.'

Gina took a breath and smiled. 'That doesn't sound good.'

The man chuckled. 'It's not all bad, I assure you, and Rainey's nieces will always be part of the family here.'

After her melodramatic dash through the streets this was especially comforting. She perched on an old oak settle that happened to be handy. Now her anxiety to get away from Egan had faded and she remembered she'd only been going to the centre to see what was new and meet some of the dealers she hadn't met before. Getting to know this elegant and kindly gentleman was a very good start. 'How very kind of you!'

'I'm Bill Morrison, by the way.' He took her hand

and shook it. 'We haven't coincided before. I'm not here that often as I have things in a couple of other centres and have to keep my eye on them.' His eyes twinkled. 'It must have taken you a while to catch up with us all here.'

She nodded. 'It has – though it shouldn't.' She frowned. 'I should have made a point of meeting everyone. I still haven't.'

He shook his head slightly. 'No one else has ever done that. There is no reason why you should.'

She was about to tell him that she had plans to shake the centre up a bit but decided she shouldn't do that just yet. She smiled and shrugged instead.

'Actually, I am very glad to run into you at last,' he went on. 'I was at an auction the other day and picked up this job lot at the end. Much of it is rubbish but there are a couple of items in there I knew Rainey would have liked.' He smiled and held out his hand. 'Yours for a tenner. But if you don't want it, no hard feelings.'

She took the hand and closed the deal, although she hadn't seen what was in the box yet. She felt it would be churlish to ignore this sweet gesture. After all, he knew a lot more about the business than she did. 'That is so kind of you.' She found her bag and, eventually, her wallet and the aforementioned tenner.

'Rainey and I used to buy things for each other quite often,' he said. 'After all, you can't be at every auction.'

Gina felt rueful. 'It'll be a while before my sister and I know nearly enough to buy things for you at auctions, I'm afraid. I can't even reliably buy things for our own stall.'

'Ah.' He inclined his head. 'But I hear you can sell – very much more important ultimately.'

What had Matthew told him? Had they all been discussing the two new arrivals?

'I was just lucky. But after all those scent bottles went, we're now low on stock so your contribution is very gratefully received.' Thinking about the scent bottles reminded her about seeing Egan in the shop but she pushed him out of her mind. She had a new life now. 'Actually, Bill . . .'

'Yes, my dear? Anything I can do to help?'

'I have this plan to put on a special event, before Christmas, to get people into the centre who wouldn't usually come in . . .'

Later, having had a quick look at what was in the cardboard box, Gina decided to see if Matthew was in. He might have arrived without her noticing. She needed help with pricing up and she wanted him to know that Bill Morrison was definitely on side with regard to the Christmas event. She'd also had another idea she wanted to run past him and the box was a good excuse. She'd met most of the dealers now, but going on what Bill Morrison had said, most people would be keen to do anything to get more business into the centre which had once thrived. Although Bill was too discreet to say as much, Gina got the impression that everyone believed Matthew had lost heart, but as Bill hadn't said that directly, she couldn't ask why he thought it.

As she went up to the next floor with her box of bits she found herself wondering slightly why Bill, who seemed to be doing better from his other spaces, should still keep a stall in the French House. It seemed the French House had a lot of loyal dealers but why were they loyal? And was it to the centre, or to Matthew? Or even the memory of his father? The more she talked to people the more she realised what big boots Matthew had to fill. She knocked on the door of the office and opened the door when he answered.

'Hello!' she said brightly, rubbing Oscar's chest, flattered that he'd got up to greet her. 'Bill Morrison kindly bought me a job lot at an auction and I wondered if you'd help me sort it out and price up what's suitable. I've got an idea to share with you too.'

Matthew put down his pen. He seemed to have been buried in the accounts again. 'Of course. Fire away,' he said from behind his desk.

Gina decided he must have been a headmaster in a previous incarnation. She couldn't bring herself to accept his authority unchallenged, however. He brought out a devilish desire in her to keep prodding at the hornets' nest. She spotted something. 'Why do you have that ghastly china dog up there? It's hideous.'

'Is that your idea? To tell me you think the Foo dog is hideous?'

'No. It just struck me as odd. It did the first time we came but I didn't know you then. It seems odder now. Everything else sort of fits in. Not the dog.'

'I'm very fond of it,' he said, putting an end to the matter. 'But now you've shared your feelings perhaps you could show me your box or tell me about your idea. Otherwise I've got things to do.'

Gina drew a breath. She'd never had a client so difficult to get through to. 'You know about my plans for a Christmas event?'

He sighed. 'Not intimately but we are almost on Christian name terms.'

Gina ignored his lack of enthusiasm. 'Well, I thought we should have regular events, throughout the year.'

'An idea is for life, not just for Christmas?'

She refused to acknowledge this attempt at humour. It was just too dry for her taste. 'Yes. I thought: Why not set up meet-the-expert events?'

'What sort of expert?'

'An antiques expert, you dummy.' Gina's patience expired. 'I'm not suggesting people bring in their bicycles to have them checked over. I'm suggesting we leaflet the town and the surrounding areas with something like "Is that perfectly hideous dog on your mantelpiece really valuable? Bring it in and find out."'

'It's not valuable, I'm just fond of it.'

'Right. In which case the expert will say, "It's a very appealing item but the true value is in what it means to you."'

Gina sensed the tiniest glimmer of interest in his expression but realised she might have imagined it.

'So what would a good outcome be?' he said. 'Supposing it isn't a Foo dog but a genuine carriage clock or something?' he asked.

Clutching firmly at this possible warming to the idea on his part, she said, 'It would depend, but the expert might say, "I'd be very happy to offer you a hundred pounds for it." Or even, "I suggest you put it into a good auction house" – and say which one – "to see what it raises."' She leant forward and put her hands on his desk, going in for the kill. 'The point is, there doesn't necessarily have to be a sale or money changing hands but the visitor has to have a good experience while here.'

'We're not a theme park.'

She rolled her eyes in a good imitation of the Foo dog. 'Are you kidding me? Wow, I bet you have loads of people coming in here looking for the rollercoaster.'

'No need to be sarcastic.'

'Sorry. It's catching.' She glared at him. She was trying so hard to help and she knew her ideas were good. Why wouldn't he accept a little upset to his ordered world?

Matthew shook his head. 'I do see where you're

coming from but the meet-the-expert thing really is something an auction house would do.'

'It doesn't mean we can't do it too,' she growled in frustration. 'It would get people through the doors. And auction houses can seem a bit daunting. Lots of little old ladies would rather go into a nice house which is really a shop. But if you think we'd be stepping on the auction houses' toes, we could invite an auctioneer along. We could do food.' She was not going to give up.

'I'm not sure that would be cost effective but I do know a very nice auction house. Anthea Threadgold might come in.' At last! He rummaged in a box on his desk and produced a card. 'Here.'

Gina took the card and decided not to mention providing food and nibbles again. He'd given her a contact name and hadn't said no. She was ahead.

'So we can do the meet-the-experts thing?'

He shrugged. 'It would mean people coming in on extra days or we might run out of experts.'

'I don't think they'd mind if there was going to be something in it for them.' Really, this was like trying to shift Stonehenge a little to the left. 'I've had another idea for the Christmas event too—'

'You want me to have a pole fixed so Santa's Little Helpers can dance round it?'

Gina ignored this. 'It would be a spot-the-object competition for the children. Like a treasure hunt—'

'No. Definitely not. It would be a disaster. I'm not

having children trooping round here trying to spot the cuckoo clock.'

He was so adamant Gina decided it was time to show him her box. In her job it was important to know when to push and when to stop pushing. She would bring her idea up again when he was in a more receptive mood – which would probably be some weeks after hell had frozen over. She got up and lifted her box on to the desk.

'So, have I bought ten pounds' worth of rubbish? Or is there a profit in here?'

Matthew pulled back the flaps of the box. 'If Bill thought it was worth you having it, it is. He and Rainey used to buy for each other sometimes. He had a soft spot for her which you seem to have inherited.'

'Talking of inheriting things, have you told the solicitor we've made a profit and so can get our bit of extra cash?'

'I have actually.' He seemed pleased with himself. Then looked rueful. 'And sadly, I've found out how much the extra cash is, which isn't very much.'

'Well?'

'Another two hundred and fifty each.'

Gina took this in. Not precisely a life-changing amount, but better than nothing. 'Well, if I can make money out of ten pounds' worth of junk, that seems substantial.'

He laughed. 'Let's have a look at the junk then.' He pulled out something wrapped in newspaper and revealed a jug. 'Oh, this is nice. Bill's done very well . . .' He was back where he felt comfortable.

He sorted through the box and Gina made a list of the contents and how much Matthew thought it should sell for. It came to well over a hundred pounds so Gina was very pleased.

'But no scent bottles,' he said when the box was empty.

'No. But Carmella Romera, the woman who bought them all, has started setting up her shop. I saw it as I came through and had a peek.' She frowned, wondering if she should mention seeing her ex-boyfriend there but decided not to. Her personal life was nothing to do with him. She was curious, though, as to why Egan had been there.

'Well, let's hope she can start up a new business in these hard times,' he said, suddenly bleak.

'Luckily the French House is already established,' she said buoyantly. 'We're not starting from scratch.' She paused. 'Are we all set for the centre to open this Sunday?'

He sighed, but the bleakness seemed to lift a trifle. 'If you absolutely must. But you'll have to get Jenny to brief you about the locks and the alarm system.'

'That's fine. I'll sound out the others on being experts. And I'll get in touch with the auctioneer.'

Chapter Twelve

Gina took her laptop on Sunday morning, just in case no one came in – proving Matthew right. She could then get some work done and not waste her time completely. She could have a look at the website again and see if it could be improved. She had been slightly surprised the centre had a website at all – Matthew seemed so embedded in the Dark Ages.

It took her a while but eventually she had unlocked the doors, disabled the alarm and set herself up in the front of the centre so she could see if anyone approached the front door.

As she waited for her laptop to boot up she thought about her encounter with Egan. She hadn't told Sally and she hadn't quite worked out how she felt about it. Seeing him had been a shock, there was no doubt about it, but did she really care? She was well over him and although the fact he still owed her money jarred was he really a threat to her new way of life? And what was his connection to Carmella? She couldn't help speculating that he'd found a new and obviously more lucrative source of income but was he playing her for a fool too? Somehow she couldn't imagine him daring to do the dirty on Carmella – she'd eat him alive!

It wouldn't be good if she had to see Egan often, but she thought him turning up in the same town was probably OK; they might never see each other again. She pushed out of her mind the fact she'd told Sally he was hard to avoid in London. He was probably just down for the weekend.

She heard a sound and looked up from the screen. The noise had come from behind. Had someone actually come in to help her man the (silent) barricades? She glanced at her watch and saw it was only five to ten. The centre wouldn't actually be open for another five minutes.

'Hello,' said Matthew. Oscar, trotting beside him, sighed and flung himself to the floor.

Gina suppressed her delight at seeing them both. 'Are you the only person who could make it in today?'

'Don't sound so disappointed or I'll go away again. Actually I was the only person I asked. I didn't have much else on.'

Gina got up, trying not to smile. Considering how grumpy he always was she was surprisingly pleased to see him. 'I'll make you some coffee. And I brought croissants. I thought if I was dragging someone away from domestic bliss I should offer some reward.'

As she found a mug, milk and plates for the croissants she wondered *why* she was pleased it was

Matthew she'd be working with. It couldn't be because of his upbeat personality, that was for sure. It was probably because he knew she was almost entirely ignorant about antiques. She wouldn't have to pretend with him.

'The croissants are going to make hideous crumbs,' said Matthew, accepting his plate.

'Fortunately, Eeyore, I know how to use the hoover,' she said and sat down with her own plate. 'And I'm sure Oscar will do his best to help out.'

Matthew had taken her chair, cutting her off from her laptop. It made her feel faintly unsettled but she was determined not to show it.

'I see you've been looking at the website,' he said. 'See, we do have an online presence, of sorts.'

Gina finished her mouthful. 'Ye-es.'

'I suppose you see a lot wrong with it.' Matthew took a bite.

'Would you like me to tell you what?'

'Can I stop you?'

'You asked. You want to know really,' said Gina firmly. 'First of all, it looks dated.'

'We're an antiques centre. That's our USP.'

'Antique and dated are not the same thing. What you want is it to be easy for people to find out things. And I really do think you should make it possible to buy online.'

'No. At least not now. If you're going to drag us into the present please do it in stages.' Half of his mouth smiled. His smiles were so rare it reminded Gina of the sun coming out from behind the clouds after a stormy day: it wasn't exactly blazing sunshine but it lifted the spirits.

'OK. But could I ask my mate who does websites to have a look? I could make a start, change that ghastly font for example—'

'That's old English! It's supposed to look antique.'

'It looks dreary. You want something that is stylish if not modern. This ye olde stuff just looks naff.'

'You're telling me our website is naff?' He was outraged.

'Only a little bit . . .'

If Oscar had looked at Gina like that she'd have got something between them double quick; Matthew's scowl was terrifying. 'How much do you think it would cost?' he said eventually and Gina suddenly understood he wasn't so much scowling at her but scowling at life. The sun had gone in again.

Gina did sums in her head. 'I think we should budget for five hundred but I could ask my friend what she could do for, say, three hundred.'

He sighed. 'Get her absolute best on it then.'

Gina looked at him, almost shocked at the weariness of his tone. Why had she never before appreciated what it must be like to be Matthew with all his responsibilities? It wasn't just the financial side of it, there was the personal side, too. Some of the dealers had been part of the centre for decades. If Matthew couldn't make it work, these people – old friends of his father's – would be devastated. From what some of the other dealers had let slip and from her own observations she knew that things weren't rosy – far from it: the French House was barely ticking over. Why then was Matthew stubbornly wedded to keeping things exactly as they always had been rather than accepting that life had moved on and the centre had to move on with it? He wasn't stupid by any means, so presumably he had his reasons, but as far as she could see all they led to was him burying his head in the sand. Well, she wasn't going to let him ruin himself. It was personal now.

Movement caught Gina's attention. Someone was about to open the door of the centre. 'Typical! Visitors and the floor is covered in crumbs.'

She ran for the vacuum while Matthew did his usual welcoming speech, which amounted to 'do feel free to look around and ask for help if you need it'.

When she'd done the floor she moved her laptop to the office. Matthew could watch for visitors if it all went quiet again and she could work in private.

She and Matthew met again in the little kitchen, both needing coffee. It was early afternoon and they'd been surprisingly busy and – on behalf of the absent dealers – sold a respectable number of items. Gina had even managed to sell a couple of the items she had bought from Bill.

'We were just lucky those people had moved into an empty house and needed furniture,' said Matthew before Gina could say anything.

'They were lucky we were open. Otherwise they'd have had to go to Ikea,' she retorted instantly. Then she smiled.

For a split second they shared a moment of delight, smiling at each other. A part of Gina she had smothered for months reminded her it was there. She put the mental cushion back firmly. There was no point in having feelings – anything beyond friendship – for Matthew. That flutter of excitement was just a blip. She would ignore it.

At the end of the day, once they had locked up, Gina ran round with the vacuum again – glad to be doing something she understood at last – while Matthew did the paperwork.

'Would you like to come up for something to eat?' he said when they'd both finished. 'I know it's still early but I'm starving.'

'You don't have to invite me for supper just because you're hungry,' she said.

'No, but I owe you something, even if it's just cheese on toast. I see now Sunday opening is a very good thing.'

Gina chuckled, as pleased by his approval as she was about being right. 'OK.'

His flat was very much as she would have

imagined it – a lot of dark furniture, leather sofas, ancient Persian rugs – but what did surprise her was that it was well lit. There were no bright lights but nor were there dingy corners. She went to the window and saw his view over the town. 'It's nice up here,' she said.

'Not too ye olde worlde for you?' he asked with that dry humour that he usually hid so successfully.

'Well, it is full of old things, as my sister would say, but it's comfortable and stylish.'

'Thank you. Now sit down and relax. Read the paper. I'll just feed Oscar and then get started on the meal.'

'I thought we were having cheese on toast?'

He shook his head. 'I think I can do a bit better than that.'

He handed her a glass of wine before getting out bags of dog food for Oscar. Gina settled herself in the tatty but very comfortable leather sofa. She picked up a magazine about antiques and adjusted a cushion. Eventually she called, 'Need any help?'

'No thanks. There's only room for one of us in here.'

As she settled back down with the magazine, she reflected that Egan had never done much cooking. If he'd felt obliged to for any reason he'd just send out for a pizza or Chinese.

The kitchen smelt wonderfully of frying garlic

when Matthew came out a little later with some knives and forks. He cleared a space for the two of them at the old gate-leg table.

'Are you sure there's nothing I can do?' she said. 'I feel lazy not helping at all.'

'You're all right,' he said. 'Have some more wine.'

Gina had already decided to call a taxi. Even one glass of wine on an empty stomach after a long day had gone to her head. She accepted another glass.

'This tastes as good as it smelt when you were cooking it!' she said a few mouthfuls in. 'What is it?'

'Just a version of a carbonara. It's a bit variable. Sometimes it's nicer than others.'

'Well, this is really nice. So, did you do any good business today? I saw a woman very interested in that gorgeous little table you've got. Is it French? And did she buy it?'

'Yes to both. And well done for spotting it was French.'

Gina felt pleased. 'You were right when you said you had to do it to learn it – the antiques business, I mean. I feel I'm just beginning to get my eye in. It's not that I think I know anything but I can imagine that one day I might.'

He smiled. 'Like when you're learning to ride a bicycle and you first push the second pedal. You fall off but, just for a minute, you had the feeling.'

'It's exactly like that! I know it'll take years – far

longer even than it took me to learn to ride a bike – but that does describe it.'

He laughed softly. 'I've got pudding.'

'Now I'm really impressed.'

'And so you should be, but we'll have some cheese to finish our wine off first.'

He came back with some soft blue cheese Gina didn't recognise and a packet of water biscuits. 'This goes very well with this wine,' he said, putting down his burdens.

It did, Gina found, and when Matthew got up to open another bottle she found herself having a wild fantasy where, emboldened by more wine, she and Matthew found themselves entwined on the sofa. That must definitely not happen, she told herself.

'No more wine for me,' she said, 'or I'll have a thick head in the morning.'

'Fair enough. I'll get the pudding.'

The pudding turned out to be a pair of Magnums. 'My favourite,' said Gina, forgetting to be cool and off-putting. 'I *love* them.'

'Go and sit down and be comfortable,' he said when they'd finished eating. 'I'll put the kettle on. Would you like tea or coffee?'

Gina was about to say, 'Ooh, cup of tea please,' when she realised if she wasn't careful, in about five minutes she'd be snuggled up on the sofa with Matthew watching the *Antiques Roadshow*.

No! She mustn't do that. It would be too awkward,

too intimate. She might doze off and wake to find her head on his shoulder with her mouth open.

'Actually, I think I'd better ring for a taxi. Busy day tomorrow and all that. But thank you very much for a lovely meal.'

Just for a moment she waited for him to press her to stay: it was still early, there was no real reason why she should get home before eight o'clock; but he didn't.

She should have been relieved and not disappointed.

'I'll call you a cab,' he said.

On the way home in the taxi Gina examined her conflicting feelings over and over again without managing to resolve them. It was an argument of head versus heart. Or maybe – she reluctantly acknowledged – head versus a healthy woman's need for physical affection. Which was another way of saying she was sex-starved, a very worrying conclusion.

She didn't want to have a thing with Matthew. For a zillion reasons, the most important being it would make things impossible at the centre if it all went wrong. And her recent experience didn't make her optimistic. Egan had been a disaster.

She sighed. She'd felt all this before she got involved with the antiques centre. That was another reason not to lose focus. To have feelings – and she couldn't really bring herself to decide what these were – for Matthew made the whole thing even more insane.

Then a moment later she forgot this sensible reasoning and accepted there was something about Matthew – in a purely physical sense – that she found very attractive. She wanted to feel his arms around her. She wanted to bury her face in his neck and inhale his scent. She wanted to have his mouth on hers, so hard their teeth clashed. She also wanted him to pull off her clothes and make love to her.

It's just a physical thing, she thought, and then worried she might have actually said it out loud. As the driver of the cab – mercifully taciturn – didn't comment or move, she assumed her private thoughts were still private.

It's just because you haven't had sex for ages. And he's not a bad-looking bloke – it's no great surprise you fancy him a bit. And he'd probably be horrified if he even knew you were having these thoughts.

She asked the cabbie for a card so she could get him back if she needed him.

Chapter Thirteen

The trouble with working on a Sunday meant you felt you hadn't really had a proper weekend, Gina thought as she yawned and made herself a cup of tea, ready to start Monday morning in earnest. She was just settling down to some emailing when the phone went. It was Sally.

'Hi, hon. What are you up to?' her sister said.

'Well, bits and pieces, you know.' Gina felt that Sally had never quite got the concept of working from home.

'Any chance we could meet up? The girls are in nursery and we haven't had a catch-up for ages.'

'Actually, we should do that. I've got loads to tell you.' Gina realised she hadn't told Sally about the shop or about seeing Egan and her sister always got dreadfully huffy if Gina hadn't told her something she felt she should know. 'Would you like to come here?'

'Actually, I'd like to go to the centre. I haven't been for a while. Meet me there?'

'Could you pick me up from here then? I left my car there.'

'Why?' Sally demanded.

Gina took a breath. She might as well tell Sally now – any prevarication and Sally would make even more of it than she would anyway. 'I had a meal with Matthew. He came to do the Sunday opening with me and we were both starving. I felt I deserved a couple of glasses of wine so I cabbed it home.'

There was an ominous silence while Sally kept everything Gina knew she was thinking to herself. 'Fine. I'll be right over.'

Matthew rang soon afterwards. 'I was wondering about how to get your car to you. I could drive it over with Jenny driving my car if you'd like.'

Gina was extremely touched and surprised. Her recent experience of men hadn't led her to expect such thoughtfulness. 'That's terribly kind but there's no need to do that. Sally's coming over. She can drive me into town so I can pick up my car after we've had a chat.'

'Oh good.' He paused as if he was going to say something else but he obviously changed his mind. 'I'll let you get on then.'

'Thank you very much for the thought though. I appreciate it.'

'That's fine. Goodbye.'

When he'd disconnected she went upstairs and put some make-up on. She needed to give herself a bit of a talking-to. The self-lecturing that had gone on the previous evening had done nothing to quash the little crush that had been forming recently. When she'd heard

Matthew's voice on the phone she'd found herself getting all fluttery. If Sally found out about it her life wouldn't be worth living. She'd be arranging for his car to run out of petrol so they were stranded by darling little boutique hotels and had to stay the night. She knew her sister. Sally was relentless when she got the bit between her teeth. She was also very good at spotting when Gina was trying to keep anything from her.

'Hello, darling!' said Sally when Gina opened the door shortly afterwards. 'Oh, going to a meeting? You've got your corporate look on again.'

Gina's black trousers and white shirt ensemble was her pulling-herself-together outfit, as well as her one for meetings. 'I've got nothing booked apart from you, but I was thinking of calling in on someone later, when I've got my car. I want to check out a venue for my client. The do isn't for ages but I like to see as many places as possible for him.'

'Oh.' Sally had never quite got what Gina's job entailed. 'So, kettle on? Bickies out? Then tell me about how the Sunday opening went.'

Sally's desire to go to the centre wasn't that pressing then. Gina filled the kettle. 'It was brilliant but there's something much more interesting than that! Carmella is fitting out her shop. And you will never, in a million years, guess who I saw in there.' Describing it like this to Sally made seeing Egan fun and not the ghastly shock it had seemed at the time.

'Who?'

'Egan.'

Sally was suitably awed. *'No!* I can't believe it. What was he doing there?'

'No idea. I was peeking between the sheets of paper they'd put over the windows to stop people looking in—'

'They should have put that white stuff—'

'I just wanted to see if they had any stock yet, to see if your lamps would work for them. They didn't, before you interrupt me again: they're just decorating. But there was Egan.'

'Did he see you?'

'Yes! I legged it. I absolutely didn't want to talk to him and I fled up to the French House as fast as I could in case he was following me.'

'And was he?'

Gina shrugged. 'I shouldn't think so actually, which made me feel a bit silly. But I met a lovely man called Bill Morrison who was obviously big friends with Rainey because he'd bought us a box of stuff from an auction. For only ten pounds. Which I thought was really sweet of him. And he's keen to do events.'

As Gina had intended, this distracted Sally from thoughts of Egan. Gina didn't want to go through the how-do-you-feel-about-him-now conversation which Sally was prone to having.

'Like the Christmas one?' said Sally.

'Yup. And I thought we could have a meet-the-expert thing. Matthew's not keen of course but he did give me the name of an auctioneer whom we could invite too.'

'I really don't think we've got time to fit it in before Christmas if we do the Christmas thing,' said Sally.

'We haven't, but I thought we could combine them.'

'What: "Sell your tat and buy a nice Christmas present with the money"? Catchy.'

'People do clear out their houses at this time of year. They want to put up the fairy lights and get out the baubles, and they want to get rid of the junk first. And everyone needs money at Christmas, especially if it's for something they don't want.'

'"Sell your tat and buy something nice for the kids."'

Gina giggled. 'What about "Tat for Turkey! Make the swap now! You know you want to!"? We could have a big banner made and hang it in front of the French House.'

'Not even I would go that far,' said Sally. 'But I do think we could do it at the same time, and if it seems popular, we could do it again in the New Year – same message only not the turkey bit. "Overspent over Christmas? Make some money back now!"'

'Matthew wasn't at all keen on the treasure-hunt thing.' Gina put her elbows on the table. 'I can't decide if I should push it, or leave it.'

'I don't think you told me about a treasure hunt. I think you've been making all sorts of plans without me.'

'I probably have. The trouble is it's my job to make businesses more profitable. It's only natural that I should want to improve the one I'm involved with. If only Matthew wasn't so stubborn! He nearly bit my head off when I said the website was a bit dated. He did agree to let me ask Serena to look at it. She's my web-designer friend.'

'Have we a date for the event? I think early in the month is best, while people are still in the mood for Christmas and haven't done all their shopping.'

Gina got out her diary. 'What about Saturday the first of December?'

Sally made a face. 'That's in a fortnight. Would you be able to set it up in time?'

Gina sighed. 'I think so. I need to get going on it immediately. But I know Matthew would want me to run it past all the dealers. I mean, they seem keen in principle, or at least most of them do, but I haven't managed to speak to them all and I didn't discuss timings or anything with them.'

'Maybe we should have a little do and lay it all out for them then? People are much more likely to be enthusiastic if they've had a glass of wine and a vol-au-vent. We could do it at the centre and I can provide nibbles as long as they're simple.'

'Matthew might come up with the wine. It's not for all that many people, after all.'

'Sor'ed!' said Sally. 'You're the best PR ever.'

Gina laughed. 'I guess! But you know what? It's the antiques I'm really into now.'

Sally was amazed. 'Really? I mean I know you like

a challenge but surely it's not what you want to be doing forever?'

Gina shrugged. She rather thought it might be. It hadn't been a sudden realisation; it had crept up on her. She knew she was good at PR, it's what she'd been doing for years, but it no longer thrilled her. She didn't yearn to find out more about it. But with antiques and the French House, she just wanted to learn more and more. However, for some reason she didn't want to admit that to Sally – she'd assume it was all because of Matthew, and it really wasn't. Her feelings for him – whatever they were – were quite separate. 'I'd better run all this past Matthew.'

'Right. Now, shall we go? We could have a bite of lunch while we're in town . . .'

That evening when Gina rang Matthew, to her surprise he agreed to providing the wine without a fuss. 'We always used to have a get-together for the dealers around this time of year. It would be nice to revive the tradition. And if Sally doesn't want to do the canapés herself we can buy them from the supermarket.'

'Oh! Well, that was a lot easier than I expected.'

'I don't always say no to any suggestion, you know.'

Gina decided not to argue the point.

'You can't beat a sausage roll,' said Harold, the brass dealer, taking two. 'And these don't look as if they came out of a shop.'

'My sister Sally made them,' said Gina proudly. It was six thirty in the evening a few days later. Matthew had duly invited all the dealers, and Jenny, for drinks in his flat.

'They are really good,' said Jenny as Gina topped up her glass with the hot apple juice and ginger that was the non-alcoholic alternative to wine. 'I'm so glad we managed to serve the eats hot. They're so much more appetising. I'm glad you're doing this. Matthew's father did it every year but Matthew hasn't for the past couple of years and it's a shame. It does us good to all be here together. It never happens in the normal course of events.' She took another sausage roll. 'It's unlike him to want to do anything social.'

Gina glanced across at Matthew, who was perched on an oak coffer nursing a glass of wine. He was paying courteous attention to one of the older female dealers, Margaret. She had known Matthew's father and specialised in clocks and silverware and was one of the remaining people Gina hadn't yet met. 'I was quite surprised too. But pleased, obviously.'

When she gauged everyone was suitably softened up by alcohol and hot snacks she tapped her glass with a fork and found a place to stand where she could see almost everyone.

'People!' She waited until most of the conversation ceased. Only Margaret, who was bending Matthew's ear, was still murmuring. Matthew kept nodding as if he was engrossed, giving Gina rueful glances.

'On behalf of Matthew, I'd like to thank you all for coming to this little gathering. I think you all know by now that my sister and I have taken over Rainey's spot. As we know less than nothing about antiques—'

'You're learning,' said someone. Gina recognised Tiggy's warm, smoky voice.

'—we wanted to bring something to the centre that we do know about. As most of you will also know, I'm a PR person in my real life and I felt – we felt – that there were some things we could do to help the centre do a bit better.' She sipped from her glass of fizzy water. 'It does involve change and we all hate that.' This was a slightly sweeping assumption but she made it anyway. 'But if you can put up with these ignorant new girls, with their pushy ways, we will be very grateful and also fairly certain that business will improve.

'I have spoken to some of you about this – my apologies to those of you who haven't yet met me and my sister, let alone heard about our plans . . .'

She went on to explain her ideas for the Christmas event, throwing it all in, including the treasure hunt, and then stood back, hoping they wouldn't fling the remaining canapés at her. Those she had spoken to before about the event might have changed their minds now they knew exactly what was involved.

Someone at the back started clapping, and soon everyone was. 'Well done,' said Harold. 'Rainey would have been proud of you. She was always shaking us up in her way and I know she'd like to think of you carrying on shaking. I'm happy to be an expert, and to organise the treasure hunt, if you'd like me to.'

Everyone joined in, offering to help in one way or another. Gina found herself deeply moved and spotted Sally wiping her eyes over in the corner by Jenny.

'Thank you so much, everyone. And thank you, Matthew, for letting us in,' she said, her throat a little constricted. 'We were rather forced on him but he accepted us for Aunt Rainey's sake. We're going to make sure neither he, nor any of you, has cause to regret it.'

The applause, while not thunderous, was fervent and sincerely meant.

'You know,' Gina overheard Jenny saying to Matthew in the little kitchen a while later, 'I think we'll find those girls are a real asset. They'll bring a bit of youth and beauty which will do everyone – us and the business – the world of good.'

Gina, who'd been bringing in a tray full of dirty glasses, stayed out of sight until a suitable time had passed. Deep down she'd been waiting for Matthew to say, 'You're absolutely right, Jenny,' but he didn't. He muttered something she couldn't hear.

Chapter Fourteen

Typically, just when she needed to focus on the Christmas event, Gina's one client decided he wanted her to arrange a cocktail party at short notice. While this wasn't really her job, she didn't like to refuse and it didn't take her long but it did mean she had to work hard, knocking out a press release at midnight one night. But Sally had designed some lovely posters and her leaflet, which included her own line drawings, was a masterpiece. It was being printed and Gina had arranged for the local paper to put one in every copy, along with a picture of the French House and possibly its owner (if Gina could persuade Matthew to pose in front of it). She and Sally then went round the local shops asking them to put up posters.

They were just wondering if it was lunchtime when they turned the corner into the main square. 'Hey, will you look at that. Carmella's shop. It's open.'

'It looks amazing,' said Sally after a stunned few seconds. 'Come on.'

Sally dragged Gina across the road. Reluctant, Egan's face filling her mind, Gina dragged her feet slightly, but Sally's jaw was hanging slightly open and her eyes were glazed. It was a clear case of retail-lust.

'We have to go in,' announced Sally, taking a step towards the door.

'No! I mean – yes. But can you check that Egan's not in there? If he is, you can have a look round on your own.'

'Gina, you told me you were OK about him months ago. Before you even moved down here. Why are you bothered?'

'I'm not sure really – I just feel weird.'

Sally marched into the shop and marched out again quite quickly. 'It's OK, there's no sign of either of them.'

It was a temple to the house beautiful. From its Farrow-and-Ball-painted exterior to its lush interior, it exuded style and splendour. Such a contrast to the French House, Gina thought ruefully. Carmella, with her floor-length, species-endangering coat, had immaculate taste, Gina had to concede. As Matthew had predicted, there were rugs that looked like zebra skin, but there were others like pale grass sprinkled with wild flowers that would make one's sitting-room floor look like a meadow. There was furniture made of mirrors and lamps of every kind. Clocks, objets d'art, cushions, scented candles (costing a fortune, Gina noted), the despised throws, pouffes – in fact anything the most indulged heart could desire. Gina fell in love with a pink velvet chaise longue, grateful it would never fit into her rented cottage, even if she had been willing to take out the mortgage necessary to pay for it.

'Oh God, this is so perfect for my crystal lamps!' said Sally, almost orgasmic with pleasure. 'This shop could have been created to sell them. I've died and gone to heaven!'

Gina nodded. Her sister was right, her lamps would look right at home here. 'Have you got a business card?'

Some of the gleam went from Sally's eye. 'Of course I haven't got a business card. But I have got some fantastic lamps that would look great here.'

'OK, Sal, calm down. I completely agree with you but I think it would be better if you made an appointment to tell Carmella about them and didn't just bounce in.'

Sally took this as a knock-back. 'And I need a card to do that?'

'Not strictly speaking but I just think . . . well . . .' Gina glanced around to make sure they weren't being overheard. Apart from an immaculate young woman – Carmella's clone and able assistant for sure – who was wrapping up a cream cashmere throw for an immaculate young man, the shop was a haven of tranquillity. Unlike at the French House, this didn't necessarily equate to the business being on the slide. Gina went on, 'Carmella is a bit formal. She'll be more likely to take your lamps if she thinks you're a proper business who's been making them for ages and they're not just something you knocked up in your spare room because you had a few chunks of chandelier that needed a home.' She took hold of her sister's arm. 'I know it wasn't like that. And those lamps are fabulous. But you want them and you to look really professional. Get some cards done – you can do it off the internet – and make an appointment. And then think what you'll do if she wants twenty of them, or reorders.'

'God I hate it when you're right.'

Gina smiled in sympathy. 'I know.'

They were just about to leave when a little glass cabinet caught Gina's eye. It had jewellery in it and some things she recognised: Rainey's scent bottles.

'I've just got to check something,' she said to Sally. 'Won't be a tick.'

She was only half a tick. 'I do not believe it!' she said as she dragged Sally from the shop. 'She's selling the scent bottles for nearly half as much per bottle as she paid me for the whole lot! What a mark-up! If people only had a look on eBay and saw what you can get old scent bottles for—'

'But people don't want to do that. They don't think, "I want an old scent bottle," they want to buy a piece of that style. I'm sorry to say this but I'm far more enthusiastic about this shop than I am about the centre.'

Once at home again Gina's shock had subsided enough for her to acknowledge there was nothing intrinsically wrong with putting a huge mark-up on something. She'd made a very good profit on the bottles herself and she shouldn't grudge Carmella doing the same as she sold them on. But Sally's enthusiasm for the new and stylish over antiques was a bit unsettling.

Before the drinks party Gina had realised that learning about antiques gave her a buzz; now she had to admit that she'd fallen in love with the business: the quirky people, the beautiful objects, the thrill of the chase that seemed to accompany almost every transaction, whether buying or selling. She had really hoped Sally would join her in this. But it wasn't as if Sally spent much time at the centre anyway and the less she was there the more she wouldn't be able to try and get Gina off with Matthew. Although Sally had tried not to question Gina too much about Matthew, Gina had sensed her ready to pounce. Not that there was anything for her to pounce on: Gina certainly hadn't had time to any more suppers *à deux*.

Before Gina knew it, it was 1 December: the day of the Christmas event. She was in that just-before-it-starts, slightly apprehensive mood.

'It doesn't matter how well you prepare things, make lists, be organised, ask people, tell people, you can never be absolutely confident that the planning will all work until the day,' said Anthea, the surprisingly glamorous auctioneer, who had come to the event a bit early, a sympathetic smile on her face. She patted Gina's arm. 'But it always does.'

Gina, who had liked Anthea on sight, nodded. 'I know that from every do I've ever arranged, yet I'm always really nervous just before.'

'That's a good thing,' said Anthea. 'If you ever got complacent, you wouldn't be so good at your job.'

Gina grinned ruefully. 'You don't know if I'm good at my job.'

Anthea smiled reassuringly. 'I have faith.'

Anthea was about Matthew's age and Gina had initially wondered if they'd ever had a thing – they obviously got on well, Gina saw that the moment Anthea arrived – but Anthea had put paid to that thought by saying, as they'd been chatting earlier over a cup of coffee, that she'd always liked Matthew and respected him hugely but she'd never fancied him. It was a shame really, she'd said, as he was a really nice chap under his grumpy exterior and attractive if you liked the dishevelled look. He'd got rather more grumpy and certainly more dishevelled since he'd got divorced.

'Divorced?' Gina had squeaked.

'Yes,' Anthea had said. 'I'm sorry, I didn't mean to gossip. He was married to a Frenchwoman – Yvette. They split up – oh, a little while ago now.' Something about the way she said it made Gina think she had not liked this Yvette. Unfortunately she had said no more, and Gina did not know her well enough to dig further.

'Sally and I got everyone to chip in a bit towards expenses, but we didn't manage to persuade them to dress up,' Gina said now. 'One or two were quite keen – there's a lovely guy who's very into Gilbert and Sullivan; he and his wife were well up for it – but the others said no, basically.'

'Shame. I love a good dress-up myself.' Anthea laughed. 'Any excuse to rummage in the dressing-up box!'

'My sister is just the same. Have you met Sally? Come over and I'll introduce you before we open. She's been brilliant. It was her idea to get the nursery where her girls go to put leaflets in the children's bags. They'll be a bit young but they might bring their wealthy parents. You never know.'

As they went to look for Sally, Anthea said, 'That was a lovely piece in the paper and a really good picture of Oscar. Matthew looked quite good too.'

Gina nodded. It had been a major triumph to even get Matthew to agree to it let alone spruce up the paintwork and the sign outside. But Gina had felt it was worth it: the French House looked positively upbeat in the picture.

'Ah, here's Sally. Sal? You haven't met Anthea, our star auctioneer.'

'Hi!' said Sally. 'You were in *Bargain Hunt* once, weren't you?'

'*Flog It*, actually,' said Anthea, 'but same difference.'

Gina looked at her watch. It was five to ten. 'OK, guys!' she said.

Jenny came forward with Matthew and Oscar, who was sporting a smart new collar. Everyone stood in a line. There was the odd pirate and wench amongst the usual tweed and pearls.

Everyone had picked the smallest and most gift-like items they had. Sally's chandelier decorations and their other stock were in Tiggy's care, who promised to sell them as enthusiastically as if she were making money from them too.

All the 'experts' were in place. Anthea was ensconced in the middle of the centre prepared to do her best.

'OK, here goes!' Gina went forward and unlocked the door.

'So where is everyone then?' demanded Matthew on the dot of ten, ten seconds after Gina had turned the sign to 'Open'.

'Be reasonable!' hissed Gina, terrified no one would come and it would all have been a horrible waste of time and money. 'Remember Sunday opening? That turned out all right.'

'This is different,' hissed back Matthew.

Sally, never known for her patience, grabbed a tray of mince pies. 'OK, I'm going to get them in.' She whisked out of the door before anyone could suggest she might need a coat.

By ten past ten the first family trooped in. Although

it was still early, they fell on the snacks and mulled wine or hot apple juice with enthusiasm.

Gina's hand shot out with a couple of competitions. 'If you can spot all these items on the list,' she said, 'you can have a prize!'

She thought she heard Matthew sigh from behind her but decided to ignore it. As she watched the family rush up to the cuckoo clock which was first on the list she thought how great everything was looking. The centre really had livened up lately since the dealers had been bringing in more stock and with the success of the Sunday opening. She felt proud to be part of it. The inside was decidedly less gloomy these days. Now, with all the decorations and every possible form of lighting on display it positively sparkled. Today, at least, it was a place one might actually want to spend time in rather than hurry past or ignore.

Their second visitor was a man in a raincoat bearing a plastic supermarket bag before him like a bouquet of flowers. 'I need an expert,' he said nervously.

'Well,' said Jenny once he'd been directed to the dealer who specialised in ceramics, 'I really hope that what's in there is valuable. It'll break his heart otherwise.'

A harassed-looking couple with three children came in. They looked like they'd wandered in seeking something – anything – to keep the children safe and entertained.

Sally and Gina exchanged glances, both recognising exhaustion and despair when they saw it. 'Good morning!' said Gina. 'Have a hot drink and a nibble.'

'Would you like to enter the competition?' said Sally, to the children, a little boy and two slightly older girls.

'If you like, we could take the children on the treasure hunt while you have a browse on your own?' Gina addressed their mother. 'They'll be fine with us. My sister has twin girls of her own.'

It was fun taking the children around, encouraging them to spot the carved owl up on a high shelf and getting them to tick it off. They soon got into it and were looking intently at everything, vying with each other to be the first to see the statue of a man with a lion at his feet.

Harold had planned the treasure hunt carefully, not encouraging children into areas where they could break things. Even so Gina found it a little nerve-racking and was relieved to take them back to their parents so they could choose a prize.

'Thank you so much for that,' said the mother, looking calmer and wearing a little ring that her husband had bought for her.

'It was fun,' said Gina. 'Wasn't it?'

The children jumped up and down. 'Yeah! Can we do it again?'

'No, we need to get off now. Granny's this

afternoon!' The woman's enthusiasm was a little forced. 'That'll be fun, won't it?'

'No,' said the eldest child, a girl of about six.

'But at least we found her a present she'll like,' said her mother, clutching a package and not bothering to argue. 'Thank you so much,' she said again before taking her family away.

'You know, I think we should offer escorted treasure hunts as standard,' said Sally. 'I bet people would be so grateful to have a few minutes' child-free time that they buy something out of gratitude.'

Matthew too had been doing child duty, but with two boys who were really a bit big for treasure hunts. Gina spotted him enthusing them by encouraging them to spot samurai swords and vicious-looking nutcrackers.

As she went to fetch some wine she had to acknowledge that he was very good at it. It was a shame he'd never had children, he was so good with them. He was one of those people who didn't know anything about children so treated them just like adults – to very good effect.

'Never put me through that again,' he said to Gina, biting into a pasty a little later, duty done. 'I had no idea what I was doing.'

'You were brilliant,' she said. 'Really. I was following you round so I could mock, but they loved you!'

Matthew tried very hard not to look pleased.

* * *

At about four o'clock the centre emptied of the public and Gina and Sally went round to the dealers to see how they felt the day had gone. They'd grinned at each other when they'd overheard a couple commenting on how much better this place was to so many of the other antiques shops in the town. They'd never noticed it before but they would definitely be back. However, the most pressing thing now was to find out if the other dealers felt it had gone well. And they did. Almost everyone had sold a bit more than they would have expected to, which meant the day's sales were already well up.

'And I discovered a couple of nice pieces,' said Harold, who'd got into the festive spirit and was wearing a twinkling bow tie powered by a tiny battery. 'I passed them on to Anthea to put in the next auction, but I'll go along too in case they don't make what they should.'

'Why didn't you just buy them yourself?' asked Sally.

'I thought the lady who'd brought them in would get a bit more for them at auction and although they were nice, they weren't exactly what I prefer. But as I say, I'll make sure they don't go for nothing when sale time comes.'

'That's really very kind of you,' said Sally.

Tiggy, extra draped in strings of beads and shawls in honour of the season, broke in. 'Anthea will make sure they do. She's good at her job.'

'So how was it for you, Tiggy?' asked Gina. 'Did you find anything wonderful?'

'I didn't buy anything but I think it was thoroughly worthwhile. A couple of people said they had things they'll bring in after Christmas. I think we showed people we're just the same as they are and they shouldn't be nervous about coming in.'

Gina nodded. 'That's brilliant.'

'Sally's crystal decorations all sold and I did sell quite a lot of smalls myself,' Tiggy said.

Harold grunted. 'No one calls the little items "smalls" these days.'

Tiggy laughed. 'Well, I like the old terms.'

Gina and Sally moved on leaving Harold and Tiggy arguing gently about the terminology of the antiques trade. They found Matthew talking to the dealer who had the largest pitch, John Webster. It had taken all Sally's girlish charms to get him to agree to the upheaval. Gina broke in on them, knowing he was key: if he'd done well Matthew would be satisfied it had been worth it.

'How did it go?' she asked.

John looked at her thoughtfully. 'Not bad at all,' he said at last. 'I must confess I'm surprised. Sold a tallboy I've had for years. Bit odd really. People don't usually buy furniture at Christmas.' Then, not wishing to be too upbeat, he went on, 'The trouble is, we've got to do it all again tomorrow.'

'I knew Sunday opening was a bad idea,' said Matthew, partly, Gina was sure, to wind her up.

'No it's not,' said John. 'It's an excellent idea. But these events are tiring for an old man.'

'You don't have to do tomorrow,' said Matthew. 'I'll stand in for you if you like. It would stop Gina making me take round packs of children.'

Gina made a face at him.

'But you're not an expert in furniture in the way I am,' said John. 'And I saw you with those kiddies. You looked in your element. That said, I'd quite like your opinion on this bonheur du jour. Haven't seen you since I bought it.'

Gina and Sally, who had thought the item he was indicating was just a fancy desk, made faces at each other and then went to gather used glasses.

Chapter Fifteen

'Hey! You'll never guess who came in!' They were having to do it all again the next day, which was partly good because they knew what to expect and partly bad because they were tired. Sally, however, was jumping up and down with excitement, all signs of fatigue gone.

'Who? The Queen? The *Antiques Roadshow* team? Madonna? Tell me.'

'Carmella! She came in. With Egan. Of course, I didn't know it was her but Egan introduced us. And' – she held up her hand so she wouldn't be interrupted – 'I gave her my card. And better, I had pictures of the lamps on my phone. She loved them.'

'I knew she would,' said Gina, thrilled for Sally but feeling a bit odd. Did she feel Sally was being disloyal to her having anything to do with a shop connected to her horrible ex-boyfriend? She pushed the feeling away.

'I'm coming to the shop tomorrow to show her and have a proper interview. Oh Gina.' Sally's eyes were wide and ecstatic. 'I haven't been so excited about anything for years.'

'That's lovely,' said Gina, still fighting her negative feelings.

'You don't mind, do you?' Sally obviously expected Gina to say no. 'I mean – Egan and everything?'

'There are absolutely no feelings left between me and Egan. The only thing I can't understand is what Carmella, who seems to have everything, sees in a loser like Egan.'

'He is good-looking,' said Sally.

'Yes.'

'Hon? Are you sure you're over him? He and Carmella might just be friends, although I did think from, you know, body language that they are an item.'

Sally's concern was typical but a bit irritating. 'I'm absolutely over him as a person. I am not over the whole horror of being in a bad relationship and being such an utter fool,' said Gina, a little more forcefully than she had intended. 'Now let's stop talking about my so-over relationship and think about your lamps. You must track down a chandelier bits shop.'

'Oh, I have already. This is me, Gina. I want to make fabulous, individual decorative pieces. It's something I can do at home and be good at. I've discovered what I want to do when I grow up.'

Gina smiled fondly. 'Any idea when that might happen, Sal?'

Sally pushed Gina affectionately. She was in love.

Nothing anyone could say would affect her new-found joy.

As Gina drove home she tried to be happy for Sally but she couldn't avoid a tiny finger of sadness touching her. As she had feared, Sally and she would not be running their Aunt Rainey's antiques business together. As a self-employed person she had looked forward to being part of a team and not having to bear all the responsibility herself. When she'd started out in the world of PR she'd worked for a company and she did miss the camaraderie.

But she'd still have Sally as a sister, she reminded herself, and the event had been such a roaring success. She had proved she was good at her job – something she knew intellectually but had to be reminded of from time to time. Everyone – except Matthew, who was apparently hard-wired to be despondent – was thrilled with the extra boost to their business at a time that traditionally was very hard for antiques dealers. So as she parked her car outside her cottage, she decided she was definitely going to have a glass of wine. She bloody well deserved one.

Gina hadn't seen Matthew since the Christmas event. He had been visiting friends and dealers a little further afield, Jenny informed her. And Gina herself had been busy: she'd got a little bit more PR business, and had also been to Anthea's auction house to restock, which meant she wasn't in the centre as much as she'd hoped to be.

However, today, Gina was at the French House, rearranging her new stock to look appealing in the cabinet, when she realised Matthew was locking up.

'Hey, I didn't think anyone else was still here,' he said. 'I haven't seen you for ages. How are things?' He leant against a table to the side of Gina's stall.

'Good. How are things going for you?' she asked nonchalantly, locking the cabinet and squirrelling away the key. She was ridiculously pleased to see him.

'OK,' he said non-committally.

Matthew was always bleak, Gina reminded herself, she shouldn't regard it. But somehow she heard herself saying, 'You don't sound very cheerful. Business has really picked up around here, hasn't it? Shouldn't that perk you up a bit?'

He chuckled. 'You make me sound like a hairstyle that needs some gunk or other to improve it.'

'I'm sure we can find that gunk if we look on the internet.' She smiled. 'Or is it the time of year that's getting you down? Not everyone loves Christmas and when the whole world is supposed to be feeling jolly . . .' A thought occurred to her. 'What are you doing for Christmas anyway?'

Afterwards she could have kicked herself. She really didn't want to look as if she was prying into his personal life, which she now knew included an ex-wife whom no one ever mentioned.

He hesitated. 'Last year I went to Jenny and her family. They have a big old farmhouse with all sorts of animals. They've got a pair of Jack Russells called Nunc and Dimittis. They adore Oscar.'

'So you're going there this year?'

There was a tiny pause. 'No. They're all going away somewhere. I shall have a peaceful time here, getting ahead with my paperwork.'

She spoke without thinking. 'Why don't you come to Sally's? It's utter chaos but always fun. I know she'd love to have you.' Even as she heard herself say this she wondered how on earth they'd fit another person and a huge dog into Sally's tiny cottage.

'I wouldn't dream of intruding.'

'You wouldn't be intruding. The more the merrier. And Sally loves it if someone who's not family comes because she says it makes the girls behave better. You'd be a very useful addition.'

'The girls are terrified of Oscar.'

'They'd get used to him. Do come.'

'I couldn't possibly. Really. I'll be fine.'

'If you don't come I'll end up doing all the washing-up on my own. It happens every year.'

'So you want me to help with the washing-up? That's the only reason you've invited me?'

She nodded, trying not to smile and knowing she'd have to examine all the other reasons she might have for inviting him the moment she was on her own.

Was she imagining things or had he been pleased she'd asked him?

'In which case I'd be delighted to accept.'

'Good. I know Sally will be delighted.'

'But on the condition you let me invite you to something.'

Gina frowned. 'A particular something? Or just some random something that might come up?'

'A particular something.' He smiled but didn't elaborate.

'What then?' Gina urged.

'I want you to visit an old friend with me. I think you'd enjoy it. I will need to check first though. He lives in an amazing house. It'll be shortly after Christmas – if it comes off.'

'It sounds wonderful – and very intriguing. Can you give me more details?'

'I could but I prefer not to. It might not happen.'

'You're being very mysterious, Matthew.'

'And usually I'm a miserable old man resistant to change?'

Gina nodded. 'You're not that old though.'

Matthew laughed. 'Come on, it's time you went home. I'll let you out.'

Rather than phoning Sally she decided to drive to her house so she could tell her face to face about inviting another guest for Christmas to her tiny house. She caught Sally at a good moment. The girls were ensconced in front of CBeebies and Alaric was in his studio.

'Come and talk to me while I cook. This is so nice. I can open some wine,' Sally said when she'd given Gina a huge hug.

'I won't have any—'

'You don't have to. But your presence in the house means it's OK for me to drink.'

'You might throw it at me when I tell you why I've come.' Gina pulled out a chair and sat at the table pulling the bowl of half-peeled potatoes towards her. 'Sally, I've asked Matthew to spend Christmas with us. He was going to spend it on his own,' she said in a rush.

Sally sighed as she pulled open the fridge door.

Gina held her breath, and then let it out again as her sister said, 'Well, I can't blame you. I would have invited him too if I'd known he was going to be alone. I am a bit surprised by you though, hon. I thought you wanted to keep things strictly business between you.'

'On the whole, yes, but I have my share of the milk of human kindness. I'm peeling your potatoes although I'm not staying for supper.' She realised she wasn't being completely honest with Sally but if Sally got wind of her crush on Matthew and the possibility (or foolish hope on her part) that he might feel something for her in return she would have no peace. Gina got up from the table and took the potatoes over to the sink to rinse them. To stop herself mentioning something that was beginning to take over her mind she said, 'Let's think about Christmas. How many other people are coming? Or is it just us and Matthew?'

'I wish. No, we've got all Alaric's lot, including the mad aunt who sounds a lot of fun but who really isn't.' She bit her lip and looked at Gina. 'Auntie Rainey was a proper mad aunt, generous, fun . . .'

Gina nodded. 'Always drank too much at Christmas.'

'Exactly. She was proper.'

'So where are you going to put people?' said Gina after a moment's silent reflection on their dead aunt.

Sally looked around her. 'Well, I thought if we took out every single moveable bit of furniture apart from the table we could just about manage to eat in here. That was what I planned to do.'

Gina felt that there would be no room for chairs. She was overcome with guilt. 'Oh God, Sals, I'm so sorry. Now I've added Matthew that will be just impossible. I'll uninvite him.' Just for a second the thought of inviting him to her own little cottage and having a romantic Christmas for two flittered into her head like a cobweb to be chased out again by her mental broom of good sense.

'Don't be silly, we'll manage.' Sally rubbed her sister's arm in reassurance. 'It's not as if he's bringing Oscar.' Then she caught Gina's rueful gaze. 'He's bringing Oscar.'

Gina nodded. 'I will uninvite him. He'll understand—'

'No. I refuse to think of him – anyone that we know – being alone at Christmas when we could have done something about it. Us'll manage,' she added. 'That's what Alaric always says, coming from the West Country, loike.'

Chapter Sixteen

Gina was delighted when Sally asked her if she could come over a couple of days before Christmas Eve to help her get ready. She was unexpectedly excited about Christmas this year: although she didn't really want to admit it, she knew it was because she would be spending the day with Matthew.

In spite of his mysterious invitation she wasn't sure how he felt about her, of course, but sometimes she caught him looking at her in a way that gave her a frisson of hope.

She set off for Sally's with a packet of chocolate Hobnobs and a pair of rubber gloves.

Sally was wearing a thick jumper and dungarees with a scarf wrapped round her head. 'The kids are with my dear friend and her kids and Alaric's off somewhere, which is a shame because we could do with some muscle, but you and I are going to create our Christmas space.'

Gina hugged her sister hello. 'One of the things I love about you is the way you dress for the part – whatever that part might be.' Warned she was going to get dirty, Gina had on tracksuit bottoms and a jumper which had once belonged to Egan. (As she'd given it to him in the first place she felt it was sort of hers anyway, and it was the only thing of his that she hadn't wanted to throw on the fire in a fit of anger.) 'Can I come in? Why aren't we in the kitchen with the kettle on?'

'I'll make you a hot drink if you want one but we're not going into the kitchen.'

Gina shook her head. 'Sal, you'll never be able to clear all the furniture out of the sitting room—'

'We're not having Christmas dinner in the house. We're going in the garage.'

Sally led the way down the front path to the garage and, with as near to a flourish as she could manage given she was dealing with something quite heavy, she pulled up the door. 'Alaric agreed it's too good a space to keep the car in. All we have to do is clear out the rubbish and then decorate it.'

Gina inspected the space. It was quite large. She remembered when Sally and Alaric bought the house – a tiny if picturesque ex-farmworker's cottage – they'd mentioned turning the garage into a studio. Lack of money had stopped them ever doing it. Alaric had a shed in the garden.

'God, Sal, we haven't got a lot of time, have we?' said Gina, trying not to dampen Sally's enthusiasm.

'I know, but I only had the idea the other day and then had to arrange childcare. We'll be fine.'

'Of course we will!' said Gina brightly, quashing her doubts. 'Where are we going to put the rubbish?'

'We'll drag it out of the door in the back into the garden and have a bonfire. It's mostly wood. Look, I've bought us gloves.'

Accepting that her sister had thought everything through, Gina put on the gloves and started pulling at some hardboard. 'Goodness. There's an inspection pit in here. I wonder how you get into it?'

Sally took hold of the other end. 'I don't know, but you'll be pleased to hear I've decided against having Father Christmas rising up out of it. I thought it would be confusing for the girls as they think of him as coming down things.'

'Like chimneys?'

'Exactly.'

Synchronising their efforts, they heaved the plywood on to the bonfire. 'That looks a bit too good to burn,' said Gina.

'It does. I might just leave it here until after Christmas. Or let Alaric decide.'

They went back into the garage. 'So what are we going to eat off?'

'That's easy. We use the plastic picnic table and put a bit of fibre board or something on top of it.' Sally giggled. 'I was going to ask Alaric if I could have that really big canvas he's never got right but thought someone might poke a hole in it.'

Gina restrained her amusement better. It was all right

for Sally to be disrespectful about her husband's paintings but it wouldn't do for her to be so. 'It wouldn't be rigid enough anyway.'

'The absolute joy about having earned a bit of money of my own is that I can spend some of it at least on Christmas.'

'Well, I'll provide the alcohol as usual,' said Gina. 'And as it's my fault you're having to do all this' – she indicated the garage and its contents – 'I'll do the turkey as well. Although it will be frozen. Free-range but frozen.'

'That would be wonderful. Alaric's parents always give us a bit of money towards it. Of course, they think they're getting a posh fresh one from some farm or other but really, they never can tell the difference and there's plenty of other things to spend money on.'

'Now, let me get a broom so we can sweep the floor and see what we've got to deal with.'

The floor was not inspiring. Concrete and dirty even after a brisk sweeping, it definitely needed some sort of covering.

'I don't suppose Matthew has a huge supply of antique kilims we could borrow, do you?' Sally looked at her sister.

'Oh God, Sal. Don't ask me to ask him. They might get damaged.'

Sally sighed. 'OK, I'll scrub that idea. What about tarpaulins?'

'Well, they are quite expensive,' said Gina.

Sally thought for a moment. 'Right, fall-back position. We'll paint the floor. If it's light and bright it'll be fine. You can get emulsion in bulk for not a lot of money.'

'But will it dry in time? Imagine: little footprints permanently on your floors.'

Sally shuddered. 'We'll have to do something about heating anyway, that would help it dry quicker. I'd better get looking. There's bound to be something on the internet.'

'While you do that, I'll start on the walls. We should maybe do them first, if we're doing them. What do you think we should tackle first?'

'Actually I think we need tea. Come into the house.'

By the time Sally had made tea and put a hazelnut and chocolate chip biscuit by Gina's side, Gina had found out that portable gas heaters were hideously expensive too.

'Oh!' said Sally, crunching in Gina's ear a few moments later. 'Lightbulb moment. Alaric's got a friend who spray-paints cars. He won't be working over Christmas. I bet he'd lend us his industrial heaters. I'll go and phone him.'

She came back shortly afterwards. 'Result. He's shutting up shop this afternoon and I can pick up the heaters at five.'

'Yeah! So that's the heat and the floor decided if not actually done . . .'

'We need to go back and see what else needs doing. I'm really enjoying myself.' Sally hugged her sister.

They stood side by side inspecting the garage walls. The building was wooden and the construction meant the walls consisted of small shelves as wide as the two-by-fours that kept the building rigid.

'No, we can't paint them,' said Gina. 'It would take forever.'

'I'm thinking tea lights,' said Sally. 'Masses and masses of them, on every shelf. It would help keep us warm, too.'

Gina sighed. 'I hate to be an older sister but what about fire?'

Sally nodded slowly. 'Hmm. Annoyingly, I think you're right. OK, we'll just have some where we can reach them and maybe' – her expression lightened – 'little buckets of sand? In case of emergencies?'

'Good idea, and for the rest of the shelves, battery-operated fairy lights,' said Gina. 'There's bound to be a website with a deal on.'

'Excellent. Let's go and look,' said Sally as they went back to the house. 'And as fairy lights are one of my addictions I don't mind buying them with some of my Carmella money.'

As they looked online for the best deal Gina said, 'You won't give up on the antiques entirely, will you? I mean I know you really prefer new things to old but I need you!'

'Oh hon. I'd never abandon you if you needed me.

I won't ever get into the fusty old stuff like you have but we're still a team.'

Gina tried to smile although her sister's words told her that Sally's support was going to be more emotional than practical. Well, so she would be on her own with the antiques. She'd just have to manage. She was managing without a partner in her personal life, she'd do the same professionally. Matthew would go on supporting her, she was sure. Resolutely she pushed an image of his smile – so charming because it was so rare – from her mind. Focus. 'Look. Bargain. Four sets for a tenner. Will that be enough?'

'Gina, there is no such thing as enough fairy lights. We'll have eight sets.' A quick phone call that guaranteed next-day delivery and they went back to the garage.

'Now,' said Gina. 'With the table in the middle and all the chairs round, there'll still be a bit of empty space in the corners. You need Christmas trees.'

Sally shook her head. 'I need white-painted branches stuck in pots displaying my lovely crystal decorations. With fairy lights, obviously.'

'Oh! And you've got those already, have you? That's very *Blue Peter* of you, if I may say so.' Gina was impressed.

Sally looked smug. 'Actually I had to make some for the shop and I went on until I'd used all the stuff. After all, the plaster of Paris would have had to be dumped anyway. But there was only room for two in the end.'

'Oh?'

'It's all right, Miss Honesty Box, Carmella didn't want the extra ones. She was a bit annoyed there wasn't room for more, though. That shop is a bit small really for some of the stuff she's got in there. It's not displayed to its best advantage.' Sally snapped back to the job in hand. 'Anyway, we get the benefit.'

When Gina fell into bed that night, she was exhausted and paint-spattered, but pleased with the result of their hard work. Sally had insisted in tiptoeing over the still-damp floor and setting up the Christmas trees. They were stunning.

'All we need is a centrepiece in the middle,' Sally had declared. 'Otherwise it's all too bloody tasteful.'

As she headed for the shower the next day, Gina wondered what her sister had in mind. Sally was no minimalist.

Chapter Seventeen

Christmas Day arrived. Matthew was going to collect Gina. It wasn't really on his way but, as he said, there was no point in taking two cars and it would mean she could at least drink. They were to arrive at about midday to give the girls time to open some presents and have hysterics in private, Sally said.

So, thought Gina, wearing a towel and looking at the cardboard carry cases that she'd never got round to unpacking, what should she wear?

The trouble with Christmas was that it was quite hard to get the balance of practical and festive right. She needed to be able to schlep things in and out of the oven – she always shared responsibility for the meal with her sister – but she also wanted to look attractive.

Gina had stopped pretending – to herself at least – that she didn't fancy Matthew. She did. And she wanted him to fancy her.

She ended up in black jeans with a fitted cardigan that showed off her waist and her cleavage – practical and sexy – and added a necklace of bright glass beads for the festive part.

Then, remembering where they were to have dinner, she found a looser cardigan to go on top and a scarf. Chattering teeth and blue lips was never a good look. She wasn't absolutely convinced by the industrial heaters Sally was borrowing. She added a extra spritz of perfume to offset the less glamorous part of her outfit. Now she had to wrap Matthew's present. Finding a Christmas gift for him had felt impossible. She didn't want to be either over the top or mean. While she was looking she decided the problem wouldn't have been much easier had she had loads of money – anything expensive would definitely be over the top. In the end she had bought something useful; she had got two dozen pencils printed with the name of the centre on them. They were very stylish, with rubbers at the end, plain wood with the printing in gold. She found a suitable pot (courtesy of one of the other dealers) and felt pleased with the result. It wasn't something he could dislike even if he preferred pens. They were personal but neutral. Anyway, they would have to do.

When the pencils in their pot were duly, if untidily, wrapped and she was satisfied with her make-up she realised he'd be here at any moment. She thrust the organic dog biscuits she'd got for Oscar into a bottle carrier, stapled the top together and added a bow. Oscar's present looked far classier than Matthew's but there was nothing she could do about it now.

'This is not a date,' she told the mirror as she leant in, checking for surplus eyebrows, 'it's a family Christmas. He's only coming because he didn't get a better offer.'

She was concentrating so hard on breathing deeply and being calm that when he knocked she jumped. She pulled open the door immediately, even though she was sure she should have waited a certain amount of time, so as not to seem too keen.

'Happy Christmas,' she said brightly.

'Happy Christmas,' he echoed and kissed her cheek.

She caught a whiff of cologne. He smelt divine and she was unexpectedly affected by it. 'Get a grip,' she ordered silently.

'Shall I take your things? Oscar's in the boot but these will be safe on the back seat.'

'I took most of my presents and stuff over yesterday,' she said. 'This is just for you and Oscar.'

'We're honoured,' he said gravely.

Gina had long since suspected that his gravity was often a disguise for amusement but she didn't feel she could call him on it.

He opened the passenger door for her. 'Hop in.

'I've brought a bottle of port and some cognac,' he said as he started the engine and they pulled away from the kerb. 'My contribution to the feast. I found a nice little book about Cézanne for Alaric – quite old but with charming notes – and for Sally one of those cut-glass scent bottles with bulbs and silk tassels.'

'Oh, she'll love that.'

'The girls I struggled with a bit but we'll see.'

'As long as whatever you've got is far too old for them and is pink and sparkly, it'll be fine.'

He laughed. 'I've probably hit it on the head then. I've also brought a few tins of biscuits for anyone else who's there.'

'And what about me?' said some imp using Gina's voice. 'Have you got me a present?'

He gave her one of his looks. 'Of course. But I'm not going to tell you what it is, am I? It's a surprise.'

Gina accepted this happily, and the fact that she seemed to have temporarily changed into a teenage girl going on a date with her crush.

'I'm going to leave Oscar in the car until I've got the lay of the land a bit,' said Matthew. 'We don't want the girls having hysterics immediately. Better to postpone it by half an hour at least.'

'You'd be surprised. The girls are now really excited about having Oscar in their house. Alaric told them he was like the Gruffalo and wouldn't hurt them. Which is true.' Another similarity between master and dog, thought Gina.

'He certainly wouldn't hurt them. In fact, what

he'd like best is a quiet corner where he can lie down and snooze. He's had a walk today and in spite of being huge, he doesn't need much exercise.'

'I'm sure Sally has it all in hand. She's well into the Christmas spirit this year.'

Sally was bouncing around in the garden giving instructions before they'd even got out of the car. 'Hello! Happy Christmas! We're going straight into the garage if that's all right. And, Matthew, we've lit the fire in the sitting room, so if Oscar would like to go there he won't be disturbed.'

'That's very kind,' said Matthew, kissing Sally's cheek. 'I'll bring him in when we've had a chance to say hello.'

Gina did wonder if Sally was treating Oscar like the crotchety uncle but then realised she had her father-in-law for that role.

'Come in, do,' said Sally, who had been joined by her daughters. 'I can't wait for you to see everything!'

'Gruf'lo,' squeaked Sephie as she and Ariadne excitedly pointed at Oscar, who was peering out of the back window.

Sally led the little party towards the garage, the girls skipping along beside her. Gina almost broke into a skip herself.

Even though she'd been part of the transformation, Gina was amazed. It was like Santa's Grotto with furniture. And up the far end, between the white-painted branches (now decorated with baubles and yet more fairy lights) was a diorama. Sally had bought every single available chocolate creature and created a Nativity.

There were bears, kittens and rabbits propped up with cocktail sticks. Behind were giant gold foil bunnies and deer with bells round their necks. A choir of angels (six of them) supported the shepherds, who looked strangely like the angels only they had bits of wool and felt stuck on them. The Three Kings, once in the dreary garb of Father Christmas, were now bedecked with gold and silver and edible baubles. Their gifts, gold-covered chocolates, in three colours, were stuck to their midriffs.

There was a stable made of gingerbread, thatched with chocolate flakes and supported by Curly Wurlies. Icing sugar snow, sweets like jewels and flashing fairy lights added to the general exuberance. Even Mary and Joseph were made of chocolate. Only baby Jesus had once been a sugar pig, and lay in a manger borrowed from some generous Sylvanian Family.

'Sally! I absolutely love it!' exclaimed Gina, hugging her sister and jumping up and down. 'It's so kitsch it's not true.'

'I know! Alaric's parents are going to hate it.' Sally was just as excited. 'I had such fun doing it. The girls were so good. They made the snowflakes that are stuck to the wall and decorated the stable.' She paused, aware of the tall, silent figure standing behind her sister. 'What do you think, Matthew?'

'I think it's stupendous,' he said. Gina checked for sarcasm but didn't spot any. 'And I definitely think we should have something like this at the centre next year.'

Both sisters were inspecting him very carefully by now but before they could decide if he was mocking them Alaric appeared wanting to know what they wanted to drink, reeling off a range of options, including punch.

Matthew opted for a glass of elderflower cordial which Gina seconded. Sally had hurried off to the kitchen to 'check on something', the girls in tow. Alaric followed his wife with their orders.

'You're not driving,' said Matthew when they were alone. 'You could have had the punch if you'd wanted.'

Gina looked up at him, touched again by his thoughtfulness. 'I might have to drive the oven though. Sally and I always share it but with her in-laws coming she may hit the bottle a bit. Don't blame her. They are not easy guests. I'll move on to the hard stuff later, when I know it's safe.'

'You're very close to your sister, aren't you?' he said.

Gina nodded. 'We're very lucky. We really like each other. I can't imagine anything happening to change that.'

'Goodness, full of the Christmas spirit and you haven't even had your first glass of wine,' said Matthew.

* * *

Gina and Matthew happened to be present when Alaric's parents (the mad aunt had thankfully decided to visit a friend – 'One less pedant,' Sally had whispered to Gina) came into the garage. Although she pretended she wanted to shock them and part of her did, Gina knew that Sally secretly hoped that one day they would say something nice to her. Gina felt her sister was doomed to disappointment.

They came into the garage through the back door, ushered in by their son, who was so unlike his parents, Sally always insisted he had been swapped in the hospital.

'Good God!' said Alaric's father, his eyes on stalks. 'It's like the Blackpool Illuminations!'

Even the little girls, who hadn't heard of the Blackpool Illuminations, realised he wasn't paying a compliment.

Alaric's mother stood in front of the Nativity in silence for several, long, heavily laden seconds. Then she said, primly, 'You do know, don't you – or maybe you don't – that the Wise Men shouldn't be placed by the crib until Twelfth Night. They weren't there at the birth.'

'Oh, I know,' said Sally tightly, 'but I just thought it would be rather fun to have them. Darling! Do get your parents a drink. And Matthew? Would you like to bring Oscar in now?'

Possibly only Gina deduced from this how much

Sally wished Oscar was an attack dog and would tear her in-laws limb from limb should she give the command.

Alaric's parents had strict rules about Christmas. Presents in the afternoon, after lunch, after the washing-up. Rather than take them head on, Sally and Alaric had special, small and educational presents to give their children after lunch. Their real presents were opened at breakfast with a lot of screaming and spilt drinks. If the grandparents made any comments about these presents, the children were trained to say, 'But Grandma, we've had these ages!'

After lunch, which had been cleared away in record time, Gina, the girls and Oscar escorted the grand-parents up and down the road for some post-prandial exercise. The girls took it in turns to hold Oscar's lead and Gina did her best to make conversation. It was hard work and she wished she was back at the house, clearing up, but Matthew had insisted on doing it.

When they came back the garage had become a sitting room. Some of the furniture had been moved back into the cottage and the dining chairs (borrowed from the village hall) were all facing the same direction. There was even space for Oscar: his bed had been laid regally in front of the chimenea, which was now filled with rows of tea lights to simulate an open fire. The industrial blowers were doing a good job – aided by the mild weather – and it was pleasantly warm.

'Now! Presents!' declared Alaric, almost as excited as his daughters.

Matthew's presents were very well received: especially by the girls who fell upon the nail varnish designed to drop off shortly after being applied. He seemed very pleased with his presents too, the pencils being admired by everyone as well as him.

While Sally was making a note of everything the girls were given so they could write thank-you letters afterwards (in fact, only the grandparents got these) Gina opened her present from Matthew. It was large and square and at first she didn't know what it was.

'It's a lap desk,' he said. 'Papier-mâché, mid nineteenth century. Open it.'

Gina lifted the lid and saw how it formed a slope. There were spaces for pens and two little ink bottles. The whole thing was painted with roses and inlaid with mother of pearl.

'It's beautiful!' Gina was hardly able to speak. It seemed far too valuable a present – especially as she'd given him pencils. He'd obviously put a lot of thought into choosing it for her.

'If you look closely you'll notice it's been restored quite a lot.' He paused. 'I did really well on it.'

Gina smiled up at him, wanting to kiss him but not wanting to do it in public. 'Thank you so much,' she whispered.

Chapter Eighteen

After a long, dull afternoon with mince pies and cake and stilted conversation, Gina got up to go, feeling her sister would be tired and want to enjoy the rest of Christmas Day with her nuclear family.

'Sally, thank you so much.' Gina hugged her. 'It's been such a lovely day.'

'You're not going home already!' said Sally. Gina guessed she didn't want to be left with Alaric's parents, but she hoped if she and Matthew left, they might take the hint.

'I need to feed Oscar,' said Matthew, 'but it has been wonderful. Thank you so much for including me.'

Their leave-taking included a frantic, private conversation between Gina and Sally about whether Alaric could just ask his parents to leave (they decided not), but finally, Gina and Matthew, with Oscar lying in state in the back, drove away. Neither of them spoke until they were nearly at Gina's house.

'So, what will you do now?' asked Matthew as he pulled up. 'Write your thank-you letters?'

Gina smiled. 'No. I'll put something rubbishy on

telly and eat crisps. Maybe have a glass of wine. Then I'll fall asleep.'

'That sounds cosy,' said Matthew.

'Join me?' said Gina impulsively. 'You don't have to have wine. I could make tea. Or cocoa.'

Matthew didn't answer immediately. 'I've only had one glass of wine all day. I think I could risk another now. There was Christmas dinner in between.'

'But what about Oscar's dinner? You said we had to go because he needed feeding.'

Matthew picked up a foil-wrapped packet from the floor by his seat. 'Sally gave me a doggy bag. She said otherwise they'd be living on turkey for weeks.'

Gina felt excited and nervous as they went down the path to her door. She put her key in the lock.

'I'll go and get Oscar – if you don't mind him coming in?'

'Of course I don't mind. He's been here before and besides, he was such a saint today. Being dressed up as a boar's head, "bedecked with bays and rose-marree" like that – what a star.'

This made Matthew smile. 'I think he has a previously untapped streak of showmanship and fondness for children. I'll get him.'

Maybe his master had too, thought Gina as she let herself in and deposited her loot – including her beautiful and thoughtful present from Matthew. She stroked it lovingly and felt a flutter of excitement. Then she plumped the sofa cushions, shoved wrapping paper, sticky tape and scissors that were on the floor under the sofa and set a match to the fire, thanking God that she had laid it previously. She'd fluffed up her hair and checked under her eyes for stray mascara before she realised how cold the cottage was. She went into the sitting room to feel the radiator. It was icy.

Gina stood in the middle of the room feeling absurdly disappointed. How could they possibly have a cosy evening with no heating? While the open fire would begin to help soon, it would be chilly while they waited. Matthew wouldn't want to stay and freeze to death.

She was just wondering if she would ever be able to find the instructions for the boiler when he came back.

'I took him for a little trot, just in case,' he said.

'Good idea,' she replied. 'We have a problem though. The heating's broken.'

'Ah. Would you like me to look at the boiler?' he said. 'I mean, you can probably sort it out yourself if it just needs rebalancing or anything . . .' He stalled, obviously torn between wanting to be helpful and revealing himself as a sexist.

Gina felt she would be letting down the sisterhood if she admitted to not knowing what 'rebalancing' meant, but on the other hand she needed heat. 'I haven't been here that long. If you thought you might be able to sort it, that would be great.'

While Matthew was investigating the appropriate cupboard full of spiders, Gina found a couple of throws that they could snuggle under if necessary. Then she moved the furniture round so the sofa was much nearer the fire. She didn't ask Oscar to move. Matthew could do that if it became necessary.

'Well, I've done something that might help,' he said coming back into the room. 'We'll have to wait and see. I'll feed the brute now.'

While he was fiddling around in her tiny kitchen, Gina lit more tea lights. Then she went upstairs and brushed her teeth. She didn't use toothpaste because she didn't want Matthew to know she'd brushed her teeth – it would look as if she was expecting something. But she also didn't want her breath to smell of mince pies and Brussels sprouts. She only hoped she hadn't misread the look he'd given her when she'd opened his present.

Gina joined Matthew in the kitchen, watching him fill the bowl with turkey.

'Have you got a stool or something I can put the bowl on?' asked Matthew. 'It's not good for dogs this size to eat at floor level.'

In the end she found a bucket which held the bowl at the perfect level. Then when Oscar had finished eating Matthew took him into the garden and she cleared up the mess.

'Right!' she said when he'd come back in. 'You go and make yourself comfortable, I'm just going to find us drinks. What would you like? Wine? Tea? Cocoa?'

'Actually have you got anything stronger? Rude of me to ask . . .'

'Not at all rude. You sit down. I'll bring you a whisky mac.' More out of panic than anything she picked up the *Radio Times* Christmas edition. 'Here. I only ever buy this at Christmas – you know how you do. See if there's anything on.'

She hurried through to the kitchen. If he was opting for something stronger then that meant he wasn't intending to rush off. Perhaps her dream of a cosy – and possibly something more – evening in front of the fire might actually become a reality. Then nerves overtook her again. The looks he had been giving her all day made her feel her hopes weren't based on wobbly foundations but then again Matthew was terribly difficult to read.

She brought out the drinks and handed one to Matthew. They both took a sip but Gina still couldn't sit down. 'I'll just find us something to nibble. We shouldn't drink on an empty stomach.'

Not sure where this had come from – she often drank without food and they'd eaten a feast today – she went back into the kitchen and rummaged in the cupboard for a box of cheese straws. 'Clutching at straws,' she muttered to herself as she put them into a tall glass. Why on earth was she nervous about going back into the sitting room with Matthew? She'd invited him – it's what she wanted, wasn't it? But did he? That was the thing.

She found Matthew standing by the fireplace. She put down the cheese straws and then went to adjust the curtains. Then she went back out into the kitchen. Once there she realised she didn't have an excuse and so filled a couple of glasses with water. She was just about to take them through when Matthew appeared. He took the water out of her hands and set the glasses on the side.

'I've fixed the boiler and fed Oscar and you've mixed drinks and found nibbles. Now I wish you would stop fiddling about and come and join me.'

She followed him out of the kitchen. 'Why—' she began, looking up at him as they reached the sitting room.

'So—' He hesitated as they heard Gina's pocket break out into song.

'Ignore it,' he said.

The ringing stopped and then started again. Then the main phone went.

'Someone's persistent . . .' Matthew said as the answering machine kicked in and they heard, 'Gina, Gina, are you there, I'm sorry, there's been an accident, Sephie, can you come – Al, she's not there . . . I'm leaving a message.' There was a muffled sob. 'I *have* tried her mobile . . . Gina, please come . . .' Then the phone went dead.

Gina scrabbled for her mobile. 'Oh, God, what's

happened?' she cried as she fumbled with the keys. Matthew already had his coat on and was handing her hers. 'Come on, you can phone from the car.'

When Gina got through, Alaric was able to reassure her that whilst it had been a nasty fall, bones might even be broken, Sephie would be fine. The little girl had been playing with her sister when she'd slipped off a chair 'she shouldn't have been standing on in the first place' and fallen awkwardly on her arm, knocking her head on the side of a table. Sally had taken her to the hospital – contrary to Gina's predictions, she'd been on soft drinks for most of the day. They needed Gina to come and look after Ariadne for them. Alaric wanted to get to the hospital as soon as he could. His parents *had* left shortly after Gina and Matthew and he knew Ariadne would be much happier with her aunt than her grandparents.

Once at the cottage, Matthew asked Gina if she wanted him to stay, but since he'd offered to drive Alaric to the hospital, which was in the direction of the French House, she said no. Having reassured Ariadne that her sister wasn't going to die and would be home soon, she read her stories until her eyes drooped and she finally fell asleep. Gina tidied up a bit and then sank down on the sofa with a sigh and a glass of wine from a half-empty bottle she'd found in the fridge.

Shortly after midnight the others returned, Alaric carrying a very sleepy Sephie, her arm in a sling (it wasn't broken, her wrist was just badly sprained), a butterfly plaster on her forehead. They went straight upstairs. When Sephie was safely tucked up in bed, her parents returned and Gina handed them each a generous glass of brandy, which was gratefully received. The three of them chatted for a little while before heading for bed. Gina borrowed a toothbrush and settled down on the sofabed, her mind whirling. What an evening! Her emotions were all over the place. And Matthew had been about to kiss her, hadn't he? She hadn't imagined it, surely?

Alaric dropped Gina off at her cottage shortly after breakfast the next morning. Sally had said she was very welcome to stay but Gina felt the family needed some time together, particularly after the shock they'd had.

Making herself a strong cup of coffee, she rang her parents. They had already heard about Sephie's accident and after reassuring them that all was OK, Gina gave them an expurgated but entertaining account of the previous day pre-accident, and promised she'd be over to visit as usual at this time of year.

After disconnecting Gina slumped down on the sofa, feeling rather flat. It was probably just tiredness but she couldn't help wondering what Matthew was doing. Was he alone or had he decided to visit friends? And had something been about to happen between them before Sally had called? She slipped into a reverie, imagining her and Matthew entwined on the sofa, and later in bed . . . She shook herself. This was no good; perhaps she should do a bit of work? But then she felt that would be far too sad on Boxing Day. She was just wondering about going for a walk to blow away the cobwebs and any lingering, lustful thoughts when her phone rang.

She blushed. It was Matthew. After filling him in about Sephie there was a pause.

'Are you still at Sally's?' Matthew asked.

'No, I'm back home. Why?'

'You remember me mentioning wanting to take you somewhere?' He hesitated, as if unsure, which made Gina smile; he wasn't usually given to insecurity. 'To visit my old friend with me?' he finished.

Gina's heart fluttered. 'No, I mean, yes, I do remember you mentioning your friend. Although you were very mysterious about it all.' She felt some of her confidence return.

'Didn't want to spoil the surprise. Well, I've been in touch with him and I think he's up for it.'

'Oh. When?'

'Don't know that yet. Anyway.' He was silent for agonising seconds – long enough for Gina to wonder if they'd been disconnected. Then he said, 'Have you got something wonderful planned today or do you fancy a dog walk and a pub?'

'Um—'

'You're probably doing something . . .'

'I was planning on having a quiet day, at home,' said Gina, hoping she didn't sound too like the spinster aunt, sadly sitting at home on her own, or more to the point too off-putting.

'I'm here at home alone too and there's nothing much to eat. I thought you might be in the same situation.'

'I was about to make toast . . .'

'Come to the pub instead. I'll pick you up.'

'Oh, OK, that would be nice,' flustered Gina.

'Nice!' He laughed and her heart did another flip. 'I'll swing by in about twenty minutes. I know a lovely pub—'

'Where they like Oscar?'

'That's the one!' They disconnected and Gina hugged herself with joy and excitement.

As she got out of her sloppy sitting-at-home wear and into jeans and a jumper – and put on make-up – she tried to tell herself she was only going because she needed to eat, it would be nice to go out on Boxing Day and she was bored with Christmas specials and her own company. She knew she was lying though: really, she just wanted to see Matthew again, on whatever terms.

She and Matthew had had a very pleasant time. After the hectic and traumatic Christmas Day, Gina found she'd run out of nervous energy and could only be relaxed and chatty. After a lunch of soup and home-made bread they set off into the cold with a slightly reluctant Oscar.

Walking together was a great way to get to know someone, Gina discovered. Not being face to face meant it was easier to talk about books, music, influences, and generally talk about things. He told her about the buying trip to France he had coming up. He also talked about his ex-wife and how demanding she could be – typically French and dramatic, he'd let slip at one point. He was gentlemanly enough not to go into too much detail but she did gather the divorce settlement had been a very generous one, for her, which he now slightly regretted. He owed her quite a bit of money which was taking far too long to pay off, he felt. He was going to talk to her about it when he went to France.

She felt immensely privileged that he had shared even this much information with her when he was such a private man, and the topic was clearly painful. She understood a little more why he was so gloomy so much of the time. He did not simply have the responsibility of keeping the centre going in a recession, of maintaining the livelihoods of his loyal dealers, of living up to his much-loved father: he was dealing with the aftermath of an acrimonious divorce. She remembered how hard it had been to get over Egan; how much harder was it to move on from a failed marriage? Especially when he couldn't really do so until he had paid her off.

Perhaps 'gloomy' was the wrong word – an unkind word. She could see now that there was a well of sadness in him, which he capped with dry humour and thoughtfulness, but which was always there, deep and occasionally overwhelming.

By the time he dropped her off at the end of the day she felt she could definitely count him as a friend. Annoyingly, for her anyway, he had people to see in the evening so she didn't get the chance to find out if that flicker between them on Christmas Day had been real. Whilst he obviously enjoyed her company he probably didn't want anything more, not while he was still suffering so from the fall-out from his marriage. One day, she told herself, when her silly crush on him had passed, his friendship would be special.

Chapter Nineteen

Gina was sitting at her desk pretending to work. She'd booked her flight for her visit to her parents and was now trying to interest herself in some filing. It was two weeks after Christmas and she was waiting for Matthew to call to make the final arrangements for the visit he'd promised her. In spite of herself, she was very excited about going to see his old friend. She kept her feelings from Sally though. 'You know,' she'd said, 'he's just taking me so he doesn't look like Norman No Mates. It's nothing remotely like a date. It's two friends going to visit an old man.'

Fortunately Sally bought this. Much as Gina was upset by Sephie's accident, she was pleased it had diverted Sally's attention away from her and Matthew nicely. It had also stopped Sally speculating about his divorce, which she had done occasionally since the Christmas event, when Gina had told her what Anthea had said. Gina had not passed on any more details. Part of her longed to discuss her feelings for Matthew with her sister: they rarely kept anything from one another. But somehow it all felt too new, too tentative and too precious. Sally's Labrador-like enthusiasm, desperate to dissect every detail, could make it all vanish and send Gina back into no-men-for-me mode only too easily.

'I'll pick you up at about five,' Matthew said when he rang. 'We won't stay for dinner.'

Gina was intrigued. She'd managed to tease a few more details out of Matthew: that it was a gorgeous old house and she'd love it; she'd love his friend, too. Apart from that he'd been frustratingly unforthcoming, not wanting to spoil it for her. 'Will he even offer dinner?'

'He might, but it would be difficult for him. He has a man who looks after him – a cross between a butler and a carer, great bloke – but he doesn't do catering.'

'Five o'clock,' said Gina. 'So is that tea or drinks? And does "he" have a name?'

'"He" does, it's Nicholas. And it'll be drinks probably but do you need to know?'

'Of course,' said Gina. 'If it's tea I'll wear a tea gown!'

Matthew laughed.

Gina suppressed her *Downton Abbey* fantasies and wrapped up warmly. She wasn't in the habit of visiting stately homes but her sketchy knowledge and imagination led her to feel they would not, unless owned by millionaires, be well heated. Thus she put on thick tights under her dress with a wrap-over cardi and her Uggs. Trousers would have been warmer but she knew old gentlemen tended to prefer young women in dresses.

When Matthew picked her up she still hadn't got her coat on. He stood in her sitting room and looked at her. She tried not to feel she was being checked over.

'Will I do?' she asked a little tartly.

'You will. You look delightful. Nicholas will be enchanted.'

Gina frowned slightly. 'Do you want me to enchant Nicholas?'

He nodded. 'I do, rather. I only took Yvette – my ex – to meet him once and it didn't go well.'

'Oh?'

'She just didn't get him. Consequently he didn't get her. There was no point of contact.'

'Did it matter to anyone?' Gina was beginning to wonder if perhaps this Nicholas was like a father figure for Matthew and he felt he needed to get his approval before entering a new relationship.

Matthew shrugged. 'Not really, I suppose. Anyway, get your coat. We don't want to keep Nicholas waiting.'

As they got out on to the main road, Gina asked, 'So, remind me, who is Nicholas, exactly?'

'I told you he was an old friend of my father's? Well, they met because Nicholas – who got out a lot more in those days – bought a sideboard from him and Dad delivered it. He lives in the most amazing house. Fairfield Manor.'

'In what way amazing?'

'Mostly because no one's ever allowed in it. Well, none of the societies who have wanted to see it for years. It's a lost gem – *the* lost gem almost – of Georgian architecture.'

'Wow!' She looked down at her outfit and wondered if a tea gown might have been appropriate after all.

'Nicholas says he doesn't want people ferreting around what is his home and exclaiming about the pedimented portico when they should be talking to him.'

Gina gulped. 'I promise, I won't mention it. I won't even recognise it if it gets up and bites me.'

'You would recognise it – will rather – and I think he's slightly less defensive about it now. I think part of it is he likes to buy pieces that aren't strictly in period. He says it's ridiculous to imagine any house would only have one style of furniture in it.' He frowned. 'I think he said this to someone in the Georgian Group who was a purist and who disagreed. Nicholas felt he was being told off.'

'I completely understand then. I hate being told off.' She paused. 'Has it all gone to rack and ruin, then?'

'Oh no, it's not lack of cash. Nicholas is very proud of his house really. And actually, all this was years ago. I think he might feel differently about it now.'

'Which is why you're bringing me?'

'Oh no, he would always have wanted to meet you. He loves his pieces to be admired. He's got some wonderful things – a lot of which my father found him, and some I did. He's not ashamed of the house so I'm not entirely sure why he still won't let people see it. Anyway, I thought you'd appreciate it, you've really taken to the antiques business. We'll make a fine dealer of you yet.' He smiled across at her and it felt like being given a medal. She was delighted he'd noticed her growing passion for the business and, whatever his reason for taking her today, she was thrilled he finally saw her as an equal.

'Well, I feel very honoured to be invited. And more intrigued than ever,' she said.

Matthew drew up in front of a house definitely big enough to be described as 'stately'. There *was* a fine portico, Gina noted, with pillars and a triangular top which she assumed was the pediment. The black-painted front door had a huge lion's head knocker and generally the house had an air of grace and substance, not to mention history. Her excitement increased.

'Bernard,' said Matthew when the door had been opened by a man Gina assumed was Nicholas's general factotum. He stepped aside and they entered as another man appeared, leaning on a stick.

'Nicholas, hello. Let me introduce you to Gina Makepiece. She and her sister have taken over Rainey's case at the centre.'

'Good evening, my dear. How delightful!' Nicholas slapped Matthew on the back, almost toppling over in the process. Matthew steadied him as Nicholas took Gina's hand and kissed it. Wearing, among other things, a velvet jacket and monogrammed slippers, he was dressed for effect. 'Come into the drawing room and have a glass of sherry.'

Gina found herself ushered into a beautifully decorated room that made her feel she was on the set of a costume drama. Palest blue walls were decorated with delicate plasterwork that reminded Gina of Wedgwood china or cake icing. She glanced up at the ceiling and saw more plaster mouldings depicting flowers, swags and garlands. She spotted a gathering of classical nymphs and shepherds in the middle.

What on earth was wrong with Matthew's ex-wife that meant she wasn't enchanted by Nicholas and his wonderful house? He might have been a bit of a showman and a flirt but he was lovely. And his house was heavenly. She tried, rather unsuccessfully, not to gawp.

Nicholas led her to a chair by the fire which crackled merrily in a huge marble fireplace. 'Now, what sort of sherry do you prefer?' He indicated a silver tray with glasses and three decanters.

Gina was a bit stumped. 'To be honest I don't know anything about sherry but I'm sure I'll like whatever you choose.' She hoped she didn't sound as if she was trying to suck up to him but sherry really was a bit of an unknown to her.

'I think an amontillado then.' He handed her a glass and waited while she sipped it. 'Nice?'

'Delicious!'

Nicholas poured more sherry and then they all sat down.

'So, Nicholas,' said Matthew, sitting back in his chair, glass in hand. 'How have you been?'

'Still creaking on. Mustn't complain, gets damn boring. What about you?'

'I'm well, thank you. I must tell you about a little French side table I came across the other day.'

'Well, I'm not exactly short of side tables, God knows . . .'

Gina, fascinated by her surroundings, couldn't focus on a discussion about furniture Nicholas might or might not want, and found her gaze drawn to the paintings.

Noticing this, Nicholas said, 'Gina my dear, why don't you take your sherry and have a wander round? Go through the double doors if you want – there are more things in there. Then Matthew and I can discuss my furniture needs and tear apart some joint acquaintances without boring you to death.'

Gina got up immediately. 'Would that be all right? I'd love that.'

Nicholas had some amazing works of art, she decided, after circling the room and then going into the second room. There was a very fine collection of porcelain displayed in a cabinet that she felt belonged in a museum, and another whole cabinet devoted to Chinese blue and white pottery. But it was the paintings that most fascinated her. Here her lack of knowledge didn't matter, only her eye had to be satisfied.

Many were family portraits but there were also some lovely landscapes: views from the house from a much earlier period, a couple of little watercolours and views of classical ruins, which were possibly done by someone on the Grand Tour.

She drew to a halt in front of a full-length portrait of a young woman in evening dress. The woman had soft, light brown hair and was laughing, in a pose far less formal than in the other paintings. A group of spaniels gathered at her feet and behind her was a horse being led by a groom. Gina found herself wondering about her. Was the horse hers, or had it been put in because it balanced the painting? If she looked out of the window in daylight, could that view still be seen? She was still in front of the painting when Matthew and Nicholas joined her.

'That's Lady Mary, my grandmother,' said Nicholas.

'She's very pretty,' said Matthew.

'She reminds me rather of Gina here.' Nicholas scrutinised Gina for a moment or two. 'Yes, the likeness is quite pronounced.'

Gina felt embarrassed. 'I don't know why that should be. We can't be related.'

Matthew peered at her. 'I do see what you mean, Nicholas. And it's a lovely picture.'

'Hmm.' He stared at it for quite a bit longer. 'Do you know? I think I've still got the dress. Gina, you should have it.'

'No I shouldn't!' Gina said instantly. 'It's yours.'

'Oh, do take it. It's only mouldering away up there.'

'I couldn't possibly. It will be extremely valuable and I wouldn't fit into it anyway.' Gina hoped that this last protest would put an end to this embarrassing conversation.

It didn't. Nicholas and Matthew both stared at her intently as if calculating her measurements and comparing them with those of the woman in the portrait. It made her even more uncomfortable. 'I think you might,' said Nicholas. 'You're only a slip of a thing and she was pregnant when the portrait was painted.'

It got worse and worse. 'Now I wonder if I should take offence,' said Gina, blushing.

'Well, don't do that,' said Nicholas. 'Have some more sherry. Or shall we move on to wine? I've got some very acceptable burgundy in the cellar. I'll ask Bernard to bring it up.'

'Well, that was one of the most enjoyable evenings I've ever had,' said Gina as she and Matthew drove away.

'Nothing to do with the fact that you and Nicholas sank a bottle of burgundy between you?' said Matthew, smiling.

'That is part of it, of course,' said Gina, making sure she didn't slur her words. 'But it was just lovely. Nicholas is so funny and kind. And he knows so much about architecture and art and stuff.'

'Well, he obviously took to you.'

Gina couldn't tell if he was being disapproving or not. She took a look to check. 'He did rather ply me with alcohol. Only with no ulterior motive,' she added, not wishing to imply criticism. She really had liked Nicholas. She paused. 'I'm dying for a cup of tea.'

'Before I drop you off—' he said.

'You won't join me in a cuppa? I've got some biscuits and half a Christmas cake Sally made me take.' She tried not to sound too eager.

'I won't, if you don't mind, but I do want to ask you a massive favour.'

'Oh! Ask away then.' She wondered why he couldn't stop for a quick cup of tea and if he was trying to avoid a full-of-potential moment alone with her.

'Well, I told you, didn't I, that I usually have Christmas with Jenny but that she had to go to relations this year?'

'Mm.' Gina was still fighting her disappointment. Was he worried she might try to jump on him the moment he was through the door? Had he been trying to put her off by telling her about his ex-wife?

'Well, the relations in question can't be left. It turns out they're struggling to cope. I had a call from her this morning to tell me she can't come back to the centre until she's found a care home and has settled them into it. It might take weeks, months even.'

'And?' She had a hint where this was going now.

'Well, you know she does an awful lot for me but what she does most and is the most important thing, of course, is look after Oscar when I'm away.'

Gina's heart sank just a little. The thought of Oscar in her tiny cottage was daunting. 'You want me to look after him?'

'More than that—'

'There's more? You have a flock of sheep you never told me about?'

He chuckled. 'No, but there is a bloody great antiques centre that you know all about already.'

'Sorry, I don't get you.'

'I'm asking if you'll move into the centre and look after it, and Oscar, while I'm away in France on this buying trip.'

'When?'

'In about a fortnight.'

'I told you I was staying with my parents for a while, didn't I?' Gina asked.

'You did. Remind me when you'll be back?'

'At the end of the month. I don't go over very often so when I do, I stay.'

'I won't need to go until the first week of February.'

Gina swallowed. 'How long for?'

'Two weeks tops.'

'Where would I live in the centre?'

'In my flat, of course. Is it asking too much?'

'No, of course not,' she said after frantically thinking of a good excuse to say no. 'I don't see a problem.' This was no time to tell Matthew it wasn't the problems she could see that were the issue – it was ghosts. The thought of sleeping alone in that huge old house, full of antiques, scared her witless. But if she admitted that, Matthew would utterly despise her. She realised she'd also half hoped he was going to suggest she came with him on his trip as 'good experience'.

'Thank you, Gina. I knew I could depend on you.'

Gina made a pathetic attempt to laugh cheerily. Why had she ever felt being 'just good friends' could ever be a good thing?

Chapter Twenty

After a lovely, lazy time with her parents, Gina came back to England. The next day she set off early for the French House.

Matthew had left Oscar with one of the dealers on the morning Gina was due to arrive. He was leaving at the crack of dawn for the ferry.

Although he hadn't mentioned it since, Gina couldn't help remembering that Matthew was planning to visit his ex-wife to see if she'd be reasonable. As she put her case in Matthew's bedroom she wondered if this would work.

If she were an ex-wife and the judge had said she was entitled to an amount of money but it meant her ex-husband was forced to cripple himself financially, would she hold him to it?

She decided that it would depend on why the marriage had broken up. If she'd felt sufficiently resentful she might take all that was due her, but otherwise? It was hard to tell. No one knew what went on inside someone else's marriage. She then found herself worrying if Matthew still had feelings for

Yvette. Maybe that was why he hadn't made a move or given any indication that he'd like to recently – he was perfectly friendly but that spark she was sure had been smouldering between them at Christmas seemed to have disappeared.

The more she thought about it the more she was certain that had her phone not rung he'd have taken her in his arms on Christmas night. And he hadn't sounded like a man still in love when he'd spoken about Yvette – more a man beleaguered by an irritant he wanted to get rid of.

And thinking of irritants and exes, she set up her laptop on Matthew's desk and sent Egan an email. It was something she'd meant to do ages ago but now she felt the time had come to get tough.

Dear Egan,

It's been a while but I'm writing to ask you for the five thousand pounds you owe me. I hope I have given you enough time to find the money.

A cheque care of the French House would be the best way of getting the money to me.

Best, Gina

She made a cup of coffee feeling proud of herself. She suspected wounded pride and the ghastliness of what he'd spent the money on – other women – had held her back from asking before, but she was a lot stronger now.

She looked again at the long list Matthew had left her and smiled. He was very thorough, but it was very much a note one might leave one's cleaner. Not even one 'x', she noticed with a pang.

Gina enjoyed her day at the centre, relishing being in charge even if it was only temporary. She chatted to the dealers when they weren't busy, and entertained some children so their parents felt free to browse and buy. She definitely felt the centre was busier – with both locals and tourists – than when she and Sally had first seen it and this was pleasing. Although she realised Matthew would have to sell an awful lot of antiques to finally be free of Yvette's grasping hands. She sighed. Maybe on this trip he would find the piece that no one recognised as valuable and sell it for a fortune.

Harold handed Oscar into her care and she took him for a walk along the river. She found it more like holding someone's hand than having a dog on the end of a leash, and she enjoyed it: she felt she was bonding with Oscar, which was surprising, considering he didn't say much.

When it was time to close up and go upstairs to the flat she decided she was going to enjoy her time here. She'd tell Matthew so if he rang.

She cooked supper, cleared up and then settled on the ancient leather sofa to watch Matthew's tiny television. It was only after she'd taken Oscar into the garden for a last wee and they were walking up through the empty house that she remembered her fears about being there on her own.

'But I've got you, Oscar,' she said aloud and then wished she hadn't. Her voice in the building made it seem emptier than ever, especially when it had been fairly busy and noisy during the day.

She ran up to the flat and pushed open the door. She'd feel safe when she was there and Oscar was with her. He was taking longer to get up the stairs than she had, not being fuelled by the fight-or-flight instinct that had suddenly infected Gina.

It was a bit better once she was in the flat and the door was closed but she couldn't help thinking about the big empty space below her. She poured herself another glass of wine and switched the telly back on. Something soothing would help. Then she realised, after clicking every number she could find on the remote, that for some reason the signal in Matthew's flat meant she could only get three channels; she had a choice between a gloomy documentary about the polar ice cap melting resulting in the end of the world – probably by next week – a terrifying Scandinavian crime thriller with subtitles and a serial killer, and a programme about brides whose mothers were even scarier than the Swedish axe murderer.

Maybe an early night was a good idea. If she was asleep she couldn't get frightened, could she? She wished Matthew were here – and not only so he could keep away any spirits that might be lurking in the shadows. She thought she'd enjoy being in his space with his things around her but in fact it just made her miss him more than ever.

Oscar was very good about having his rug dragged into the bedroom and lay down the moment he could. 'OK, Oscar,' she said. 'I'm going to turn the light out now and go to sleep. I'll be able to get up early to take you out.'

She wasn't sure what woke her. It might have been the church clock which she could hear beginning to chime. She counted the dongs. Midnight. It was only midnight and here she was, all her sleepiness gone and the whole night ahead of her.

The she heard a thump. Something or someone had moved on the floor below. She stifled a scream, knowing she would scare herself even more if she screamed out loud.

'Oscar, what should I do?'

Oscar barely raised his head. He'd obviously heard the bang and ignored it.

'OK, I know what I have to do. I have to go down there. It is not like in a gothic novel. I'm going down to check everything is all right. And everything will be. This is real life. But Oscar, you have to come with me.'

She put on her slippers and her dressing gown and then she found the torch Matthew had left for her.

Oscar was not inclined to follow her. He clearly wanted to go back to sleep.

'I know you must think me dreadfully neurotic

and a scaredy-cat, but I can't go down there alone. Sorry!'

She bent and held on to his collar, ready to pull him up if she had to. Fortunately he took the hint and got up on his own: she wouldn't have been able to make him if he'd refused to move.

She turned on all the lights in the flat before she left and propped the door open so she could make a quick dash back if she had to. Quite what she was expecting to find she didn't know, but doing nothing when there was a noise was not an option: Matthew was relying on her. She may be a complete wuss but she didn't want Matthew knowing that.

Oscar groaned as she hung on to him as they went down the stairs. 'Oh Osc. I'm sorry, but I need you.'

She let go of him once they'd reached the floor below and looked around using the torch. Then she decided the torch made everything seem a lot worse – like an episode of *Scooby Doo*, where there were always monsters. She went over to the light switch.

The room looked as it normally did. No animate shadows or intruders. She saw nothing that could have woken her. Could the maker of the noise be hiding behind anything, waiting to knock her out and steal the antiques? Or break into the safe with all their takings? With the light on, with Oscar, evidently bored, this seemed fairly unlikely. Although if it was an intruder, she'd have to hope just the sight of Oscar would scare him – Oscar wouldn't actually do anything. As a guard dog he was a very good chocolate teapot – useless, in other words.

Then she spotted the culprit. Over in the corner were some mechanical toys. She could see where a toy soldier with a coggly leg had knocked over a wooden ball – part of a set of skittles. It must have shifted slightly. The ball in turn had thumped on to the uncarpeted floor and woken her.

'Oh, for goodness' sake!' she said to Oscar. Cross with herself for being so scared of a toy, she stomped across the room, put everything back in place, propped up the soldier's leg more securely and, making sure that nothing would touch anything else, she then turned off the lights and went back upstairs to bed.

She was woken the next morning by Oscar's beard in her face. He'd had a drink of water first, so as a waking mechanism it was extremely efficient.

'Is it that time already?' She wiped her face and looked at the clock. 'Do you always wake at six? Or is it only when I'm looking after you?'

She got out of bed and put on her slippers and dressing gown. Then she took Oscar down to the garden. Matthew warned her that although it was very rare for him to have an accident, if he did, she would be dealing with absolute lakes of wee.

Later, when she'd opened up and got the coffee machine going so it would be there for the dealers who were due in that day, she saw a man come through the doorway.

Maybe she was still jumpy from the night before but Gina felt instantly that something was wrong. He didn't look like a browser although she had learnt by this time that you couldn't tell what people were like by their clothes or accent or bearing. And yet he gave her the creeps. She had just dismissed this feeling as a hangover from last night when he came up to her.

'Good morning. I've come to value the premises.'

Gina stood stock-still. Her mind was whirling but she tried not to let this show. Matthew hadn't mentioned anything about this. She was alone – what should she do?

'Do you have the authority to do that?' she asked, wishing she had the confidence to send him away.

He produced a sheaf of papers. Gina glanced down them. 'I'm sorry, I don't recognise any of the names on there. You'll have to wait until Mr Ballinger is back at the beginning of next week.' Gina was expecting him a bit sooner than that but if this man was authorised to value the place, Matthew would probably like some warning. Was he though? And who had authorised it? She felt sure Matthew couldn't have done, not without telling her.

'I'm acting under instruction from Mr Ballinger's ex-wife. See? That's her name here. If you check the deeds you'll see her name on them.'

Gina frantically tried to think of something else she could do.

'I don't suppose the deeds are here. Doesn't the building society usually hang on to them?' Gina suggested.

'Only if the property is mortgaged,' said the man firmly, as if she was an idiot for not knowing this.

She sighed, knowing her broken night meant her brain wasn't fizzing along as it should be.

'Can you hang on while I ring Mr Ballinger to check? I'll get you some coffee in a minute. The machine is on.'

'You can ring if you like but it won't make any difference. I have strict instructions.'

This was all she needed. She prayed one of the dealers would arrive soon. Bloody woman, Gina thought as she ran upstairs to the office so she could ring in private. Yvette had obviously waited until she knew Matthew wasn't here to get all this done. Then again, maybe Matthew had forgotten to tell her. Surely he wouldn't do that? No, of course he wouldn't. There was no reply from Matthew. She left a message, and then thought what to do. She didn't want to leave the man alone for long, but she had to do everything she could.

Should she look for the deeds? The man was so confident he had the right to value the house, would finding them make any difference? She took a breath. A valuation didn't necessarily mean it would automatically go on sale. Yvette was probably seeing how much value was in the property and how much more she could extract. She just had to keep calm.

Led by her own need she decided to sort the coffee out first, and then, with luck, someone else would be there to keep an eye on the man while she tried to find the deeds. She felt she had to do everything she could to stop Matthew being taken advantage of.

Bill Morrison was in by the time she got downstairs and the valuer had already got his electronic tape measure out and was making notes.

She took Bill by the arm. 'Can you keep an eye on him while I get us all coffee? I'm sure he won't steal anything but you never know.'

'Who is he?' asked Bill.

Suddenly aware that she couldn't confide in Bill about the centre being threatened (Matthew might not want the others to know, never mind her) she said, 'Oh, I think Matthew's thinking of having new carpets or something. He told me to expect someone to measure up.'

She went right up to the flat this time and went into Matthew's study. It felt all wrong opening the desk and looking for papers but this was no time to be squeamish. Needless to say there was no file marked 'Deeds' but she pulled out the top folder anyway. If she didn't find anything quickly she'd give up.

Nothing remotely like deeds to an ancient building appeared but a sheaf of bank statements were on the top. Knowing she should just put them back, she was compelled to look through them. One standing order leapt out at her. It was for five hundred pounds a month, payable to Yvette Dupont – his ex-wife.

She put it all back as quickly as she could and rushed downstairs again. She gulped the now-cold coffee and followed the valuer like a collie at the heels of an errant sheep.

She ran out to buy a Danish pastry in lieu of breakfast the moment the valuer had gone. She was just stuffing the last of it in her mouth when she saw Carmella come into the shop. She was wearing her floor-length suede coat and her caramel hair was swept up in a chignon that reminded Gina of Grace Kelly with her timeless beauty. This was all she needed. Although if Carmella was on a buying trip Gina was ready to do some hard bargaining.

She checked her mouth for crumbs before coming forward. 'Good morning,' she said in her best PR-girl voice. 'May I help you?'

Carmella cast a practised and calculating glance over the room. 'Just looking round,' she said.

For some reason Gina got the impression it wasn't the antiques she was looking at. 'I'm afraid I haven't had a chance to source any more scent bottles yet,' Gina said, 'but I'm sure there are lots of other things that might catch your eye.'

'Oh I'm sure,' said Carmella.

Gina didn't feel she could actually follow her, so she just watched. She was poised to swoop in with a really high price on anything that wasn't clearly labelled. But Carmella showed no interest at all in the antiques.

Gina had retreated to the kitchen to wash up some mugs when Carmella reappeared.

'Actually, I'll be frank with you. I'm not interested in buying things here. I'm interested in buying the building.'

'*What?*'

Carmella smiled, but she didn't repeat her words. Gina suddenly felt sick and her mouth went dry.

'It's not for sale,' she managed. But was she right? What was that valuation all about then? Things must be worse than she thought.

Carmella raised a perfect eyebrow. 'Are you sure?' She shrugged in a way that indicated that Gina was a fool. 'Anyway, I'd like you to show me round. I may want things moved so I can see better.'

Carmella's faint foreign accent seemed to add emphasis, but Gina became firm. 'I'm sorry, I can't possibly move things around. I'm not the owner and I've been given no instructions about selling the building. You'll have to come back when Matthew is here.'

'I know when Mr Ballinger is due back, thank you, and I don't want to wait that long. And if it's not for sale now, it soon will be.'

'You can't possibly know that.' Gina was doing well with her haughty, I'm-in-charge stance but this was a blow.

'Oh, but I can and do know it. I am friends with

Yvette Dupont and she assures me it is going on the market any minute, for a very good price. It's just the sort of property I'm looking for.'

'But why do you need another property? You already have a shop in the town.'

'You have obviously seen my shop. It's tiny. I always knew it would be too small but I heard that the French House was going to be for sale so I came here anyway, to establish myself.'

Gina was quietly furious. How could Carmella have possibly known the French House would definitely be going on the market? Gina knew Matthew owed Yvette money – probably a lot of money – but surely things hadn't come to this? Remembering that Matthew had told her a lovely old antiques guy had been shoved out of the way for Carmella's shop that she 'always knew would be too small' enraged Gina further. She became even more icy to compensate. 'Why did you do that? What a waste of money. If you knew the French House was going to be for sale, why didn't you wait for it to come on the market?'

'I'm going to keep the other premises, just for jewellery. And why should I wait? I wanted my name to be known before I make a big splash.' She paused. 'What is all this to do with you anyway? You just work here, no?'

Gina felt desperate. It was nothing to do with her really, she just cared about it enormously. She couldn't think of anything to say so she shrugged.

'So, please show me round,' went on Carmella crisply. 'Otherwise things may be damaged when I move them about.'

Gina speculated for a few seconds on the wisdom of calling the policc to get Carmella thrown out but she realised it was a ridiculous overreaction. Should she ask Bill to help her strong-arm Carmella on to the street? No. By the time she'd explained her reasons to him Carmella would either have left, or taken her frustration out on the stock and flung a Staffordshire figure of the Queen of Prussia across the room.

'OK. I will show you round but you have to pretend it's because you're interested in old houses. I'm not having the dealers disturbed by thinking the building might be for sale.'

Carmella shrugged but nodded in agreement.

'Of course it is a listed building,' said Gina. 'Grade One starred, which means you can't make any alterations at all, outside or in.' Then she remembered that only proper stately homes, or buildings like Westminster Abbey, were Grade One listed and hoped Carmella wouldn't know this. Although she was fairly confident she was right about the alterations.

Carmella smiled that supercilious smirk. 'Not a problem. Each small room will showcase a different part of my collection.'

'Of course, it's terribly damp in here,' said Gina, hurrying Carmella past Tiggy, and showing her into a pretty room that smelt of lavender and beeswax.

'Really?' Carmella's sharp upward inflection told Gina that Carmella knew she was lying. They went through the rest of the building in silence.

When she left Carmella said, 'It's absolutely perfect. Do make sure Mr Ballinger knows I'm willing to make an offer. No need to put it on the market first.'

Gina nodded, biting back a bitter comment about Carmella and Yvette having stitched him up already. 'I will make absolutely sure he knows.' Then she shut the door behind her with a little slam that set the bell above it ringing.

'What did she do to annoy you?' asked Bill, coming up. 'It's not like you to be snippy with the customers.'

Gina sighed. 'I know. She was an exception.'

That night, Gina resolved to ignore any bumps in the night. She had real things to be anxious about: she didn't have nerves to spare on the supernatural. She told Oscar this as they went up to the flat after his last excursion into the garden. He seemed to agree with this plan.

Fortunately for Gina, she was so tired after her previous bad night and everything that had gone on she slept like a log. She had two last waking thoughts, somehow simultaneously: Burglars, take what you like but don't wake me up! and 'Matthew, please just come home.'

Chapter Twenty-One

'I can't believe you just did that!' said Sally, holding on to her daughters – Sephie now sling-less – as Gina put a cheque in the drawer. 'You just sold a desk and it sounded like you really knew what you were talking about.'

'Not just a desk, sweetie, a cylinder bureau, and yes, he did notice it was a bit damaged but when I pointed out he couldn't have afforded it if it wasn't, he paid up like a lamb.'

It was nearly the end of Gina's tenure and she'd gained a lot of confidence over the time she'd been in charge – with regard to the antiques anyway.

'I'm still impressed by your knowledge, Gines,' said Sally as Ariadne tried to escape her grip. Sephie, usually the leader, seemed a bit more clingy since her accident and it had meant that Sally hadn't had time to come to the centre recently. When she wasn't looking after the girls she was making decorative items for Carmella's shop.

Gina brushed off the compliment. 'I do know a tiny bit more than I did before. We both do.'

'I think Rainey would be very proud about how well we're – you're – doing,' said Sally, catching hold of the escapee before she could launch herself on to an eighteenth-century chaise longue.

'I think she would. Selling has never been a problem but I actually bought a collection of bits and pieces the other day,' related Gina proudly. 'I'll show you in a minute.' She bit her lip. 'I hope I didn't rip the seller off – a nice woman – but she seemed more than happy, so I expect it's all right. Of course, we won't know exactly what I've got until Matthew gets back. Er – Ariadne! Don't touch anything, will you, darling?'

'When are you expecting him?'

'I'm not exactly sure. I had a text earlier and he said it depends what ferry he gets. I'm hoping for first thing tomorrow.'

'Are you desperate to see him, or desperate to get home?' asked Sally teasingly.

'Enough with the matchmaking!' said Gina. 'And neither. Though it will be good to hand back the responsibility.' And to see him again, but she didn't say this out loud.

'So, has he been in touch much?'

'Some.' Gina made out she was fine with this but in fact she was a bit miffed that he hadn't been in touch more often. She had been thinking about *him* constantly. He'd sent her a text in reply to her phone message about the valuer and the second one she had left about Carmella, telling her not to worry, but there'd been nothing since.

'You don't think he's got back with his wife, do you?'

'Of course I don't think that. And it's nothing to do with me if he has. Silly woman!'

'It's only what I'd be thinking, that's all,' said Sally.

'Well I'm not,' said Gina firmly, although now the idea had been put into her head, she was, slightly.

'And there's nothing else you're not telling me?'

'No!'

'You just seem a bit shifty to me.'

Gina gave her sister a hug. 'Oh, that's just me being edgy. All this responsibility, it's getting to me.' Although this was true, she hadn't told Sally about Carmella's visit. It wasn't her secret; it was Matthew's.

'Well, you'll be able to hand it all back soon.'

Gina nodded. 'I'll miss Oscar though. He's more like a best friend now than a dog.'

Everyone else had gone home and Gina was just about to lock up when she thought she'd check the ledger. She was leaning over it when someone came up behind her and put one hand over her eyes and another round her waist.

She screamed and struggled free, using a backward jab of her elbow to get her assailant off her.

'Holy shit, Gina!' said a voice she instantly recognised. 'No need to overreact.'

Heart racing, Gina turned round. 'Egan! You bloody idiot. What the hell do you think you're playing at?' She was incandescent – it wasn't possible to overreact to being jumped on from behind. Although her brain now accepted that this was Egan, her ex, and not someone likely to harm her, her heart still pounded.

'I just thought it would be fun to give you a surprise. And not that much of a surprise – I saw you peeking into the shop. You knew I'm in the area now.'

'Anyone coming up behind me like that would make me think I was being attacked!'

He sighed. 'I'm sorry. I didn't mean to scare you. I just came up for a chat.'

'I was just about to close the shop,' she said crisply, still feeling shaken.

He looked at his watch, which Gina couldn't help noticing was a gold Rolex he hadn't owned when she knew him. 'What? At just gone four? Things not going well here then?'

'They're going just fine. Thank you.'

Egan shook his head. 'Not the word on the street.'

'Oh, for God's sake. This is the Cotswolds, not an American TV cop show.'

'Calm down, old girl.' He held up his palm. 'I come in peace!'

Belatedly remembering she'd emailed him asking for her money back, Gina tried to shake off her shock and anger. 'Oh, OK then.'

'I thought I'd come in person and write you that cheque – any chance of a cuppa?'

Gina didn't particularly want to spend any longer with Egan than she had to but she did want that cheque. If that meant having to make Egan a cup of tea then so be it. She felt badly in need of something herself.

'All right. Tea, or would you prefer coffee?' she asked, resignedly.

'Coffee would be great, thanks.'

When she had made two drinks she led Egan to a desk where they could sit down.

She studied him briefly as she moved her chair further away from his and sat down. She would be the first to admit he was good-looking, in a conventional sort of way. She found she now preferred something more rough-hewn if not actually unkempt. She also realised he was much shorter than Matthew and she wondered what she'd ever seen in him. He had pursued her relentlessly though, and now she supposed she had been flattered.

'Sorry about earlier,' said Egan with the smile that so often got him what he wanted, but no longer worked with her. 'I never thought you'd be so scared of me.'

'I wasn't scared of you, Egan. I was just scared.'

He nodded and sipped his coffee, maddeningly slowly. He was obviously determined to stay a while. 'So how do you get on with the proprietor? Seems a bit of a nonentity.'

Gina ordered her hackles to lie down. 'Not at all, he's very – he's surprisingly dynamic.'

'Really?' With a single word he managed to imply Gina was telling the opposite of the truth.

'Oh yes.' She wasn't going to be tricked into giving an example of his dynamism.

'So, are you and he – er – an item?'

Gina was incensed. How dare he! It was none of his business! But just as she was about to deny it, it occurred to her it might be a good thing for the centre if Egan – and thereby Carmella – thought she and Matthew were together. 'Um . . .'

'You're still holding out, are you? You always did like to play hard to get.'

Trust Egan to put everything down to sex. And how had she put up with his clichés so long? She smiled, hoping to look enigmatic as she couldn't think of anything to say that Egan couldn't purposefully misconstrue.

'The thing is,' Egan went on, 'you know Carmella wants this place? It would be so perfect for her shop.'

Her stomach clenched in protest at the thought of beautiful, pampered Carmella having something just because she wanted it. 'It's pretty good for antiques, too.'

'Yes, but the antiques aren't paying the bills, are they?'

'What makes you say that?' Gina felt the antiques

would pay the bills just fine if Matthew's ex-wife weren't bleeding the centre dry.

'Carmella and Yvette go way back. She'd really like Carmella to have the house.'

'It's not hers to dispose of though, is it?' Gina felt she should avoid being hostile for all sorts of tactical reasons but knew she wouldn't be able to keep it up for long.

'You know as well as I do that Yvette is entitled to half the house.'

'Really?' It was her turn to sound incredulous, even if she did partly believe him. She now knew Matthew was paying her a certain amount a month and had hinted that she was very demanding but would she really be legally entitled to half the house? Perfectly possible, she thought, if she'd sent a valuer round.

'OK then, half the value of the house. You know what divorces are like and Yvette has a very good lawyer.'

Gina shrugged. 'It's nothing to do with me.' She wished Oscar would be a bit more proactive. It would be very satisfying if he would bark or growl or do something to get Egan out of the centre feeling thoroughly intimidated, but he was fast asleep in Jenny's room.

'I'm sure it's more to do with you than you like to pretend.'

'You think what you like, Egan. Now, what about that cheque?'

'Ah, yes, well, I seem to have forgotten my cheque book.' So it had been just a ruse to see what he could find out. 'If you give me your bank details I'll pay it directly into your account.'

For some reason Gina didn't like the thought of Egan having her account details. 'I'd prefer a cheque, actually.'

'You always were old school, Gina.'

'Old school enough to think people should pay their debts.'

'All right, all right. I'm on it. You'll get your money.'

'Good.' He seemed to expect her to be grateful to get her own money back but she wasn't going to oblige him.

'So, what will you do when this place packs up?' he went on.

'I don't think it will pack up. Why are you so sure?'

'Because Yvette wants her money and Carmella is keen to buy.'

'How much is Carmella hoping to pay?' It was a blunt question but Gina had done with tact now.

He named a figure so low that even Gina, who wasn't up on current property prices, realised it was ridiculous. 'Why on earth do you think Matthew might sell for that price? It's ridiculous.' She didn't think Yvette would be happy with that price either.

Egan gave a sneer combined with a shrug that made her want to throw something at him: it was smug, superior and patronising, all in one easy facial expression. 'Who else is going to buy it in this market?'

'At that price anyone would. If Matthew wanted to sell he'd just put it on the market. He'd get more than that.'

'Wake up and smell the coffee, sweetheart.' He waggled his now-empty coffee cup at her. 'It's going to be a private deal. Yvette will name her price and Carmella will offer it. Matthew will have to just accept it.'

Gina got up from her chair. She'd had enough. 'I really don't see why. If he's prepared to sell it for so little he could sell it to anyone – for more probably.'

Egan stood up too. 'He's got to sell immediately. Yvette's waited for quite a while already and he's not going to find another buyer – cash buyer' – he paused for emphasis – 'as quickly.'

Being in PR meant you had to be able to act. She put on her very best sceptical smile. 'Oh really?' She imitated the upward inflection that he had used earlier, implying that everything he said was complete rubbish. She sounded convincing but inside she was desperately asking herself if all this could be true.

'Yes, really. And you could make things easier for everyone, including Matthew.'

'How, exactly?'

Egan came up behind her, put his arm round her shoulders and squeezed her to him. 'By being nice to me. I have influence over Carmella.'

Gina was too stunned to react but when he rubbed her cheek with his chin and went to kiss her, she recovered herself.

'Get off, Egan! What are you doing?'

Egan stepped back a little, looking incredulous. 'I'm being nice! You used to like it when I kissed your neck.' He moved towards her again, his intent obvious.

She stepped sharply out of the way, shuddering. 'Well, I don't like it now.'

'What? Not even when Matthew does it?' He grabbed her.

Gina lost it. She was tired of this. She pushed at him to get him away. 'I said, get off, Egan! And get out!'

Her anger seemed to excite him. 'I don't think you really mean that. You loved me. I haven't forgotten how wild you could be in bed.'

Gina felt physically sick. She felt ashamed to think she had once loved this revolting specimen and had had sex with him. And why hadn't she asked Bill – or even Tiggy – to stay a little longer? Egan would never have dared to make a pass if they'd been there or she could have at least called out for help. She covered her face with her hands to blot him out.

He seemed to think this was an invitation; he put his arms round her and started to kiss her. She pulled away but he pressed on, as if trying to suffocate her into submission. She struggled but he was a lot bigger and stronger than she was. 'Come on now, you know you're enjoying this really,' he said when he stopped to draw breath.

She kicked out at his shins but his wide stance meant she didn't make contact. He had moved from her mouth to her neck now, burrowing down between her shirt and her skin, working his way down to her breast with his mouth and tongue.

'Get off!' she said, panting with the effort to free herself.

And suddenly he was off and sitting on the floor looking as if he didn't know how he'd got there. Matthew stood over him. 'I think Gina's made her wishes clear,' he said.

Oscar, who'd managed to sleep through Gina's struggles, heard Matthew's voice and appeared like a giant in the doorway. He gave one deep, low bark, jumped up and put his paws on Matthew's shoulders.

'Bloody hell!' said Egan. 'What the fuck is that?'

Matthew pushed Oscar down and turned to Egan who had now got to his feet. 'That's my dog. And now I think you should leave.'

Matthew, Gina and Oscar all watched as Egan got to his feet, never taking his eyes off Oscar. Matthew opened the door for him and gave him a little push to hurry him through it. Then he turned to Gina. 'Are you all right?'

Gina found she was weak-kneed and feeling sick.

'No, I don't think I am!' and she stumbled into his arms.

He held her much more tightly than Egan had only this time being nearly suffocated by a man seemed like a lovely way to go. She felt safe at last.

She clung to him as if they'd been parted for years. When she broke away Matthew said, 'What did that bastard do to you? You're shaking! He didn't—'

'No – no, nothing dreadful,' she whispered, and let go of his jumper which she hadn't been aware of clutching.

'So why are you so upset? Shall we go upstairs where we can talk?'

'The centre—'

'Bugger the centre,' he said, 'I've got a bottle of brandy in my bag. I'll open it.' He turned the sign round, clicked the lock, picked up his bags and, motioning for Gina to go first, they went upstairs.

She curled up on the sofa with her feet under her. She was holding a glass with a very large amount of brandy in it. As well as the brandy, Matthew produced a broken baguette and some very ripe cheese. 'I don't know about you but I'm starving. Food might help?' He looked at her anxiously before going back into the kitchen for plates and knives.

It seemed to take forever before Matthew sat down next to her. He spread cheese on a piece of bread and added more brandy to her glass. He handed her the plate. Oscar stretched himself out at their feet with a contented sigh.

'So, what happened?' he asked. 'You were really upset. I need to know what he did to you. If I'm going to kill him, I need to know exactly why.'

She chuckled as the horror of Egan's mauling waned and she began to relax. 'Actually it wasn't what he did that upset me. I could have handled that. It was what he said before – and Carmella. They implied that Yvette could just sell the centre – to them – for a ridiculously low price, and you couldn't do anything about it.'

He peered into his brandy for a few seconds before answering. 'Ah.'

'Does that mean they're right? She can sell it over your head?'

'I think she would if she could and she probably can.'

This was more upsetting than anything that had happened before. 'Really? That's awful.' To think that Egan had been right made it all worse, somehow.

'She's waited quite a long time for her money. She said as much when I saw her. I was hoping to reason with her . . .' He paused. 'She could probably find a court who would say it was time I finally paid up the last chunk.' He drained his glass and then smiled. 'I might have to sell the house, but I'm darned if I'll let it go to that bloody woman for half nothing.'

Despite his bravado he looked so sad, it made her

heart turn over. She yearned to comfort him – it must be awful to have such a harridan of an ex-wife. And she couldn't bear to think that all her hard work to make the centre more profitable had been a waste of time.

He was looking at her intently and Gina found she couldn't meet his gaze. She wasn't sure she could conceal how she felt about him. She'd suddenly realised that what she felt for him wasn't just a crush. It was much, much more than that. You didn't pine for someone you simply had a crush on; you didn't want to protect them, to save them from marauding gift-shop owners and grasping exes. She'd fallen in love with him.

But she didn't know how he felt about her. He'd been wonderfully protective when he'd rescued her from Egan, but he might have been like that with any woman in that situation. She just didn't know and unless he told her, she couldn't find out.

He didn't speak for what seemed like hours. Gina heard the clock in the background. Then he said, 'How would you like to come to France with me?'

This seemed like a complete change of subject but she went with it. 'One day, I'd love it. Why do you ask?'

'Because I need to go back and I'd like to take you with me this time. I think you're ready. I took a quick look at the ledger and Tiggy told me you'd been brilliant.'

She laughed. 'You were checking up on me!' So he'd phoned one of the others, but not her. But never mind, he thought she was doing well. 'Why do you need to go back so soon?' she asked. 'You've only just got home. And what about Oscar? The centre?'

'It does sound crazy,' he said, 'but it's not unheard of. The reason I have to go back is I left some pieces being restored. They're for Nicholas so I want him to have them quickly. He'll pay me for them for one thing. And Jenny phoned me. She's sorted out her relations and is desperate to get back here.'

Hope flickered like a just-lit tea light, tiny yet optimistic. 'Getting back to normal is one thing but will she want to take on Oscar and the centre?'

'Oh yes, I asked her.'

'You *asked* her?' Another person he'd been in touch with when he hadn't even sent her a text.

'Yes. I knew I had to go back for the pieces and couldn't have asked you to go on looking after things here.' His eyes narrowed. 'I didn't tell her I was planning to take you to France with me, although I was.'

'Oh.'

'Gina,' he began but then stopped, gazing at her. She hardly dared breathe as his look intensified. She kept very, very still, not taking her eyes from his. They were so close, facing each other on the sofa. He leant in and gently kissed her. She closed her eyes as the kiss deepened. He pulled gently away, cupping her face with his hand. 'Oh, Gina. I can't tell you how long I've been wanting to do that.'

'Why didn't you?' said Gina, with a sigh.

'I . . .' He raked his hands through his hair. 'I've been so preoccupied with the centre and keeping Yvette off my back. And I wasn't sure . . . I mean at Christmas I thought, but then Sephie had her accident . . .'

'I know, but . . .' She hesitated. She had been about to say that there had been plenty – well, not plenty, but a handful at least – of moments since then when he could have swept her into his arms. She had been more than ready and willing. Although she was an independent, modern woman, she was romantic enough to want the man to make the first move. But she might have nudged him along earlier if she'd known how he felt. Once more she vowed she'd never play poker with him. And perhaps her pride had got in the way, making her keep things light between them so he wouldn't see how she felt and giving him the impression she liked him only as a friend. What fools they'd both been.

He kissed her again, for a very long time, then he pulled her up from the sofa. 'Come on,' he said and led her to the bedroom.

Sally was beside herself when she called the next day. Gina felt she had to tell her sister about going to France, although she didn't go into too much detail about what had happened after Matthew's invitation. She'd mentioned kissing but nothing else, not the fact that she'd spent a wonderful couple of hours with him before he'd reluctantly put her into a taxi – at her insistence. Staying the night would involve too much embarrassment the next day. She didn't feel she could let the other dealers know about it at the moment.

'Back up, back up,' Sally said. 'I thought you weren't keen on a relationship – you sly thing! You did all that without my help! I'd better get on with ordering Sephie and Ariadne's bridesmaids' dresses . . .' She sighed as the romance of it all took her over, then went on, 'I knew it, I was only saying to Alaric. I knew you were getting on well, but you kept telling me you were just friends. Honestly, Gina! I can't wait to tell Mum.'

'You won't tell the other dealers,' said Gina, 'will you?'

'Of course not! You know me. Discretion is my middle name!'

'Actually, your middle name is Maud, and I'd rather you left it to me to tell Mum and Dad.'

'Oh, OK, spoilsport. But hey! Just imagine! France!' Sally went on excitedly. 'Some darling little hotel with shutters and a smelly shower and croissants for breakfast! The perfect setting for a first time. So sensible of you to wait. Was he cool with that?'

'Um – not actually the first time . . .'

Gina held her phone away from her ear while Sally screeched her excitement. 'Even better,' said Sally after she'd calmed down. 'First times are always crap.'

Gina didn't comment. Her first time with Matthew had been anything but crap. She hugged the memories of last night to her before changing the subject. 'So, what have you been up to? Anything new to tell me?'

'Well, not on a level of what you've just told me, no. And we did see each other the other day. But I have made some lovely cushions with some fabric I got at a car-boot sale.'

Chapter Twenty-Two

Gina and Matthew were going to France in three days' time. They were not going in the Transit van Matthew usually hired for his trips and as Gina had expected, given he had furniture to bring back. They were flying and Matthew would arrange transport for the furniture, after he had checked on the restoration. While this seemed a bit extravagant, Gina didn't complain. It would have been a very long drive, Matthew explained, and would mean him being away from the centre far longer than really necessary. Nicholas would be paying for the furniture to be shipped, after all.

As Gina waited for Matthew to pick her up and take her to the airport she felt she had never been so happy in her entire life. The man she loved was taking her away on a holiday where he would make love to her, take her on romantic walks, to French antiques markets and wonderful little restaurants known only to the locals. It would be absolute bliss.

And even though Matthew's idea of the right time to arrive at an airport wasn't quite the same as hers she was able to reason that he'd done this journey hundreds of times and anyway it would be his fault if they were late so she could relax.

She'd packed and dressed carefully, hearing Sally condemning some of her initial choices as 'corporate' in her head. Thus she ended up packing a couple of jersey maxi dresses, an old but still lovely silk dress with a selection of shrugs and cardigans in case as it was still so early in the year, a couple of pairs of jeans with a choice of tops and – after a bit of internet panic buying – a bright yellow raincoat that would be perfect to travel in and could never be described as corporate. She'd managed to reassure Sally that she didn't need to come over and inspect her suitcase.

'Good morning!' he said softly when she opened the door to him.

'Hello!' she whispered back after a very satisfying kiss. 'This is so exciting!' Then she remembered it wasn't quite so exciting for him and hoped she hadn't sounded childish.

The smile he responded with reached every part of his face, from his dark eyes with crinkly corners and long lashes to his generous, slightly crooked mouth and straight teeth. Gina felt the sun had come out just for her. 'Let me take your bag. Oh, you travel light!'

'I thought I might not travel quite so light on the way home. I've left room for some French bits and pieces. You know, now I'm an expert and all that.'

He chuckled. 'Anything big you can have put in with Nicholas's stuff. That's what I'll do with anything that I might buy.'

Gina locked her front door, turning away from him so he wouldn't see her blush. For a moment she had forgotten that for him buying things in France didn't mean squashing some knick-knacks into a suitcase – it probably meant large pieces of furniture.

As they drove through the countryside on the way to Bristol Gina relaxed so she could enjoy every moment. She hadn't asked any questions about where they would stay – she wanted it all to be a surprise – but she had fantasised about little French hotels with shutters, tables on the street with umbrellas, with a pâtisserie on every street corner. She realised it was not yet March and even in the Dordogne it wasn't going to be baking hot, but she could dream.

'It's so strange it being so sunny but there being no leaves on the trees,' said Gina. They had picked up a hire car and were driving out of the Bergerac airport. 'I haven't been to France for ages although I'm a Francophile. It's so gorgeously French, isn't it?'

'Pretty much,' he agreed with a glancing smile that made her stomach flip. Just for a moment she tried to work out if her feelings for him really were true love or just extreme lust. Then she decided that she couldn't separate them out and that it didn't matter anyway. Whatever it was, it was lovely.

'So, what's the plan?' she said, having looked at the passing scenery with the pleasant sensation of being in a Cézanne painting. The sky was bright blue and the trees, bare of leaves, stood out against it like children's drawings. The vines in the passing vineyards consisted of just one shoot, giving no inkling of the lushness that would follow later in the year.

'Well, I thought we'd book into a nice hotel I know. It's right in the centre of town but in the back you'd never know that, it's so quiet. There's a pool, a lovely garden, everything you could want, really.'

Gina might have said she'd share a single bed in a brothel with him – if such a thing existed. It would look so needy. 'It sounds perfect.'

He parked the car in a small street in the middle of the town. 'There's the hotel,' he said, pointing up to what looked to Gina like a mansion.

'Wow!' she said. 'Weirdly, it reminds me of the French House.'

'Not weird at all. The French House is called that for a reason.' He got out and opened her door for her. 'Come on. Let me get your bag.'

Matthew opened the huge old front door and they went in. The reception area was a large hallway, well lit and beautifully decorated, and completed the French-chic picture.

A woman came out from behind the desk. 'Ah! Matthew!' She kissed him on both cheeks. 'How delightful to see you again,' she said with only a hint of a French accent. 'And who is this? Should I be jealous?' As she said this with a broad smile and kissed Gina with almost as much affection, Gina didn't take this too seriously.

'Gina, this is Céline, who owns this wonderful hotel. Céline, this is Gina, my . . .' He paused for a moment. 'My friend – and colleague.' Gina tried not to feel disappointed he hadn't said girlfriend, or, even better, lover, but she thought Céline would probably assume this.

'Come in. Come in. The formalities we can deal with later. Let me show you your room.'

As Céline found keys Gina looked down the hallway. At the end she could see doors open on to a garden and beyond that a swimming pool.

'Follow me, then when you've had time to freshen up, we can go in the garden. It's time for a little glass of something.'

As they followed Céline up the stairs Gina reflected that it was still quite early in the day for little somethings, but then decided she was on French time and to just go with it.

When they reached the spacious landing Gina paused to look around her. 'You do have some lovely things.'

'Thank you,' said Céline. 'I have always been a collector and was lucky enough to inherit some good furniture from an old uncle. And Matthew found me some pieces also. *Voilà!* Your room,' she went on, opening a door. She ushered them into a huge room with two tall windows. A splendid four-poster bed stood opposite, its height from the floor meaning that one would enjoy the view the moment one opened one's eyes.

Gina stood still, not daring to look at Matthew. Was his room next door? She hoped not, but he might have booked two rooms, not knowing at the time how things might stand between them.

'This is beautiful. And so large,' said Gina.

Céline crossed the room and opened a door. 'Here are the facilities. A bedroom is one thing, but no woman should ever have to share a bathroom with a man. However, this is a hotel.' She sighed.

'We'll be fine,' said Gina, smiling. So they were sharing a room.

'Well,' he said when they were alone. 'Will this be all right? I did presume rather . . .' he asked and took her into his arms.

'Mm,' she said into his shoulder. 'Think so.' She held on to him tightly, hardly believing her luck. She was in France, in a beautiful boutique hotel with a man she was very much in love with.

A little later, after a very happy time, they both had a shower and as they were getting dressed, Gina said, 'Tell me about the house.'

'Well, it's very old, obviously, and was in bad condition when Céline bought it. She's done a great deal of work on it – a lot of it herself.'

'Really? And is there a Mr Céline?'

Matthew shook his head. 'No, she has a shit-hot lover instead.'

Gina giggled slightly, surprised at Matthew's wording. 'I love that. Tell me more about the house. It's so beautiful!'

'It was used as a hospital during the war and of course it's haunted.'

Gina, who had, quite recently, believed in ghosts, knew that if she had Matthew in bed with her, she wouldn't notice a complete skeleton and dangling chain, and even if she did, she wouldn't care.

'I do wish you wouldn't look at me like that,' he said.

'Like what?' she replied indignantly.

'Oh, I think you know.'

Gina turned away to hide her smile.

'Come on, you wanton woman, Céline will be wondering what's happened to us. We'll have a glass of something, then I'll show you the sights.'

'So where are you taking me?' Gina asked a little later after a very pleasant drink with Céline in the hotel garden.

'Saint-Émilion,' said Matthew. 'It's a World Heritage Site, but if you don't fancy that, we could just go for a walk. It is beautiful down by the river.'

'I think I ought to see Saint-Émilion. I'm not sure I've ever seen a World Heritage Site before.'

'OK. Let's go. You won't regret it.'

Matthew didn't so much park the car as stop it dead in the street. 'It's early in the season and there's space so why not?' He gave a shrug.

Gina observed that Matthew was becoming very Gallic all of a sudden but decided she liked it.

The little town was beautiful: steep cobbled streets, wonderful old houses perched where no house should manage to stay upright and tantalising glimpses of the hills beyond. They wandered slowly up the hill, investigating the little shops and enjoying the stunning views.

There were some amusing sights: lovely young women all dressed up in high heels who hadn't been warned about the cobbles, shiny with many hundreds of years of use. Finding themselves unable to stay upright they were now either carrying their shoes or clinging on to their escorts – wonderfully endearing. Gina was glad she'd put on her sensible, brightly coloured pumps.

They passed some enchanting clothes shops, and stores that sold the sort of fabric you instantly wanted to redecorate your house for. Her own feet slipped sometimes but Matthew's arm was firmly round her. She felt she was in a travel magazine.

'Oh, macaroons.' She drew to a halt outside a very enticing window with a bright-pink-and-chocolate-coloured awning. There were macaroons to match displayed in the window.

Matthew stopped beside her. 'Shall we go in? They are a local speciality.'

'They were invented by the nuns,' said the beautiful girl behind the counter.

'I must buy some. Maybe for Céline? She's been so kind to us.'

Matthew shook his head. 'Her guests often buy them for her. Do you know what she says?'

'No.'

'"I 'ate bloody macaroons!" he said, imitating Céline's accent perfectly. Gina laughed and, having bought some macaroons for herself, they headed back up the hill.

They reached the church at the top and stood and admired the view. On the far hills were endless acres of vineyards but it was the roofs beneath them that fascinated Gina. They seemed to face every angle and with their stone tiles looked like a sophisticated patchwork quilt. If only she could have bottled this moment . . .

'Come on, let's have lunch,' said Matthew, breaking into her reverie. 'I know where to take you.'

Right in the middle of the square, the bar was surrounded by shops and cafés. Awnings and window boxes added brightness and beauty and it was a place Gina would happily have spent hours in.

'What do you want to do now?' he asked after they'd eaten.

Suddenly, a yawn she wasn't expecting overcame her. 'Well . . .'

'We did get up early,' said Matthew.

'And a nap is always OK when you're abroad.'

'Do you know what the French for nap is?'

She shook her head.

'*Sieste amoureuse.*'

'Oh!' Gina was impressed. 'Fancy you knowing that!'

'You'd be surprised at what I know.'

'Not as surprised as I once was,' she said.

'Shall we test the breadth of my knowledge?' He took her hand and his look made his intentions perfectly clear.

'Very good idea. I'll let you know if you pass.'

As they drove back to the hotel Gina found she couldn't stop smiling.

Chapter Twenty-Three

'I'd love to see a proper French market,' said Gina the next morning as they left the hotel. She felt wonderfully decadent after breakfast in bed and a languorous morning.

They got into the car and he started the engine. 'Brilliant idea. I know one that's not far. It's quite big, too.'

'Excellent,' said Gina and she sighed happily.

It wasn't long before they were turning into the slightly larger town where the market was.

'Gosh, you really know your way around the area,' Gina said a bit later after Matthew had dived up and down the back streets and found an impossible space to squeeze the car into.

'I have been fairly often on buying trips. It's always a bit tricky on market days but this will do us.'

Gina felt she was in heaven or was the star of the best sort of romantic film. Walking along a French street, hand in hand with the man she loved, all her cares left behind in England, had to be the most delightful situation a girl – or woman – could be in.

'This market sells everything,' he said as they approached row upon row of awnings. 'And, as you see, is fairly enormous. Shall we do the brocante first?'

'Oh yes, there's something about French junk – see, my French isn't too bad – that is so much more glamorous than English, isn't there?'

He laughed and pulled her close.

It occurred to Gina that she and Matthew had never gone looking at antiques together in this casual way before. Now, she didn't feel she was being tested or had to prove knowledge she didn't have, she could just browse and look at things she liked as well as a lot of things she didn't. One stall sold a lot of medical apparatus for example.

'I really don't see who would want someone's old prosthetic foot!' she laughed. 'Let alone the glass eyes. Do you think they're used? Or new?'

'New, I should imagine, although I don't know. But there is a market for that sort of thing. Look at this case of surgeons' instruments, for example. It's beautifully made and the steel is first class.'

They were nearly at the end of the antiques bit of the market when they came across some small silver items.

There was a little swan that drew Gina's attention. 'Oh that's pretty. What is it, do you think?'

Matthew picked it up. 'It's either a salt or a pepper shaker. It is nice.'

'It's dreadfully expensive,' said Gina, catching sight

of the label hanging round its neck and swiftly putting it back down again. She spotted some clothes hanging on a rail further into the market. 'Do you mind if I look? You stay here if you want. I won't be long.'

She was long enough to buy a couple of lovely linen dresses and a pair of espadrilles she'd seen in England for twice the price, and she was pleased that she'd managed to do it all in French. She only hoped they had a halfway decent summer in England.

Matthew cruised up and took her arm. 'So you've bought something?'

'Yes. Amazing bargains. I'll show you later.'

'Good. And you didn't need a translator?'

'Oh no, GCSE French did the job.'

'I think you deserve a drink. Come with me.'

He led her through the rows of clothes, amazing vats of food – some of which looked and smelt delicious, others that looked like steaming tubs of sewage that smelt of fish – to an indoor market.

'What is that?' asked Gina, failing to hide her distaste as they passed a particularly disgusting tub.

'It's called *lamproie à la bordelaise*. It's a regional speciality. It's lampreys – similar to an eel. It's cooked in its own blood for about twenty-four hours. Only for the very brave.'

'I certainly can't imagine eating a surfeit of them like that bloke in Shakespeare did.' She shuddered.

He kissed the top of her head and then led her into the covered part of the market.

'Drink first, then you can look round,' said Matthew firmly as she pulled on his arm, dazzled by arrays of fish, most of which she didn't recognise.

He took her to a bar with three or four tables outside. Then he went to the counter. The woman behind it obviously knew him, or was a very fast worker, because she came out and embraced him warmly, kissing him on both cheeks. They chattered in French for a few seconds before Matthew drew the woman forward.

'Gina? This is Monique – an old friend of mine.'

Gina accepted the woman's warm embrace.

'You are so pretty! Now sit, sit, I'll bring snacks and, Mathieu, your favourite? Yes?'

'Yes please, thank you, Monique.'

Monique appeared with little rounds of toast with something spread on them. Gina took one. It was delicious but she couldn't decide what it was. 'This is lovely, but what is it? It's salty, slightly fishy but also creamy?'

'That about sums it up. It's smoked fish made into a sort of pâté. Monique has her own recipe.'

A couple of minutes later Monique came back with a tray. On it were two glasses of what looked like champagne. 'Kir *à la châtaigne*,' she said as she put them down and then glided over to the next table. The bar was obviously very popular and they'd been lucky to get a table.

'What is it?' asked Gina picking up her glass.

'Try it and see if you can tell.'

Gina took a tentative sip and then smiled. 'It's delicious! Champagne but with something else?'

'Not actual champagne – sparkling wine – and with *crème de châtaigne* – which is chestnut liqueur. Monique introduced me to it years ago and I always have it when I come here.'

The woman in her forced her to ask, 'Did you ever come here with Yvette?'

He shook his head. 'No, Yvette doesn't quite get market bars like this.'

'Her loss,' said Gina happily and took another sip.

Matthew bought Gina another Kir *à la châtaigne* and then, having said goodbye to Monique, who now seemed like a long-lost friend, they explored the indoor market. The enormous, strange fish, obscene-looking sausages and cuts of meat that looked quite different to what Gina was used to were absurdly exciting. Then they went outside and Matthew found Gina a hat which he put on her head and paid for. Then they walked back to the car.

'I thought we'd have dinner within walking distance of the hotel.' He looked at her with eyes that held a disturbing twinkle.

Gina blushed.

After a leisurely breakfast the following morning – the day of their departure – and which they ate on the little balcony outside their room, Matthew said, 'I have to go and check on the pieces I'm having restored for Nicholas and if they're OK – which I'm sure they will be – arrange transport. Do you want to come and meet Henri, who's doing the work? Or would you rather relax here or explore the town?'

'I'd like to come. As an antiques dealer I feel I should find out about restorers.' Actually she didn't want to spend a second away from him if she could avoid it, but she didn't say so. He needn't know everything.

He grinned. 'Great!' He put his arm round her shoulders, and kissed her.

Henri the restorer's workshop was in a little back street in a nearby town. As Matthew parked with the panache she had come to expect, Gina noticed a little clothes shop with a very pretty dress in the window. She was in the mood to buy a pretty dress.

'Can I meet you here in a little while?' she asked. 'I just want to pop into that shop.'

'Sure. There's a café a little further along, do you see it, with the red check tablecloths? I could meet you there.'

Gina nodded, kissed his cheek before she got out and sighed happily.

Three-quarters of an hour later, having had a cup of coffee and feeling she'd waited long enough for Matthew, she decided to head towards the restorer's. Matthew had obviously got caught up. She hoped there wasn't a problem.

The door to the workshop was ajar and she pushed it open.

It took her a moment or two to work out what she was seeing. Matthew was glaring at a woman who was looking back at him with narrowed eyes. Neither of them was speaking but they were both clearly furious, like two cats about to hiss and strike.

A little sound escaped her and they both turned.

'Oh, Gina, it's you,' said Matthew. His face was thunderous.

The woman, who looked very French, said, 'How do you do? I am Yvette, Matthew's ex-wife.' She sounded very Gallic too.

Gina didn't know how to reply. 'Hello,' she said. She had to admit Yvette was very attractive in that well-groomed style Carmella had. She felt scruffy beside her but was confident Yvette no longer held any sway over Matthew – at least not romantically. Not judging by the look on his face now.

'I have heard about you. You are the girl who took over Rainey's spot? Now Rainey, she was a woman.' Yvette laughed. It was a strangely deep laugh, at odds with her petite, rather girlish frame.

Gina nodded. 'She was my aunt.'

'Yes? Interesting.' Yvette's look said 'unlikely'. 'Now,' she went on. 'I must go. Henri . . .' She broke into rapid French. Henri nodded and murmured and at last she stopped. 'Matthew? I have told you how things are. Goodbye!'

She swept out of the workshop, the picture of elegance in silk trousers, blouse and chunky gold jewellery.

Matthew said something to Henri in French and then, taking her elbow, ushered Gina out of the workshop. She realised things must be bad because he'd forgotten to introduce her.

They got into the car and still Matthew hadn't said anything. Eventually, after they'd driven for a few minutes, Gina asked, 'Were you expecting to see Yvette there?' She wanted to ask much more but hoped he would tell her unprompted.

He growled. 'No, but I told her about Henri so I suppose I shouldn't have been surprised.'

Another few kilometres passed. 'Things didn't go well between you then?' she prompted.

'You could say that.'

Gina was dying by inches from the desperate need to know what was going on. She waited until she couldn't bear it any more. 'Tell me what she said then. Please. I'd like to know. It's obviously upset you.'

He shook his head. 'It's not your problem.'

This was at once hurtful and deeply frustrating. 'Yes it is. We're in this together. And I hate seeing you like this. Please tell me,' she added gently.

'It's not your problem. This is something only I can sort out.'

It was so typical of Matthew to feel he had to take on all the burdens alone. 'If you have to sell the French House we'll all be affected,' she said quietly.

'In which case, you're all affected. I do have to sell it.' Matthew looked and sounded as forbidding and distant as the day she'd first met him.

Gina took time to breathe. Getting cross with Matthew or even Yvette would not help. 'OK. When?'

'As soon as possible.'

'Matthew, could we stop? We need to talk about this properly. You're too angry to drive right now.'

'OK.' He stopped at a viewing point and pulled on the handbrake. 'Right. What do you want to say to me?'

Gina decided to be blunt. Pussyfooting round the issue wouldn't help. 'How much do you owe Yvette?'

'It makes no difference. I need to pay her. If I don't sell the house voluntarily she'll sell it over my head.' He paused. 'All our heads.'

'Is there anything legal that says you have to sell the house? Or do you just have to pay Yvette half the value of it?' She remembered what Egan had intimated.

'No, I only have to sell it because there's no other way of raising the money. I've sold my own home, cashed in my pension. The house is all I have left.'

'Do you mind me asking how much you owe? I mean it seems mad to sell the house, which must be worth over a million, surely, to raise twenty quid.'

'Thirty thousand pounds. A bit more than twenty quid.'

Gina's spirits lifted slightly. 'Yes, but not a fortune. Surely to goodness we can raise that without selling the house.' A second later she regretted speaking without thinking. Of course he'd done everything he could. The house was the last resort, which was why he thought he had to sell it. 'I'm sorry.' She put her hand on his. 'That was horrendously tactless.' She paused. 'But you've got me on the case now. I'm a PR girl. I work miracles for a living.'

'Is that what they do? I've often wondered.'

Gina was so used to having her work dismissed she was only slightly offended. 'Come on, fair's fair. Think how much more business we've done since I've been here.'

'That's true. Having you and Sally involved has added a lot.'

She was touched. 'And I'm still involved. I think we could raise the money without selling the house.'

'So you say, but I don't see how.'

Gina thought frantically for an idea. 'I'll come up with something, you'll see. And Sally's brilliant at these things too. We'll sort it! It will be hard work but anything is possible.'

'But why should you work hard to save the centre? You could take Rainey's stuff – your stuff – to another centre and do just as well. Better possibly.'

In spite of all they'd shared she didn't think she

could just tell him the reason was because she was in love with him and would donate a kidney to him if he needed one, without thinking twice.

'OK,' she said, in PR-girl mode. 'Well, for one reason, I don't want you to have to give in to blackmail. Two, I do think it's an amount we could raise. Three, think of all the dealers who might not find other outlets – or bother to look for one – who've been there since your father's time. We – you – can't just abandon them.'

He nodded. Weariness was etched on to his face. 'It's because of them I haven't sold the centre already. You're not telling me anything I don't know, Gina. I have tried very hard to raise money. *Very* hard – so you must forgive me if I've no confidence left. Yvette has the law on her side; she's entitled to the money.'

'But you haven't had me on the case, as I said. Trust me, we can do this.' She paused. 'How long have we got?'

He looked at her blankly. 'Two months.'

Chapter Twenty-Four

'Do you mind if we go to the French House first? There's something I need to pick up and then I've got someone to see near you.'

They were on their way back from the airport after an almost silent journey. For once Gina hadn't been able to think of a solution to this problem immediately: how to raise thirty thousand pounds in two months. And Matthew had barely registered her, let alone touched her. After he'd told her about his predicament, he seemed to shut down. A couple of times she tried to lighten the mood but to no avail. Eventually she felt the best thing to do was leave him alone. Where was the loving, romantic man she'd spent three glorious days with? Had he gone forever?

'Can't you even stop for a cup of tea before you have to go back to work?' She tried again to lift the gloom that had settled on both of them.

He gave her a brief smile. 'We can certainly have a cup of tea but if I'm going in that direction, it seems silly not to deliver that little table. Saves fuel.'

He sounded friendly enough but to Gina it felt as

if he was saying, 'Don't think we can go back to the shagging at every opportunity we've been doing in France,' only more politely. She felt like someone had thrown a bucket of water over her.

She cheered up when they got through the door of the centre. Things were bustling although it was early afternoon, which wasn't always a very busy time. She saw Andrew, the Gilbert and Sullivan fan, and went over to talk to him.

'How are you doing?' she asked him.

'Can't complain. Business is doing quite well, actually.' He smiled. 'All thanks to you and your sister.'

Gina brushed this aside; it was very nice of him to say so, but it hardly mattered now. 'And how's the Gilbert and Sullivan going?'

Andrew sighed. 'Well, not quite such a rosy picture. Our latest production was a bit disappointing.'

'Oh, why's that?' asked Gina, wondering if she should go and find Matthew.

'Well,' Andrew said, launching in, 'we borrowed this little theatre to do it in and although it was a gem, it only seated about a hundred people, which meant lots of the company's family and friends couldn't get tickets.'

'Oh?' Although no one would have guessed it, Gina was only listening with half her attention. She spotted Bill moving out a big table and wasn't sure if he'd sold it or was taking it out of the centre. Was he moving out altogether? That would be very bad news. She would never describe him as a rat, but if he'd found out the ship was sinking, she could hardly blame him.

Before she could get too gloomy Jenny appeared with a mug of tea. 'Matthew said you wanted this. He'll be down in a minute.'

He was hurrying her off the premises, she thought, as she sipped and nodded and tried to focus.

'. . . we had such beautiful costumes and were singing better than we ever had done, and all for a couple of hundred.'

Gina frowned. 'I thought you said the theatre seated a hundred?'

'Two nights. It would have been OK if we'd had it for a week, but we couldn't.'

'What a shame!' she said, looking round.

Matthew was coming towards them carrying a box. He was smiling. Not grinning from ear to ear or anything like that, but with a definite stretch in his mouth. It was a decided improvement on the last few hours.

'This came for you while we were away,' he said, handing it to her.

'What is it?'

'I have no idea. Open it and see. It came from Nicholas.'

It was an old-fashioned dress box from Harrods. It was in good condition but the Harrods lettering hailed from another decade; the 1940s possibly, thought Gina.

'Here, put it down on this table,' said Andrew. 'I'll find my knife so you can get in it.'

Eventually the tape was cut through and the box opened. Several layers of yellowed tissue paper were revealed. Carefully Gina lifted them and exposed layers of silk and lace. Confused, she lifted it out of the box.

'Ah ha,' said Matthew. 'Now we know what it is.'

'What?' asked Andrew, together with Bill, who had joined the group.

'I took Gina to see Nicholas Davenport the other day. He took a definite shine to her and said she looked like his grandmother.'

'It's the dress she was wearing in the painting,' said Gina, awed by the ancient beauty in her hands.

'There's a note,' said Jenny, who had been passing and had stopped to see what they were all looking at.

Gina picked it up. It was a sheet of headed writing paper. *My dear Gina, I know you said you didn't want me to give this to you, but I feel you should indulge an old man sometimes. I hope one day to see you in it. With very best wishes, Nicholas.*

Gina held the dress up against her, admiring the delicate silk and lace.

'Try it,' said Jenny, clapping her hands. 'Let's see what it looks like on.'

'I'll never get into it. Women were tiny in those days.'

'Don't forget she was pregnant when she had that portrait painted. Nicholas told us,' said Matthew.

Gina gave him a look. If he was saying she was fat he would live to regret it.

'Do let us see you in it,' pressed Bill. 'It's a beautiful dress. Worth a few bob, I'd have thought.'

Still Gina hesitated although by now she was dying to see what she looked like in it.

'Come into my room,' said Jenny. 'Go on. I think you'll get into it just fine!'

In fact it didn't quite do up at the back but Jenny insisted it could be let out.

'It would be a shame to spoil it though,' said Gina. 'Currently it's original and valuable. I shouldn't accept it really.'

'Oh, don't be silly,' said Jenny briskly. 'Now let's show the chaps. I'm sure Matthew – and the others,' she added quickly, 'would love to see you in it. You're quite decent. I'll just adjust the sash to hide your knickers. There.'

Gina gathered up her skirts and walked back into the main part of the shop. She realised Jenny must know about her and Matthew – or maybe she was just wondering. Did the others know? And would they mind? If Jenny was fine about it it would be such a relief. She was so important to Matthew and the centre. But then after what Matthew had said earlier perhaps it didn't matter at all anyway. Their romance might have ended before it had really begun.

'Hey, look at you!' said Bill.

'Gorgeous!' whistled Andrew.

Gina looked at Matthew. He was smiling at her, obviously approving, but with the sadness that caught at her heart. 'You're a delight,' he said.

And as he drove her home, with the little table in the back of the Volvo, there were no more smiles. She couldn't help feeling he was detaching himself from her.

'Matthew,' she said, 'are we all right?'

'What do you mean?'

'I mean – like we were in France?'

The fact that he hesitated told her what to expect.

'I'm sorry, Gina, this whole business with Yvette and the centre . . . I'm likely to be left with nothing. I can't seem to think about anything else.'

'But I can help you with that, like I said.'

'You can't dig me out of this hole, however much you want to.'

'And what about us?'

He sighed. 'I can't pay you the attention you deserve while I've got this hanging over me. And I can't expect you . . . I'm hardly a good prospect. Let's just see . . .'

They pulled up outside Gina's cottage. He took her bags out of the boot and handed them to her. 'I've got to go, I'll call you.' He kissed her on the cheek and left her standing there by the gate wondering what had hit her.

* * *

Slowly Gina carried her bags and the box with the dress in it into the house and put the kettle on. What on earth happened there? It couldn't just be Yvette's threat hanging over him that had made him so distant, could it? Surely he didn't think his money problems would mean she didn't want him?

She hadn't been dumped. She refused to be dumped. When she thought of all they'd shared – the wonderful, tender, passionate, thoughtful sex – she couldn't think they were finished. She wouldn't let his pride ruin something that had been so lovely. She just couldn't.

She pulled out a bottle of wine she'd bought for Sally and opened it. She wouldn't despair, she'd just think bloody hard and work out a solution. She'd show Matthew. She could be as stubborn as he was.

After the first glass of wine she rang Sally. She told her how wonderful France had been but not what had happened at the restorer's or afterwards. She didn't want sympathy just now. And while she was willing to mentally hurl every insult she could think of at Matthew, she didn't want anyone else to say a single bad word about him. This was a blip, it was not the end of the affair.

In the night she had an idea so crazy she actually jotted it down just in case it wasn't quite as crazy as it seemed. In the morning she looked at the words 'Iolanthe' and 'Fairfield Manor'.

She took the old receipt, which had been the only bit of paper she could find in the middle of the night, downstairs so she could think about it with a clear head. Just how mad was the idea?

It was pretty off the wall, she admitted, as the kettle boiled and she transferred the words on to a foolscap pad. But it had merit. She listed the merits too, so when she talked to Matthew about it she would have all her ducks in a row.

First on her action list was to ring Nicholas. She had the perfect excuse. She had to thank him for the dress. She would have written as she felt such a wonderful present deserved something more than a phone call, but she wanted to invite herself to tea – or drinks if that would suit him better. She wanted to get back inside his house. Her mind was now fizzing with ideas. It was a good distraction from Matthew. He hadn't phoned.

She caught up with other work until eleven o'clock when she felt a telephone call might be acceptable. Bernard gave her the impression that Nicholas would be pleased to hear from her and eventually he came on the line.

'I'd really like to thank you in person,' she said. 'It was such a generous present.'

'Darling girl, it would be delightful to see you. Drinks?'

'Can I come to tea? I'll bring a cake.'

'A home-made cake? I can't remember the last time

I ate one. Come at four. We can always move on to sherry if it seems appropriate.'

Baking wasn't one of Gina's most practised skills and she considered buying a cake, or scouring the local WI markets for one. But as she wouldn't be able to lie to Nicholas, and trying to buy a decent one would probably take up more time than actually making one herself, she called in at the Spar shop and bought ingredients. She opted for chocolate and then any failures in the actual baking could be disguised with icing.

Her cake really looked very nice, she thought as she stood on the doorstep of the magnificent example of Georgian architecture that was Nicholas's home. She just hoped it helped her cause.

It was delightful seeing Nicholas again. He was so charming and flattering Gina felt uplifted just setting eyes on him.

'I do hope chocolate cake is all right,' she said as Nicholas ushered her into a room she hadn't seen before. 'Bernard took it away but I couldn't tell what he thought about it from his expression.'

'We love chocolate cake. And I've brought you in here because it's so cosy. If I'm having tea I like to have it here.'

It was warm and inviting but it was hard to think of a room this size as cosy, thought Gina. But she was delighted to think there was yet another reception room. It would make her plan easier to carry out.

Eventually, after two slices of cake, two cups of tea and a glass of sherry, Gina got to the point. 'Nicholas, I have a very big favour to ask you.'

Nicholas, who had eschewed tea and drunk sherry with his cake, was in a good mood. He obviously enjoyed Gina's company and smiled benignly at her.

'Anything in the world I can do for you, I'll do in a heartbeat.'

Gina laughed nervously. 'I won't hold you to that. It is a very big favour indeed.'

He inclined his head in query and Gina realised she would have to explain her plan, out loud, and it might turn out to be completely ridiculous. She took a deep breath and began.

Eventually, after listening to Gina's request, which became very like pleading by the time she got to the end, Nicholas spoke. 'As long as you wear the dress,' he said. 'I would so love to see you in it.'

She just about managed to leave Nicholas without flinging herself at his feet with gratitude. Once home, she rang Andrew and put her plan to him. He was ecstatic and kept her talking far longer than she would have liked, thinking of the different ways in which it could work. He was convinced he could work everyone up to the same pitch of enthusiasm.

Eventually she had to bring the call to a close.

'That's absolutely fantastic. But I've still got to get it past Matthew.'

She decided to ring him the following day. She wanted to arrange a time so she could talk about it to him face to face. She convinced herself this was so she could read his body language and if necessary seduce him into accepting her plan, but really she knew she just wanted to see him. And although she knew she could just pick up her phone and be connected with him in two clicks of a button, in her heart she was an old-fashioned girl: she wanted to give him time to ring her first.

However, she didn't want to leave it too long so when she hadn't heard from him by the evening, she picked up the phone.

'Matthew? Hi, how are you?'

'Gina. I'm OK. You?'

But he didn't sound OK. She sighed silently. 'So, what have you been doing?'

'Dealing with paperwork mostly, which was a bit depressing, but later I got a call from Bernard to say that Nicholas's furniture had arrived so I went over to help him place it.'

Shit! Supposing Nicholas had told him her plan? Had she sworn him to secrecy? Was this why he was being a bit off? Was he being off? Maybe he was just being his normally gloomy having-to-sell-his-house self?

'That was quick!' she said brightly. 'And did the furniture look nice *in situ*?'

'It did, once he decided where to put it. I swear we tried every reception room – and there are several – and every bedroom, hallway, bay or passage before he was happy. He had some fixation about leaving enough room for God knows what.' His tone softened a little. 'How are you?'

She decided to keep it light. 'Oh, same – I mean I've been catching up. Doing stuff. Nothing remotely exciting.' She hesitated, then she said, 'Matthew, can we meet?'

His pause seemed to go on forever. 'Of course. But I am very up against it. It would have to be during the day.'

Gina forbore to point out that if he was really up against it evenings would make more sense than daytimes. 'Great! Tomorrow?'

'Not until teatime.'

'Perfect. But I won't offer to make a cake.'

'Why on earth should you? Although Nicholas had some very good chocolate cake someone had given him.'

'Really?' she squeaked. 'I'll come over to the centre.' She hesitated. 'Unless you're going to be in my area?'

'No, the centre is better.'

'Fine.' She softened her tone. 'Bye then.'

'Bye.' His goodbye wasn't exactly brisk but it wasn't full of love and longing as she rather thought hers had been.

Chapter Twenty-Five

The following morning she had her calculator, her pad, her list of contacts who might be persuaded to sponsor champagne or the catering, or give raffle prizes – always a good idea to have a raffle – and was halfway through a letter of invitation when the doorbell rang.

Sally stood on the doorstep, her eyes shining. 'Oh God, I am so happy and excited I can hardly speak. I had to come straight round and tell you. Alaric's got the girls.'

Gina couldn't help smiling, infected by the sheer joy her sister embodied. 'How lovely. Come on in. Tell all!'

Gina led them into the kitchen and put the kettle on. Sally pulled out a chair and sat down. 'I've got a job – and it's just sooo perfect! I can do all the things I'm good at: creating beautiful things, selling them, having mad ideas and making them happen . . .' She got up again, obviously too excited to sit.

'A job – how fab! But what about the girls? Alaric has to work too.' Gina poured water on to tea bags.

'That's the beautiful part. I can pretty much choose

my own hours. Three days a week to begin with and more when I have time. If Alaric wants some time away from work – or pretending to work – he can have the girls more. And, get this, his parents are paying for one day of nursery because they see it as a proper job. How brilliant is that?' She was practically skipping round the room now.

'Totally brilliant. I'm so thrilled for you, Sal. So who are you doing all this making and selling for?'

'Carmella. You know, the one I sold my lamps to?'

Gina's excitement drained away as if someone had pulled the plug out of a sink. 'Carmella?'

'Yes. She's buying the French House and is going to expand hugely which is why she needs me. Gines, what's wrong?'

Gina found that her mouth had gone dry and she felt sick, exactly as she had done when Carmella told her she wanted to buy the building. It was as if someone had died. Matthew hadn't sold the centre already, had he? Before she'd even put her plan to him? He couldn't have, not without telling her, surely. 'What about the antiques centre?'

'What about it?' Sally flung her arms into the air as if anything was possible. 'People can sell their antiques anywhere. It's not as if there aren't about a zillion antiques places in Cranmore.'

'Does she have to have her shop in the French House?' She couldn't bear to think of Carmella there.

She remembered the proprietory way she'd looked round that time.

'Well, yes!' said Sally impatiently. 'There's nowhere else as good. It needs to be quite big, you see.' Sally frowned as it dawned on her that Gina wasn't also dancing about in ecstasy. 'Why are you so upset? I know you were really getting into antiques – God knows why – but there are loads of places who'll give you space. You don't have to give it up.'

Gina couldn't believe Sally didn't see the problem. 'That's not the point. There are dealers there who *will* give it up if the centre closes.'

'Then they'll be happy to retire! People are. And if they don't want to retire, they can move. What is the matter with you, Gina? It isn't like you to be so negative.'

'It's not that I'm being negative, I'm just pointing out that if the French House closes lots of people would give up dealing in antiques.'

'But why would you care? They're not really your friends, you know, only acquaintances.'

Gina's mouth dropped open. She'd never known Sally to be so . . . so appallingly insensitive. 'What about Matthew?'

'What about him? He knows he's got to sell to give his ex-wife her money. Carmella's a cash buyer. It's a gift for him. He'll be relieved to get rid of the centre. It's a millstone around his neck.'

Gina let out her breath. She had told her some of

that, but only the basics. Carmella must have been incredibly indiscreet.

'That's not what I said! The French House is Matthew's life! He'll be devastated if he has to sell. I care about it, and I thought you did too. When we had the Christmas event you threw yourself into it.'

'Yes, well, that's because it was fun and I like a challenge. But half the dealers have other outlets and it's only a building.'

'It's not just that. Aunt Rainey loved the French House. She loved Matthew. She lumped us all together in her will. And it's his home. You can't just get him turned out!'

'I'm not getting him turned out of his home. He has to sell it. Carmella's doing him a favour by making it quick and easy.'

'But she'd be robbing him of its proper value! Her offer is bound to be well below the market price. I told you what she said when she came round that time. Anyway, the French House *isn't* for sale.'

'How do you know? Even if Matthew hasn't accepted Carmella's offer – and I know for a fact she's putting it in today – he will. He has to; he needs the cash.'

Gina tried to keep calm. Carmella really was a devious cow. Yvette had obviously been straight on the phone to her the moment she'd left Henri's. 'That's as may be but there are other ways he can raise money.'

'Really?'

Gina noted the upward inflection of incredulity. Had everyone been practising it? Now it made her wonder if everything she'd been planning was hopeless even before she'd written a press release or told Matthew about it. 'Of course. He doesn't owe that much.' She gambled on Sally not knowing the amount. Carmella might not know herself.

'So how much does he owe?' asked Sally.

'I'm not really sure,' Gina lied, 'but not enough so he has to sell the house.' Although it might be. Could the event she had in mind raise enough?

'Are you sure?'

'Yes. Pretty much. I'm organising an event to raise the money.'

Sally narrowed her eyes. 'What sort of event?'

'A Gilbert and Sullivan evening.'

Sally stared at her for several seconds, her mouth hanging open. Then she laughed. 'Oh, Gina, really? That is the lamest thing I have ever heard. Most people don't even know who Gilbert and Sullivan are.'

Gina was starting to get angry now. 'Yes they do. Certainly more than know of Puccini! Anyway, I'm not aiming this at people who are that thick!'

'Even so, I'm sure you've got to make a lot of money. How much are you planning to charge? A hundred quid a ticket?'

'Yes.'

'Look, Gina, I know you're good at this sort of

thing, but how on earth are you going to raise what has to be a substantial amount, even charging that much for tickets? And how many people do you think are going to readily hand out a hundred pounds when we're in the middle of a recession? Be realistic.'

Gina couldn't believe this was her sister talking. She was always so upbeat and supportive. What had got into her? Surely Carmella hadn't taken over her brain?

'I do know about the recession – there's no need to be patronising – but there are plenty of rich people out there who are still prepared to pay that sort of money. They've hardly been affected by the recession. You know that.'

'And really rich people like Gilbert and Sullivan, do they? Strange you never read that in *Hello!* magazine. I thought opera would be more their thing.'

'If I had opera we'd have to pay the singers. Gilbert and Sullivan comes free.' Sally's attitude was really beginning to grate.

'Honestly, Gina, I don't think you've really thought this through. You think you can save the French House just by putting on a musical evening? It's ridiculous.'

Even Gina, who knew all the other things the evening was offering, felt it was a bit ridiculous, but she wasn't going to let her sister know that. 'I have to try!'

'Why? Who are these people who are more important than your sister?'

'Don't be silly. It's not like that.'

'Yes it is. If Carmella can't buy the French House I don't have a job.'

'Oh, for God's sake, Sal, Carmella can find another house to put her bloody shop in.'

'She can't, as a matter of fact. She's looked everywhere – all over the area – and can't find anywhere else suitable. That's when Yvette told her about the French House being about to go on the market.'

'So those bloody women have been plotting. I knew it.'

'What do you mean, plotting? It's all above board – Matthew owes Yvette money, has done for bloody ages, and now she wants it. She's setting up her own business in France. She and Carmella—'

Gina knew this all too well but she hated the fact that Sally seemed to be on the side of the enemy, using it as an excuse to see Matthew homeless and the French House forced to become yet another 'chic' boutique for the rich and idle.

'Will you shut up about Yvette and Carmella,' she practically shouted, really cross now. 'What those women are doing to Matthew—'

'Matthew? What about Matthew?'

'Sally, I told you! We went to France – we – you know—'

'Shagged each other's brains out? Well, bully for you. But Gina, I am your sister. If the French House isn't sold, I won't get my dream job.'

'It's Matthew's home – his business – his life!'

'I can't believe you're blowing me off for a man. You don't even like men. When you arrived down here it was all "Oh Sally, don't you dare matchmake" and now it's all "It's Matthew's home"! Get your priorities right, for fuck's sake!'

Gina drew in a sharp breath: she very rarely heard Sally use bad language; but this wasn't getting anyone anywhere. And Sally had a point. In the past there would never have been any question of her putting a man before her sister, and she hadn't told her how she really felt about Matthew. 'Look, calm down. I'll find somewhere else for Carmella to go.'

'What on earth makes you think you could? It's not as if she hasn't looked. Carmella wants to be in Cranmore-on-the-Green. It's perfect for her. And I want to work there too: it's near, it's convenient and it has a really good nursery.'

Sally was beginning to sound dangerously like her three-year-old daughters when they weren't getting what they wanted. This wasn't the Sally she knew and loved but this job obviously meant the world to her. 'No need to get upset. I'll find somewhere just as good, just as convenient—'

'Carmella used a professional search agency and they couldn't come up with anything,' Sally said petulantly. The resemblance to Sephie having a paddy was now uncanny.

'There might be things that have come on the market since then.'

Sally slumped in her chair. 'I need tea. This is so horrible. I thought you'd want me to have my dream job. It never occurred to me you'd do something as underhand as try to stop me.'

Gina slammed the kettle down on its stand having filled it with water. Their row had stopped her in her tea-making track. 'I'm not doing anything underhand!'

'Do you hate Carmella? Are you jealous of her? Is this because of Egan?'

'Egan? No. Why on earth should this be to do with Egan? Look, Rainey loved Matthew. Of course she did or why would she involve him in her will? She loved the centre. Otherwise why would she want us to take on her space? This is *family*, Sally!'

'No, actually,' Sally bit out the words, her eyes sparkling with anger or tears, '*I* am family! Your sister!'

Then she slammed out of the kitchen and out of the front door.

Gina felt sick all over again. She and Sally hadn't had a proper quarrel since they were teenagers. Her head was swimming and she wanted to cry only she couldn't. Her tears were all balled up in her chest and wouldn't come out. Then her phone rang, jolting her out of her stupor.

She answered it automatically. It was Nicholas.

'Darling girl, I think you should come over. Matthew's a bit upset.'

Chapter Twenty-Six

When Gina saw Matthew she felt Nicholas's description of 'a bit upset' was a huge understatement. Matthew seemed bigger and darker and chillingly controlled.

As soon as she'd arrived, Bernard had ushered Gina into the Orangery, where Matthew was waiting for her, so they could 'thrash out their differences alone', as Nicholas put it. Gina got the impression that if there was thrashing going on, Matthew would be the one doing it. If she'd thought him headmasterish when she first met him, it was nothing to how he came across now. What on earth had happened?

'What the fuck did you think you were doing?' he said, emphasising each word.

Gina had never heard him swear before and the unfamiliarity gave it terrifying impact. Two people she cared deeply about had sworn at her in the space of an hour. 'You obviously know,' she said, as calmly as she could and not allowing herself to flinch.

He went on in the same icy, relentless tone. 'Nicholas was one of my father's best and most loyal clients and now he is my client. You know how important his privacy is to him. I brought you here because I trusted you, assumed you would respect how he felt about his home, and now you've done this.'

Gina found she was shaking and couldn't tell if it was anger or nerves. Being accused for the second time of something appalling when actually she was only trying to do good, she found she couldn't be calm and soothing as she was trained to be. 'I haven't actually done anything,' she said, matching her tone to his. 'I have merely made a proposition and Nicholas agreed.'

'Well, you had absolutely no right. I gather you wanted to raise money to save my house. Well, it's my house, thank you very much, and if it's going to be saved, I'm the one to do it!'

'And what were you planning to do to save it? Anything? Or were you just going to sell the bloody thing – to the lowest bidder!'

'I don't think abusing the trust of a very old client and friend is the way to behave under any circumstances.' His look of disdain made her feel like a worm but she wasn't going to let him see that.

'Give me some credit,' she said. 'Obviously I asked Nicholas first. He's very happy to help.'

'Are you sure? Are you sure he really wants this thing or is he just indulging you?'

Suddenly she wasn't certain. Perhaps Nicholas *was* just indulging her, but she still felt insulted that

Matthew would think that she would let him without a thought for his welfare. Did he think so badly of her? 'He's a grown man – he's not going to do anything he doesn't want to do.'

'And when were you going to tell me about it?'

'Tonight! Or have you forgotten we have an *appointment*?'

'So why am I the last to know?'

She had been so excited by her plans and the thought of revealing them to Matthew. She might have known he'd throw cold water over them before she'd had a chance to tell him. Her resolve strengthened. They were good plans; Nicholas was keen – no matter what Matthew was implying. She'd help him even if she was beginning to wonder if he really deserved her help. Well, she'd do it for the other dealers and the memory of her Aunt Rainey.

'You're not the last to know,' she said, 'but I had to ask Nicholas first and then make sure that Andrew could do it. I haven't been in touch with sponsors yet, or with all the architectural societies who'd pay almost anything for a chance to look round this house.' She drew breath. 'But you know what? I wish I didn't have to mention it to you at all. You're so bloody negative. I'm doing this for you, you know.'

'I don't remember asking you to!' Matthew blazed back at her.

'You didn't ask me to. I decided to just do something because if I left things to you the French House would be sold, for peanuts, to a bitch of a woman who doesn't care who she stomps over to get what she wants. A bitch-woman who is in cahoots with your wife, I have to point out.'

'My *ex*-wife.'

'She won't truly be your *ex*-wife until you no longer owe her money and she stops hovering over you like a vulture, waiting for you to show weakness, so she can swoop in and tear you apart.'

He ignored this. 'What do you mean, Carmella is in cahoots with Yvette? And how on earth do you know?'

'You know she is. I told you about her visit that time. Well, it seems that Yvette could hardly wait to tell Carmella the French House was hers. She must have been on the phone the moment she left the restorer's. Why on earth you signed such a stupid divorce settlement is beyond me – such a gentleman, and now you might be thrown out on the street.' She had a horrible thought. 'Unless there's something you're not telling me – that you've put the house on the market already and it's a done deal?'

'Of course I haven't, but she's right,' he said, a little more quietly now. The anger was leaching out of him, leaving that air of exhausted misery that she had seen before. But Gina was too angry herself to let him get away with what he'd just said.

'God, why are you so defeatist? You're stuck in the

past, you're too sodding honourable to breathe and you will do fuck-nothing to help yourself. And then you accuse me of bullying your friend, when you know full well I'd never do anything to hurt Nicholas. You're an idiot, and I'm fed up with it!'

She turned around and strode out of the room, bumping straight into Nicholas, who managed to catch her without falling over.

'Little chat not going well?' he asked, holding her shoulders and looking down sympathetically.

Gina started to laugh – it was either that or cry. 'You could say that.'

'Matthew is a very proud man,' he said. 'He won't accept help easily.'

'Well, he doesn't need to accept mine, not any more. I'm done with him – as a person, as a colleague, in every possible way you can be done with someone.' Her desire to laugh was turning into a need to sob. Two major rows in twenty-four hours was more than she could stand. 'I'm going to say goodbye, Nicholas, and thank you. We're obviously not going to be having a Gilbert and Sullivan concert now.'

'Now wait a minute. It's time I stepped in. Bernard! Bring the champagne and then go and fetch Matthew. If he's escaped into the garden, get him back. We haven't heard a car so he must still be on the premises.'

Gina watched as Nicholas undid the wire on the bottle he had obviously had waiting for the moment. 'It's a bit early to start drinking, isn't it?'

'The joy of champagne, my dear girl, is that it is always the right time of day for it and eleven a.m. is absolutely perfect. Besides, I think you need a bit of a stiffener.'

Silently she agreed.

Bernard appeared with Matthew following. He was tight-lipped and unrepentant, Gina could tell. Only respect and fondness for Nicholas kept him in the room. Her too, for that matter. He reluctantly accepted a glass of champagne.

'Now,' said Nicholas when they all had glasses and Bernard had gone. 'I gather there has been a difference of opinion.'

'Yup,' said Matthew.

'And because I'm ancient and therefore infinitely wise, I would like to be the peacemaker.'

'You'll have a job on your hands,' said Gina. She sipped her drink and glowered at Matthew over her glass.

'There has been a misunderstanding,' Nicholas went on. 'But that doesn't mean a bit of explaining couldn't make everything all right again.'

Gina wished she had the same confidence in him that Nicholas appeared to have in himself; she thought it would take more than a very charming and endearing old man to melt the icy disapproval and disdain that was coming off Matthew in almost-visible waves.

'The plan is,' said Nicholas, 'to have a travelling concert. Now, Matthew, listen to me.' He put up a hand. 'You can have your say at the end. I know you want to protect me and I love you for it but I'm not such a frail old bird that I can't think for myself. I haven't felt this energised in years.' He beamed at Gina and she couldn't help feeling deep affection wash over her.

'So,' Nicholas went on, 'each room will have its own musical event, and people will go from one to the other. For example' – he made a sweeping gesture which indicated just how enormous was the room they were currently in – 'here we could have quite a chorus – maybe half a dozen singers – a couple of musicians and room for what, fifty guests?'

'That many?' asked Gina. This was good news. She felt her spirits lift a little. Matthew glowered but kept silent. At least he hadn't started ranting again.

'Oh yes. In my mother's day we used to have parties for three hundred people.' Nicholas said this in a casual way that indicated a certain amount of pride. 'And from here,' he went on, leading them across the vast expanse to some double doors that led into another reception room of equal size and magnificence, 'our guests would move on to something of equal charm. I love Gilbert and Sullivan, don't you?' he said to Matthew. 'I know it's considered lowbrow but really, the music is so charming and the words so clever.'

He led them about the house describing how he pictured it all happening – often using words and expressions that Gina had used when she had been trying to convince him it was a good idea. She could have hugged him. They ended up in the Orangery. Gina had pictured this full of fairy lights – slightly reminiscent of Sally's Christmas garage – although she doubted if Sally would let her borrow her lights now they had quarrelled.

'. . . So you see how utterly lovely it could all be,' said Nicholas at last, obviously completely enchanted by the idea himself.

'What I don't quite understand,' said Matthew after a few agonising moments of silence, 'is why you're willing to do this when you've been so intent on keeping your house secret for all these years.'

'Well, I'll tell you what it is. When Gina came and told me her vision and I saw it all through her young eyes I thought, Why don't I let anyone share in the beauty of this house?' Nicholas said.

'I understand that you might be willing to share it with a few chosen people, who'll appreciate the architecture and the history – but why all this carry-on?'

'Do you know? I think I prefer to have people who

won't particularly appreciate the architecture, but who just think how beautiful, how special and what a treat the evening is.'

Matthew was still unconvinced. 'I'm not sure I really believe you. It'll be such a major intrusion.'

'Ah, but you see, Gina promised me she would wear the Dress!' Nicholas beamed, and there could be no doubting his sincerity.

There was another excruciating pause.

Matthew looked at his friend, and then down at her, his expression completely unreadable. 'If she can get into it!'

Gina narrowed her eyes at him, aware this was his way of saying he had forgiven her to some extent. 'You're forgetting that Lady Mary was pregnant when the portrait was painted.'

'And it can always be let out a little more,' Matthew went on, raising one eyebrow.

Gina practically snarled at him, but inside, she was rejoicing.

'If you two want to do something so bonkers, I can't stop you. But it is a completely mad idea, you know that,' he went on.

'All the best ideas are!' said Nicholas with a flourish. 'All is well in paradise again. Shall we have another bottle?'

Gina laughed. 'No, thank you. I must go. But thank you so, so much!' She put her arms round his neck and kissed him.

Only slightly taken aback he said, 'Well, you did bring me chocolate cake – it seemed the least I could do.'

Matthew and Gina left the house together, on speaking terms if not yet quite on the terms they had been on in France.

'I wondered where that cake had come from,' said Matthew, as they got outside.

'I think I want to marry Nicholas,' said Gina, ignoring the cake remark. 'Do you think he's gay?'

Matthew laughed. 'You keep your hands off him! He's a poor old man and you've put him to enough trouble. And he's not gay.'

'I was only joking!' She became serious. 'I am really sorry I didn't run the whole thing past you first but I never thought Nicholas would agree to it. If he hadn't been keen I would have forgotten the whole thing. I didn't want you to worry for nothing.'

He looked down at her again, fond but stern. 'I'm sorry I was so brutal – I was worried about Nicholas and with everything that's gone on . . . just don't ever do anything like that behind my back again, please? And I'm not saying I like the idea of you doing this for me. I still think it's my problem, to sort myself, but I don't think we can convince Nicholas to back out now – I've never seen him so excited.' He looked thoughtful for a moment. 'And don't go offering yourself in marriage to anyone either, just because they are kind and enormously wealthy.' He opened her car door and pushed her into it.

Once seated she wound down the window. 'I'm not making any promises about that, Matthew,' she said, and shot off in a shower of gravel.

Chapter Twenty-Seven

Gina was immensely cheered that she and Matthew were friends again, although she wondered when they'd be lovers again too. However, her main concern now was her row with Sally.

She wasn't ready to forgive Sally for what seemed like a major betrayal, yet felt she had to do *something* to make things right for her if she could. She had one friend who might be able to help. If he couldn't, she'd let Sally and Carmella and Yvette sort it out for themselves.

As it was the quickest of the many tasks she had on the mental list she had begun at Nicholas's house, she did it first. Still in her coat, she found her phone and went through her contacts.

'Is that the best property search consultant in the whole wide world?' she began.

'Is that the very best schmoozer and flatterer in the whole wide world?'

'It might be. But only if you are indeed the best.' Gina found herself smiling. It was lovely to be talking to an old friend.

'You know I am. And that's why you're ringing me after months of silence. How's your cottage?'

'Oh Dan, it's bliss, and it's bliss to talk to you too. I need some help . . .' She went on to describe Carmella's requirements in detail and then added, 'But if you come across a property called the French House – not yet on the market—'

'Nothing I find is yet on the market, sweetheart. It's how I operate.'

'Well, it's not for sale. If you could find its clone, that would be perfect, but the French House is spoken for.'

'OK. So who is my client? And who is paying my fee?'

'Can we just leave that for a bit? You will get paid somehow. It's all a bit up in the air . . .'

'Not like you to be so vague.' Dan sounded surprised.

'I know, but I just haven't had time to work out the details yet.'

Fortunately he seemed to accept this.

They talked for a while about what they'd both been up to and then Gina disconnected. Dan really was a genius at finding property for people. That done, Gina made a proper list. It was horribly long.

She sent an email to a selected group of people and was gratified to get one back from Anthea, the auctioneer. She telephoned almost immediately afterwards.

'I can't believe you're putting on an event at Fairfield Manor!' she said the moment Gina answered. 'I've been trying to get myself through those doors for years. And so has my mother-in-law. You can put us down for at least six tickets, but she might want more. Such a coup – getting her friends in there.'

'Oh, I am glad you're so keen. We'll need plenty of enthusiasm if we're going to raise enough money.' The moment she'd spoken she realised she shouldn't have said that. Her professionalism had been knocked off balance by recent events. Matthew might not want anyone else to know what the event was actually in aid of.

'What are you raising money for?' asked Anthea, unaware that Gina had made a gaff.

Gina looked at her watch. 'Actually, Anthea, would you be up for a quick meeting? In town? Are you free?'

'I could be free and I'm already in town. What time would be good for you?'

'I'm meeting Matthew at four.' He hadn't cancelled so she assumed this was still on.

'Three o'clock then?' said Anthea.

As she sat across from Anthea at a table in the café around the corner from her office, it occurred to Gina that auctioneers probably needed counselling skills, at least sometimes.

'What's up, Gina? I presume from the urgency you didn't just want a girly catch-up.'

Gina thought for a moment. Now she was here should she confide in Anthea? She needed another woman to talk to, someone she trusted. Her brief acquaintance told her Anthea was such a woman. 'I know we don't know each other very well but I need an ear,' she said. 'I'd ring my mum but as it's about my sister, I can't really do that.'

'Oh, families. Who'd have 'em? Come on, give. You'll feel better for it.'

Gina did feel much better having told Anthea all about her row with Sally and she appreciated that Anthea saw both sides but didn't judge.

Anthea had proved such a good listener she'd ended up telling her about the real reason behind the event and her determination to help save the French House. She didn't go into all the details about why Matthew had to sell – she didn't feel it was her place to wash his dirty linen in public – but Anthea was sympathetic and thought it was in a good cause. She thought everyone would be so keen to see inside the house they wouldn't care if it was 'save the bankers' they were contributing to.

'I know it will be all right eventually,' Gina said, 'especially if I can find somewhere else for Carmella to go. Mostly we get on really, really well; we're there for each other. But now suddenly, when I really need her, she's not.'

'And you need her to help you with this Gilbert and Sullivan thing?'

'Not so much practically but for support, you know? I'm not convinced that even if we charge a fortune, sell every ticket and really cram them in, we'll raise enough.'

'Have you thought of having an auction in the middle of the evening? Have a supper break, make sure they've had plenty to drink and you'd be surprised what people are willing to pay for things.'

'Tell me more.' Gina sat up, her enthusiasm beginning to return. Perhaps it wasn't too ambitious after all.

Anthea flung out a hand. 'Nothing to it. I've done loads of them. I'll do it for you too if you want. You have to make sure the lots are really attractive gift items. You know, jewellery, sports memorabilia . . .'

'I've got you. And away days, and treats, like theatre tickets, helicopter trips, things like that.' Gina's enthusiasm dwindled again. 'Only nothing we have to pay for. I can probably drum up a few free items but not a whole auction's worth.'

'Why don't you skip that part and just stick to selling things?'

Gina nodded. 'I'll think about it. But we'd definitely like the auction and it would be wonderful if you could do it for us.' Matthew and Nicholas couldn't possibly object, could they?

'I'd be happy to,' said Anthea. 'And don't worry

about Sally. She loves you just as much as you love her. It'll be sorted out soon, I'm sure.'

Gina wasn't quite as sure as Anthea that she and Sally would sort out their issues. Nor was she certain of her welcome as she made her way up to the office to see Matthew at four.

'Hi!' she said breezily as she entered his office. 'How are you?'

Matthew looked up, his expression customarily serious, but then he smiled. 'Currently I'm fine. Just waiting for the other shoe to drop.'

'What do you mean?'

'I'm just wondering if there's anything else you want to tell me – confess, even.'

She laughed. 'You are suspicious.' But she realised to her relief he was teasing her again.

'Hmm. Tea or a drink?'

'Neither, thanks. I've just had tea with Anthea. Don't let me stop you though.'

'And what did Anthea have to say? I take it you didn't just meet her for a gossip?'

It was now or never. 'Never let it be said that I don't learn from my mistakes,' she said. 'Anthea suggested we have an auction in the middle of the evening. She said it would raise extra money.' Gina looked as innocent as she could. 'But I wondered how we'd source the right sort of stuff without spending more than we'd make.'

'And what did Anthea think the right sort of stuff was?' He was either deliberately ignoring her hint or genuinely didn't realise what she was trying to get at.

'Gifty things. Jewellery, memorabilia, the sort of things people might buy for their wives or girlfriends – or husbands, I suppose – if they've had a few glasses of champagne.'

'I see. Tell me, Gina, how is this extravaganza going to make money? I get that we charge for tickets and the music is free – more or less. But you'll have to feed people, give them champagne and all the extras or they won't pay enough for the tickets. I don't think a paying bar is appropriate.'

At least he was talking to her as if it was a viable proposition. That was a start. 'Absolutely, I agree with you. Once people have paid for their vastly expensive ticket it will all be free. And of course we have to get caterers in. This isn't the sort of thing we can do ourselves.' She saw his expression change. 'What?'

'This probably isn't useful at all but there's a residential catering college not far away. Knowing you, you might be able to sweet-talk them into doing the catering more cheaply than professional caterers.'

Gina had her notebook out before she drew breath. This was even more promising – Matthew was actually giving her some help. She leant forward in her chair. 'Address? I'll get on to them. That could save loads of money. Thank you for the heads-up.' She could afford to be gracious now she no longer felt she was in the headmaster's office about to be chastised.

Matthew looked at her. 'I know you probably don't believe it,' he said wryly, 'given that I live in the past and am a very negative person, but I am actually on your side in this, now I'm convinced that Nicholas really likes the idea.' His self-mocking expression faded and once again his face became unreadable. 'I'm touched that you want to help me so much but I'm sure you could devote your talents to a better cause.'

A better cause? What did he think their time – their glorious, loving time – in France had meant to her? Had it meant nothing to him? No, that wasn't possible; she wasn't that poor a judge of people.

'Matthew, I—'

His phone went and he stayed Gina with his hand. 'Sorry, I need to take this, I'm expecting a call.' He answered then put his hand over the receiver. 'Americans, I've got to plan a buying trip for them. Look, I'll sort the items for the auction, don't worry.' He smiled and then returned to his call, 'Hello, Bob, yes, just need the dates . . .'

Gina quietly left the room, went back to her car and drove home. Bloody phones! Yet again a call had interrupted a critical moment. If mobiles had never been invented she might have got to the bottom of what was going on in his head by now.

Chapter Twenty-Eight

The following morning, she had just made an appointment to visit the principal of the catering college later that day when she had a call from Dan, her property-search contact.

'Dan? That was quick! Surely you haven't found somewhere already?'

'Well, nothing is ever certain,' said Dan, 'but I think I may have found the perfect location. It's not actually on the market yet, and it isn't actually a shop.'

'Oh Dan.' This didn't sound as if it was suitable at all.

'Trust me. It's got a change of use to become a commercial premises and the town is fantastic.' He gave her a bit more detail and mentioned one of the larger claimants to the title 'Queen of the Cotswolds' – Middleford.

Gina gasped. It must be perfect after all. 'That sounds amazing! Is there a link? I can't wait to have a look.'

'Not on the net yet. You could do a drive-by though and take some pictures on your phone. It's a winner,

I'm sure. I had a look at the French House and this is very similar. Same period, more or less, and a bit smaller but in a great position.'

'I really hope you're right.' Gina was worried about the 'bit smaller' aspect.

'I am right. I'm an expert.' He gave her the address. 'Now you go and take some pics and print them up on decent paper. I can email some details and a floor plan. This woman will bite your hand off for it.'

'Can I put her in touch with you if she's interested?'

'Yup.'

When she'd disconnected she looked at Google Maps and found Middleford wasn't far from the catering college. She could do her drive-by after her meeting. She noted that the town was far nearer the M4 than Cranmore-on-the-Green. It could indeed be a much more commercial prospect.

As she ate some toast for lunch she thought of ringing Sally. She hated them not speaking. But then she decided to check out the alternative premises first. If it was perfect and Carmella liked it she could say sorry to Sally and present the solution at the same time.

Matthew had phoned to say he was going to be away for a few days, at another antiques fair. She quelled the disappointment that he hadn't asked her to go with him but she couldn't spare the time anyway. She had too much to do.

She missed Matthew desperately, the way they'd been in France, but couldn't see a way to bridge the gap. He had withdrawn from her – she didn't know why – while she found her feelings had become stronger. She'd never felt this way about a man before – this aching, yearning feeling, and it was pathetic. She'd been self-sufficient all these years; she couldn't let herself become a needy female now. Especially when she wasn't sure if he'd retreated because it had been a brief fling he was now regretting, or because he was so preoccupied and just couldn't concentrate on more than one thing at a time, or even because he thought he wasn't the right person for her. What was that he had said when they got back from France – something about not being a good prospect?

Her thoughts sped on. Was he letting her go ahead with this event just to humour her and Nicholas or did he really hope it would help him out? Was he desperate and therefore now willing to let someone else help him at last? *She just didn't know.*

And it wasn't that he wasn't friendly, but their easy intimacy had gone. Until the Yvette issue was resolved, Gina felt they would never be free of her and her looming influence. She was casting an ominous shadow over both their lives and she hated it.

She shook herself mentally. She couldn't answer all these questions while he was away, and she had work to do. At least Egan had returned her money, which was something. She realised just how low her own bank account had got. It would at least keep body and soul together if not her heart.

She went to her meeting with the catering college with her shoulders back and her negotiating skills sharper than ever. She came out an hour later hugely impressed, very pleased with the deal and with a contact for a local wine merchant.

But even with a truly fabulous venue and entertainment for nothing, the food and wine would have to be paid for even if nobody came. However, persuading people to come to events and bring their friends was what she was good at. She just had to keep the faith!

Three days later she had her phone in her hand, her finger hovering over a number. Then she pressed it and put the phone to her ear, waiting for it to be answered.

'Is that Carmella Romera? Hello. It's Gina Makepiece.'

There was a tiny pause and Gina pictured a perfect eyebrow rising in surprise – just as far as the Botox permitted. 'Yes?'

'I have something I'd like to talk to you about. Can we meet?' She could be short and to the point too.

'Is this about the French House?' Carmella asked suspiciously.

'No.' It wasn't, directly. 'But I think you'll be interested.'

The pause was longer this time. 'Very well. If you can be at Le Bistro in town for about half past six, I'll meet you there.'

And so here she was, walking up from the car park in her favourite silk dress, slightly unsteady in heels which weren't designed for outdoor use, towards a brightly lit bar and restaurant. She could see Carmella by the bar from across the street.

'Hi!' she said as she came in.

It was only as she reached Carmella that she saw Egan. She cursed herself for not realising he'd be there. Of course he would! He was Carmella's partner.

But she was the one who had something she needed them to agree to, so she smiled politely and hoisted herself on to a stool, pleased she managed to do so without flailing around for something to hold on to.

'What can I get you?' asked Egan. 'We're drinking Bellinis.'

'How very Venetian of you!' said Gina, forestalling Egan's inevitable description of the drink. He always thought he knew more than anyone else did and it was intensely boring. 'Just sparkling water for me.' She smiled, determined to be completely detached and professional.

'So, why have you called this meeting?' asked Carmella. 'You say it's not about the French House?'

'No. Nor scent bottles.' Gina hooked her bag

round and took out the file. 'I have a property that might interest you.' She held on to the file, ignoring Egan's outstretched hand. This was nothing to do with him.

'Why do you think I would be interested in property?' asked Carmella. 'I have my plans in place.'

Just as Gina had taken a breath to deliver her spiel, her drink arrived. She took a re-energising sip.

'You're a businesswoman,' she began, 'and while you obviously have artistic interests, you really want your business to be successful. For that to happen, you need the perfect venue.'

'I have my venue and while nothing is perfect, it is the best available. And such a bargain price.' Carmella's eyes glittered in delight.

Gina took another sip to regroup. 'Have a look at this.'

'What is it?' asked Egan.

'The most desirable retail space in the country. Once you've looked at that you will think the French House isn't quite as good as it seems – rather small rooms, difficult to alter because of its listing, not really near enough to London.'

She handed over her envelope and then tried to control her breathing.

It took Carmella an agonisingly long time to peruse those few sheets of paper. Thanks to Dan, Gina had managed to get a fairly good description of the principal rooms, she had a floor plan and a list of other shops in the area. But there wasn't a lot of material – not nearly enough, Gina felt.

'Well,' Carmella said eventually, just as Gina thought she would have to demand an answer or threaten her in some way. 'It is a very lovely property and in many ways it would be just perfect.'

The 'but' hung in the air like a neon sign.

'There's just one teeny tiny problem—'

'I'm sure it's nothing that can't be sorted,' said Gina, all her PR positivity to the fore.

'I doubt if you can do anything about it being leasehold,' said Carmella.

'But why is that a problem?' Gina was baffled. 'It's a ninety-nine-year lease or something.'

Carmella shook her head. 'I only ever buy freehold.'

Gina made a mental note to see if it was possible to turn a property that was leasehold into one that was freehold, but she wasn't optimistic. It would probably have needed to happen ninety-nine years previously.

'It is such a beautiful building,' she said out loud, trying not to sound desperate. 'It makes the French House seem so – so ordinary!' She had picked the word deliberately and saw Carmella react to it. To one with such a sense of style as Carmella it was a damning description. Mentally she crossed her fingers. It had to work. So much depended on it. Not least, her relationship with Sally.

She caught movement from out of the corner of her eye. Had that grey, loping shape been Oscar? She didn't know, and she had to concentrate on Carmella making the right decision. Deliberately she relaxed her fingers – they were revealing her desperation.

'No, I don't think so,' said Carmella decisively, shutting the file but holding on to it.

Throughout it all Egan had sat there quietly. It indicated clearly who was the dominant partner. It made things a bit easier. She wouldn't have wanted to deal with two of them. She also was obscurely pleased to see Egan powerless again. Seeing him sitting passively on his stool underlined his utter irrelevance in her new life. She was – as she had been protesting for so long – finally over him.

'I will keep these details if you don't mind,' Carmella went on, 'in case by some remote chance I can't buy the French House, but I don't think anyone, with any sense of style at all, could refer to that fine old listed building as *ordinary*.'

Honesty forced Gina to agree. She nodded, deciding there was nothing to be gained by staying. She'd done her best. She shot out her arm and said, 'Ooh, is that the time? Sorry. Got to go.' She pulled her coat off the stool but didn't take time to put it on.

She was out of the building before Carmella could notice she wasn't actually wearing a watch. She hurried down the road, hampered by her heels, and as she rounded the corner she saw him. Matthew. So it had been Oscar she'd spotted. Matthew was looking in a shop window while Oscar sniffed. 'Wait!' she called, panting hard.

He turned. She ran up to him and put her hand on his arm. 'So lovely to see you.'

'Hey! Are you OK?'

'Fine,' she muttered. 'Do you have a moment? Can I come home with you?'

'Of course,' he said. 'But put your coat on, do. You'll get cold.'

She did this and then hooked her arm in his and, for the time it took them to reach the French House, all seemed right with the world.

But by the time they'd got upstairs and Gina was sitting hunched by the fire while Matthew fed Oscar, her recent failure dimmed her joy at being with Matthew again.

He handed her a glass of wine. 'What's up? What were you running away from?' He frowned. 'Not that bastard ex-boyfriend of yours again?'

'No. He was there but this wasn't to do with him.' She thought for a moment. She'd better tell him. He'd told her never to go behind his back again. Did this qualify? 'I went to meet Carmella. Egan was there too but he was irrelevant.'

'And why were you meeting Carmella?'

She didn't need to look at him to sense his disapproval. She suddenly had the feeling that he always thought the worst of her. Well, she wasn't going to lie to him. 'I was trying to convince her to buy another property instead of the French House.' There, she'd said it.

'Oh?'

Just a single syllable and he could condemn her.

'I thought if she had another property Yvette wouldn't nag her to buy the French House which might take the pressure off you a bit.' Why did her genuine and perfectly logical efforts to help seem like interfering and busybodyish? Why did he make her feel she was in the wrong? If it hadn't been for her, he'd probably have sold the French House weeks ago.

'I can deal with my own pressure, thank you.' He sounded clipped.

'Really?' Gina choked back anger that was mixed with tears. She was doing her very best to save his house. He didn't seem to be doing much about it.

'Yes. And what was the property?'

She gave him as many details as she could remember.

'I know it,' he said. 'Not all that suitable, I wouldn't have thought.'

Silently she cursed him for being so knowledgeable but then realised of course he would know all the important historic houses in the area. 'I think it would make an excellent shop,' she said, stubbornly. 'Just what Carmella needs.'

'I'm not saying it couldn't be converted but if

Carmella wants to be here, Middleford isn't going to attract her.'

'Why not? It's handier for London and so should do far better trade.'

'But I thought Sally wanted to supply Carmella?'

Gina frowned. 'How do you know that?'

'She came in when I was flying out of the door with my Americans.'

Gina felt a little relieved. She couldn't bear the thought of Sally and Matthew talking about her.

'She was checking on your cabinet. She told me she was better at creating new things really and hoped Carmella would sell them. If Carmella moved to Middleford, it would be quite a bit further for her to travel.'

Gina wanted to kick herself. She had been so thrilled that Dan had tracked down a property so quickly that she hadn't thought about Sally needing somewhere near her home. And while Middleford probably had nurseries, it wouldn't work if Alaric had to drive miles to pick them up. She had been so stupid she just wanted to howl. 'Sally and I aren't speaking. Did she tell you that too?'

He frowned. 'No. And why aren't you?'

Gina sighed deeply. 'I don't want to go into it. I thought finding a property for Carmella might fix it but obviously not.'

'You can't solve all the problems of the world, you know. It's very sweet of you to try but—'

Gina hated to be patronised more than anything. 'I know that. I'm leaving world peace and famine to the big boys. I'm just trying to tackle a failing business – because I care about it and the people who work in it.'

'I deeply resent that. It's not a failing business!' He glared at her.

'Not since I had anything to do with it, no.' She got up and put down her wine glass still half full.

'Gina, honestly, this really isn't your problem.'

She didn't dare answer. She was too angry. Couldn't he see? Why must he throw her help back in her face each time? She thought she'd been making progress. 'I'd better go. I've got a lot on tomorrow.'

'That is probably for the best. I've a lot of paperwork I need to do.'

'I'm sure.' She buttoned up her coat which she hadn't got round to taking off.

'But I don't want us to part on bad terms,' he said, standing now. He reached out to take her hands but she folded them round her bag and stepped away.

'We could get something to eat – start the evening again?' he tried. But it was too late.

'No. We're both tired and busy. I'll just go home.'

As she made her way out of the flat she willed him to follow her, to take her in his arms and kiss her until she forgot about Carmella, the row with her sister and the whole Fairfield Manor event, which was giving her so much work and was so high risk. But he didn't.

She was in a comforting, candlelit bath when Nicholas rang her. God, what now? If he pulled out now it would be such a disaster not even she would be able to think of a way round it.

Fortunately he was in buoyant mood. 'Dearest, I wonder if you could put me in touch with the director of music for our evening. I just want to make sure they have as much rehearsal time as they need. I'm rather thinking that if this is a success we could make it a regular event . . .'

Even though her bath was cold when she got back to it Gina felt her resolve return. Nicholas's call had been just what she needed. She could do this; she'd show them all, most importantly Matthew. And she still wanted to marry Nicholas. He was so positive. If only everyone were like him, the world would be so much more fun!

Chapter Twenty-Nine

Gina made an excuse to go and visit Nicholas the following morning. She told herself – and him – that it was to reassure him in person that all would be well. But she knew it was because he would cheer her up.

'How lovely!' Nicholas said when Bernard escorted her to where he was contemplating a large Spanish chest. 'I need your advice. Do you think we should move this out of here?'

'Absolutely not!' The chest was enormous, probably worth the price of a large family car and would be very difficult to shift. 'Why are you even contemplating doing so?'

Nicholas shrugged. 'Well, most of the other things in here could be described loosely as chinoiserie and I thought it would be rather charming to have songs from *The Mikado* in here.'

Gina nodded, wondering just how much trouble she'd be in with Matthew if Nicholas started shifting extremely valuable antiques as if they were stage props. She'd get the full-blown lecture about heritage being ruined and a frail old man put in danger, even though Nicholas knew his own mind and knew exactly what he wanted and how to get it. 'But it looks lovely in here. It goes fine with everything else, there's no need to move it.'

Nicholas nodded. 'Good. I'm so glad I asked your opinion.'

But as he led her from room to room asking what she would suggest she realised she was a bit out of her depth. She was just contemplating a charming little window embrasure that Nicholas wanted a duet in when she had a thought. 'The person we really need to help us with this is my sister.'

'Oh? And is your sister handy?'

Gina laughed but without conviction. 'Well, she's not very far away but she has baggage – namely two small daughters. And worse than that, we're currently not speaking.'

'My dear!' Nicholas was horrified. 'And is this a common occurrence? Are you often at outs with her?'

Gina shook her head. 'Never – hardly ever – and it's horrible. I tried to put it right but couldn't.'

'You mean she didn't accept your apology?'

'No. I didn't apologise, I just tried to take away the cause of the conflict.' She sighed deeply. 'We were both in the wrong, I suppose. It's not that I mind saying sorry – even if I don't believe it was my fault – but I don't know how to start. Because we never quarrel, this is all new to me.'

'If you don't mind taking advice from an old man . . .'

'I'd love advice,' said Gina quickly, hoping this didn't look as if she thought he was an old man and thereby causing offence.

Nicholas patted her arm. 'Ask for her help. Tell her we need her here. She'll be flattered, I'm sure, and very willing to forgive anything you did wrong.' He paused. 'What did you do, exactly?'

Gina grimaced. 'Doing, rather. I'm trying to stop the French House from being sold.' Nicholas knew most of this, if not every detail. 'She wants the person buying it to have it so she can work in the shop – and create objets d'art for it.' She frowned. 'I think that's what you'd call them.'

'Ah. I see your difficulty. You're both in the right really. One of you will have to give up what you want because your needs conflict.'

Gina nodded. 'It's a lose-lose situation,' she said, trying to sound lighthearted.

'I still think my solution might work. Go forth and do your best.'

As Gina walked across the expanse of gravel to her car she couldn't help feeling that Nicholas was enjoying the situation more and more. He did seem to be relishing his role as agony aunt. And he was certainly loving the thought of having his house, which he'd kept private for so long, thrown into the spotlight. Gina wondered how long it would be before it was featured in all the house-and-garden magazines with Nicholas lounging in a velvet jacket against one of the more magnificent fireplaces.

Then, without giving herself a chance to think about it too deeply, she set off towards Sally's house.

Losing her nerve a bit, she stopped at a local Spar and bought posh biscuits, fancy yoghurts the girls could ingest without the aid of a spoon, some wine and a large box of chocolates. If Sally wouldn't see her at least she could take it all back to Nicholas and they could comfort-eat in style. Although she realised Nicholas would dismiss her wine with a shudder and have something lovely brought up from the cellar.

She knew all these random thoughts that filled her head were displacement for what she should really be concentrating on: what to say to Sally.

No script appeared in her head and, just after she'd knocked at Sally's front door, she decided she'd simply say whatever seemed right at the time. It didn't help that Alaric answered.

'Oh,' he said, obviously at a loss too.

'Hello. Is Sally in?' Gina felt as if she was knocking on the door of a friend and asking if she could come out to play, only was unsure of her welcome.

Alaric didn't answer immediately, probably unaware that every second was making Gina feel worse and worse. 'Er – yeah – I'll get her.'

He didn't ask her to come in and Gina didn't know if this was deliberate or if he just assumed she would follow him in. She stayed on the doorstep, clutching her presents, on the verge of tears. Supposing Alaric came back saying Sally didn't want to see her?

After what seemed a very long time Sally appeared. She seemed to look older than when Gina had last seen her and she stared at Gina for a few seconds. 'What are you doing on the doorstep?' she said.

'I didn't know if you'd want me to come into the house.' Gina heard her voice crack and cleared her throat.

'Oh, don't be so silly! Come in.' But she spoke more with irritation than enthusiasm.

As Gina went in she felt as if Sally were the sister in charge, and as she was the elder, this felt wrong. She had hoped, and expected, that Sally would open her arms to her, they would hug and cry and everything would be better, but it wasn't happening like that. She followed Sally into the kitchen, which was exceptionally tidy.

'Where are the girls?' Gina asked.

'Nursery,' said Sally.

'Oh. I bought them squashy yoghurt and you these flowers, and biscuits and wine. Bit early for the wine though.'

Sally looked her in the eye for the first time. 'Shame.'

Gina nodded. 'We could have tea and biscuits though.'

Sally put the kettle on.

'So, what have you been up to?' said Gina, having seated herself at the kitchen table.

'Cleaning mostly.'

'Why?' Gina was amazed. While Sally wasn't slovenly, cleaning was never her first priority. As long as her house wasn't a health hazard she usually had something more interesting to do with the time she didn't spend looking after her daughters.

Sally shrugged and then sighed, turning to face her sister. 'Actually, I've been so miserable I haven't been able to do anything creative. There's only cleaning left.'

'Why miserable?' said Gina, carefully.

'Because I've fallen out with you, dork!'

Then they were in each other's arms, hugging and crying and patting each other.

'I've been so unhappy!' they both said at once.

'I've tried really hard to make things right,' said Gina.

'Have you?' said Sally. 'I didn't notice.' But there wasn't a trace of anger left in her voice.

'Silly! I tried to find Carmella another premises so she could have her shop and you could have your job and the French House could stay as it is.'

'Really? That's amazing!' A few crumbs escaped as Sally enthused.

'Yes, but don't get too excited, I failed.'

'Oh.'

Gina sighed. 'The other shop had a lot going for it. Further away from here, sadly, so not as perfect for you, but it should have been good for Carmella. Slightly nearer the centre of the universe, too. I mean the M4,' she added.

'What a shame. I do understand why you want to keep the French House as an antiques centre, especially now you and Matthew seem to be making a go of things.'

Another sigh escaped Gina.

'Don't tell me you've split up while my back was turned?' said Sally, outraged.

'I don't know, Sal. We haven't seen much of each other. We've both been busy. You know how it is.' She didn't like to admit how things were – or rather weren't – between Matthew and her right now.

Sally looked at Gina. 'Hm. I thought when you first get together you can't keep your hands off each other.'

Gina made a little gesture. 'Well, it's not like that for everyone. At least, not for Matthew.' Then, because she knew her sister loved being an agony aunt even more than Nicholas did, and, unlike Nicholas, wouldn't hold back if she felt Gina was in the wrong, she went on. 'Actually, Sally, I really need your help. Not with Matthew.' She gave a little 'as if!' laugh. 'It's with this event I'm arranging. The massive fund-raiser for the French House – Gilbert and Sullivan. You know, the event you despised.'

'I never said that . . .'

Clutching fresh cups of tea and more biscuits, Gina filled Sally in.

* * *

'God, I'm so glad you two are friends again,' said Alaric a little while later, 'it's been bloody hell here.'

'It has been awful,' Gina agreed. 'I'm so proud of everything Sally does, I felt dreadful standing in the way of her big chance. She's so ace the way she fits it all in round you and the girls.'

Sally didn't speak but put her hand on Gina's. 'I didn't know you felt like that,' she said after a few moments.

'Of course I do!' Gina got up and they hugged again.

'I'm going to open some baked beans,' said Alaric. 'I think you two need food.'

'And I'm really proud of you, too!' said Sally. 'You've really got behind the antiques thing and now this event – it sounds amazing.'

'I hope it is. After lunch' – Gina sent a grateful smile towards her brother-in-law who was tipping beans into a saucepan – 'I'll take you to meet Nicholas. He'll love you, and you can advise us as to what should go where.'

'Oh God, I'm so excited,' said Sally. 'Shall I open the wine?'

'No. We have work to do.'

'Bloody hell, Gines. It's like Chatsworth has relocated to the Cotswolds.'

Gina chuckled. She and Sally were negotiating Fairfield Manor's impressive drive. 'I know what you mean but it's nothing like as big.'

'And no one knew it was here?'

'They knew about it but Nicholas has never let anyone look over it before.'

Sally shook her head in amazement. 'I have to say, I knew you were good, but snaffling this venue has to be your best yet.'

'I know. The house is amazing, but getting this event to actually make money is going to be tough.'

'Why? The house is free, the entertainment is free, you've only got to pay for the food and wine.' Sally was back to her old optimistic self.

Gina pulled up in front of the house and turned off the engine. 'Yup. And advertising, and insurance, and loos: all those little extras that send your overheads up like a rocket. I'm not sure we can do it, frankly.'

Sally gave her sister a sharp dig in the arm with her elbow. 'Of course you can. Now come and get me shown round this gaff.'

Just having Sally on side did make Gina feel much more positive and she loved watching Nicholas showing off his home to a very appreciative Sally. As Gina followed the two of them, making expansive plans for doing the Balcony Scene from *Romeo and Juliet* – just so they could take advantage of a very handsome specimen – she felt a lot more positive.

She had suppressed Sally's and Nicholas's more extravagant plans, taken note of Sally's other, very good suggestions and driven Sally home when her phone rang. Her heart leapt when she saw Matthew's name appear. She made herself let the phone ring a couple of times before she pressed the button.

'Hi,' she said, trying to make her voice sound relaxed but pleased to hear from him rather than desperately overexcited. Her ache for him hadn't diminished. It was like a dull headache, always there, always interfering with what she was doing. He had sent her a couple of texts since they last saw each other, but always work-related – did she want to pay Bill fifty quid for his latest auction bargains, things like that – but he had sometimes added a cross indicating he didn't actually hate her. If he asked her out now, she'd say yes like a shot.

'How are you?' he said.

She could tell from his voice that he was going to say something she wasn't going to like. 'Fine. Busy. You?' Please don't let him start telling her off again. She couldn't bear it.

'Gina, I've got to go to Edinburgh for a while.'

'Why?' She felt instantly abandoned.

'An old friend of my father's has just died. He was an antiques dealer and his wife wants me to help her sort through the stock. Sort everything really.'

'Right.' She tried to sound bland, as if it didn't matter to her one way or another that he was going away, leaving her to run a massive event – entirely for his benefit – without even his moral support, let alone any actual assistance.

'I'm terribly sorry,' he said, as if reading her mind. 'There is a good side to it. We'll get whatever pieces we want and at a good price. I'd go out of kindness for my father, but it's good business too.'

'Good.'

'And I'll be back in plenty of time for the event, I promise.'

'Oh.'

'If there was anyone else I could send – and if she hadn't asked me particularly – really, if I could I'd stay, but her husband left things in an awful mess. If I don't go she could lose everything. Her home, the lot.'

'That's OK. I quite understand. You have to go. It must be awful for her.' And he could lose everything too, his home, the lot. She loved him for being so kind at the same time it made her want to shake him.

'I knew you'd understand,' he said. 'Thank you.'

After he'd rung off she tried to convince herself that she did understand and wasn't at all jealous of some poor woman who'd just lost her husband. France now seemed something that had happened to another person – a prettier, more lighthearted version of herself. But there was no point dwelling on that. She had to set things up so she could also sell tickets for the event online.

Only Gina seemed to realise just how important it was to sell enough tickets. Nicholas was just enraptured by the thought of his house being thrown into glittering centre stage. The Gilbert and Sullivan group were focusing on polishing their performances and Matthew was in Edinburgh. However, she was used to this and just got her head down. It helped her forget Matthew for a bit.

First she set up a PayPal account so people could buy tickets online. Then she worked out discounts for various people. Anyone booking a table from a historical society, or connected to the Gilbert and Sullivan group, got a deal. She also decided to offer discounts to anyone else helpful – but not too many, of course. She included the catering college and the wine merchant and Anthea's auction house.

She rang Anthea to tell her. They had become good friends. 'I really hope people won't be frightened off by the price. But we only have one chance at it – we have to make all the money in one hit.'

'Which is tough,' agreed Anthea.

'Although I think Nicholas is planning to have salons and things all year. He might feel differently when it's actually happened but now, well, he rang me to see if I think the Bach Choir would come down and sing in little groups. I told him I had no idea and he should ask them.'

'Lordy. Poor love. So who have you been in touch with so far?'

'Every historical society for whatever architectural period that anyone has ever heard of. Andrew has given me a list of people who'll be interested in the music, and of course he's planning to get at least a coachload of tickets sold.'

'Mm. It's a pity Gilbert and Sullivan is a bit, well, Marmite. Some people hate it,' said Anthea.

'I know, and everyone thinks opera would be better but as I told Sally, I'd have to pay opera singers. This way we're getting our singers free. And for all those who don't like them, there are plenty who'll just come for the house.'

'True. Well, I'll do my best to help. And hey, I've just remembered my mother is friends with a woman who's very high up in the National Trust. She might bring some people.' Gina heard Anthea scribbling on a pad. 'Good luck with this, Gina!'

Gina made a chart with the break-even mark on it so she would know the moment they started making money. She had numbered tickets printed and made a careful note of who had which numbers to sell. Then she set up a dedicated Twitter account and Facebook page, and when she wasn't doing anything else, she sent links to her page to anyone she thought might be interested.

'It's probably just as well Matthew's away with his Scottish Widow,' she told Sally on the phone later. 'I'm so busy I wouldn't have time to see him.' She still hadn't confessed how things were between them. 'And I haven't done much on the antiques front lately. When I popped into town to see how ticket sales were going I realised we were dreadfully low on stock. We have sold quite a bit which is good but we need some new things. Bill got me some, but we're still low.'

'Let's go to a car boot this Sunday. There's one near here, I noticed a leaflet when I was doing the weekly shop,' said Sally. 'We can take the girls and have a jolly time and maybe pick up some things for the stall.'

Gina opened her mouth to say there wouldn't be anything suitable at a car-boot sale and she was far too busy to take a morning off just for fun when she realised how very boring she had become. 'Well, that would be nice. I'll have to be back quite early though. The first few bookings from the online site should start to trickle through by Sunday and I'll need to post the tickets off.'

'You'll be fine. Car boots are early, remember. I'll pick you up at eight. Well, maybe half past. And bring bags.'

As they walked along the field full of stalls, eating hot dogs and laden with carrier bags, the girls holding on to the pushchair, Gina realised it had been good for her to get out of the house. She'd done a fair bit of dashing about, delivering packets of tickets to people who thought they might sell them, meeting with the caterers to check on the menu, persuading a local firm to provide fresh apple juice at cost price and all the other thousands of jobs that her role seemed to consist of, and now this time out, in the fresh air, was very reviving. Also, in among the vast quantity of plastic toys her nieces picked up for pennies, she and Sally did find a few pieces of china that would go well with their other stock at the centre.

'While Matthew-the-Antique-Nazi is away, he won't be able to be picky about things being not quite old enough.'

Gina laughed but suddenly discovered she had become quite picky about these things herself and determined to do some research when she got home. One of their car-boot bargains had been a *Miller's*, only just out of date and so potentially extremely useful. And it meant she could return Matthew's copy.

Once she had been delivered home by Sally, who was off to Sunday lunch with her in-laws, Gina took the box of things to the kitchen so she could give them all a good wash and then went to her laptop to see what, if any, response there had been since her site had gone live.

She was thrilled. Twenty tickets, mostly in pairs, had been sold. It wasn't much but it was a very encouraging start. Feeling she was being very childish, she filled in twenty lines on her chart after she'd addressed the envelopes. She would take this first batch as a good omen. The tickets *would* all sell. The event *would* be an enormous success.

Chapter Thirty

Gina woke horribly early. It was still pitch dark but she knew she wouldn't go back to sleep again. There was too much on her mind. The morning of the event had dawned. It was make-or-break day and she still didn't know if the numbers worked out.

She made herself a bowl of porridge. Until she got to Fairfield Manor she couldn't do anything more. After her breakfast she felt calmer and went up to pack her bag. She might not have time to come home and change so she wanted everything with her. Then she had a quick shower and washed her hair before getting dressed, packing the car, and setting off. Bernard would be up and about by eight and would let her in.

The caterers had arrived very early. They had already set up a couple of huge vans when Gina got there. The vans connected with the kitchen, which Bernard had confided was designated as 'service only' – which meant it wasn't fit to cook in.

'They said it would cause less disruption,' said Bernard, 'although how there could have been more disruption I cannot tell you.'

'Oh, Bernard, I'm awfully sorry. This must be ghastly for you,' said Gina, mentally putting him on her list of 'people to be publicly and heartily thanked'. 'Of course it's a huge amount of work for you. I never gave that a thought when I suggested it.'

Bernard inclined his head gracefully. 'Well, it isn't what we're used to, but it's given Nicholas such a new lease of life I'm inclined to forgive you. Although I've told him if he starts opening the house regularly, he'll have to take more people on.'

'Would you hate that? When you're used to it just being the two of you?'

'No, I don't think so. As long as Nicholas is happy, so am I.'

Gina had her arms round his neck, giving him a hug, before she checked to see if he would be OK with this expression of affection and gratitude. Fortunately he didn't leap away in disgust.

The person in charge of catering was a student, but to Gina's private and extreme relief, she was a woman in her thirties, retraining after a life in advertising, and was extremely well organised.

'Well, you have to be, when you've got children,' she said to Gina when Gina complimented her on her clipboard and series of lists which rivalled even Gina's. 'How up to date are we on numbers?'

Gina shrugged. 'There's a friend of someone's mother who said she was bringing a table's worth but she hasn't confirmed. I couldn't say it's all too late because she'd be a good contact if we ever did anything like this again.' She heard herself say 'we' although up to now, whenever Nicholas had got overexcited about another performance-with-food she'd mentally, if not audibly, distanced herself from something so unwieldy. This time she had a real incentive to work so hard for nothing – even if the real reason had become somewhat blurred. Was it her love of the French House that she was doing all this for, for the dealers who worked there, or was it for the love of its owner?

Matthew had, by text, promised he would appear with the lots for the auction, complete with a written programme, in plenty of time. Gina had rung Jenny who promised her this was so and she would bring plenty of copies. Anthea had told her it was a slight shame that people wouldn't have time to study the list of items beforehand, but she promised to do her best to get every penny out of them.

'Honestly, with a few glasses of champagne on board, people get very into the whole auction thing,' she had explained. 'First of all they bid to make sure things don't go for nothing, and then they end up buying something they didn't know they wanted. But that's for charity auctions. At least this time they'll get some lovely antique.'

'You think?'

'Oh yes. Matthew has a wonderful eye for quality.'

Since despite his long absence Gina was still feeling

that inconvenient yearning for Matthew, she got a little frisson of pleasure to hear him praised. 'As long as he's not late. Jenny told me he's on his way back from Edinburgh right now.'

'He won't be late, trust me.'

Everyone who should be there had now arrived so Gina went to see how Sally was getting on with the flowers. Gina hadn't foreseen a need for flowers until relatively recently. It was only when they realised the fires couldn't be lit without everyone roasting and risking their costumes bursting into flames that Gina and Nicholas agreed some of the fireplaces had to have something in front of them. He sent Bernard into the attics and produced some fire screens, but in the great hall, where people would congregate for champagne, they decided a fire screen would detract from the marble mantelpiece.

'Surely you know someone who does flowers?' Gina had said to Nicholas. 'For the church? Something like that?'

'No,' Nicholas had replied. 'Don't you have a contact?'

After ringing round everyone she could think of, she asked Sally if she knew anyone.

'Gina,' Sally declared indignantly. 'I could do the flowers, no problem. But they'd need to be huge and they'd be very expensive.'

Gina took a breath. 'No, they'd be free, but you'd have to get them from Nicholas's estate and I happen to know he's let the garden go horribly.'

'Don't worry,' said Sally. 'As long as I can hack away, I'll find things.'

'God, Sals, it would be so brilliant if you could do it. I don't know why I didn't think of asking you straight away. I know you're fantastic at that sort of thing.'

'It's all right. I'm not offended. You've got too much on your mind to see the bleedin' obvious.'

'It was so awful when we weren't speaking. It was like I was missing an arm. I even lost my appetite.'

'It was horrible,' said Sally. 'But I'm back on the team now.'

Now, Gina found her sister in a pantry, surrounded by foliage. 'Have you discovered anything to put in the vases that's not green?'

Sally turned, secateurs in hand. 'It's been amazing! The garden is full of wonderful things – even at this time of the year – and so enormous I can be really lavish. Look at my arrangement for *The Mikado* room.' She gestured to a Chinese vase containing branches which appeared to be covered in blossom. 'I know *The Mikado* is Japanese but we're not being too purist.'

'I'm not either. I promise,' said Gina. 'What is that plant?'

'*Viburnum bodnantense*,' said Sally, slightly smug. 'And Bernard found me some amazing vases.'

'Nothing too valuable, I hope,' said Gina.

'No. The beauty is, they are all damaged. Bernard said they were hardly worth anything.'

Gina left chuckling at her sister being so pleased to be working with damaged goods. Then she went to check the loos. By the time she'd gone back to Sally to ask her to put flowers in the Ladies, it was time to see if the wine had all arrived. The portable loos were arriving later. She'd make sure they got flowers too.

She had employed a firm of cleaners – an expense she felt was justified knowing it would be far too much for Nicholas's regular cleaner – and now she felt her decision entirely justified. The woman in charge was managing her team with calm efficiency and they were cracking on at an impressive pace.

Having told the team what a brilliant job they were doing and mentioning casually that they shouldn't spray polish on to the antique furniture – just in case they didn't know that already – Gina went to the kitchen to see how Bernard and Nicholas were coping. She found only Bernard, who explained that he'd sent Nicholas for a rest – mostly to keep him out of the way.

'Tea?' asked Bernard, holding up a kettle.

Gina nodded and sat down at the table and found her clipboard.

'It all seems to be going well,' said Bernard, putting a mug near her hand. 'Don't you think?'

'Yes. I just wish we'd charged more for the tickets.'

'Really? They seem quite expensive enough already.'

'I know. Everyone thinks so but the costs really

mount up. Still, I'm sure it'll be fine.' In her heart she had stopped hoping to make masses of money and just wanted to break even. That seemed a high enough target at the moment.

At five o'clock, when Gina was just going to make her rounds again, Sally came and found her. 'Come on, missus, you're getting changed now.'

'Oh, Sally, no need for that. I don't need to be ready until about quarter to seven. No one will be here until seven.'

'Time to do as you're told for once. I'm going to do your hair.'

Sally had taken hold of Gina's arm and was leading her firmly towards the stairs.

'It doesn't take a minute to do that. I washed it this morning.'

'What were you planning to do with it?'

'Just put it up in some sort of bun. I've got a scrunchie somewhere.'

'Thank God you have a sister who takes these things seriously. Come with me.'

There had been a bedroom allocated for their use and Gina now saw there were things on the dressing table she had not put there.

'Sit down,' said Sally, pushing Gina firmly on to the stool in front of the triple mirror. 'I borrowed an anglepoise so we can see what we're doing. I got you a hairpiece.'

'No need for that,' Gina exclaimed. 'It doesn't matter what I look like. As long as I look reasonably elegant—'

'And wear the dress—'

'Oh shit, the dress!'

'What? Did you leave it at home?'

'No! It's in my case, but I completely forgot to get it altered. It won't fit, Sal!'

'Don't worry. I've got needle and thread and loads of ribbon and things in case we need it for your hair. Now sit down and let me turn you into an Edwardian lady.'

'I think I should be looking Georgian, or Regency, really.'

'But the dress is Edwardian and no one will know the difference anyway. Both styles are fairly high-waisted and not too sticky-outy.' Sally picked up a strand of Gina's hair. 'It's a pity you washed it really, it would have been better for a bit of grease. Still, I've got hairspray.'

'I never use hairspray!'

'You do now!'

Three-quarters of an hour later, Gina looked at herself. Her hair was swept into an elegant chignon that wouldn't have looked out of place in the drawing room at Downton Abbey. 'I would never have thought I could look like this,' she said. 'You're amazing.'

'I looked up how to do it on YouTube,' said Sally,

obviously very pleased with her efforts. 'And I bought the kit. Now, let's try the dress. I must say, it would have been good if you'd taken it out of the case. But never mind. I borrowed a steamer to get the creases out.'

Sally, obviously not trusting Gina to do anything, swung her case on to the bed and took out the dress. She held it up. 'It's survived quite well, considering.'

'It's been on a hanger since I got it,' Gina said, sounding apologetic.

'We'll give it a good steam and then you can put it on. Go and have a very careful shower or a good wash while I work.'

'You've got awfully bossy lately, Sal,' said Gina, going to the bathroom.

When she got back a little later the dress looked perfect. 'I don't think it can have been worn much,' said Sally. 'Maybe only while the portrait was painted. Now, let's get it on.'

'It won't fit, I know!' said Gina, nervous now. She stepped into the dress Sally was holding out for her.

'There!' said Sally, stepping back. 'It fits perfectly.'

'I can't believe it. Are you sure it's really done up?' Gina put her hand to her back to check for a gap.

'Yes! I knew you'd lost weight. I've also bought these shoes as I knew you'd only have your boots.'

Gina grinned at her sister and took the shoes. They

were almost flat but decorated: a perfect combination of comfort and glamour. They fitted perfectly.

'Now check your make-up and you're done!' said Sally.

Gina couldn't help being impressed. She really saw the similarity between herself and the portrait now. She just hoped Nicholas would be pleased.

Sally was in the bathroom, getting into her own dress so, as time was getting on, Gina set off downstairs alone. She had gone along the corridor and was at the top of the stairs when she realised the lighting, which had taken a lot of thought and planning, was on.

Gina, and Nicholas had agreed with her, felt that when people entered the hall they should have the sense of going back in time. Other rooms would be well lit for the performances, and supper would have enough light for everyone to eat by, but this first impression would be as it would have been when the house was built.

There was a huge fire crackling in one of the two fireplaces (the other couldn't be used because of a faulty chimney and risk of costumes going up in flames but they'd agreed this one needed a proper fire with good-sized logs) and very carefully placed candelabra lit the space. Although she had planned it all and knew what to expect, Gina still felt there'd been some sort of magical transformation. She set off down the stairs with a smile on her face.

She had been aware of two tall male figures talking but it was only when she was halfway down the curving staircase that one of them turned, and she realised that the man talking to Nicholas (who was wearing a velvet smoking jacket and cap) was Matthew. She stopped and the two men regarded her in silence. Suddenly self-conscious, she set off again.

Matthew took her hand as she reached the bottom but didn't speak. He didn't need to. His normally inscrutable face was alive with admiration and – was Gina imagining it? – longing.

'My dear girl,' said Nicholas, 'you look sensational. I shall have your portrait painted and hang it next to my grandmother's.'

Gina smiled and looked at Matthew who still said nothing but searched her eyes with his own. Then he kissed her mouth. 'I've missed you.'

'Really?' she breathed.

Nicholas cleared his throat. 'Just going to check on the wine.' Then he limped off.

Matthew took Gina into his arms and kissed her properly.

All the tension and anxiety that Gina had been living with for the past weeks – ever since France – seemed to melt into his kiss. It was only when his hands started creeping into her hair that she realised this wasn't the moment.

'I've missed you too, Matthew,' she whispered

huskily. 'But about two hundred and fifty people are about to arrive and I have to look after them.'

'So no chance of carrying you back up the stairs and ravishing you in the master bedroom?'

She giggled. This was so unlike Matthew she was tempted to call his bluff and say, 'OK then,' gather her skirts and lead him to the bedroom at a run. But she couldn't. 'Later – maybe?'

She saw his throat move as he swallowed. 'Later, definitely.'

Just then, Sally appeared. 'Hey, you two, get a room!'

'We've got a room,' said Gina, 'but unfortunately no time to take advantage. Matthew, have you got the items for the sale?'

'I have. Anthea's having a look at them now.'

Nicholas walked back into the hall, Bernard behind him with a tray of filled glasses. 'I think we should all have a quiet drink together before battle commences.'

Although she never usually drank when she was working, Gina took a glass. 'Here's to Nicholas and his beautiful house and to a successful evening.'

'And here's to Gina and the French House and to a successful evening,' said Nicholas, raising his glass to her.

Chapter Thirty-One

'Do you mind running me through what's going on?' said Matthew after they had finished their champagne. 'I feel rather out of the loop.'

'Of course. Follow me. How did Edinburgh go?'

'Well, really. Not ideal timing, of course, but things are fairly well sorted out now and I got some very nice items, some of which you'll see at the auction later.'

'You must let me know how much they cost. We hope to make money – lots – on the items but we do need to keep proper accounts.'

'They're my donation. Is that all right for your accounts?'

Gina decided she had to pull herself together. She had been trying to suppress her feelings for Matthew since they'd been apart, burying them beneath activity and worry, but now he was with her and the show was about to begin she found they had all rushed back in a very inconvenient way. Everything he said seemed to have a hidden meaning and if it didn't, it made her insides melt anyway.

'That's fine,' she said briskly. 'And while people are having drinks I'll walk you through it all. Carefully – don't tread on my train!'

She took him first to the Chinese Room, set up for *The Mikado*. The parquet floor shone, reflecting the fairy lights that Sally had threaded through branches. Little paper lanterns, some lit (bought from Sally's favourite supplier), some not (made by Sally), combined to make the room the perfect mix of stage set and beautiful historic salon.

'Before you say anything, we know *The Mikado* is Japanese and this is Chinese but we're not being picky,' she said warningly. She went over to where three musicians were warming up. 'Are you OK, guys? How are you going to manage to get to your next venue?'

'We've got a bit of time before we need to be in the conservatory,' one of them – hardly more than a boy really – said.

'So where do you come from?' asked Matthew.

'We're music students. Andrew asked us to come. It's a good gig so we're doing it for nothing. And a meal, of course.'

'Of course,' agreed Gina, who hadn't been told about this. 'And a glass of wine. But only one – at least until we're sure all the paying punters have enough.'

As they walked through to the conservatory, Gina said, 'It's brilliant to have musicians – especially for nothing – but I'm not sure I factored in all the extra meals and wine. It's all an added expense.'

'I'm sure it'll be fine. How many tickets have you sold?'

'I'm not absolutely sure. Some of the people who booked for parties might not have a full table of twelve. It's a bit of a weak spot in the organisation. It would have been easier if we'd had more time to arrange it all in.'

Matthew opened the door to the conservatory. 'Oh wow!' he said.

Gina was pleased. The conservatory had been done up like a ship, first for *HMS Pinafore* and later for *The Pirates of Penzance*.

'What I don't get is how you'll fit everyone in? Even without seating, you wouldn't get more than, say, fifty people in here.'

'There's a shift system. You have a programme and you go to each room as instructed. Everything is performed twice. It should work.' She wasn't completely convinced but Andrew was very certain. 'Then we have a break for supper and then the auction.' She winked. 'Come and let me show you why we're really pleased it's not raining.'

She led him out of the conservatory and across a drugget that led down a long path to a temple. 'People will have to hurry,' she said, 'or they'll freeze.' She couldn't herself though; there was something about wearing a gorgeous vintage gown that demanded she walked slowly, with decorum.

When they arrived she said, 'This is one of the

largest buildings in the garden and we're having a soloist singing "The Moon and I". Which is, in my humble opinion, a very lovely song. And look. A fake moon.'

'This is really very atmospheric,' said Matthew huskily, having given the building and the stage set within a brief inspection, before pulling her into his arms.

When Sally saw Gina a little later, she whisked her into the Ladies to touch up her chignon.

From an organisation point of view, Gina realised, the evening was not brilliant. People were not following their programmes and moving from one room to another like the well-oiled machine Gina had hoped for.

On the other hand, everyone was having a very good time. A few of the architectural interest groups had wandered off into other rooms but when Gina realised they'd been led there by Nicholas, she didn't worry too much. The singers all had enthusiastic audiences and – she was extremely grateful for this – they didn't go over time beyond the extra time Gina had allocated.

However, when the time came for supper and the auction, Gina had the house searched. She wanted everyone to be there, fed and tipsy enough to be slightly more generous than they would be had they drunk less champagne.

The catering was pretty faultless. Vegetarians had been issued with fabric daffodils to put by their places so the staff would know and everyone else ate the chicken with good grace. Gina was constantly searching the room for signs of upset so she could glide over and soothe the situation but she didn't need to. She began to wonder if the tip she had put in an envelope for distribution later was going to be big enough.

Anthea was a star. She stood at the rostrum (which she had brought with her) in a long, low-cut sequinned dress. She effortlessly drew the attention of the room. Gina found a chair at the back of the room to watch an expert at work.

Matthew's items were perfect. There was some nice jewellery: nothing too valuable but he'd found a stunning diamanté necklace which, according to Anthea and the catalogue, was a copy of the one Audrey Hepburn wore in the film of *My Fair Lady*. It was possibly a bit over the top for most people normally, but now, when everyone was wearing their most glamorous clothes, it seemed a lot of people were willing to bid for it.

A few antique brooches and tie pins came up and were bid for by couples, and the good-tempered rivalry meant the prices were healthy. Gina sat back, arranged her skirts and thanked Anthea silently for having the idea and for doing such a good job with it. She even bid for a pretty little necklace herself, just because it would have looked so right with the gorgeous dress she was wearing, which was making her feel so special. But she was outbid early on and told herself that was just as well.

At last, the gavel came down for the last time and a cricket bat signed by a long-gone but obviously very successful team was sold for a huge amount of money.

The evening was over. Gina could go home just as soon as everything was tidied up.

Sally came up and flung her arms round her neck. 'I've got to go because my taxi is here but, honey, it was amazing. A billion, trillion times better than I could ever have imagined. The girls will be wild with jealousy when I tell them all about it.'

Gina hugged her hard. 'Thank you so much for the flowers and all your help.'

Gina never left anything she had organised until she was sure all was in order. And so, half an hour later, she was still shooing people out of the house, finding bags, ringing for taxis. Finally they were free of the paying public and could get on with sorting out the caterers.

'You were absolutely bloody brilliant!' said Gina as she handed over her envelope, into which she'd added some extra notes, to the woman in charge. 'I'm going to give you a fabulous testimonial.'

'I'm very pleased you're happy. There were a few

hiccups that you didn't need to know about, we've all learnt a lot and got a lot of useful experience. And what a fantastic venue.'

At last it was only Nicholas, Gina, Matthew and Bernard left. Gina was retrieving glasses from far-flung corners, Matthew was in the kitchen and Nicholas had opened a bottle of brandy.

Bernard found her. 'Gina, I've put sheets on the bed in the bedroom you got dressed in. Nicholas says you're to come and have a brandy and then stay the night. You must be exhausted.'

Gina's stock refusal to accept stuck on her tongue. Bernard took her arm. 'Come on, the others are on their second brandy already.'

It was lovely to sit in the kitchen, a plate of leftover pudding and a bottle of brandy on the table, her shoes off, but Gina had been awake since before dawn and she was beginning to sway.

'It's been really nice to end the evening like this, but I really have to go to bed now.' She stood up.

'I'll show you the way to your bedroom,' said Matthew.

'I know the way perfectly well, thank you,' she said primly, and walked out of the room, suddenly feeling shy at leaving the room with Matthew in front of Nicholas and Bernard.

Two seconds later she was back. 'Actually, Matthew, could you help me with my dress? I can't get out of it on my own.'

Nicholas raised his glass to her, a mischievous look in his eye, and even Bernard smiled benignly at her.

Matthew put his hand in the small of her back as they went up the stairs together. She was glad of the support.

He unhooked her dress while she pulled hairpins from her hair. When she was free of the hairpiece and had brushed her teeth she realised something.

'I haven't got a nightdress. I wasn't expecting to stay overnight.'

'I'm sure you'll manage,' said Matthew.

He pulled back the heavy bedspread and she got in, wearing her bra and pants. 'It seems sort of out of period to sleep in my underwear in this bed. I should have a nightie buttoned up to my neck.'

'I'm not going to ask Nicholas if he's got one he can lend you but I am going to see if Bernard can rustle up a toothbrush.'

'Use mine,' mumbled Gina. Then she fell asleep.

Gina was alone in the bed when she woke up. Had Matthew stayed the night? If so, why hadn't he woken her up to ravish her? And she was equally cross she'd fallen asleep before she could ravish him. She looked at the world blearily and spotted a cup of tea steaming on the bedside table.

She struggled upright and picked up the tea. She thought she'd drink a bit of it before she looked at her watch. Once she knew the time she'd probably have to leap out of bed and get dressed.

There was an envelope and a small parcel behind the mug, as she discovered when she picked it up. She picked up the envelope with a rather heavy heart. Was it from Matthew? Although he'd been very pleased to see her and they'd kissed, he hadn't made love to her last night, or stayed for a romantic morning in bed together. So she still didn't really know what he thought about their relationship – if they had one.

It was a sheet of Fairfield Manor writing paper.

I'm sorry to wake you, if I have. I have to get back now and it broke my heart to leave you sleeping but you deserve as much sleep as you can get so I didn't disturb you. The parcel is a little thank-you present. You may remember we saw it when we were together in France. I had it made into a key ring by a silversmith I know in Edinburgh. It reminds me of you, serene on the surface but batting away like mad underneath.

See you soon

Matthew

She smiled but felt sad and a little put out that he hadn't woken her: she would have swapped a bit of sleep for what might have happened.

The parcel, wrapped in a twist of tissue paper, was the little silver salt (or possibly pepper) shaker in the shape of a swan. She couldn't help smiling. It was a lovely thing, useful and beautiful, and most importantly a present from Matthew.

She lay back on her pillows and finished her tea. When she got up she'd have to go home and do the sorting out. Had they made any money, or hadn't they?

Chapter Thirty-Two

In the end it was some days after the event before Gina could finally work out the accounts. Money had come in and gone out and she needed to track it all.

Apart from bills and payment for tickets there had also been many, many emails and letters congratulating the team on the event. Almost everyone had really loved it and – much to Gina's relief – felt they'd got their money's worth.

Nicholas had been ecstatic. He wanted to employ Gina to arrange more events: operas, music hall evenings, murder mysteries in fancy dress. He even wondered if ballets would be popular. Gina had been firm during the phone call. 'Let's see how this one has worked out financially. There's no point in putting on huge entertainments if they don't wash their faces – cover their costs and make some money.'

'We could charge more. People will pay almost anything for this sort of thing. They couldn't have loved it more. Oh – Noël Coward! How about Coward and Novello evenings?'

Gina laughed although she was trying to be firm

with Nicholas's new-found passion for theatricals. 'I'd be absolutely delighted to help you with anything you want to do, but, as I said, please first let me work out if they are remotely profitable. You could certainly take parties from the historical societies, give them lunch and a private tour and charge really quite a lot.'

'Maybe Bernard should go on a cookery course. That could save us money. I must ask him how he feels about becoming a cordon bleu.' He paused. 'Though really, *au fond*, what I loved was seeing the house all dressed up. It wouldn't be nearly so much fun if it was just normal.'

'Well, we'll see, shall we?'

'Goodbye, my love,' he said after a bit more discussion.

Sally had similarly been in love with the whole thing. 'God, it was amazing. Whoever would have thought it could have worked out so well? You actually got people to move from one room to another without the use of a loudhailer. You're a genius.'

'Or a sheepdog,' said Gina, whose anxieties about the numbers was dampening her enthusiasm very effectively.

'No, but really, it was fab. So pretty. It would be a real shame if it didn't happen again in some form.'

'Promise not to talk to Nicholas, who thinks exactly the same, until I know if we've made money or not.'

'We must have. We must have sold every ticket

and they cost a hundred pounds. Surely to goodness we've made a profit when so many people were working for nothing.'

'I don't know. An awful lot of people got a discount and all the people who worked for nothing had to be fed and watered – or wined even. Until I've done the figures I can't tell where we stand. But if we've made a loss the French House will have to be sold and quick.'

Sally didn't speak for a few seconds. 'What does Matthew say about it all?'

'I haven't actually talked to Matthew about it much.'

'Why on earth not? You're together, aren't you?'

'If this has failed, well, I'll feel he'll think I'm just a failure too. All fur coat and no knickers – you know the sort of thing.'

'He was lovely at the do, though. I saw him being really chatty with a group of old ladies.'

Sally's surprise at Matthew's ability to make conversation amused Gina. 'Just because he's not gobby like you—'

'Or you. By the way, you looked sensational. You must wear that dress again.'

'The opportunities don't come up that often and it is a bit fragile . . .'

'I'll copy it for you. I saw Matthew look at you with his tongue hanging out.'

Gina giggled again. 'That doesn't sound like Matthew.'

'You know what I mean. He obviously fancies you like mad.'

'Good. Now, Sal, I must get on with my arithmetic.'

'You know how to turn your phone into a calculator, don't you?'

'Yes. But I've got a calculator.'

'Let me know when you've got the answer. If we've won we'll have champagne.'

'Absolutely. Now goodbye.'

Gina set off for the French House late the following afternoon. She'd rung to check when Matthew would be there and this was the earliest time. She'd been quite happy to have their meeting postponed, though. She didn't have good news to impart.

'Is he in the flat?' Gina asked Jenny, who was dusting a table of figurines, presumably before she closed up the centre.

'Yes.' Jenny smiled. 'It was a lovely evening, wasn't it?'

Gina returned the smile. 'Yes, really lovely.'

'Everyone enjoyed themselves so much. And what an amazing house! I knew about it, of course, from Matthew and his father, but I never thought I'd get beyond the front door. It was brilliant.'

Inside, Gina was slowly dying, but she had to keep on chatting to Jenny as if everything was fine. Jenny would find out soon enough everything wasn't but Gina had to tell Matthew first.

'Shall I just go up?' she said eventually when Jenny had finished saying what a triumph the event had been.

'Do. He knows you're coming.'

As she made her way up the stairs Gina was just grateful Andrew wasn't around. They'd spoken on the phone, of course, and he was more than thrilled with everything. Gina had withheld Nicholas's telephone number from him 'for reasons of confidentiality' but she knew it was only a matter of time before he and Nicholas got together, and then they'd be staging a musical version of *A Midsummer Night's Dream* on the lawn and rigging up wires so the fairies could really fly. Until Matthew knew the bad news she didn't want to talk to anyone else about it.

'What's that dog doing there?' she said, the moment she was in Matthew's sitting room. Oscar got up and gave her a reproachful look. 'I don't mean you, Osc. That bloody Foo dog!' It was sitting in the middle of the coffee table and the sight of it twanged her already pinging nerves.

Matthew picked it up protectively and put it on top of a bookcase. 'You've never liked that dog.'

Gina sighed and tried to smile. 'I know. It just isn't you, somehow. It jars on me.'

He stood looking at her. 'Am I right in thinking you've got bad news?'

She nodded.

'I can't say I'm surprised. Now, come and sit down.'

His matter-of-fact tone maddened her. 'What do you mean?'

'I mean, I'm not surprised we lost money. Did we at least break even?'

Gina had been putting on a brave and positive front for everyone except Sally. She'd been dreading telling Matthew they didn't raise as much as they needed but his calm assumption the whole event had been a huge, exhausting waste of time was too much for her. Didn't he trust her at all? As she hadn't slept much or eaten for some days she lost it.

'Yes, we fucking broke even. We made money. Just not quite enough money.'

'No one's denying you did a really good job—'

'Don't patronise me. I know just how good a job I did. I know how hard I worked to get as much as possible for nothing. And I know how easy it would have been to lose money. But I didn't. I made money.'

Matthew stood looking at her. She couldn't know what he was thinking but she could guess. He thought she was a foolish woman who thought she could save the world just by putting on a party. He obviously knew better.

'Just not enough.' He paused. 'Gina, I know how hard you've worked, you've been brilliant, but we have to face facts. I can't hold out any longer. I know you think I've been sitting on my hands but I have been doing my best to delay things legally. Well, I've used up my last tactic. The French House has to be sold.'

He was trying to put it kindly but Gina felt she was being stabbed. 'There must be another way! Can't you talk to Yvette?'

He shook his head. 'I *have*! But I've done all the talking I'm going to do and I won't beg. It's time to let go.'

She became aware of a number of boxes. He appeared to have started packing already. 'Have you already spoken to Carmella?'

'Not yet. I will soon.'

So it had all been a horrendous waste of time and energy. She had worked so hard to save the French House and it was going to be sold anyway. It was too much. She either had to burst into tears or lose her temper. She went with the temper option. She strode across the room and picked up the Foo dog from the bookcase. Then she dashed it to the floor, at the last minute aiming for the corner of the room where it wasn't likely to damage anything else. The noise it made was hugely satisfying. 'I'm sorry,' she said, not remotely apologetic. 'It was either that dog or me.'

'Rainey gave me that dog.'

'I can't imagine why. It's hideous.' She refused to apologise although she did feel guilty.

Matthew stood there like a statue, refusing even now to show any emotion. 'There is no point in getting upset and throwing things. I've known for a long time I'll have to pack up and sell the house.

Yvette wants her money. I just have to get on with it.'

'Well, at least you won't have to pack that bloody ornament.' Gina was still furious – with Matthew, with Yvette, with the world.

'I'll get you a drink. It might help you calm down.'

Gina realised there were no words less likely to make anyone calm down than those. 'You know what? You're bloody lucky I didn't throw the dog at your head! I did everything I knew how to do to make that event a success—'

'It was a success – a huge success! No one is denying that.'

'And it was hugely hard work.'

'I'm not denying that either.' He was starting to pick up on her anger now. He stalked across the room to the table where the drinks were kept. He took out a bottle of whisky and poured two large measures.

'But you're not prepared to do anything yourself to help? You're just going to roll over and sell the house?'

'I've just told you I tried! Anyway, you don't know anything about it.' He handed her a glass.

She didn't much like whisky but she took it anyway. 'Then explain. Why couldn't you get a mortgage, for instance?'

Matthew spoke slowly, as if she was an idiot. 'When my father died there was a huge amount of inheritance tax to pay. I had to raise a mortgage for that and it's a struggle to keep up the payments every month. The extra thirty grand would make everything impossible, even if the bank would increase the amount I owe. It was bad enough when I had to sell my cottage to pay off Yvette. And now she's after the house. I've fought long enough to keep it and recently I've wondered why.'

'You've wondered why? Isn't it blindingly obvious? It's your home, your business – you were brought up here. Other people need it for their businesses. And anyway, we did raise something. It's a start; it might help with the bank.'

'What do you mean?'

'The event raised five grand.'

'I didn't realise. I just assumed you'd—'

'What? Raised a hundred quid or something? Wrong, Matthew.'

'I said I was sorry!' He frowned. 'Although I realise I don't exactly sound sorry. And although it's impressive, it's still not enough.'

'Well, I'm quite sorry about the dog. Not extremely, but a bit. I didn't realise Rainey gave it to you.'

'You don't sound sorry.'

Gina nodded ruefully. 'I know. I'm just so angry that you seem to be giving in.'

'There's hardly anything I wouldn't do to prevent having to sell the French House and I have done an awful lot – sacrificed an awful lot, actually. But you can only go on banging your head against the wall for so long. I'm exhausted, Gina. Even with the money from the event – and I'm not sure I should take it, honestly, not now. I still owe Yvette twenty-five grand. She won't wait any longer. It's better for me to sell the house so I can start again.'

Gina understood what he was saying and her heart ached to see the weariness settle over his impassive, handsome features. But she still wasn't satisfied. 'I always prefer to be pig-headed to giving up myself.' She took a sip of whisky and while she didn't like the taste she liked the jolt of courage it gave her. She no longer felt as if she might cry, but she felt cheated and let down.

She got up. 'If you tell me where to find a dustpan and brush I'll sweep up the bits of Foo dog.'

'I'll do it.'

'No, let me. I threw it, after all. Is there a brush and things in the kitchen?' She went into the kitchen to look and found them quite easily.

Matthew stood by the empty hearth, nursing his whisky, brooding in a way that made Gina want to throw something else. He was like someone in a play, being strong and silent and proud. Gina thought being proud was all very well – she could see how integral it was to personality – but she thought he should be angry too, and do something proactive.

But of course throwing things wasn't the answer and as she knelt and began clearing up she realised that however bad she felt about the French House being sold it must be a trillion times worse for Matthew. She reached for one of the bigger shards and then stopped. 'There's something – papers – in among the bits!'

'What?'

'I don't know!' She picked up the paper carefully and tipped the bits of china that were on it into the dustpan.

'Let me look.' Matthew was by her side in seconds. He took the papers from her.

Gina was torn between finishing the job and demanding to know what the papers were. But she didn't let herself hope for anything much. She straightened up. 'So? What is it?'

'It's two things. It's a letter—'

'From Rainey? God, Rainey and her letters. And what's the point of writing one if you hide it in a china dog? It might never have been found.'

Matthew muttered something about a strange conversation he'd had with Rainey before she died now making sense. 'The other bit is in French and written in really difficult handwriting,' he said to Gina.

'Oh. How disappointing.'

'It was never going to be a treasure map, now was it?' Setting the letter aside he went on perusing the paper that was in French.

'Maybe if I had a look at it? I've got French GCSE,' she snapped when she could bear the suspense no longer. Then she remembered Matthew spoke it fluently and took another gulp of whisky.

He took the letter over to where the light was better, under a standard lamp. She followed him and tried to read over his shoulder. 'I see what you mean about it being difficult,' she said a couple of moments later. 'It looks like it's a poem or something. It has a title, and it's obviously work in progress because of all the corrections and things. Is there a signature?'

Matthew turned the paper over. 'Yes. It seems to have been added later because the ink is different but it's the same writing. And it's dated.'

'What do you reckon it says?'

'Jean something,' said Matthew after a bit.

'I'd got that far. I meant, what's the surname?'

'Something beginning with R,' said Matthew. 'Not enormously helpful. I suspect this is a poem dedicated to Rainey by one of her many lovers. A French one, obviously.'

'Hang on, I've just thought of something.' Threads of memory were gathering in Gina's mind. 'I think I remember there being a family story about Rainey and a French pop star of some kind. And Clare said Rainey had a secret lover in France, remember. I'll ring Dad, he might know.'

She saw Matthew opening the letter while she was dialling, but when she heard her mother answer the phone she lost interest in what Matthew was doing. 'Mum? I don't suppose you can help me. What was the name of Aunt Rainey's French lover who was a bit of a sleb? If you can't remember can you get Dad? I need to know.'

'Gina darling, hello. I'll get Dad, but why do you want to know? And how was France?'

'Oh, fabulous, and I'll tell you why I want to know about Rainey's wicked past when I have a bit more information. How are you?' Suddenly it seemed churlish to ring up her mother and not actually speak to her.

'We're fine. You?'

'You know, busy, but well generally.' Churlish or not, she didn't really want to talk just now. 'Could you get Dad? This is urgent!'

She had long enough to wonder why Matthew was looking amused before her father was on the phone. 'Jean Reveaux,' he said immediately. The name of Rainey's secret lover had been known to her family, at least.

'Thank you, Dad. And was he famous?'

'Oh yes. In his day, he was enormously famous. He still has a huge following. Why do you want to know?'

'I'll get back to you,' she said and disconnected.

'Jean Reveaux,' she said. 'He was terribly famous and still has a following.'

'We'll Google him,' said Matthew, who was no longer smiling but was wiping his eyes. She wondered why. 'I'll get my laptop from the office. In the meantime, you'd better read that.' He handed her Rainey's letter.

Dear Matthew,

If you're reading this you or someone has broken the Foo dog you hate so much. I know you wouldn't be able to live with it for long! Don't feel guilty. I only left it to you to see how long you could stand it, and because it was hollow.

I'm not sure if what else in there – lyrics written to me by the love of my life – will be valuable or not, but they are rare. I had to force him to let me keep them; he always insisted on burning all his drafts. If they are valuable, sell them. Money is always useful.

The other reason for this letter is to do with my niece Gina. The business side you already know about but I'm just hoping that your own innate good sense has meant you've got over that ghastly Frenchwoman and have discovered what a lovely girl Gina is.

She's always been a bit overshadowed by her more flamboyant younger sister in my opinion, but she's got the courage of a lion and a heart of pure gold.

This note is just to give you the heads up in case you haven't noticed. Not that I would ever dream of match-making, of course. (Not much!!!)

With very much love from beyond the grave,

Rainey, née Doris Ivy Rainbow

Gina found she was crying. She got up and fetched her whisky and drained the glass. And what did Matthew think about Rainey's words about her? Would he curse his old friend for meddling? Or be pleased that she'd helped to bring them together? It would be easier to work out if she knew how Matthew felt about her. And where on earth was he? It didn't take that long to get to the office and back. She sniffed hard and composed herself.

'Right,' said Matthew, reappearing a few minutes later. 'Where shall we start? Wikipedia?'

'It's as good a place as any but then let's look on eBay to see if his artefacts have a value.'

'Let's just put his name into Google and see what comes up.'

A few seconds later Gina gasped. 'I can't believe it. He was obviously really famous. I feel I should have known about this.'

'Me too,' said Matthew, looking over her shoulder.

'She used to talk about her life as a rock chick in a general way but I didn't realise it had been with a French rock god. Mind you, she was good at keeping secrets. So now what do we do? We need to find out if song lyrics are remotely valuable,' said Gina.

'They are, definitely – for certain people.'

Gina chewed her lip for a moment. 'I'm going to ring Anthea. She'll have an idea. Or know someone.'

By the time she disconnected, Gina's ear was sore and her cheek sweaty from being pressed against her phone for several minutes.

'So?' asked Matthew.

'Well, there's good news and bad news. Anthea

does know someone and they could be incredibly valuable. And, possibly better news, there's a suitable sale coming up at Christie's but it's terribly soon.'

'I see the problem. If we could get them into that sale, they might not have time to advertise them enough, get them into the online catalogue and drum up interest.' He paused. 'When's the next sale?'

'Not for months.'

'We haven't got months. And song lyrics aren't the sort of thing you can borrow money against.'

'Maybe I could—' Gina started.

'No. Absolutely not.'

'You don't know what I was going to say,' she protested.

'Not exactly, but I bet it involved you borrowing money on your credit card or something.' He paused, looking stern, almost angry. 'I've accepted a great deal of your kindness, in many ways, but I won't do that.'

Gina could tell there was no point in her trying to say anything else on the subject. She was frustrated by his refusal to let her help but she admired the fact that he wouldn't let her go into debt for him.

'So what are we going to do?' she said when she felt it was safe to speak.

Matthew took a breath. 'We're going to eat something, drink tea, more whisky possibly, and then we'll decide. I'll cook; you carry on searching the internet.'

While Matthew was making scrambled eggs Gina

created a file. She put everything useful she found into it. If Matthew decided to put the lyrics into the sale in spite of the short notice, Gina wanted to have all the relevant details to pass on to Anthea's contact. Just to make her tough job a little bit easier.

'So, have you decided?' she asked when he came back into the room with plates, a tea towel over his arm and a bottle of wine tucked under it.

He nodded and deposited the plates on the coffee table. 'It's a no-brainer. We risk not getting enough for them but on the other hand we'll get something. And if we're only a tiny bit short – well, I'll sell Oscar or something.'

Oscar, hearing his name, raised his head and then lowered it again, as if it was too heavy to hold up if food wasn't going to be involved.

'Sounds good. Apart from selling Oscar. There'd be something else we could sacrifice before him.'

Matthew sat down next to her, having collected knives, forks and glasses. 'Tuck in. I changed my mind about the tea and the whisky. Wine seemed a good compromise.'

'I'll make a cup later. I shouldn't drink any more really.' She was still feeling the effects of the enormous drink he had given her earlier.

'Of course you can have tea if you want to. It's up to you, but there is no need to worry about drinking and driving.' He looked at her in a way that made her blush and giggle at the same time.

'No?'

'No,' he said firmly. 'You are going nowhere. I'm not letting you slip through my fingers again. Rainey was right. You have the courage of a lion and a heart of gold – and her letter made me cry. I never cry. But you're worth crying over. So I've decided you're staying here with me all night – or at least until I've given you twenty-seven orgasms.'

Gina found herself a bit breathless. 'Twenty-seven? That's a very specific number.'

'I'm a very specific sort of man. Now eat up.'

Chapter Thirty-Three

Oscar's nose in her face woke her the next morning. Having disentangled her foot from between Matthew's she looked at the clock next to his bed. It was seven o'clock – a perfectly respectable time to be woken.

'Morning, Osc,' she said, and rubbed his chest.

Matthew groaned and then pulled her to him. She hadn't actually counted but Gina felt he might not have been far off when he'd said he wanted to give her twenty-seven orgasms. It had been blissful. She would have been even happier if they hadn't fallen out since France but perhaps it had made the sex even more wonderful. And she understood now what had been happening. He'd got some ridiculous notion into his head that if he lost the French House and all his money she wouldn't – or rather shouldn't – be with him. Poor prospects. It was utterly Victorian. Antique even. But so like Matthew. She had informed him that he was an idiot and she wouldn't care if she had to live in a tent as long as she was with him (although she had a perfectly good rented cottage of her own, of course). This had produced a thoroughly satisfactory response from him, and she giggled at the memory.

'It's time to get up!' she said now, removing his hand from her breast.

He wouldn't be put off. 'This bed is quite valuable. It might be the last time I can make love to you in it.'

She kissed him but was firm. 'Unless you're planning to sell it today, I don't think we need worry about that. But I must get on. I have to go and see Sally for one thing.'

'Why particularly?' He sat up on one elbow and watched her as she slid off the bed and began gathering her clothes.

'I didn't tell her how much money we made at the event – or didn't make. And I must tell her about the lyrics and the letter.' She looked over her shoulder at him for a moment before realising she was in danger of being hauled back into bed.

'I still wonder why Rainey didn't include you and Sally when she left me the lyrics.'

'What do you mean?'

'Why did she leave them to me exclusively?'

Gina shrugged. 'I don't know. She was a woman of mystery. But I'm very glad she did.'

'Oh?'

She nodded. 'Because if she hadn't, you'd have insisted on splitting what they make three ways, which might not leave enough to pay off Yvette.

Then you'd get all huffy about us giving you our share.'

He frowned. 'Are you sure you don't want a shower, at least?'

Gina shook her head. 'I'm a bit wary of taking all my clothes off for one thing and I really want to get out of here before anyone sees me.' She gave him a rueful smile. 'I'm sure most people know we're – well – together by now, but I still don't want to do the walk of shame in between the Chippendale and the Sèvres.'

He chuckled and she leant over to kiss him. 'I'll see you later. And if Anthea rings you instead of me, you will tell me, won't you?'

'Of course.'

It took a few minutes, but she managed to leave him and exit the French House without being seen.

'Oh my God, look at you,' said Sally, as she opened the door, still in her pyjamas.

'What?' Gina hadn't showered but she'd brushed her hair and teeth and washed her face.

'Shagged senseless. It's obvious.'

'Oh God, is it?'

'Course. You're glowing. Come in. I'll make you some tea. I'm just giving the girls their breakfast.'

'I was wondering if I could have a shower. I was going to wait until I got home but now you say you can tell what I've been up to . . .'

'Help yourself, but be quick. Alaric might want it soon. Currently he's reading the paper.'

Gina was quick but she was thorough and by the time she appeared in the kitchen she was damp but clean and wearing a pair of Sally's knickers. 'I hope you don't mind,' she said, after confessing to borrowing them without asking.

'Just as long as you tell me everything the moment Alaric's got the girls off to nursery—'

'I thought you were going to take them?' objected Alaric.

'I was, but I'm not now. I have business to talk about with Gina.'

'Auntie Gina,' said Sephie. 'Do you like Ready Brek?'

'Not much, hon,' said Gina, finding a mug and a tea bag.

'I like it velly, velly much,' said Sephie.

'Do you think it's a problem that she can't say her "r"s?' said Alaric.

'No,' said Sally. 'Come on, girls, shoes on and into the car.'

'Hang about. What about my shower?' said Alaric.

'Have it when you get back. I need to talk to my sister, now!'

Alaric shrugged. 'I don't know what can be so urgent . . .'

When Sally had finally shooed her family out of the door she sat down opposite Gina. 'First things first, I gather things are going well between you and Matthew?'

Gina nodded encouragingly. 'Oh yes. Velly, velly well, as Sephie would say.' Gina sighed reminiscently for a second. She wondered if she should tell Sally about Rainey's letter and then thought no, she wouldn't. That was between her, Matthew and their late aunt. 'But there's more news,' she went on. 'Do you want the good or the bad?'

'Oh, the bad. Let's get it out of the way. The event lost money and now everyone's in even bigger debt than they were before?'

'No! Honestly, you're as bad as Matthew. We did make money – five thousand! – just not enough.'

'Oh, well done. So is that the good news?'

Gina shook her head. 'You know that horrible Foo dog that Matthew was so attached to?'

'I think so.'

'I was forced to throw it at him – well, not at him, but anyway, it broke.'

'It would, but what has this got to do with anything?'

'There was something inside—'

'No. Tell all. Was it details of a secret bank account Rainey had and we're all going to be millionaires?'

'No, Sal, stop interrupting. Something much more romantic. Do you mind if I finish the toast?'

'Of course not, but you've got to tell me everything!'

By the time Gina had given Sally all the many details she required, Sally had made more toast.

'So these lyrics are worth money?' she said.

'We think so. It's all a bit risky though because although there's a specialist auction next week, which is an amazing stroke of luck, they might not be able to enter them at such short notice. And Anthea says if they can't drum up enough interest they won't go for their full value, which would be a disaster.'

'Oh no. How tantalising. When will you know?'

'About what?'

'About everything. If you can get it in – with enough interest – and when would the next auction be if you can't.'

'Anthea is on the case. She's going to ring me or Matthew.'

'But hey,' Sally said. 'I forgot in all the excitement. You're not the only one with news. Carmella has bought a shop.'

'Really? Tell *me* everything.'

'Bizarrely it's the one you found for her. She went for a look and has put in an offer. How about that? So I'm going to have my dream job after all, if just a bit further away.'

Gina got up and went round the table so she could hug Sally. 'I'm so happy for you.'

'And me you! I mean, you and Matthew.'

The sisters hugged until they realised their tea was getting cold.

Gina had gone home, caught up with some work, cleaned her house and made a cake and still there had been no word from Anthea. Gina sent her a text.

The reply was a terse *I'm on the case and will be back to you ASAP.* She harrumphed around with the hoover for a bit longer and then got in the car and went back to the French House.

Matthew was maddeningly sanguine. He'd cooked a meal and welcomed her with a glass of wine and a kiss. 'Hello, you.'

'Hello!' A few fond moments later she said, 'Hello, Oscar. How was your day?'

'He's been fine,' said Matthew.

'Anthea didn't ring you?'

'No. I told you I'd call if she did.'

'I know but I just couldn't wait so I sent her a text just now but she was very short when she replied.' Gina sighed, and took out her frustration on some nuts.

At nine o'clock Anthea finally rang Gina's mobile. Matthew and Gina had been playing Pontoon to, as she put it, stop her eating the cushions.

'OK, here's the deal,' said Anthea. 'I rang my friend who put me in touch with the auctioneer. Apparently song lyrics by Jean Reveaux are so rare they are nearly unheard of. I forwarded her the information you gave me, which was helpful. There are loads of collectors out there but she's not a hundred per cent sure they could advertise the lyrics sufficiently to get their absolute top price. She asked me to ask you if you want to wait and put it into the next sale, which is in September, when she can almost guarantee you top whack, or take a chance on this sale.'

'Can I ring you back? In about ten minutes?' She needed to tell Matthew the score. It was for him to decide if they should go ahead or wait for the next sale.

'OK, but not much later. I'm heading for a hot bath and a cold glass of wine in fifteen.'

Gina told Matthew what Anthea had said. They regarded each other in silence for a few minutes.

'We don't have a choice really,' said Matthew. 'As I said before, I think we should put them in and risk not getting what they're worth. We ought to get enough anyway. We have to trust Christie's to do their best.'

'You're absolutely sure?'

He nodded. 'Yes. I'd like to know where I am at last. All this uncertainty – which has been going on for years really – has got to end. It's driving me mad and making me behave like an idiot – as you have so kindly pointed out. And I can't put Yvette off any longer. She's sent another email – and a text. She won't give up until she gets her money. And even if Carmella doesn't want to buy the French House, plenty of other people will.' He gave Gina a look that made her heart thump. 'Losing the house would be sad but it wouldn't be the end of the world. If these lyrics save it, fabulous, but if they don't . . .' He paused and took her hand. 'Well, we'll face the future together.'

She squeezed his hand back and gave herself a moment before replying. 'OK, I'll ring Anthea.'

Matthew had made up the fire and refilled their glasses while she had told Anthea his decision. She came and flopped down on to the old leather sofa and picked up her glass. 'This is so nice.'

He sat down beside her and nodded. 'Better than any mansion could possibly be.'

'And we could recreate this in a starter home on a new estate if we had to.'

He frowned. This was obviously stretching his sense of the romantic too far. 'A simple worker's cottage maybe, but I'm not sure a Barratt home would work for me.' Then he laughed. 'Although maybe we could get Sally to give it a makeover.'

Chapter Thirty-Four

A week later, Matthew drove Gina and Sally to the station. 'I'm so sorry I can't be with you, but my Americans booked a while ago.' He sighed. 'I'll keep my phone on, so ring me as soon as you know.'

Gina kissed his cheek. 'Don't wait. It's awful waiting for other people's trains to leave.'

Having been upbeat and positive ever since the lyrics went into the auction she felt she could express her worries freely now she was alone with Sally.

'This is so nerve-racking,' she said a few minutes later as she took her seat on the train opposite Sally. 'Supposing they go for half nothing?'

Sally sighed and put her hand on Gina's wrist. 'They won't.'

'It's all right for you, you've got your dream job. If Matthew has to sell the French House—'

'Then you and he will start up somewhere else. Which is what he says.'

Having considered the worst-case scenario, Gina began to make plans. 'I suppose we could sell what stock we have at antiques fairs. I'll still work, of course. It might be fun. But what about the other dealers?'

'They'll be fine. But honestly, Gina, you're worrying for nothing. It won't come to that.'

'How do you know?'

'I don't for one minute believe you haven't done anything to stir up a little interest among suitable buyers.'

Doing her job was so much second nature to her Gina wondered if it was a sort of obsessive/compulsive disorder. 'I only sent a press release to the fan site, and got the details of collectors from Anthea and told them, just in case the auctioneers didn't do their job.'

'Given they are one of the top auctioneers in the world I do think that's unlikely, but I know you: a job can't be said to be done unless you've done it.' Sally sounded resigned.

'Am I really like that?'

'No one's saying it's a bad thing. And it's only in your work life. You're relatively normal the rest of the time.' She stood up and extracted her purse from her bag. 'I'll get us drinks. Do you want tea or coffee? Or, as we're on holiday, hot chocolate?'

'We're not on holiday. What are you talking about?'

'I'm not working, I haven't got the girls – I'm on holiday. What's it to be?'

The auction was in progress when they got there but their lot wasn't due for a little while. They bought a catalogue and found somewhere to stand at the back in case they wanted to make a quick exit.

The room was much quieter than Gina had imagined. It didn't have the same casual, slightly ramshackle air as the general auction houses she'd seen so often on the many TV programmes devoted to them, and there was an electricity in the air that was exciting. The buyers – or onlookers – were far smarter than they were in country auctions too. Most of them wore suits of some kind apart from the odd very arty type in flamboyant clothes and smudged lipstick, or ageing rockers, pin-thin with lined faces and dyed hair. There were a few beautiful young things with floppy hair and long legs on the phones who clearly worked there.

'I wonder how many people here are bidding on our lot,' whispered Sally.

'I don't know how we'd tell which they are,' Gina whispered back. 'None of them are wearing berets or strings of onions round their necks to indicate they're French.'

'Fool.' Sally gave her a little push.

The lyrics had an estimate of five thousand pounds. It wasn't nearly enough to cover the shortfall but Anthea had assured Gina that a lowish estimate would entice the buyers. But how much would the buyers pay? Would it be enough?

Suddenly they came to their lot number. 'Oh God, I feel sick,' said Sally, 'and it doesn't even affect me, really.'

Gina couldn't even speak.

The auctioneer looked at the book in front of him and then at the computer screen. 'Right, lot number 751, song lyrics from Jean Reveaux. This is a late entry to the sale but there's been a lot of interest in this very rare item. How are we with the phones?'

He looked up and a couple of the young men with floppy hair nodded to indicate they were in touch with the bidders.

'OK, who'll start me at ten thousand pounds?'

Gina gripped Sally harder.

'You knew the estimate was just a guess – they told you that,' Sally whispered.

'But to start at double!'

'Shush,' whispered Sally.

The phones, the internet and people in the room all seemed keen. The price rose. Gina wanted to run from the room but she was wedged in. Besides, Sally would never forgive her if she fled now.

'I'm selling now . . .' said the auctioneer. 'All out on the phones, it's with you in the room now – selling at . . . forty thousand pounds.' His gavel came down. Bang. 'Lot number . . .'

Sally led a stunned Gina out of the room and across the road to an Italian restaurant. 'Two espressos and two brandies, please,' she said.

'I can't believe it,' said Gina when she'd taken a sip from each drink and found her voice again. '*Forty thousand pounds!*'

'Way over the original estimate. Ring Matthew.'

Gina looked at her watch. 'He's got the Americans until four. I can't disturb him while he's driving.'

'Gina!' squeaked Sally. 'Are you sure? He must be in agony wanting to know too.'

'I suppose I could text him. He could pull in.' She retrieved her phone and composed a text, and then they waited.

At last Gina's phone broke into song. It was Matthew. She picked it up. 'Forty thousand pounds! Isn't that amazing!'

'That really is amazing. And it's all down to you!'

'No it's not. It's not down to me at all. They're just really rare, that's all.'

'It was you who alerted the fans and the collectors.'

'You weren't supposed to know about that! Anyway, we're going to go for our train now. Will you be there when I get back?'

'Realistically, probably not, but I'll get there as soon as I can.'

Alaric and the girls met them at the station and drove Gina to the French House. She felt slightly flat. Her initial euphoria at the lyrics going for so much money had faded. Something was missing. She tried to rationalise her feelings. Of course she'd feel down. Everything she'd been working towards, seemingly for months, had been achieved so it was as if her motive for living had been taken away from her. And she was tired. She'd been working ridiculous hours and hadn't been sleeping all that well – for various reasons; she probably needed a holiday. She could go and stay with her parents for a few days.

When they pulled up in front of the centre, Gina clambered out of the car past the sleeping twins and said her goodbyes. She looked up at the French House with fondness. 'You'll stay as you are,' she said to it silently. 'I do hope you're pleased.'

She had wanted to see Matthew and celebrate but now she wasn't sure, and if he got stuck in traffic he might not be back until the early hours. A tiny part of her acknowledged she was nervous. Supposing Matthew thanked her hugely for her help in saving the French House and then, in a very gentlemanly way, dumped her? Maybe he didn't need her any more. Oh heavens, that was just neurotic. She really must be tired.

Perhaps the best thing to do would be to see Jenny and tell her the good news before picking up her car and going home. No point in waiting in case Matthew was really late. He would ring her or send a text when he got in, surely. It would be nice to see him when they weren't stressed and anxious.

'Hi, Jenny!' she said as she entered the centre. 'Have you heard the good news?'

Jenny was smiling broadly. 'I have. Matthew sent me a text. It's wonderful. You must be so pleased.'

'I am, of course. But tired. I just came to pick up my car and go home.'

Jenny shook her head. 'I think you should pop up to the flat. There's something there for you.'

Gina felt her legs could have done without the walk up through the centre to the top floor but she could hardly say so. It felt churlish to feel so lacking in bounce when the French House was going to be saved.

The door to the flat was ajar and she saw there were lights on. She went in and saw it was illuminated by dozens of candles and tea lights. The fire was lit and Oscar was asleep in front of it. She had hardly taken in this unexpected sight when Matthew appeared and took her into his arms.

He hugged her hard, lifting her off her feet and turning round and round with her. 'Darling girl, you are so clever. I am so proud of you.' Then he kissed her.

It was a couple of minutes later before she could speak. 'Matthew! I didn't think you were going to be here. I thought you'd still be in Leamington Spa or somewhere.'

'I managed to get away early. The Americans completely understood. They agreed I had to be here to welcome you.'

Now Gina noticed not only candles but a huge arrangement of flowers and a bottle of champagne in a bucket.

'It's lovely that you're here,' she said. 'I was feeling a bit anticlimactic.'

'Of course I'm here. I'll always be here.' He looked down at her, his gaze searching. 'You do know that, don't you?'

Held captive by the sincerity in his normally inscrutable face, Gina smiled and nodded. Her paranoid fears melted away.

'Now, glass of champagne?' he went on.

'Yes, please. This is so nice. The candles, the flowers and everything.'

'I'm glad you like it. You see, I can be romantic. I'm not always a grumpy old Eeyore.'

He squashed her to his side in another hug. 'My Americans were very insistent I get the setting absolutely right,' he went on.

She frowned. 'Setting for what?'

He paused. 'Well, you know, your triumphant homecoming. The Americans were so thrilled to hear about everything.'

He was being a bit obscure. 'About the French House?' said Gina, checking. 'I bet they were. This was the group you've known for years?'

Matthew nodded. He took out the bottle and began to unwind the wire. 'They've seen me through a lot.'

'It's because you've always been utterly straight and not done anything other than be a complete star.' She watched as he eased the cork out with a gentle phut and began to pour.

'It always annoyed Yvette. She thought I was mad. But I don't think it does me any harm. The dealers get in touch if they have anything special. It all works out. Now.' He handed her a foaming glass. 'Here's to you.'

'And here's to you. And the French House. May she continue to reign as the star of the town's antiques shops!'

'You've put so much of yourself into saving her, everyone really appreciates it. It turns out they all knew everything, but didn't want me to know in case it made me worry about them.'

'Well, they obviously care about you. And I do love a project,' she said and sipped her champagne.

'But do you love it as much as I do?' he asked.

'Of course I do! I worked so hard to save it. Although admittedly that was because—' She stopped.

'Yes?'

'Well, you know, the greater good. All those small dealers who need it. Stuff like that.' She took refuge in her champagne, aware she had been about to confess to loving him, which, while not a bad thing, wasn't for her to say first, she felt. 'So,' she went on, to change the mood a bit, 'apart from paying off Yvette, what are you going to do with the money? You do realise there are fees, seller's premiums, things like that?'

'Of course. Once those are paid, I'll do some repairs

to the building, maybe a bit of refurbing, and of course restocking.' He paused. 'Actually I've spent some of it already.'

'Really? On an antique? What? I can't wait to see. Is it in the shop already?'

'No, it's here.' He led her to the sofa and sat her down. Then he sat down opposite her. 'Darling Gina, I don't have a brilliant track record with marriage but after I met you – and fell in love with you – I found I really wanted to do it again. Do you think you might consider it?'

Gina found she couldn't breathe properly. In spite of everything that had happened between them, this was a shock. 'I'm not sure I'm following you. Are you asking me to marry you?'

'Yes, but I wanted to make it so you could refuse if you wanted to.'

'I don't want to. Refuse I mean. But I'd like it if you asked me in plain English. I wouldn't want to say yes to the wrong thing.'

He smiled his rare smile that was like the sun coming out just for her. 'Gina, will you marry me?'

She nodded. 'Yes please.'

The smile grew even wider, if that were possible. He burrowed in his pocket. 'I've got you a ring but if you don't like it I can easily—'

'Sell it on. And I'm not to worry, you got a really good deal on it.' She found she was laughing and crying at the same time.

He laughed gently with her. 'There is a certain pragmatism about antiques dealers, but I hope I've shown you I can be romantic.'

She remembered their time in France together and how he'd had the swan-shaped salt (or pepper) shaker made into a key ring. 'I know.'

He opened the little leather box. In it was a ring with several stones in a band. He took it out and found the right finger. 'It's a Georgian regard ring. That means there's a ruby, emerald, garnet, amethyst, another ruby and a diamond in it. If you'd rather have a simple solitaire I do have a jewellery friend . . .'

'No! I love it. It's so pretty.' She looked at it on her hand. 'I've never seen one like it before.'

'I can't believe you said yes. I'm so happy.' He reached for the bottle and topped up their glasses. 'When you met me I was in a very dark place. It was as if I was frozen – you'd probably say fossilised. That's why I found it so hard to take on all your innovations. You must have found it infuriating. And I was determined not to let myself fall in love again. But you blew that plan out of the water. And when I saw you on the stairs in that dress, well, I knew. I can't believe you love me. I know I'm not easy – although when the threat of homelessness isn't hanging over my head I am a lot more cheery.'

She giggled. 'I'll have to take your word for that.' Then she sighed. 'I was going to stay single forever, too. After Egan I thought men were just horrible.' She bit her lip. 'You changed that.'

'I loved the way you threw yourself into the antiques business. You didn't know a thing but it didn't stop you.'

'That makes me sound incredibly crass.'

'Not at all. You worked so hard and learnt everything you could. I loved that breathless enthusiasm. In fact, I love everything about you. And I will do, forever.'

'I've just thought of a huge advantage to being married to someone who likes antiques: I'll get more and more valuable the older I get.'

Matthew nodded. 'I'm really glad you like them too . . .'

Then Oscar groaned, as if bored with this conversation, and Matthew and Gina decided not to talk any more. They settled into each other's arms. It felt like the place where they belonged.

Get to know

Katie Fforde

Read on to learn more about Katie, with an exclusive Q&A, Katie's top tips for budding writers and an insight into how Katie's novels get published.

About Katie

'I live in the beautiful Cotswold countryside with my family, and I'm a true country girl at heart.

I first started writing when my mother gave me a writing kit for Christmas, and once I started I just couldn't stop. *Living Dangerously* was my first novel and since then, I haven't looked back.

Ideas for books are everywhere, and I'm constantly inspired by the people and places around me. From watching TV (yes, it is research) to overhearing conversations, I love how my writing gives me the chance to taste other people's lives and try all the jobs I've never had.

Each of my books explores a different profession or background and my research has helped me bring these to life. I've been a porter in an auction house, tried my hand at pottery, refurbished furniture, delved behind the scenes of a dating website, and I've even been on a Ray Mears survival course.

I love being a writer; to me there isn't a more satisfying and pleasing thing to do. I particularly enjoy writing love stories. I believe falling in love is the best thing in the world, and I want all my characters to experience it, and my readers to share their stories.'

Q&A

Did you always want to become an author?

No, I didn't know I wanted to be an author until my late twenties. Before that I ran a narrowboat hotel business with my husband and then had babies, but I would have liked to be a counsellor if I wasn't a writer.

Do you miss anything from your life before?

I had a very good life before I became an author, with a lovely husband, children and house. But when I started writing I realised what I had been missing. I think it's to do with having an over-active imagination and wanting to communicate (which can be a posh word for chat!).

What's the best thing about being an author?

The best thing is getting to try out lots of jobs I could never have had in real life through my characters. It's also lovely to hear from people who have enjoyed my books – it can give me the impression that I'm doing something worthwhile, even though what I write is for entertainment.

How do you start writing a new novel?

I start with a theme. I have several subjects I long to explore bubbling around at any one time and when one comes to the top I start to think about my characters. Then comes the plot. I don't usually know at the beginning what the ending will be – I have to wait and find out! Although I know that it will be happy.

What are the essentials of creating a good romance?

I think a good hero is absolutely key, and then a heroine who the reader can recognise – not too perfect, but likeable. Plot is very important, so then it's a case of creating a few really romantic scenes. Not necessarily hearts-and-flowers romantic but unexpected romance in surprising places.

Why is research important?

It's hard enough to write a book as it is, let alone without knowing about your theme – you need to know your stuff. That said, some things can be impossible to research, like the judging at the Chelsea Flower Show, or when the Queen visits! I do quite a lot of research personally. I remember a writer friend saying to me, 'But you write contemporaries, you don't need to do research', but that is very far from the truth. My early books were set around my own life – working in a cafe and being a cleaning lady were things I had actually done. However, eventually I ran out of life experience and had to do research. I love finding out fascinating things about subjects that interest me.

Do you ever suffer from writer's block? How do you try and relieve this?

Writers block happens often in a small way. A change of scene helps to relieve it for me. This might involve shopping, a drive in the car (scenery often gets my creative juices going) or just being with friends. Luckily it never lasts for long with me and is often caused by being a bit tired.

Can you tell us about the Katie Fforde Bursary?

I created the Katie Fforde Bursary because I was a 'nearly there' writer for a long time. I found it a bit of a struggle to pay my annual subscription to the Romantic Novelists' Association so when I finally became published, I wanted to give something back. That's the bursary, a year's subscription and a place at the conference. It does seem to give people a valuable boost to their confidence. People can find out more about the Romantic Novelists' Association at www.rna-uk.org.

BEHIND THE SCENES WITH
Katie Fforde

Katie takes us behind the scenes and into her writing study as she describes the process of writing her new book, *The Perfect Match.*

I work in my study which, though small, has a nice view. I do have to stand up to look at it in full, but if I turn to the right I can see the Gloucestershire hills, and trees and sky. I spend quite a lot of time with my head turned to the right.

I like to get up early and 'get ahead' – the mornings are my best time for writing – although I have to admit I often find myself playing Spider Solitaire on my computer while I get my thoughts in order. Sometimes I toy with the idea of taking Spider off my computer but the thought is so terrifying I never do it.

If I get about a thousand words done a day, I'm happy. I'm even happier if it's two thousand but that's more likely towards the end of the book when I know what's going to happen and I'm on a roll. If I'm really stuck I'll have a change of scene. Sometimes just a walk round the garden will do it, or a walk with the dogs. If things are really bad it might take a shopping trip or tea with a friend so I can talk about it to get things going again. If none of these work, a day off is called for.

I get ideas from almost anywhere. I used to worry about running out, but not any more. I know they are everywhere! I never know when they're going to hit, though. It can be a bit inconvenient if I'm a mile from home and absolutely have to make a note of something that's just popped into my head. I could carry a notebook but then I think the ideas wouldn't come.

The idea for my latest novel, *The Perfect Match*, came at me from two directions. The first was my addiction to TV property programmes (because I'm terribly nosy) and the second was the fact my sister and brother-in-law were looking for a house in my area and they took me along for viewings. I just had to write a book about an estate agent. Apart from anything else, I wanted to make it clear that not all estate agents are villains – Kirstie and Phil, for example – but of course some of them are, for the sake of a good novel at least.

If you've ever watched *Location, Location, Location*, you'll know the whole thing about house hunting is compromise. What you can put up with and what you can't. So we saw the near-perfect rectory with a lovely garden, a really interesting old house and within budget, but so close to the motorway you could hardly hear the birds. I can hear the road from my own house but even I couldn't have put up with that. Quite often there was a lovely garden with a horrid house not even Sarah Beeny could make nice, or a really lovely house with a folded-pocket-handkerchief garden. My sister loves to garden and wanted one of a reasonable size. But I still came away with the conclusion that she is possibly the fussiest house buyer ever. I am pleased to say they have now bought a house near me and are very happy. (They chose a lovely large, level garden and are doing a lot of work to the house.)

This was always going to be a difficult book because there was a long-planned two-month trip to Australia and New Zealand involved. Usually my books grow organically, one event following another, further ideas coming as I write, but this time my editors and I felt we should know what was going to happen from beginning to end even if I wouldn't be doing as much writing as usual for a couple of months. This meant a fairly detailed synopsis.

I'd been lucky up till then, and mostly avoided anything too detailed in the synopsis line. This was going to take a special effort. I needed reinforcements. So I called in my friend Jo Thomas. She is brilliant at ideas and she is also huge fun. We'd already had a few mad adventures together (mostly doing research for her books) and so she was up for coming to a health farm with me. I needed a place away from the usual distractions of home and family. A health farm would provide meals and pleasant surroundings and there would be no excuse not to work. Not everyone I told what I was up to was convinced we wouldn't just lie around having our nails done, but hey, I knew what I needed to do.

Thrashing out a plot with other writers, or one other writer, is always fun. There is an awful lot of arm-waving and finger-pointing and being unable to get out the latest idea because it's too exciting. Then there's some frantic typing and 'What did I say happened then?'. I find it an incredibly productive part of my writing process too.

Thus it was while we were at Cedar Falls, near Taunton, that we dragged out one idea after another for *The Perfect Match*. Jo has definitely paid me back for the times she took me husky racing (freezing cold Scotland) and oyster farming (also freezing cold Scotland and very wet but even more fun), all in the name of research.

After that, armed with my synopsis and my laptop, my husband Desmond and I set off for the Antipodes. We travelled all through Australia, including a trip on a very small plane, and all through the South Island of New Zealand. Then, after a ferry trip to Wellington, disaster. My beloved husband spilt coffee on the keyboard. And no, I hadn't backed up anything recently. Once home the hard drive was at a specialist place for a while, to no avail, and I had to resign myself to rewriting the missing work. It's a funny thing about authors: we always feel that any work we have lost was absolutely brilliant, but never feel like that about work we've saved and printed and sent off!

It's always terrifying sending work off to editors. It's like really important homework. You think you've done your best work but have you? And when it comes back with red writing all over it you feel very fed up. This is because you feel you should have done a better job, you've been incredibly dense not to notice all those points they've made and, basically, you're not very good at what you do. And then there's the 'No one understands me!' bit, when you feel like a small child kicking at the floor with frustration.

When giving talks and workshops, I always explain about the editing process, how it's impossible to see your work clearly because you're just too close to it. You must learn not to beat yourself up about getting edits, and realise that you need someone with a bit of vision to see what's going on. So I like to think of the editor as the diamond-cutter. You offer them the rough (although I hope not too rough!) stone and they carve and chip it into something beautiful. Sometimes they make a suggestion and I think grumpily, 'This isn't all that good', but make myself write the scene or use the idea, and then I'm amazed at how well it works. It's one of the things that make my job the best in the world. Magic can happen at any time.

Katie Fforde

To find out more about how Katie's books get published, visit the behind the scenes blog on www.katiefforde.com. *The Perfect Match* is out in hardback March 2014.

TOP TIPS FOR AUTHORS

I first became a writer because my mother gave me a writing kit. I'd been talking about wanting to write for years, but thought because I had three children, a dog, two cats and a husband who was away at sea a lot of the time, I wouldn't have time to write. Nevertheless, my mother bought a kit full of paper, dictionaries, a thesaurus and Tipp-Ex, wrapped it up in a big bow and gave it to me for Christmas. It was the big kick that I needed. My New Year's resolution for that year was to start writing my novel, and I'm ashamed to confess it's the only New Year's resolution I've ever kept.

EVERYONE IS DIFFERENT, BUT MY THREE TOP TIPS FOR ASPIRING WRITERS ARE:

1. **READ A LOT:** You learn more about writing from reading than you would believe. I think it's very hard for people who don't read to become writers. Read anything and everything.

2. **PERSEVERE:** It took me eight years to become a published novelist. I just refused to give up. I think if you're really determined and you really want it enough, you will do it, but you have to want it more than anything. I've wanted other things in my life, like to be a size 10, but I haven't achieved them because I didn't want them enough. I did want to be a writer enough and I persevered and eventually I made it.

3. **LISTEN TO CRITICISM:** Learn to see when criticism is helpful and when it's not. If somebody says 'I can't get into this book because it's boring in the beginning', don't disagree with them and say, 'But that's how I wrote it, I want them to know all that!' but listen. The fact is, people aren't going to want to read it if it's not compelling enough. There are, however, people who will say 'No one wants to read a book about a girl who goes climbing without equipment; who would?' But if you know differently, if you know that there are people who would be interested, then take no notice of that criticism. When it comes to editorial criticism, usually people are telling the truth and it is best to listen to it.

THE MAIN THING IS TO REALLY PERSEVERE AND YOU WILL DO IT. ANYONE CAN IF THEY WANT IT ENOUGH.

ALSO BY KATIE FFORDE

From Scotland with Love

When Daisy travels to Scotland to confront notorious author Rory McAllan, little does she know that within hours she'll be snowed in with him. But surely she's not going to have to spend her precious New Year's Eve with him too?

A digital short story, available to download online now

ALSO BY KATIE FFORDE

Recipe for Love

Take one aspiring cook . . .

When Zoe Harper wins a coveted place in a televised cookery competition, she can't wait to put her cooking skills to the test. But as the competition heats up, she realises she's developing an inconvenient crush on one of the judges, the truly delicious Gideon Irving.

All too soon there's more than canapés, cupcakes and cordon bleu at stake. Will Zoe win the competition, or is Gideon one temptation too far?

ALSO BY KATIE FFORDE

Summer of Love

What might happen in a summer of love?

Sian Bishop has thrown herself into a new life in the country. With her young son, her picture-postcard garden and her small thriving business, she's happy and very busy. She is not – repeat not – looking for love.

And then, Gus Beresford arrives, ridiculously exciting, wonderfully glamorous – and, Sian tells herself, completely wrong for a romantically cautious single woman like her. But she and Gus have met before. And, despite Sian's best intentions, it isn't long before she's falling for him all over again. . .